Everyone's talking about the FALLEN series . . .

'Insanely unputdownable. It's the kind of book I'd read over and over again and still fall in love with each time'
~ Jonne Bombita, Australia

'One of the most alluring, sexy, thrilling books since *The Mortal Instruments*' ~ Juliette Walkuski, USA

'Captivating. Intense. Thrilling. A whirlwind series that captures the forbidden love story of star-crossed lovers. Kate takes romance to the next level as you fall into the story yourself' ~ Lydia Amy Jones, UK

'The *Fallen* book series is sure to Torment your soul with Passion, and Rapture your heart strings. You're going to get all the feels'
~ Leah Walker, USA

'Enthralling, unforgettable, spectacular, remarkable . . . Everything about the book is perfect. Lauren Kate has done it'
~ Nur Marini Binti Nazri, Malaysia

'Fall in love with this amazing series. A must-read for people who love angel stories and romance with a gothic feel to it. The ending will blow your mind' ~ Carmen Maldonado, Puerto Rico

'*Fallen* is the perfect picture of a romance that everybody wants in their life. It proves that everyone can have a happy ending. Even when you least expect them to' ~ Anja Đurđević, Croatia

'*Fallen* captured my heart from the moment I saw the cover. It exceeded all expectation. It will leave you breathless and longing for more' ~ Savanna Waters, USA

'*Fallen* lends readers their own majestic wings, and slowly transports them to the wonderful world of fallen angels' ~ Ara Hilis, Philippines

www.**laurenkatebooks**.co.uk

RAPTURE

A FALLEN NOVEL

LAUREN KATE

CORGI BOOKS

RAPTURE
A CORGI BOOK 978 0 552 56181 5

First published in Great Britain by Doubleday,
an imprint of Random House Children's Publishers UK
A Penguin Random House Company

Doubleday edition published 2012
Corgi edition published 2013

7 9 10 8 6

Set in Palatino

Corgi Books are published by Random House Children's Publishers UK,
61–63 Uxbridge Road, London W5 5SA

www.totallyrandombooks.co.uk
www.randomhouse.co.uk

Addresses for companies within The Random House Group Limited
can be found at: www.randomhouse.co.uk/offices.htm

THE RANDOM HOUSE GROUP Limited Reg. No. 954009

A CIP catalogue record for this book is available from the British Library.

Printed and bound in Great Britain by Clays Ltd, St Ives plc

FOR JASON—
WITHOUT YOUR LOVE,
NOTHING IS POSSIBLE.

ACKNOWLEDGMENTS

It is a wonderful thing to find one's acknowledgments growing with every book. I am grateful to Michael Stearns and Ted Malawer for believing in me, for indulging me, for making me work so hard. To Wendy Loggia, Beverly Horowitz, Krista Vitola, and the excellent team at Delacorte Press—you have made Fallen soar from start to finish. To Angela Carlino, Barbara Perris, Chip Gibson, Judith Haut, Noreen Herits (I already miss you!), Roshan Nozari, and Dominique Cimina for how expertly you've turned my story into a book.

To Sandra Van Mook and my friends in Holland; to Gabriella Ambrosini and Beatrice Masini in Italy; to Shirley Ng and the crew at MPH in Kuala Lumpur; to Rino Balatbat, Karla, Chad, the wonderful Ramos family, and my superb Filipino fans; to Dorothy Tonkin, Justin Ractliffe, and the brilliant group at Random House Australia; to Rebecca Simpson in New Zealand; to Ana Lima and Cecilia Brandi and Record for a beautiful time in Brazil; to Lauren Kate Bennett and the lovely girls at RHUK; to Amy Fisher and Iris Barazani for inspiration in Jerusalem. What a wonderful year I had with you all—cheers to more!

To my readers, who show me the brightest side of life every single day. Thank you.

To my family, for your patience and trust and sense of humor. To my friends, who coax me out of my writing cave. And, always, to Jason, who braves the cave when I can't be coaxed. I'm lucky to have all of you in my life.

All other things to their destruction draw,

Only our love hath no decay. . . .

⊰ ⊱

—JOHN DONNE, *"The Anniversary"*

RAPTURE

PROLOGUE

FALLING

First there was silence—

In the space between Heaven and the Fall, deep in the unknowable distance, there was a moment when the glorious hum of Heaven disappeared and was replaced by a silence so profound that Daniel's soul strained to make out any noise.

Then came the feeling of falling—a drop even his wings couldn't prevent, as if the Throne had attached moons to them. They hardly beat, and when they did, it made no impact on his fall.

Where was he going? There was nothing before him and nothing behind. Nothing up and nothing down. Only thick darkness, and the blurry outline of what was left of Daniel's soul.

In the absence of sound, his imagination took over. It filled his head with something beyond sound, something inescapable: the haunting words of Lucinda's curse.

She will die . . . She will never pass out of adolescence— will die again and again and again at precisely the moment when she remembers your choice.

You will never truly be together.

It was Lucifer's foul imprecation, his embittered addendum to the Throne's sentence passed in the Heavenly Meadow. Now death was coming for his love. Could Daniel stop it? Would he even recognize it?

For what did an angel know of death? Daniel had witnessed it come peacefully to some of the new mortal breed called human, but death did not concern angels.

Death and adolescence: the two absolutes in Lucifer's Curse. Neither meant a thing to Daniel. All he knew was that being separated from Lucinda was not a punishment he could endure. They had to be together.

"Lucinda!" he shouted.

His soul should have warmed at the very thought of her, but there was only aching absence, an abundance of what was not.

He should have been able to sense his brethren

around him—all those who'd chosen wrongly or too late; who'd made no choice at all and been cast out for their indecision. He knew that he wasn't *truly* alone; so many of them had plummeted when the cloudsoil beneath them opened up onto the void.

But he could neither see nor sense anyone else.

Before this moment, he had never been alone. Now he felt like the last angel in all the worlds.

Don't think like that. You'll lose yourself.

He tried to hold on . . . Lucinda, the Roll Call, Lucinda, the *choice* . . . but as he fell, it grew harder to remember. What, for instance, were the last words he'd heard spoken by the Throne—

The Gates of Heaven . . .

The Gates of Heaven are . . .

He could not remember what came next, could only dimly recall how the great light had flickered, and the harshest cold had swept over the Meadow, and the trees in the Orchard had tumbled into one another, causing waves of furious disturbance that were felt throughout the cosmos, tsunamis of cloudsoil that blinded the angels and crushed their glory. There had been something else, something just before the obliteration of the Meadow, something like a—

Twinning.

A bold bright angel had soared up during the Roll Call—said he was Daniel come back from the future.

There was a sadness in his eyes that had looked so . . . *old*. Had this angel—this version of Daniel's soul—suffered deeply?

Had Lucinda?

A vast rage rose in Daniel. He would find Lucifer, the angel who lived at the dead end of all ideas. Daniel did not fear the traitor who had been the Morning Star. Wherever, whenever they reached the end of this oblivion, Daniel would take his revenge. But first he would find Lucinda, for without her, nothing mattered. Without her love, nothing was possible.

Theirs was a love that made it inconceivable to choose Lucifer or the Throne. The only side he could ever choose was hers. So now Daniel would pay for that choice, but he did not yet understand the shape his punishment would take. Only that she was gone from the place she belonged: at his side.

The pain of separation from his soul mate coursed through Daniel suddenly, sharp and brutal. He moaned wordlessly, his mind clouded over, and suddenly, frighteningly, he couldn't remember *why*.

He tumbled onward, down through denser blackness.

He could no longer see or feel or recall how he had ended up here, nowhere, hurtling through nothingness—toward where? For how long?

His memory sputtered and faded. It was harder and

harder to recall those words spoken by the angel in the white meadow who had looked so much like . . .

Who had the angel resembled? And what had he said that was so important?

Daniel did not know, did not know anything anymore.

Only that he was tumbling through an endless void.

He was filled with an urge to find something . . . someone.

An urge to feel whole again . . .

But there was only darkness inside darkness—

Silence drowning out his thoughts—

A nothing that was everything.

Daniel fell.

ONE

THE BOOK OF THE WATCHERS

"Good morning."

A warm hand brushed Luce's face and tucked a strand of hair behind her ear.

Rolling onto her side, she yawned and opened her eyes. She had been sleeping deeply, dreaming about Daniel.

"Oh," she gasped, feeling her cheek. There he was.

Daniel was sitting next to her. He wore a black sweater and the same red scarf that had been knotted

around his neck the first time she'd seen him at Sword &
Cross. He looked better than a dream.

His weight made the edge of the cot sag a little and
Luce drew up her legs to snuggle closer to him.

"You're not a dream," she said.

Daniel's eyes were blearier than she was used to, but
they still glowed the brightest violet as they gazed at her
face, studying her features as if seeing her anew. He
leaned down and pressed his lips to hers.

Luce folded into him, wrapping her arms around the
back of his neck, happy to kiss him back. She didn't care
about her unbrushed teeth, about her bed head. She
didn't care about anything other than his kiss. They
were together now and neither of them could stop grinning.

Then it all came rushing back:

Razor claws and dull red eyes. Choking stench of
death and rot. Darkness everywhere, so complete in its
doom it made light and love and everything good in the
world feel tired and broken and dead.

That Lucifer had once been something else to her—
Bill, the ornery stone gargoyle she'd mistaken for a
friend, was actually Lucifer himself—seemed impossible.
She'd let him get too close, and now, because she had not
done as he wished—killed her soul in ancient Egypt—he
had decided to wipe the slate clean.

To bend time and erase everything since the Fall.

Every life, every love, every moment that every mortal and angelic soul had ever experienced would be balled up and discarded at Lucifer's reckless whim, like the universe was a board game and he was a whining child giving up when he began to lose. But what he wanted to win, Luce had no idea.

Her skin felt hot as she remembered his wrath. He'd *wanted* her to see it, to tremble in his hand when he took her back to the time of the Fall. He'd wanted to show her it was personal for him.

Then he'd thrown her aside, casting an Announcer like a net to capture all the angels who'd fallen from Heaven.

Just as Daniel caught her in that starry noplace, Lucifer blinked out of existence and incited the Fall to begin again. He was there now with the falling angels, including the past version of himself. Like the rest of them, Lucifer would fall in powerless isolation—with his brethren but apart, together but alone. Millennia ago, it had taken the angels nine mortal days to fall from Heaven down to Earth. Since Lucifer's second Fall would follow the same trajectory, Luce, Daniel, and the others had just nine days to stop him.

If they didn't, once Lucifer and his Announcer full of angels fell to Earth, there would be a hiccup in time that would reverberate backward all the way to the original Fall, and everything would start anew. As though the seven thousand years between then and now had never happened.

As though Luce hadn't at last begun to understand the curse, to understand where she fit into all this, to learn who she was and what she could be.

The history and the future of the world were in jeopardy—unless Luce, seven angels, and two Nephilim could stop Lucifer. They had nine days and no idea where to start.

Luce had been so tired the night before that she didn't remember lying down on this cot, drawing this thin blue blanket around her shoulders. There were cobwebs in the rafters of the small cabin, a folding table strewn with half-drunk mugs of hot chocolate that Gabbe had made for everyone the previous night. But it all seemed like a dream to Luce. Her flight down from the Announcer to this tiny island off Tybee, this safe zone for the angels, had been obscured by blinding fatigue.

She'd fallen asleep while the others had still been talking, letting Daniel's voice lull her into a dream. Now the cabin was quiet, and in the window behind Daniel's silhouette, the sky was the gray of almost sunrise.

She reached up to touch his cheek. He turned his head and kissed the inside of her palm. Luce squeezed her eyes to stop from crying. Why, after all they'd been through, did Luce and Daniel have to beat the devil before they were free to love?

"Daniel." Roland's voice came from the doorway of the cabin. His hands were tucked inside his peacoat pockets, and a gray wool ski cap crowned his dreads. He gave Luce a weary smile. "It's time."

"Time for what?" Luce propped herself up on her elbows. "We're leaving? Already? I wanted to say goodbye to my parents. They're probably panicked."

"I thought I'd take you by their house now," Daniel said, "to say goodbye."

"But how am I going to explain disappearing after Thanksgiving dinner?"

She remembered Daniel's words from the night before: Though it felt like they'd been inside the Announcers for an eternity, in real time only a few hours had passed.

Still, to Harry and Doreen Price, a few hours of a missing daughter *was* eternity.

Daniel and Roland shared a glance. "We took care of it," Roland said, handing Daniel a set of car keys.

"You took care of it how?" Luce asked. "My dad once called the police when I was a half an hour late from school—"

"Don't worry, kid," Roland said. "We've got you covered. You just need to make a quick costume change." He pointed toward a backpack on the rocking chair by the door. "Gabbe brought over your things."

"Um, thanks," she said, confused. Where was Gabbe?

Where were the rest of them? The cabin had been packed the night before, positively cozy with the glow of angel wings and the smell of hot chocolate and cinnamon. The memory of that coziness, coupled with the promise of saying goodbye to her parents without knowing where she was going, made this morning feel empty.

The wood floor was rough against her bare feet. Looking down, she realized she was still wearing the narrow white shift dress she'd had on in Egypt, in the last life she had visited through the Announcers. Bill had made her wear it.

No, not Bill. *Lucifer.* He'd leered approvingly as she tucked the starshot into her waistband, contemplating the advice he'd given her on how to kill her soul.

Never, never, never. Luce had too much to live for.

Inside the old green backpack she used to take to summer camp, Luce found her favorite pair of pajamas—the red-and-white-striped flannel set—neatly folded, with the matching white slippers underneath. "But it's morning," Luce said. "What do I need pajamas for?"

Again Daniel and Roland shared a glance, and this time, they were trying not to laugh.

"Just trust us," Roland said.

After she was dressed, Luce followed Daniel out of the cabin, letting his broad shoulders buffet the wind as they walked down the pebbly shore to the water.

The tiny island off of Tybee was about a mile from

the Savannah coastline. Across that stretch of sea, Roland had promised that a car was waiting.

Daniel's wings were concealed, but he must have sensed her eyeing the place where they unfurled from his shoulders. "When everything is in order, we'll fly wherever we have to go to stop Lucifer. Until then it's better to stay low to the ground."

"Okay," Luce said.

"Race you to the other side?"

Her breath frosted the air. "You know I'd beat you."

"True." He slipped an arm around her waist, warming her. "Maybe we'd better take the boat, then. Protect my famous pride."

She watched him unmoor a small metal rowboat from a boat slip. The soft light on the water made her think back to the day they'd raced across the secret lake at Sword & Cross. His skin had glistened as they had pulled themselves up to the flat rock in the center to catch their breath, then had lain on the sun-warmed stone, letting the day's heat dry their bodies. She'd barely known Daniel then—she hadn't known he was an angel—and already she'd been dangerously in love with him.

"We used to swim together in my lifetime in Tahiti, didn't we?" she asked, surprised to remember another time she'd seen Daniel's hair glisten with water.

Daniel stared at her and she knew how much it meant

to him finally to be able to share some of his memories of their past. He looked so moved that Luce thought he might cry.

Instead he kissed her forehead tenderly and said, "You beat me all those times, too, Lulu."

They didn't talk much as Daniel rowed. It was enough for Luce just to watch the way his muscles strained and flexed each time he dragged back, hearing the oars dip into and out of the cold water, breathing in the brine of the ocean. The sun was rising over her shoulders, warming the back of her neck, but as they approached the mainland, she saw something that sent a shiver down her spine.

She recognized the white 1993 Taurus immediately.

"What's wrong?" Daniel noticed Luce's posture stiffen as the rowboat touched the shore. "Oh. That." He sounded unconcerned as he hopped out of the boat and held out a hand to Luce. The ground was mulchy and rich-smelling. It reminded Luce of her childhood, running through Georgia forests in the fall, luxuriating in the anticipation of mischief and adventure.

"It's not what you think," Daniel said. "When Sophia fled Sword & Cross, after"—Luce waited, wincing, hoping Daniel wouldn't say *after she murdered Penn*—"after we found out who she really was, the angels confiscated her car." His face hardened. "She owes us that much, and more."

Luce thought of Penn's white face, the life draining from it. "Where is Sophia now?"

Daniel shook his head. "I don't know. Unfortunately, we'll probably soon find out. I have a feeling she'll worm her way into our plans." He drew the keys from his pocket, inserted one into the passenger door. "But that's not what you should be worried about right now."

Luce looked at him as she sank onto the gray cloth seat. "So what should I be worried about right now?"

Daniel turned the key, and the car shuddered slowly to life. The last time she'd sat in this seat, she'd been worried about being alone with him. It was the first night they'd ever kissed—as far as she'd known then, anyway. Luce was stabbing the seat belt into its buckle when she felt Daniel's fingers over hers. "Remember," he said softly, reaching over to buckle her seat belt, letting his hands linger over hers. "There's a trick."

He kissed her cheek, then put the car in reverse and peeled out of the wet woods onto a narrow two-lane blacktop. They were the only ones on the road.

"Daniel?" Luce asked again. "What else should I be worried about?"

He glanced at Luce's pajamas. "How good are you at playing sick?"

The white Taurus idled in the alley behind her parents' house as Luce crept past the three azalea trees beside her bedroom window. In the summer, there would be tomato vines creeping out of the black soil, but in winter, the side yard looked barren and dreary and not very much like home. She couldn't remember the last time she'd stood out here. She'd sneaked out of three different boarding schools before, but never out of her own parents' house. Now she was sneaking *in* and she didn't know how her window worked. Luce looked around at her sleepy neighborhood, at the morning paper sitting in its dewy plastic bag at the edge of her parents' lawn, at the old, netless basketball hoop in the Johnsons' driveway across the street. Nothing had changed since she'd been gone. Nothing had changed except Luce. If Bill succeeded, would this neighborhood vanish, too?

She gave one last wave to Daniel in the car, took a deep breath, and used her thumbs to pry the lower panel from the cracking blue paint of the sill.

It slid right up. Someone inside had already popped out the screen. Luce paused, stunned as the white muslin curtains parted and the half-blond, half-black head of her onetime enemy Molly Zane filled the open space.

"'Sup, Meatloaf."

Luce bristled at the nickname she'd earned on her first day at Sword & Cross. *This* was what Daniel and

Roland had meant when they said they'd taken care of things at home?

"What are you doing here, Molly?"

"Come on. I won't bite." Molly extended a hand. Her nails were chipped emerald green.

She sank her hand into Molly's, ducked, and sidled, one leg at a time, through the window.

Her bedroom looked small and outdated, like a time capsule of some long-ago Luce. There was the framed poster of the Eiffel Tower on the back of her door. There was her bulletin board of swim team ribbons from Thunderbolt Elementary. And there, under the green-and-yellow Hawaiian-print duvet, was her best friend, Callie.

Callie scrambled from under the covers, dashed around the bed, and flung herself into Luce's arms. "They kept telling me you were going to be okay, but in that lying, we're-also-completely-terrified-we're-just-not-going-to-explain-a-word-to-you kind of way. Do you even realize how thoroughly spooky that was? It was like you physically dropped off the face of the Earth—"

Luce hugged her back tightly. As far as Callie knew, Luce had been gone only since the night before.

"Okay, you two," Molly growled, pulling Luce away from Callie, "you can *OMG* your faces off later. I didn't lie in your bed in that cheap polyester wig all night enacting Luce-with-stomach-flu so you guys could blow our cover now." She rolled her eyes. "Amateurs."

"Hold on. You did what?" Luce asked.

"After you . . . disappeared," Callie said breathlessly, "we knew we could never explain it to your parents. I mean, *I* could barely fathom it after seeing it with my own eyes. When Gabbe fixed up the backyard, I told your parents you felt sick and had gone to bed, and Molly pretended to be you and—"

"Lucky I found this in your closet." Molly twirled a short wavy black wig around one finger. "Halloween remnant?"

"Wonder Woman." Luce winced, regretting her middle school Halloween costume, and not for the first time.

"Well, it worked."

It was strange to see Molly—who'd once sided with Lucifer—helping her. But even Molly, like Cam and Roland, didn't want to fall again. So here they were, a team, strange bedfellows.

"You covered for me? I don't know what to say. Thank you."

"Whatever." Molly jerked her head at Callie, anything to deflect Luce's gratitude. "She was the real silver-tongued devil. Thank her." She stuck one leg out the open window and turned to call back, "Think you guys can handle it from here? I have a Waffle House summit meeting to attend."

Luce gave Molly the thumbs-up and flopped down on her bed.

"Oh, Luce," Callie whispered. "When you left, your whole backyard was covered in this gray *dust*. And that blond girl, Gabbe, swept her hand once and made it *disappear*. Then we said you were sick, that everyone else had gone home, and we just started doing the dishes with your parents. And at first I thought that Molly girl was a little bit terrible, but she's actually kind of cool." Her eyes narrowed. "But where *did* you go? What happened to you? You really scared me, Luce."

"I don't even know where to start," Luce said.

There was a knock, followed by the familiar creak of her bedroom door opening.

Luce's mother stood in the hallway, her sleep-wild hair tamed by a yellow banana clip, her face bare of makeup and pretty. She was holding a wicker tray with two glasses of orange juice, two plates of buttered toast, and a box of Alka-Seltzer. "Looks like someone's feeling better."

Luce waited for her mom to put the tray down on the nightstand; then she wrapped her arms around her mother's waist and buried her face in her pink terry cloth bathrobe. Tears stung her eyes. She sniffed.

"My little girl," her mom said, feeling Luce's forehead and cheeks to check for fever. Even though she hadn't used that soft sweet voice on Luce in ages, it felt so good to hear it.

"I love you, Mom."

"Don't tell me she's too sick for Black Friday." Luce's father appeared in the doorway, holding a green plastic watering can. He was smiling, but behind his rimless glasses, Mr. Price's eyes looked concerned.

"I am feeling better," Luce said. "But—"

"Oh, Harry," Luce's mom said. "You know we only had her for the day. She has to be back at school." She turned to Luce. "Daniel called a little while ago, honey. He said he can pick you up and take you back to Sword & Cross. I said that of course your father and I would be happy to, but—"

"No," Luce said quickly, remembering the plan Daniel had detailed in the car. "Even if I can't go, you guys should still do your Black Friday shopping. It's a Price family tradition."

They agreed that Luce would ride with Daniel and her parents would take Callie to the airport. While the girls ate, Luce's parents sat on the edge of the bed and talked about Thanksgiving ("Gabbe polished all the china—what an angel"). By the time they moved on to the Black Friday deals they were on the hunt for ("All your father ever wants is tools"), Luce realized that she hadn't said anything except for inane conversation fillers like "Uh-huh" and "Oh really?"

When her parents finally stood up to take their plates into the kitchen and Callie started to pack, Luce went into the bathroom and shut the door.

She was alone for the first time in what seemed like a million ages. She sat down on the vanity stool and looked in the mirror.

She was herself, but different. Sure, Lucinda Price looked back at her. But also . . .

There was Layla in the fullness of her lips, Lulu in the thick waves of her hair, Lu Xin in the intensity of her hazel eyes, Lucia in their twinkle. She was not alone. Maybe she never would be alone again. There, in the mirror, was every incarnation of Lucinda staring back at her and wondering, *What is to become of us? What about our history, and our love?*

She took a shower and put on clean jeans, her black riding boots, and a long white sweater. She sat down on Callie's suitcase while her friend struggled to zip it up. The silence between them was brutal.

"You're my best friend, Callie," Luce finally said. "I'm going through something I don't understand. But that thing isn't you. I'm sorry I don't know how to be more specific, but I've missed you. So much."

Callie's shoulders tensed. "You used to tell me everything." But the look that passed between them suggested that both girls knew that wasn't possible anymore.

A car door slammed out front.

Through the open blinds Luce watched Daniel make his way up her parents' path. And even though it had been less than an hour since he had dropped her off, Luce felt her heart pick up and her cheeks flush at the sight of him. He walked slowly, as if he were floating, his red scarf trailing behind him in the wind. Even Callie stared.

Luce's parents gathered in the foyer with them. She hugged each one of them for a long time—Dad first, then Mom, then Callie, who squeezed her hard and whispered quickly, "What I saw last night—you, stepping into that . . . that *shadow*—was beautiful. I just want you to know that."

Luce felt her eyes burn again. She squeezed Callie back and whispered, "Thank you."

Then she walked down the path and into Daniel's arms and whatever came along with them.

※ ※

"There you are, you lovebirds, you, doin' that thing that lovebirds do," Arriane sang, bobbing her head out from behind a long bookcase. She was sitting cross-legged on a wooden library chair, juggling a few Hacky Sacks. She wore overalls, combat boots, and her dark hair plaited into tiny pigtails.

Luce was not overjoyed to be back at the Sword & Cross Library. It had been renovated since the fire that had destroyed it, but it still smelled like something big and ugly had burned there. The faculty had explained away the fire as a freak accident, but someone had been killed—Todd, a quiet student whom Luce had barely known until the night he died—and Luce knew there was something darker lurking beneath the surface of the story. She blamed herself. It reminded her too much of Trevor, a boy she'd once had a crush on, who had died in another inexplicable fire.

Now, as she and Daniel rounded the corner of a bookshelf to the library's study area, Luce saw that Arriane was not alone. All of them were there: Gabbe, Roland, Cam, Molly, Annabelle—the leggy angel with the hot-pink hair—even Miles and Shelby, who waved excitedly and looked decidedly different from the other angels, but also different from mortal teens.

Miles and Shelby were—were they holding *hands*? But when she looked again, their hands had disappeared under the table they were all sitting at. Miles tugged his baseball cap lower. Shelby cleared her throat and hunched over a book.

"Your book," Luce said to Daniel as soon as she spotted the thick spine with the brown crumbling glue near the bottom. The faded cover read *The Watchers: Myth in Medieval Europe by Daniel Grigori.*

Her hand reached automatically for the pale gray cover. She closed her eyes, because it reminded her of Penn, who'd found the book on Luce's last night as a student at Sword & Cross, and because the photograph pasted inside the front cover of the book was the first thing that had convinced her that what Daniel told her about their history might be possible.

It was a photograph taken from another life, one in

Helston, England. And even though it shouldn't have been possible, there was no doubt about it: The young woman in the photograph was her.

"Where did you find it?" Luce asked.

Her voice must have given something away, because Shelby said, "What is so major about this dusty old thing, anyway?"

"It's precious. Our only key now," Gabbe said. "Sophia tried to burn it once."

"Sophia?" Luce's hand shot to her heart. "Miss Sophia tried—the fire in the library? That was her?" The others nodded. "She killed Todd," Luce said numbly.

So it *hadn't* been Luce's fault. Another life to lay at Sophia's feet. It didn't make Luce feel any better.

"And she almost died of shock the night you showed it to her," Roland said. "We were all shocked, especially when you lived to talk about it."

"We talked about Daniel kissing me," Luce remembered, blushing. "And the fact that I survived it. Was that what surprised Miss Sophia?"

"Part of it," Roland said. "But there's plenty more in that book that Sophia wouldn't have wanted you to know about."

"Not much of an educator, was she?" Cam said, giving Luce a smirk that said, *Long time, no see.*

"What wouldn't she have wanted me to know?"

All the angels turned to look at Daniel.

"Last night we told you that none of the angels remember where we landed when we fell," Daniel said.

"Yeah, about that . . . How's it possible?" Shelby said. "You'd think that kind of thing would leave an impression on the old memorizer."

Cam's face reddened. "You try falling for nine days through multiple dimensions and trillions of miles, landing on your face, breaking your wings, rolling around concussed for who knows how long, wandering the desert for decades looking for any clue as to who or what or where you are—and then talk to me about the old memorizer."

"Okay, you've got acknowledgment issues," Shelby said, putting on her shrink voice. "If *I* were going to diagnose you—"

"Well, at least you remember there was a desert involved," Miles said diplomatically, making Shelby laugh.

Daniel turned to Luce. "I wrote this book after I lost you in Tibet . . . but before I'd met you in Prussia. I know you visited that life in Tibet because I followed you there, so maybe you can see how losing you the way I did made me turn to years of research and study to find a way out of this curse."

Luce looked away. Her death in Tibet had made Daniel run straight off a cliff. She feared its happening again.

"Cam is right," Daniel said. "None of us recall where we landed. We wandered the desert until it was no longer desert; we wandered the plains and the valleys and the seas until they turned to desert again. It wasn't until we slowly found one another and began to piece together the story that we remembered we'd once ever been angels at all.

"But there were relics created after our Fall, physical records of our history that mankind found and kept as treasures, gifts—they think—from a god they don't understand. For a long time three of the relics were buried in a temple in Jerusalem, but during the Crusades, they were stolen, spirited away to various places. None of us knew where.

"When I did my research several hundred years ago, I focused on the medieval era, turning to as many resources as I could in a kind of theological scavenger hunt for the relics," Daniel continued. "The gist of it is that if these three artifacts can be collected and gathered together at Mount Sinai—"

"Why Mount Sinai?" Shelby asked.

"The channels between the Throne and the Earth are closest there," Gabbe explained with a flip of her hair. "That's where Moses received the Ten Commandments; that's where the angels enter when they're delivering messages from the Throne."

"Think of it as God's local dive," Arriane added, sending a Hacky Sack too high into the air and into an overhead lamp.

"But before you ask," Cam said, making it a point to single out Shelby with his eyes, "Mount Sinai is not the original site of the Fall."

"That would be way too easy," Annabelle said.

"If the relics are all gathered at Mount Sinai," Daniel went on, "then, in theory, we'll be able to decipher the location of the Fall."

"In theory." Cam sneered. "Must I be the one to say there is some question regarding the validity of Daniel's research—"

Daniel clenched his jaw. "You have a better idea?"

"Don't you think"—Cam raised his voice—"that your theory puts rather a lot of weight on the idea that these relics are anything more than rumor? Who knows if they can do what they're supposed to do?"

Luce studied the group of angels and demons—her only allies on this quest to save her and Daniel . . . and the world. "So that unknown location is where we have to be nine days from now."

"*Fewer* than nine days from now," Daniel said. "Nine days from now will be too late. Lucifer—and the host of angels cast out of Heaven—will have arrived."

"But if we can beat Lucifer to the site of the Fall," Luce said, "then what?"

Daniel shook his head. "We don't really know. I never told anyone about this book because, Cam's right, I didn't know what it would add up to. I didn't even know

Gabbe had it published until years later, and by then, I'd lost interest in the research. You had died another time, and without you being there to play your part—"

"*My* part?" Luce asked.

"Which we don't really yet understand—"

Gabbe elbowed Daniel, cutting him off. "What he means is all will be revealed in the fullness of time."

Molly smacked her forehead. "Really? 'All will be revealed'? Is that all you guys know? Is that what you're going on?"

"That and *your* importance," Cam said, turning to Luce. "You're the chess piece that the forces of good and evil and everything in between are fighting over here."

"What?" Luce whispered.

"Shut up." Daniel fixed his attention on Luce. "Don't listen to him."

Cam snorted, but no one acknowledged it. It just sat in the room like an uninvited guest. The angels and demons were silent. No one was going to leak anything else about Luce's role in stopping the Fall.

"So all of this information, this scavenger hunt," she said, "it's in that book?"

"More or less," Daniel said. "I just have to spend some time with the text and refresh my memory. Hopefully then I'll know where we need to begin."

The others moved away to give Daniel space at the table. Luce felt Miles's hand brush the back of her arm.

They'd barely spoken since she'd come back through the Announcer.

"Can I talk to you?" Miles asked very quietly. "Luce?"

The look on his face—it was strained about something—made Luce think of those last few moments in her parents' backyard when Miles had thrown her reflection.

They'd never really talked about the kiss they'd shared on the roof outside her Shoreline dorm room. Surely Miles knew it had been a mistake—but why did Luce feel like she was leading him on every time she was nice to him?

"Luce." It was Gabbe, appearing at Miles's side. "I thought I'd mention"—she glanced at Miles—"if you wanted to go visit Penn for a moment, now would be the time."

"Good idea." Luce nodded. "Thanks." She glanced apologetically at Miles but he just tugged his baseball cap over his eyes and turned to whisper something to Shelby.

"Ahem." Shelby coughed indignantly. She was standing behind Daniel, trying to read the book over his shoulder. "What about me and Miles?"

"You're going back to Shoreline," Gabbe said, sounding more like Luce's teachers at Shoreline than Luce had ever noticed before. "We need you to alert Steven and Francesca. We may need their help—and your help, too.

Tell them"—she took a deep breath—"tell them it's happening. That an endgame has been initiated, though not as we'd expected. Tell them everything. They will know what to do."

"Fine," Shelby said, scowling. "You're the boss."

"Yodelayhee-hooooo." Arriane cupped her palms around her mouth. "If, uh, Luce wants to get out, some-one's gonna have to help her down from the window." She drummed her fingers on the table, looking sheepish. "I made a library book barricade near the entrance in case any of the Sword & Cross-eyeds felt inclined to dis-rupt us."

"Dibs." Cam already had his arm slipped through the crook of Luce's elbow. She started to argue, but none of the other angels seemed to think it was a bad idea. Dan-iel didn't even notice.

Near the back exit, Shelby and Miles both mouthed *Be careful* to Luce with varying degrees of fierceness.

Cam walked her to the window, radiating warmth with his smile. He slid the glass pane up and together they looked out at the campus where they'd met, where they'd grown close, where he'd tricked her into kissing him. They weren't all bad memories. . . .

He hopped through the window first, landing smoothly on the ledge, and he held out a hand for hers.

"Milady."

His grip was strong and it made her feel tiny and

weightless as Cam drifted down from the ledge, two stories in two seconds. His wings were concealed, but he still moved as gracefully as if he were flying. They landed softly on the dewy grass.

"I take it you don't want my company," he said. "At the cemetery—not, you know, in general."

"Right. No, thanks."

He looked away and reached into his pocket, pulled out a tiny silver bell. It looked ancient, with Hebrew writing on it. He handed it to her. "Just ring when you want a lift back up."

"Cam," Luce said. "What is my role in all of this?"

Cam reached out to touch her cheek, then seemed to think better of it. His hand hovered in the air. "Daniel's right. It isn't our place to tell you."

He didn't wait for her response—just bent his knees and soared off the ground. He didn't even look back.

Luce stared at the campus for a moment, letting the familiar Sword & Cross humidity stick to her skin. She couldn't tell whether the dismal school with its huge, harsh neo-Gothic buildings and sad, defeated landscaping looked different or the same.

She strolled through the campus, through the flat still grass of the commons, past the depressing dormitory, to the wrought iron gate of the cemetery. There she paused, feeling goose bumps rise on her arms.

The cemetery still looked and smelled like a sinkhole

in the middle of the campus. The dust from the angels' battle had cleared. It was still early enough that most of the students were asleep, and anyway, none of them were likely to be prowling the cemetery, unless they were serving detention. She let herself in through the gate and ambled downward through the leaning headstones and the muddy graves.

In the far east corner lay Penn's final resting place. Luce sat down at the foot of her friend's plot. She didn't have flowers and she didn't know any prayers, so she lay her hands on the cold, wet grass, closed her eyes, and sent her own kind of message to Penn, worrying that it might never reach her.

⚜

Luce got back to the library window feeling irritable. She didn't need Cam or his exotic bell. She could get up the ledge by herself.

It was easy enough to scale the lowest portion of the sloped roof, and from there she could climb up a few levels until she was close to the long narrow ledge beneath the library windows. It was about two feet wide. As she crept along it, Cam's and Daniel's bickering voices wafted to her.

"What if one of us were to be intercepted?" Cam's voice was high and pleading. "You know we are stronger united, Daniel."

"If we don't make it there in time, our strength won't matter. We'll be *erased*."

She could picture them on the other side of the wall. Cam with fists clenched and green eyes flashing; Daniel stolid and immovable, his arms crossed over his chest.

"I don't trust you not to act on your own behalf." Cam's tone was harsh. "Your weakness for her is stronger than your word."

"There's nothing to discuss." Daniel didn't change his pitch. "Splitting up is our only option."

The others were quiet, probably thinking the same thing Luce was. Cam and Daniel behaved far too much like brothers for anyone else to dare come between them.

She reached the window and saw that the two angels were facing each other. Her hands gripped the windowsill. She felt a small swell of pride—which she would never confess—at having made it back into the library without help. Probably none of the angels would even notice. She sighed and slid one leg inside. That was when the window began to shudder.

The glass pane rattled, and the sill vibrated in her hands with such force she was almost knocked off the ledge. She held on tighter, feeling vibrations inside her, as if her heart and her soul were trembling, too.

"Earthquake," she whispered. Her foot skimmed the back of the ledge just as her grip on the windowsill loosened.

"Lucinda!"

Daniel rushed to the window. His hands found their way around hers. Cam was there, too, one hand on her upper back, another on the back of her head. The book-shelves rippled and the lights in the library flickered as the two angels pulled her through the rocking window just before the pane slipped from the window's casing and shattered into a thousand shards of glass.

She looked to Daniel for a clue. He was still gripping her wrists, but his eyes traveled past her, outside. He was watching the sky, which had turned angry and gray.

Worse than all that was the lingering vibration *inside* Luce that made her feel as if she'd been electrocuted. The quaking felt like an eternity, but it lasted for five, maybe ten seconds—enough time for Luce, Cam, and Daniel to fall to the dusty wooden floor of the library with a thud.

Then the trembling stopped and the world grew deathly quiet.

"What the hell?" Arriane picked herself up off the ground. "Did we step through to California without my knowledge? No one told me there were fault lines in Georgia!"

Cam pulled a long shard of glass from his forearm. Luce gasped as bright red blood trailed down his elbow, but his face showed no sign that he was in pain. "That wasn't an earthquake. That was a seismic shift in time."

"A *what*?" Luce asked.

"The first of many." Daniel looked out the jagged window, watching a white cumulus cloud roll across the now blue sky. "The closer Lucifer gets, the stronger they'll become." He glanced at Cam, who nodded.

"Ticktock, people," Cam said. "Time is running out. We need to fly."

TWO

PARTING WAYS

Gabbe stepped forward. "Cam's right. I've heard the Scale speak of these shifts." She was tugging on the sleeves of her pale yellow cashmere cardigan as if she would never get warm. "They're called timequakes. They are ripples in our reality."

"And the closer he gets," Roland added, with his usual understated wisdom, "the closer we are to the terminus of his Fall, the more frequent and the more severe the timequakes will become. Time is faltering in preparation for rewriting itself."

"Like the way your computer freezes up more and more frequently before the hard drive crashes and erases your twenty-page term paper?" Miles said. Everyone looked at him in befuddlement. "What?" he said. "Angels and demons don't do homework?"

Luce sank into one of the wooden chairs at an empty table. She felt hollow, as if the timequake had shaken loose something significant inside her and she'd lost it for good. The angels' bickering voices crisscrossed in her mind but didn't spell out anything useful. They had to stop Lucifer, and she could see that none of them knew exactly how to do it.

"Venice. Vienna. And Avalon." Daniel's clear voice broke through the noise. He sat down next to Luce and draped an arm around the back of her chair. His fingertips brushed her shoulder. When he held out *The Book of the Watchers* so all of them could see, the others quieted. Everybody focused.

Daniel pointed to a dense paragraph of text. Luce hadn't realized until then that the book was written in Latin. She recognized a few words from the years of Latin class she'd taken at Dover. Daniel had underlined and circled several words and made some notes in the margins, but time and wear had made the pages almost illegible.

Arriane hovered over him. "That's some serious chicken scratch."

Daniel didn't seem deterred. As he jotted new notes,

his handwriting was dark and elegant, and it gave Luce a warm, familiar feeling when she realized she'd seen it before. She basked in every reminder of how long and deep her and Daniel's love affair had been, even if the reminder was something small, like the cursive script that flowed along for centuries, spelling out Daniel as hers.

"A record of those early days after the Fall was created by the Heavenly host, by the unallied angels who'd been cast out of Heaven," he said slowly. "But it's a completely scattered history."

"A history?" Miles repeated. "So we just find some books and read them and they, like, tell us where to go?"

"It's not that simple," Daniel said. "There weren't books in any sense that would mean anything to you now; these were the beginning days. So our history and our stories were recorded via other means."

Arriane smiled. "This is where it's going to get tricky, isn't it?"

"The story was bound up in relics—many relics, over millennia. But there are three especially that seem relevant to our search, three that may hold the answer to where the angels fell to Earth.

"We don't know what these relics *are,* but we know where they were last mentioned: Venice, Vienna, and Avalon. They were in these three locations as of the time of the research and writing of this book. But that was a while ago, and even then, it was anyone's guess whether the items—whatever they are—were still there."

"So this may end up as a divine wild-goose chase," Cam said with a sigh. "Excellent. We'll squander our time searching for mystery items that may or may not tell us what we need to know in places where they may or may not have rested for centuries."

Daniel shrugged. "In short, yes."

"Three relics. Nine days." Annabelle's eyes fluttered up. "That's not a lot of time."

"Daniel was right." Gabbe's gaze flashed back and forth between the angels. "We need to split up."

This was what Cam and Daniel had been arguing about before the room started quaking. Whether they'd have a better chance of finding all the relics in time if they split up.

Gabbe waited for Cam's reluctant nod before she said, "Then it's settled. Daniel and Luce—you take the first city." She looked down at Daniel's notes, then gave Luce a brave smile. "Venice. You head to Venice and find the first relic."

"But what is the first relic? Do we even know?" Luce leaned over the book and saw a drawing sketched in pen in the margin. It looked almost like a serving tray, the kind her mom was always looking for at antiques shops.

Daniel studied it now, too, shaking his head slightly at the image he'd drawn hundreds of years ago. "This was what I was able to glean from my study of the pseudepigrapha—the dismissed scriptural writings of the early church."

The object was egg-shaped, with a glass bottom Daniel cleverly had depicted by sketching the ground on the other side of the clear base. The tray, or whatever the relic was, had what looked like small, chipped handles on either side. Daniel had even drawn a scale below it, and according to his sketch, the artifact was big—about eighty by one hundred centimeters.

"I barely remember drawing this." Daniel sounded disappointed in himself. "I don't know what it is any more than you do."

"I'm sure that once you get there, you'll be able to figure it out," Gabbe said, trying hard to be encouraging.

"We will," Luce said. "I'm sure we will."

Gabbe blinked, smiled, and went on. "Roland, Annabelle, and Arriane—you three will go to Vienna. That leaves—" Her mouth twitched as she realized what she was about to say, but she put on a brave face anyway. "Molly, Cam, and I will take Avalon."

Cam rolled back his shoulders and let out his astoundingly golden wings with a great rush, slamming into Molly's face with his right wing tip and sending her lunging back five feet.

"Do that again and I will wreck you," Molly spat, glaring at a carpet burn on her elbow. "In fact—" She started to go for Cam with her fist raised but Gabbe intervened.

She wrenched Cam and Molly apart with a put-upon sigh. "Speaking of wrecking, I would really rather not have to wreck the next one of you who provokes the other"—she smiled sweetly at her two demon companions—"but I will. This is going to be a very long nine days."

"Let's hope it's long," Daniel muttered under his breath.

Luce turned to him. The Venice in her mind was out of a guidebook: postcard pictures of boats jostling down canals, sunsets over tall cathedral spires, and dark-haired girls licking gelato. That wasn't the trip they were about to take. Not with the end of the world reaching out for them with razor claws.

"And once we find all three of the relics?" Luce said.

"We'll meet at Mount Sinai," Daniel said, "unite the relics—"

"And say a little prayer that they shed any light whatsoever on where we landed when we fell," Cam muttered darkly, rubbing his forehead. "At which point, all that's left is somehow coaxing the psychopathic hellhound holding our entire existence in his jaw that he should just abandon his silly scheme for universal domination. What could be simpler? I think we have every reason to feel optimistic."

Daniel glanced out the open window. The sun was passing over the dormitory now; Luce had to squint to look outside. "We need to leave as soon as possible."

"Okay," Luce said. "I have to go home, then, pack, get my passport. . . ." Her mind whirled in a hundred directions as she started making a mental to-do list. Her parents would be at the mall for at least another couple of hours, enough time for her to dash in and get her things together. . . .

"Oh, cute." Annabelle laughed, flitting over to them, her feet inches off the ground. Her wings were muscular and dark silver like a thundercloud, protruding through the invisible slits in her hot-pink T-shirt. "Sorry to butt in but . . . you've never traveled with an angel before, have you?"

Sure she had. The feeling of Daniel's wings soaring her body through the air was as natural as anything. Maybe her flights had been brief, but they'd been un-forgettable. They were when Luce felt closest to him: his arms threaded around her waist, his heart beating close to hers, his white wings protecting them, making Luce feel unconditionally and impossibly loved.

She had flown with Daniel dozens of times in dreams, but only three times in her waking hours: once over the hidden lake behind Sword & Cross, another time along the coast at Shoreline, and down from the clouds to the cabin just the previous night.

"I guess we've never flown that far together," she said at last.

"Just getting to first base seems to be a problem for you two," Cam couldn't resist saying.

Daniel ignored him. "Under normal circumstances, I think you'd enjoy the trip." His expression turned stormy. "But we don't have room for normal for the next nine days."

Luce felt his hands on the backs of her shoulders, gathering her hair and lifting it off her neck. He kissed her along the neckline of her sweater as he wrapped his arms around her waist. Luce closed her eyes. She knew what was coming next. The most beautiful sound there was—that elegant whoosh of the love of her life letting out his driven-snow-white wings.

The world on the other side of Luce's eyelids darkened slightly under the shadow of his wings, and warmth welled in her heart. When she opened her eyes, there they were, as magnificent as ever. She leaned back a little, cozying into the wall of Daniel's chest as he pivoted toward the window.

"This is only a temporary separation," Daniel announced to the others. "Good luck and wingspeed."

❄❄

With each long beat of Daniel's wings they gained a thousand feet. The air, once cool and thick with Georgia humidity, turned cold and brittle in Luce's lungs as they climbed. Wind tore at her ears. Her eyes began to tear. The ground below grew distant, and the world that it contained blended and shrank into a staggering canvas of green. Sword & Cross was the size of a thumbprint. Then it was gone.

A first glimpse of the ocean made Luce dizzy, delighted as they flew away from the sun, toward the darkness on the horizon.

Flying with Daniel was more thrilling, more intense than her memory could ever do justice to. And yet something had shifted: Luce had the hang of it by now. She felt at ease, in sync with Daniel, relaxed into the shape of his arms. Her legs were crossed lightly at the ankles, the heels of her boots kissing the toes of his. Their bodies swayed in unison, responding to the motion of his wings, which arched over their heads and blocked out the sun, then throttled backward to complete another mighty stroke.

They passed the cloud line and vanished into the mist. There was nothing all around them but wispy white and the nebulous caress of moisture. Another beat of wings. Another surge into the sky. Luce didn't pause to wonder how she would breathe up here at the limits of the atmosphere. She was with Daniel. She was fine. They were off to save the world.

Soon Daniel leveled off, flying less like a rocket and

more like an unfathomably powerful bird. They did not slow—if anything, their velocity increased—but with their bodies parallel to the ground, the wind's roar smoothed, and the world seemed bright white and startlingly quiet, as peaceful as if it had just come into existence and no one had yet experimented with sound.

"Are you all right?" His voice cocooned her, making her feel as if anything in the world that wasn't all right could be made so by love's concern.

She tilted her head to the left to look at him. His face was calm, lips softly smiling. His eyes poured out a violet light so rich it alone could have kept her aloft.

"You're freezing," he murmured into her ear, stroking her fingers to warm them up, sending licks of heat through Luce's body.

"Better now," she said.

They broke through the blanket of clouds: It was like that moment on an airplane when the view out the blurry oval window goes from monochrome gray to an infinite palate of color. The difference was that the window and the plane had fallen away, leaving nothing between her skin and the seashell pinks of evening-reaching clouds in the east, the garish indigo of high-altitude sky.

The cloudscape presented itself, foreign and arresting. As ever, it found Luce unprepared. This was another world she and Daniel alone inhabited, a high world, the tips of the tallest minarets of love.

What mortal hadn't dreamed of this? How many times had Luce yearned to be on the other side of an airplane window? To meander through the strange, pale gold of a sun-kissed rain cloud underfoot? Now she was here and overcome with the beauty of a distant world she could feel on her skin.

But Luce and Daniel could not stop. They could not stop once for the next nine days—or everything would stop.

"How long will it take to get to Venice?" she asked.

"It shouldn't be too much longer," Daniel almost whispered into her ear.

"You sound like a pilot who's been in a holding pattern for an hour, telling his passengers 'just another ten minutes' for the fifth time," Luce teased.

When Daniel didn't respond, she looked up at him. He was frowning in confusion. The metaphor was lost on him.

"You've never been on a plane," she said. "Why should you when you can do this?" She gestured at his gorgeous beating wings. "All the waiting and taxiing would probably drive you crazy."

"I'd like to go on a plane with you. Maybe we'll take a trip to the Bahamas. People fly there, right?"

"Yes." Luce swallowed. "Let's." She couldn't help thinking how many impossible things had to happen in precisely the right way for the two of them to be able to travel like a normal couple. It was too hard to think about the future right now, when so much was at stake. The future was as blurry and distant as the ground below—and Luce hoped it would be as beautiful.

"How long will it really take?"

"Four, maybe five hours at this speed."

"But won't you need to rest? Refuel?" Luce shrugged, still embarrassingly unsure of how Daniel's body worked. "Won't your arms get tired?"

He chuckled.

"What?"

"I just flew in from Heaven, and boy, are my arms tired." Daniel squeezed her waist, teasing. "The idea of my arms ever tiring of holding you is absurd."

As if to prove it, Daniel arched his back, drawing his wings high above his shoulders and beating them once, lightly. As their bodies swept elegantly upward, skirting a cloud, he released one arm from around her waist, illustrating that he could hold her deftly with a single hand. His free arm curved forward and Daniel brushed his fingers across her lips, waiting for her kiss. When she delivered it, he returned the arm to her waist and swept his other hand free, banking to the left dramatically. She kissed that hand, too. Then Daniel's shoulders flexed around hers, hugging them in an embrace tight enough that he could release both arms from around her waist, and somehow, still, she stayed aloft. The feeling was so delicious, so joyful and unbounded, that Luce began to laugh. He made a great loop in the air. Her hair splashed all over her face. She was not afraid. She was flying.

She took Daniel's hands as they found their way around her waist again. "It's kinda like we were made do this," she said.

"Yes. Kinda."

He flew on, never flagging. They shot through clouds and open air, through brief, beautiful rainstorms, drying off in the wind an instant later. They passed transatlantic planes at such tremendous speeds that Luce imagined the passengers inside not noticing anything but a brilliant, unexpected flash of silver and perhaps a gentle nudge of turbulence, making little waves run through their drinks.

The clouds thinned as they soared over the ocean. Luce could smell the briny weight of its depths all the way up here, and it smelled like an ocean from another planet, not chalky like Shoreline, and not brackish like home. The glorious shadow of Daniel's wings on its hammered surface below was somehow comforting, though it was hard to believe that she was a part of the vision she saw in the roiling sea.

"Luce?" Daniel asked.

"Yes?"

"What was it like to be around your parents this morning?"

Her eyes traced the outline of a lonely pair of islands in the dark watery plain below. She wondered distantly where they were, how far away from home.

"Hard," she admitted. "I guess I felt the way you must have felt a million times. At a distance from someone I love because I can't be honest with them."

"I was afraid of that."

"In some ways, it's easier to be around you and the other angels than it is to be around my own parents and my own best friend."

Daniel thought for a moment. "I don't want that for you. It shouldn't have to be like that. All I ever wanted was to love you."

"Me too. That's all I want." But even as she said it, looking out across the faded eastern sky, Luce couldn't stop replaying those last minutes at home, wishing she'd done things differently. She should have hugged her dad a little tighter. She should have listened, really listened, to her mom's advice as she walked out the door. She should have spent more time asking her best friend about her life back at Dover. She shouldn't have been so selfish or so rushed. Now every second took her farther away from Thunderbolt and her parents and Callie, and every second Luce grappled with the growing feeling that she might not see any of them again.

With all her heart Luce believed in what she and Daniel and the other angels were doing. But this was not the first time she'd abandoned the people she cared about for Daniel. She thought about the funeral she'd witnessed in Prussia, the dark wool coats and damp red eyes of her loved ones, bleary with grief at her early, sudden death. She thought about her beautiful mother in medieval England, where she'd spent Valentine's Day; her sister, Helen; and her good friends Laura and Eleanor. That was the one life she'd visited where she hadn't experienced her own death, but she'd seen enough to know that there were good people who would be shattered by Lucinda's inevitable demise. It made her stomach cramp to imagine. And then Luce thought of Lucia, the girl she'd been in Italy, who'd lost her family in the war, who didn't have anyone *but* Daniel, whose life— however short it was—had been worthwhile because of his love.

When she pressed deeper into his chest, Daniel slid his hands up the sleeves of her sweater and ran his fingers in circles around her arms, as if he were drawing little halos on her skin. "Tell me the best part of all your lives."

She wanted to say *When I found you, every time*. But it wasn't as simple as that. It was hard even to think of them discretely. Her past lives began to swirl together and hiccup like the panels of a kaleidoscope. There was that beautiful moment in Tahiti when Lulu had tattooed Daniel's chest. And the way they'd abandoned a battle in ancient China because their love was more important than fighting any war. She could have listed a dozen sexy stolen moments, a dozen gorgeous, bittersweet kisses. Luce knew those weren't the best parts.

The best part was now. That was what she would take with her from her journeys through the ages: He was worth everything to her and she was worth everything to him. The only way to experience that deep level of their love was to enter each new moment together, as if time were made of clouds. And if it came down to it during these next nine days, Luce knew that she and Daniel would risk everything for their love.

"It's been an education," she finally said. "The first time I stepped through on my own, I was already determined to break the curse. But I was overwhelmed and confused, until I started to realize that every life I visited, I learned something important about myself."

"Like what?" They were so high that the suggestion of the Earth's curve was visible at the edge of the darkening sky.

"I learned that just kissing you didn't kill me, that it had more to do with what I was aware of in the moment, how much of myself and my history I could take in."

She felt Daniel nod behind her. "That has always been the greatest enigma to me."

"I learned that my past selves weren't always very nice people, but you loved the soul inside of them anyway. And from your example, I learned how to recognize your soul. You have . . . a specific glow, a brightness, and even when you stopped looking like your physical self, I could step into a new lifetime and recognize you. I would see your soul almost overlying whatever face you wore in each life. You would be your foreign Egyptian self *and* the Daniel I craved and loved."

Daniel turned his head to kiss her temple. "You probably don't realize this, but the power to recognize my soul has always been in you."

"No, I couldn't—I didn't used to be able to—"

"You did, you just didn't know it. You thought you were crazy. You saw the Announcers and called them shadows. You thought they were haunting you all your life. And when you first met me at Sword & Cross, or maybe when you first realized you cared for me, you probably saw something else you couldn't explain, something you tried to deny?"

Luce clamped her eyes shut, remembering. "You used to leave a violet haze in the air when you passed by. But I'd blink and it would be gone."

Daniel smiled. "I didn't know that."

"What do you mean? You just said—"

"I imagined you saw *something*, but I didn't know what it was. Whatever attraction you recognized in me, in my soul, it would manifest differently depending on how you needed to see it." He smiled at her. "That's how your soul is in collaboration with mine. A violet glow is nice. I'm glad that's what it was."

"What does my soul look like to you?"

"I couldn't reduce it to words if I tried, but its beauty is unsurpassed."

That was a good way of describing this flight across the world with Daniel. The stars twinkled in vast galaxies all around them. The moon was huge and dense with craters, half shrouded by pale gray cloud. Luce was warm and safe in the arms of the angel she loved, a luxury she'd missed so much on her quest through the Announcers. She sighed and closed her eyes—

And saw *Bill*.

The vision was aggressive, invading her mind, though it was not the vile, seething beast Bill had become when she last saw him. He was just Bill, her flinty gargoyle, holding her hand to fly her down from the shipwrecked mast where she'd stepped through in Tahiti. Why that memory found her in Daniel's arms, she didn't know. But she could still feel the shape of his small stone hand in hers. She remembered how his strength and grace had astonished her. She remembered feeling safe with him.

Now her skin crawled and she writhed against Daniel uncomfortably.

"What is it?"

"Bill." The word tasted sour.

"Lucifer."

"I know he's Lucifer. I *know* that. But for a while there, he was something else to me. Somehow I thought of him as a friend. It haunts me, how close I let him get. I'm ashamed."

"Don't be." Daniel hugged her close. "There's a reason he was called the Morning Star. Lucifer was *beautiful*. Some say he was the most beautiful." Luce thought she detected a hint of jealousy in Daniel's tone. "He was the most beloved, too, not just by the Throne, but by many of the angels. Think of the sway he holds over mortals. That power flows from the same source." His voice wobbled, then grew very tight. "You shouldn't be ashamed of falling for him, Luce—" Daniel broke off suddenly, though it sounded like he had more to say.

"Things were getting tense between us," she admitted, "but I never imagined that he could turn into such a monster."

"There is no darkness as dark as a great light corrupted. Look." Daniel shifted the angle of his wings and they flew back in a wide arc, spinning around the outside of a towering cloud. One side was golden pink, lit by the last ray of evening sun. The other side, Luce noticed as they circled, was dark and pregnant with rain. "Bright and dark rolled up together, both necessary for this to be what it is. It is like that for Lucifer."

"And Cam, too?" Luce asked as Daniel completed the circle to resume their flight over the ocean.

"I know you don't trust him, but you can. I do. Cam's darkness is legendary, but it is only a sliver of his personality."

"But then why would he side with Lucifer? Why would any of the angels?"

"Cam didn't," Daniel said. "Not at first, anyway. It was a very unstable time. Unprecedented. Unimaginable. At the time of the Fall, there were some angels who sided with Lucifer right away, but there were others, like Cam, who were cast out by the Throne for not choosing quickly enough. The rest of history has been a slow choosing of sides, with angels returning to the fold of Heaven or the ranks of Hell until there are only a few unallied fallen left."

"That's where we are now?" Luce asked, even though she knew that Daniel didn't like to talk about how he still had not chosen a side.

"You used to really like Cam," Daniel said, sliding the subject away from himself. "For a handful of lifetimes on Earth the three of us were very close. It was only much later, after Cam had suffered a broken heart, that he crossed over to Lucifer's side."

"What? Who was she?"

"None of us like to talk about her. You must never let on that you know," Daniel said. "I resented his choice, but I can't say I didn't understand it. If I ever truly lost you, I don't know what I would do. My whole world would dim."

"That isn't going to happen," Luce said too quickly. She knew this lifetime was her last chance. If she died now, she would not come back.

She had a thousand questions, about the woman Cam had lost, about the strange quake in Daniel's voice when he talked about Lucifer's appeal, about where she'd been when he was falling. But her eyelids felt heavy, her body slack with fatigue.

"Rest," Daniel cooed in her ear. "I'll wake you up when we're landing in Venice."

It was all the permission she needed to let herself drift off. She closed her eyes against the phosphorescent waves crashing thousands of feet below and flew into a world of dreams where *nine days* had no significance, where she could dip and soar and linger in the glory of the clouds, where she could fly freely, into infinity, without the slightest chance of falling.

THREE

THE SUNKEN SANCTUARY

Daniel had been knocking on the weathered wooden door in the middle of the night for what felt to Luce like half an hour. The three-story Venetian town house belonged to a colleague, a professor, and Daniel was certain this man would let them crash, because they had been great friends "years ago," which, with Daniel, could encompass quite a span of time.

"He must be a heavy sleeper." Luce yawned, half lulled back into sleep herself by the steady pounding of

Daniel's fists. Either that, she thought blearily, or the professor was sitting in some bohemian all-night café, sipping wine over a book crammed with incomprehensible terms.

It was three in the morning—their touchdown amid the silvery web of Venice's canals had been accompanied by the chiming of a clock tower somewhere in the darkened distance of the city—and Luce was overcome with fatigue. She leaned miserably against the cold tin mailbox, causing it to wobble loose from one of the nails holding it upright. This sent the whole box slanting, making Luce stumble backward and nearly hurtle into the murky black-green canal, whose water lapped over the lip of the mossy stoop like an inky tongue.

The whole exterior of the house seemed to be rotting in layers: from the painted blue wood peeling off the windowsills in slimy sheets, to red bricks crawling with dark green mold, to the damp cement of the stoop, which crumbled under their feet. For a moment, Luce thought she could actually feel the city sinking.

"He's got to be here," Daniel muttered, still pounding.

When they'd landed on the canal-side ledge usually accessed only by gondola, Daniel had promised Luce a bed inside, a hot drink, a reprise from the damp and bracing wind they'd been flying through for hours.

At last, the slow shuffling of feet thumping down

stairs inside perked a shivering Luce to attention. Daniel exhaled and closed his eyes, relieved, as the brass knob turned. Hinges moaned as the door swung open.

"Who the devil—" The older Italian man's wiry tufts of white hair stood out at all angles from his head. He had sensationally bushy white eyebrows, a mustache to match, and thick white chest hair protruding from the V-neck of his dark gray robe.

Luce watched Daniel blink in surprise, as if he was second-guessing their address. Then the old man's pale brown eyes lit up. He lurched forward, pulling Daniel into a tight embrace.

"I was beginning to wonder if you were going to visit before I kicked the inevitable bucket," the man whispered hoarsely. His eyes traveled to Luce, and he smiled as if they hadn't woken him, as if he'd been expecting them for months. "After all these years, you finally brought over Lucinda. What a treat."

❧ ❧

His name was Professor Mazotta. He and Daniel had studied history together at the University of Bologna in the thirties. He was not appalled or bewildered by Daniel's lack of aging: Mazotta understood what Daniel was. He seemed to feel only joy at being reunited with an old friend, a joy that was augmented by the introduction to the love of that friend's life.

He escorted them into his office, which was also a study of varying degrees of decay. His bookshelves dipped at their centers; his desk was piled with yellowing papers; the rug was worn to threads and splashed with coffee stains. Mazotta set immediately to making each of them a cup of dense hot chocolate—an old man's old bad habit, he rasped to Luce with a nudge. But Daniel barely took a sip before thrusting his book into Mazotta's hands and opening it to the description of the first relic.

Mazotta slipped on thin wire-framed glasses and squinted at the page, mumbling to himself in Italian. He stood up, walked to the bookshelf, scratched his head, turned back to the desk, paced the office, sipped his chocolate, then returned to the bookshelf to pull out a fat leather-bound tome. Luce stifled a yawn. Her eyelids felt like they were working hard to hold up something heavy. She was trying not to drift, pinching the inside of her palm to keep herself awake. But Daniel's and Professor Mazotta's voices met each other like distant clouds of fog as they argued over the impossibility of everything the other was saying.

"It's absolutely not a windowpane from the church of Saint Ignatius." Mazotta wrung his hands. "Those are slightly hexagonal, and this illustration is resoundingly oblong."

"What are we doing here?" Daniel suddenly shouted, rattling an amateur painting of a blue sailboat on the wall. "We clearly need to be at the library at Bologna. Do you still have keys to get in? In your office you must have had—"

"I became emeritus thirteen years ago, Daniel. And we're not traveling two hundred kilometers in the middle of the night to look at . . ." He paused. "Look at Lucinda, she's sleeping standing up, like a horse!"

Luce grimaced groggily. She was afraid to start down the path of a dream for fear she might meet Bill. He had a tendency to turn up when she closed her eyes these days. She wanted to stay awake, to stay away from him, to be a part of the conversation about the relic she and Daniel would need to find the next day. But sleep was insistent and would not be denied.

Seconds or hours later, Daniel's arms lifted her from the ground and carried her up a dark and narrow flight of stairs.

"I'm sorry, Luce," she thought he said. She was too deep asleep to respond. "I should have let you rest sooner. I'm just so scared," he whispered. "Scared we're going to run out of time."

※ ※

Luce blinked and shifted backward, surprised to find herself in a bed, further surprised by the single white peony in a short glass vase drooping onto the pillow next to her head.

She plucked the flower from its vase and twirled it in

※ 61 ※

her palm, causing drops of water to bead on the brocaded rose duvet. The bed creaked as she propped the pillow up against the brass headboard to look around the room.

For a moment, she felt disoriented by finding herself in an unfamiliar place, dreamed memories of traveling through the Announcers slowly fading as she fully awoke. She no longer had Bill to give her clues about where she'd ended up. He was only there in her dreams, and the previous night he'd been Lucifer, a monster, laughing at the idea that she and Daniel could change or stop a thing.

A white envelope was propped against the vase on the nightstand.

Daniel.

She remembered only a single soft sweet kiss and his arms pulling away as he'd tucked her into bed the previous night and shut the door.

Where had he gone after that?

She ripped open the envelope and slid out the stiff white card it held. On the card were three words:

On the balcony.

Smiling, Luce threw back the covers and heaved her legs over the side of the bed. She padded across the giant woven rug, the white peony scissored between her fingers. The windows in the bedroom were tall and narrow and rose nearly twenty feet to the cathedral ceiling. Behind one of the rich brown curtains was a glass door leading out to a terrace. She turned the metal latch and stepped outside, expecting to find Daniel and sink into his arms.

But the crescent-moon-shaped terrace was empty. Just a short stone railing and a one-story drop to the green waters of the canal, and a small glass-topped table with a red canvas folding chair beside it. The morning was beautiful. The air smelled murky but crisp. On the river shiny narrow black gondolas glided past one another as elegantly as swans. A pair of speckled thrushes chirped from a clothesline one floor up, and on the other side of the canal was a row of cramped pastel apartments. It was charming, sure, the Venice of most people's dreams, but Luce wasn't here to be a tourist. She and Daniel were here to save their history, and the world's. And the clock was ticking. And Daniel was gone.

Then she noticed a second white envelope on the balcony table, propped up against a tiny white to-go cup and a small paper bag. Again, she tore open the card, and again found only three words:

Please wait here.

"Annoying yet romantic," she said aloud. She sat down on the folding chair and peered inside the paper bag. A handful of tiny jam-filled donuts dusted with cinnamon and sugar sent up an intoxicating scent. The bag was warm in her hands, flecked with little bits of oil seeping through. Luce popped one into her mouth and took a sip from the tiny white cup, which contained the richest, most delightful espresso Luce had ever tasted.

"Enjoying the bombolini?" Daniel called from below.

Luce shot to her feet and leaned over the railing to find him standing at the back of a gondola painted with images of angels. He wore a flat straw hat bound with a thick red ribbon, and used a broad wooden paddle to steer the boat slowly toward her.

Her heart surged the way it did each time she first saw Daniel in another life. But he was here. He was hers. This was happening now.

"Dip them in the espresso, then tell me what it's like to be in Heaven," Daniel said, smiling up at her.

"How do I get down to you?" she called.

He pointed to the narrowest spiral staircase Luce had ever seen, just to the right of the railing. She grabbed the coffee and bag of donuts, slipped the peony stem behind her ear, and made for the steps.

She could feel Daniel's eyes on her as she climbed over the railing and slinked down the stairs. Every time she made a full rotation on the staircase, she caught a teasing flash of his violet eyes. By the time she made it to the bottom, he had extended his hand to help her onto the boat.

There was the electricity she'd been yearning for since she awoke. The spark that passed between them every time they touched. Daniel wrapped his arms around her waist and drew her in so that there was no space between their bodies. He kissed her, long and deep, until she was dizzy.

"Now that's the way to start a morning." Daniel's fingers traced the petals of the peony behind her ear.

A slight weight suddenly tugged at her neck and when she reached up, her hands found a fine chain, which her fingers traced down to a silver locket. She held it out and looked at the red rose engraved on its face.

Her locket! It was the one Daniel had given to her on her last night at Sword & Cross. She had kept it tucked in the front cover of *The Book of the Watchers* during the short time she'd spent alone in the cabin, but everything about those days was blurry. The next thing she remembered was Mr. Cole rushing her to the airport to catch her flight to California. She hadn't remembered the locket or the book until she'd arrived at Shoreline, and by then she was certain she'd lost them.

Daniel must have slipped it around her neck when she was sleeping. Her eyes teared again, this time with happiness. "Where did you—"

"Open it." Daniel smiled.

The last time she'd held the locket, the image of a former Luce and Daniel had baffled her. Daniel said he'd tell her when the photograph had been taken the next time he saw her. That hadn't happened. Their stolen time together in California had been mostly stressful and too brief, filled with silly arguments she couldn't imagine having with Daniel anymore.

Luce was glad to have waited, because when she opened the locket this time and saw the tiny photograph behind its glass plate—Daniel in a bowtie and Luce with coiffed short hair—she instantly recognized what it was.

"Lucia," she whispered. It was the young nurse Luce had encountered when she stepped through into World War I Milan. The girl had been much younger when Luce met her, sweet and a little sassy, but so genuine Luce had admired her right away.

She smiled now, remembering the way Lucia kept staring at Luce's shorter modern haircut, and the way Lucia joked that all the soldiers had a crush on Luce. She remembered mostly that if Luce had stayed at the Italian hospital a little longer and if the circumstances had been . . . well, entirely different, the two of them could have been great friends.

She looked up at Daniel, beaming, but her expression quickly darkened. He was staring at her as if he'd been punched.

"What's wrong?" She let go of the locket and stepped into him, wrapping her arms around his neck.

He shook his head, stunned. "I'm just not used to being able to share this with you. The look on your face when you recognized that picture? It's the most beautiful thing I've ever seen."

Luce blushed and smiled and felt speechless and wanted to cry all at once. She understood Daniel completely.

"I'm sorry I left you alone like that," he said. "I had to go and check something in one of Mazotta's books in Bologna. I figured you'd need every bit of rest you could get, and you looked so beautiful asleep, I couldn't bear to wake you up."

"Did you find what you were looking for?" Luce asked.

"Possibly. Mazotta gave me a clue about one of the piazzas here in town. He's mostly an art historian, but he knows his divinity better than any mortal I've ever met."

Luce slid down to the gondola's low red velvet bench, which was like a love seat, with a padded black leather cushion and a high, sculpted back.

Daniel sank the oar into the water and the boat slid forward. The water was a bright pastel green, and as they glided, Luce could see the whole city reflected in the glassy wobble of its surface.

"The good news," Daniel said, looking down at her

from under the brim of his hat, "is that Mazotta thinks he knows where the artifact is located. I kept him up bickering until sunrise, but we finally matched my sketch to an interesting old photograph."

"And?"

"As it turns out"—Daniel flicked his wrist and the gondola curved gracefully around a tight corner, then dipped under the low slant of a footbridge—"the serving tray is a halo."

"A *halo*? I thought only angels on greeting cards had halos." She cocked her head at Daniel. "Do *you* have a halo?"

Daniel smiled as if he found the question charming. "Not in the golden-ring fashion, I don't think. As far as we can tell, halos are representations of our light, in a way that mortals can comprehend. The violet light you saw around me at Sword & Cross, for example. I'm guessing Gabbe never told you stories about posing for da Vinci?"

"She did *what*?" Luce almost choked on her bombolini.

"He didn't know she was an angel, of course, but according to her, Leonardo talked about the light that seemed to radiate from within her. That's why he painted her with a halo circling her head."

"Whoa." Luce shook her head, astonished, as they glided past a pair of lovers in matching felt fedoras kissing in a balcony corner.

"It's not just him. Artists have been depicting angels that way since we first fell to Earth."

"And the halo we need to find today?"

"Another artist's depiction." Daniel's face grew somber. The brass of a scratchy jazz record drifted out an open window and seemed to fill the space around the gondola, scoring Daniel's narration. "This one is a sculpture of an angel, and much older, from the pre-classical era. So old, the artist's identity is unknown. It's from Anatolia and, like the rest of these artifacts, was stolen during the Second Crusade."

"So we just go find the sculpture in a church or museum or whatever, lift the halo off the angel's head, and sprint to Mount Sinai?" Luce asked.

Daniel's eyes darkened for a split second. "For now, yes, that's the plan."

"That sounds too simple," Luce said, noting the intricacies of the buildings around her—the high onion-domed windows in one, the verdant herb garden creeping out the window of another. Everything seemed to be sinking into the bright green water with a kind of serene surrender.

Daniel stared past her, the sunlit water reflecting in his eyes. "We'll see how simple it is."

He squinted at a wooden sign farther down the block, then steered them out of the center of the canal. The gondola rocked as Daniel guided it to a stop against a brick wall crawling with vines. He grabbed hold of one of the mooring poles and knotted the gondola's rope around it. The boat groaned and strained against its bindings.

"This is the address Mazotta gave me." Daniel gestured at an ancient curved stone bridge somewhere between romantic and decrepit. "We'll head up these stairs toward the palazzo. It shouldn't be far."

He hopped out of the gondola and onto the sidewalk, holding out his hand for Luce. She followed his lead, and together they crossed the bridge, hand in hand. As they walked past bakery stand after bakery stand and vendors selling VENICE T-shirts, Luce couldn't help looking around at all the other happy couples: Everyone here seemed to be kissing, laughing. She tugged the peony out from behind her ear and slipped it inside her purse. She and Daniel were on a mission, not a honeymoon, and there would never be another romantic encounter if they failed.

Their pace quickened as they turned left onto a narrow street, then right into a broad open piazza.

Daniel stopped abruptly.

"It is supposed to be here. In the square." He looked down at the address, shaking his head in weary disbelief.

"What's wrong?"

"The address Mazotta gave me is *that* church. He didn't tell me that." He pointed at the tall, spired Franciscan building, with its triangle of stained-glass roseate windows. It was a massive, commanding chapel with a pale orange exterior and bright white trim around its windows and its large dome. "The sculpture—the halo—must be inside."

"Okay." Luce took a step toward the church, giving Daniel a bewildered shrug. "Let's go in and check it out."

Daniel shifted his weight. His face suddenly looked pale. "I can't, Luce."

"Why not?"

Daniel's body had stiffened with a palpable nervousness. His arms seemed nailed to his sides and his jaw was clenched so tightly it could have been wired. She wasn't used to Daniel's being anything other than confident. This was strange behavior.

"Then you don't know?" he asked.

Luce shook her head and Daniel sighed.

"I thought maybe at Shoreline, they might have taught you . . . the thing is, actually, if a fallen angel enters a sanctuary of God, the structure and all those inside it burst into flames."

He finished his sentence quickly, just as a group of plaid-skirted German schoolgirls on a tour passed them in the piazza, filing toward the entrance of the church. Luce watched as a few of them turned to look at Daniel, whispering and giggling to each other, smoothing their braids in case he happened to glance their way.

He fixed on Luce. He still seemed nervous. "It's one

of the many lesser-known details of our punishment. If a fallen angel desires to reenter the jurisdiction of the grace of God, we must approach the Throne directly. There are no shortcuts."

"You're saying you've never set foot in a church? Not once in the thousands of years you've been here?"

Daniel shook his head. "Or a temple, or a synagogue, or a mosque. Never. The closest I've come is the natatorium at Sword & Cross. When it was desanctified and repurposed as a gym, the taboo was lifted." He closed his eyes. "Arriane did once, very early on before she'd reallied herself with Heaven. She didn't know any better. The way she describes it—"

"Is that where she got the scars on her neck?" Luce touched her own neck instinctively, thinking back to her first hour at Sword & Cross: Arriane handing over a stolen Swiss Army knife, demanding that Luce give her a haircut. She hadn't been able to take her eyes off the angel's strange marbled scars.

"No." Daniel looked away, uncomfortable. "That was something else."

A group of tourists were posing with their guide in front of the entrance. In the time they had been talking, ten people had drifted into and out of the church without seeming to appreciate the building's beauty or its import—and yet Daniel, Arriane, and a whole legion of angels could never step inside.

But Luce could.

"I'll go. I know what the halo looks like from your sketch. If it's in there, I'll find it and—"

"You can enter, it's true." Daniel nodded curtly. "There is no other way."

"No problem." Luce feigned nonchalance.

"I'll wait right here." Daniel looked reluctant and relieved at the same time. He squeezed her hand and sat down on the raised rim of a fountain in the center of the square and explained what the halo should look like and how to remove it. "But be careful! It's more than a thousand years old and delicate!" Behind him, a cherub spat out an unending stream of water. "If you have any trouble, Luce, if anything looks even remotely suspicious, run back out here and find me."

The church was dark and cool, a cross-shaped structure with low rafters and the heavy scent of incense cloaking the air. Luce picked up an English pamphlet from the entryway, then realized she didn't know what the name of the sculpture was. Annoyed with herself for not asking—Daniel would have known—she walked up the narrow nave, past row after row of empty pews, her eyes tracing the stained-glass Stations of the Cross lining the high windows.

Though the piazza outside had been bustling with people, the church was relatively quiet. Luce was conscious of the sound of her riding boots on the marble floor as she passed a statue of the Madonna in one of the small gated chapels lining either side of the church. The statue's flat marble eyes seemed impossibly big, her fingers impossibly long and thin, pressed together in prayer.

Luce did not see the halo anywhere.

At the end of the nave she stood in the center of the church, under the great dome, which let the tempered glow of morning sunlight brush through its towering windows. A man in a long gray robe kneeled before an altar. His pale face and white hands—cupped to his heart—were the only parts of his body exposed. He was chanting in Latin under his breath. *Dies irae, dies illa.* Luce recognized the words from her Latin class at Dover but couldn't remember what they meant.

As she approached, the man's chant broke off and he lifted his head, as if her presence had disrupted his prayer. His skin was as pale as any she'd ever seen, his thin lips almost colorless as they frowned at her. She looked away and turned left into the transept, the shorter aisle that formed the cross shape of the church, in an effort to give the man his space—

And found herself before a formidable angel.

It was a statue, sculpted from smooth pale pink marble, utterly different from the angels Luce had come to know so well. There was none of the fierce vitality she found in Cam, none of the infinite complexities she adored in Daniel. This was a statue created by the stolidly faithful for the stolidly faithful. To Luce, the angel seemed empty. He was looking up, toward Heaven, and his sculpted body shone through the soft ripples of fabric draped across his chest and waist. His face, tilted skyward, ten feet above Luce's own, had been chiseled delicately, by someone with a practiced touch, from the ridge of his nose to the tiny tufts of hair curled above his ear. His hands gestured toward the sky, as if asking forgiveness from someone above for a long-ago-committed sin.

"Buon giorno." A sudden voice made Luce jump. She hadn't seen the priest appear in the heavy floor-length black robe, had not seen the rectory at the edge of the transept, from whose carved mahogany door the priest had just emerged.

He had a waxy nose and large earlobes and was tall enough to tower over her, which made her uneasy. She forced a smile and took a step away. How was she going to steal a relic from a public place like this? Why hadn't she thought about that before in the piazza? She couldn't even speak—

Then she remembered: She *could* speak Italian. She had learned it—more or less—instantly when she'd stepped through the Announcer into the front lines of war near the Piave River.

"This is a beautiful sculpture," she said to the priest.

Her Italian wasn't perfect—she spoke more like she used to be fluent years ago but had lost her confidence.

Still, her accent was good enough, and the priest seemed to understand. "Indeed it is."

"The artist's work with the . . . chisel," she said, spreading her arms wide as though she were critically regarding the work, "it is like he freed the angel from the stone." Drawing her wide eyes back to the sculpture, trying to look as innocent as possible, Luce took a spin around the angel. Sure enough, a golden glass-filled halo capped his head. Only it wasn't chipped in the places Daniel's sketch had suggested. Maybe it had been restored.

The priest nodded sagely and said, "No angel was ever free after the sin of the Fall. The able eye can see that, as well."

Daniel had told her the trick to releasing the halo from the angel's head: to grasp the halo like a steering wheel and give it two firm but gentle counterclockwise turns. "Because it's made of glass and gold, it had to be added to the sculpture later. So a base is carved into the stone, and a matching hole fashioned into the halo. Just two strong—but careful!—twists." That would loosen it from its base.

She glanced up at the vast statue towering over her and the priest's heads.

Right.

The priest came to stand beside Luce. "This is Raphael, the Healer."

Luce didn't know any angels named Raphael. She wondered if he was real or a church invention. "I, um, read in a guidebook that it dates back to before the classical era." She eyed the thin beam of marble connecting the halo to the angel's head. "Wasn't this sculpture brought to the church during the Crusades?"

The priest swept his arms over his chest, and the long loose sleeves of his robe bunched up at the elbow. "You are thinking of the original. It sat just south of Dorsoduro in the Chiesa dei Piccoli Miracoli on the Island of the Seals, and disappeared with the church and the island when both, as we know, sank into the sea centuries ago."

"No." Luce swallowed hard. "I didn't know that."

His round brown eyes fixed on hers. "You must be new to Venice," he said. "Eventually, everything here crumbles into the sea. It isn't so bad, really. How else would we become so skilled at reproductions?" He glanced up at the angel, ran his long brown fingers across the marble plinth. "This one was created on commission for only fifty thousand lire. Isn't it remarkable?"

It wasn't remarkable; it was awful. The real halo had sunk into the sea? They would never find it now; they would never learn the true location of the Fall; they would never be able to stop Lucifer from destroying them. They'd only just begun this journey and already it seemed that all was lost.

Luce stumbled backward, barely finding the breath to thank the priest. Feeling heavy and unbalanced, she nearly tripped over the pale supplicant, who scowled at her as she walked quickly to the door.

As soon as she crossed the threshold, she broke into a run. Daniel caught her by the elbow at the fountain. "What happened?"

Her face must have given everything away. She relayed the story to him, growing more despondent with each word. By the time she got to the way the priest had bragged about the bargain reproduction, a tear was sliding down her cheek.

"You're sure he called the cathedral la Chiesa dei Piccoli Miracoli?" Daniel said, spinning around to look across the piazza. "On the Island of the Seals?"

"I'm sure, Daniel, it's gone. It's buried under the ocean—"

"And we are going to find it."

"What? How?"

He had already grabbed her by the hand and, with one sideways glance back through the doors of the church, started to jog across the square.

"Daniel—"

"You know how to swim."

"That isn't funny."

"No, it isn't." He stopped running and turned to look at her, held her chin in his palm. Her heart was racing but his eyes on hers made everything slow down. "It's not ideal, but if this is the only way to get the artifact, it's the way we're going to get the artifact. Nothing can stop us. You know that. Nothing can be allowed to stop us."

⚜

Moments later, they were back in the gondola, Daniel rowing them out to sea—powering them like an engine with each stroke of his oar. They sped past every other gondola in the canal, making hairpin turns around low bridges and the jutting corners of buildings, splashing water on alarmed faces in neighboring gondolas.

"I know this island," Daniel said, not even winded. "It used to lie halfway between Saint Mark's and La Giudecca. But there's nowhere to dock the boat nearby. We'll have to leave the gondola. We'll have to jump ship and swim."

Luce glanced over the side of the gondola into the cloudy green water moving fast below her. Lack of swimsuit. Hypothermia. Italian sea monsters in unseen depths of sludge. The gondola bench was freezing under her and the water smelled like mud laced with sewage. All this flashed through Luce's mind, but when she locked on Daniel's eyes, it quieted her fear.

He needed her. She was at his side, no questions asked.

"Okay."

When they reached the open channel where the canals emptied out into space between the islands' edges, it was tourist chaos: The water teemed with vaporetti shuttling tourists and their roller bags toward hotels; motorboats chartered by rich, elegant travelers; and bright, aerodynamic kayaks carrying American backpackers wearing wraparound sunglasses. Gondolas and barges and police boats all crisscrossed the water at high speeds, barely avoiding one another.

Daniel maneuvered effortlessly, pointing into the distance. "See the towers?"

Luce stared out over the multicolored boats. The horizon was a faint line where the blue-gray of the sky touched the darker blue-gray of the water. "No."

"Focus, Luce."

After a few moments, two small greenish towers—farther away than she imagined she could ever see without a telescope—came into view. "Oh. There."

"That's all that remains of the church." Daniel's paddling speed increased as the number of boats around them decreased. The water grew choppier, deepened to a dark evergreen color, began to smell more like the sea than the oddly appealing filth of Venice. Luce's hair whipped in the wind, which felt colder the farther from land they got. "We'll have to hope that our halo has not been pilfered by excavation teams of scuba divers."

Earlier, after Luce had climbed back into the gondola, Daniel had asked her to wait for him for just a moment. He'd disappeared down a narrow alley and reappeared what seemed like seconds later with a small pink plastic bag. When he tossed it to her now, Luce pulled out a pair of goggles. They looked stupidly expensive and not very functional: mauve and black with fashionable angel wings at the edges of the lenses. She couldn't remember the last time she'd swum with goggles, but as she looked out at the black-shadowed water, Luce was glad to have them to tug down over her eyes.

"Goggles but no bathing suit?" she asked.

Daniel blushed. "I guess that was stupid. But I was in a hurry, only thinking about what you would *need* to get the halo." He drove the paddle back into the water, propelling them more quickly than a speedboat. "You can swim in your underwear, right?"

Now Luce blushed. Under normal circumstances, the question might have seemed thrilling, something they both would have giggled at. Not these nine days. She nodded. Eight days now. Daniel was deadly serious. Luce just swallowed hard and said, "Of course."

The pair of green-gray spires grew larger, more detailed, and then they were upon them. They were tall and conical, made of rusted slats of copper. They had once been capped by small teardrop-shaped copper flags sculpted to look like they were rippling in the wind, but one weathered flag was pocked with holes, and the other had broken off completely. In the open water, the spires' protrusion was bizarre, suggesting a cavernous cathedral of the deep. Luce wondered how long ago the church had sunk, how deep it sat below.

The thought of diving down there in ridiculous goggles and mom-bought underwear made her shudder.

"This church must be huge," she said. She meant *I don't think I can do this. I can't breathe underwater. How are we going to find one small halo sunk in the middle of the sea?*

"I can take you down as far as the chapel itself, but only that far. So long as you hold on to my hand." Daniel extended a warm hand to help Luce stand up in the gondola. "Breathing will not be a problem. But the church will still be sanctified, which means I'll need you to find the halo and bring it out to me."

Daniel yanked his T-shirt off over his head, dropping it to the bench of the gondola. He stepped out of his pants quickly, perfectly balanced in the boat, then kicked off his tennis shoes. Luce watched, feeling something stir inside her, until she realized she was supposed to be stripping down, too. She kicked off her boots, tugged off her socks, stepped out of her jeans as modestly as she could. Daniel held her hand to help her balance; he was watching her but not the way she would have expected. He was worried about her, the goose bumps rising on her skin. He rubbed her arms when she slipped off her sweater and stood freezing in her sensible underwear in the gondola in the middle of the Venetian lagoon.

Again she shivered, cold and fear an indecipherable mass inside her. But her voice sounded brave when she tugged the goggles, which pinched, down over her eyes and said, "Okay, let's swim."

They held hands, just like they had the last time they'd swum together at Sword & Cross. As their feet lifted off the varnished floor of the gondola, Daniel's hand tugged her upward, higher than she ever could have jumped herself—and then they dove.

Her body broke the surface of the sea, which wasn't as cold as she'd expected. In fact, the closer she swam beside Daniel, the warmer the wake around them grew.

He was glowing.

Of course he was. She hadn't wanted to voice her fears about how dark and impassable the church would be underwater, and now she realized, as ever, that Daniel was looking out for her. Daniel would light her way to the halo with the same shimmery incandescence Luce had seen in many of the past lives she'd visited. His glow played off the murky water, folding Luce inside it, as lovely and surprising as a rainbow arching boldly in a black night sky.

They swam down, holding hands, bathed in violet light. The water was silky, silent as an empty tomb.

Within a dozen feet, the sea became darker, but Daniel's light still illuminated the ocean for several feet around them. A dozen feet more and the façade of the church came into view.

It was beautiful. The ocean had preserved it, and the glow of Daniel's glory cast a haunting violet sheen on its quiet old stones. The pair of spires above the surface punctuated a flat roof lined with stone sculptures of saints. There were panels of half-decayed mosaics depicting Jesus with some of the apostles. Everything was thick with moss and crawling with sea life: tiny silver fish flitting into and out of alcoves, sea anemones jutting out from the depictions of miracles, eels slipping out of crannies where ancient Venetians had walked. Daniel stayed beside her, following her whimsical course, lighting her way.

She swam around the right side of the church, peering through busted stained-glass windows, always eyeing the distance back up to the surface, to air.

At about the point that she'd expected, Luce's lungs began to strain. But she wasn't ready to go up yet. They'd only just made it down to where they could see what looked like the altar. She gritted her teeth and bore the burn a little longer.

Holding his hand, she peeked through one of the windows near the church's transept. Her head and shoulders ventured in and Daniel flattened as much as he could against the wall of the church to light the inside for her.

She saw nothing but rotting pews, a stone altar split in two. The rest was shadowed, and Daniel couldn't get any closer to give her more light. She felt a tensing in her lungs and she panicked—but then, somehow, it released, and she felt as if she had a luxurious expanse of time before the tension and panic would return. It was as if there were breathing thresholds, and Luce could pass through a few of them before things would get really dire. Daniel watched her, nodding, as if he understood that she could go on a little longer.

She swam past one more former window, and something golden gleamed in a sunken corner of the church. Daniel saw it, too. He swam to her side, careful not to press inside the church. He took her hand and pointed at it. Only the tip of the halo was visible. The statue itself looked as if it had sunk through a collapsed portion of the floor. Luce swam closer, clotting the air before her with bubbles, unsure how to wrest it free. She couldn't wait any longer. Her lungs blazed. She gave Daniel the sign to go up.

He shook his head.

When she flinched in surprise, he pulled her fully outside the church and took her in his arms. He kissed her deeply, and it felt so good, but—

But no, he wasn't just kissing her. He was breathing air into her lungs. She gasped in his kisses, felt the pure air flow into her, sustaining her lungs just when they felt like they would burst. It was as if he had an endless supply, and Luce was greedy for as much as she could get. Their hands searched each other's almost naked bodies, as filled with passion as if they were kissing purely for pleasure. Luce didn't want to stop. But they only had eight days. When at last she nodded that she was satiated, Daniel grinned and pulled away.

They returned to the tiny opening where the window used to be. Daniel swam to it and stopped, positioning his body to face the opening so his glow would shine in to light her way. She squirmed slowly through the window, feeling instantly cold and senselessly claustrophobic inside the church. That was strange, because the cathedral was huge: Its ceilings were a hundred feet high, and Luce had the place all to herself.

Maybe that was the problem. On the other side of the window Daniel seemed too far away. At least she could see the angel up ahead—and Daniel's glow just outside. She swam toward the golden halo, gripped it in her hands. She remembered Daniel's instructions, and she turned the halo as if she were steering a Greyhound bus.

It didn't budge.

Luce gripped the slick halo harder. She rocked it back and forth, putting all the strength she had into it.

Ever so slowly, the halo creaked and shifted a centimeter to the left. She strained again to make it budge, sending out bubbles of exasperation. Just as she began to feel exhausted, the halo loosened, turned. Daniel's face filled with pride as he watched her and she watched him, their gazes intertwined. She was barely even thinking about her breath as she strained to unscrew the halo.

It came off in her hands. She yelped with delight and admired its impressive heft. But when she looked up at Daniel, he wasn't looking at her anymore. He was gazing upward, far in the distance.

A second later, he was gone.

FOUR

BARGAINING BLIND

Alone in the darkness, Luce treaded water.

Where was he?

She swam closer to the crater in the floorboards where the angel had sunk through—where, only seconds before, Daniel's glow had been with her, lighting her way.

Up. It was the only option.

The pressure in her lungs built rapidly and spread through the rest of her body, thrumming inside her head.

The surface was far away, and by now the air Daniel had breathed into her was gone. She could not see her hand before her face. She could not think. She could *not* panic.

Luce thrashed away from the rotted floorboards, somersaulting in the water to face where she thought the basement window she'd used to enter the cathedral should be. Her trembling hands probed the barnacled basement walls, groping for the narrow opening she had to fit back through.

There.

Her fingers reached outside the ruin and felt the warmer water beyond. In the darkness, the passage seemed even smaller and more impossible to pass through than it had when Daniel had been there, glowing, lighting her way. But it was the only way out.

With the halo tucked awkwardly under her chin, Luce thrust herself forward, jamming her elbows against the exterior of the building to pull her body through. First her shoulders, then her waist, then—

Pain ripped through her hip.

Her left foot was stuck, snagged against something she couldn't reach or see. Tears stung her eyes and she cried out in frustration. She watched the bubbles from her mouth float up—up where she needed to be—carrying with them more energy and air than she had left in her.

With half her body through the window and half her body wedged within, Luce struggled, stiff with terror. If only Daniel were here . . .

But Daniel wasn't here.

Holding the halo with one hand, she snaked the other back through the tight window, sliding it down against her body, trying to reach her foot. Her fingers met something cold and rubbery and unrecognizable. A piece of it came off in her hands, then crumbled into nothing. She squirmed in disgust as she tried to wrench her foot free from the grip of whatever it was. Her vision was starting to cloud as her fingernails snagged and tore and her ankle grew raw from all her straining to get free—then suddenly she was loose.

Her leg jerked forward and her knee struck the crumbling wall sharply enough that she knew she'd cut it, but no matter: She furiously shimmied the rest of her body through the window.

She had the halo. She was free.

But there was no way she had enough air in her lungs to make it to the surface. Her body was shaking badly, her legs barely responding to commands to *swim,* and a haze of black-red spots swarmed before her eyes. She felt dull, like she was swimming through wet cement.

Then something amazing happened: The dark waters around her grew bright with a shimmery glow, and she was enveloped in warmth and light like summer dawn.

A hand appeared, extended toward her.

Daniel. She slipped the fingers of one hand inside his strong broad palm, hugging the halo close to her chest with the other hand.

Luce closed her eyes as she flew upward with Daniel, in underwater sky.

A second seemed to pass and they broke through the surface into blindingly bright sunlight. Instinctively, Luce gulped for the biggest lungful of air she could take in, startling herself with the raw groan her throat made, one hand around her neck to guide the air down, the other ripping off her goggles.

But—it was weird. Her body didn't seem to need as much air as her mind told her it did. She felt dizzy, struck dumb by the sudden shocking sunlight, but strangely, she wasn't on the verge of blacking out. Had she not been down there as long as she thought she had? Was she suddenly that much better at holding her breath? Luce let a surge of athletic pride complement her relief at having survived.

Daniel's hands found hers underwater. "Are you all right?"

"What happened to you?" she cried. "I almost—"

"Luce," he warned. "Shhh."

His fingers traced over hers and wordlessly relieved

her of the halo. She hadn't realized how heavy that thing was until she was free of it. But why was Daniel acting so strangely, slipping the halo away from her so stealthily, as if he had something to hide?

All she had to do was follow his dark violet gaze.

When Daniel had swum her swiftly to the surface, they had broken through in a different place than where they'd entered. Before, Luce realized, they'd seen the sunken cathedral from the front—just the twin green-gray spires rising from their sunken towers—but now they were almost precisely above the center of the church, where the nave would once have been.

Now they were flanked by two long rows of flying buttresses, which would once have held up the now-crumbling stone walls of the long nave of the church. The arched buttresses were black with moss and weren't nearly as tall as the spires of the façade. Their slanted stone tops broke through the surface of the water—which made them perfect benches for the group of twenty-odd Outcasts presently surrounding Luce and Daniel.

When Luce recognized them—a field of tan trench coats, pale skin, dead eyes—she stifled a gasp.

"Hello," one said.

It wasn't Phil, the smarmy Outcast who'd posed as Shelby's boyfriend, then led a battle against the angels in Luce's parents' backyard. She didn't see his face among the Outcasts, just a troop of blank and listless creatures she didn't recognize and didn't care to get to know.

Fallen angels who couldn't make up their minds, the Outcasts were in some ways the opposite of Daniel, who refused to take any side but Luce's. Shunned by Heaven for their indecisiveness, struck blind by Hell to everything but the dimmest glow of souls, the Outcasts made a sickening assembly. They were staring at Luce the way they had the last time, through ghastly, vacant eyes that could not see her body yet sensed something in her soul that said she was "the price."

Luce felt exposed, trapped. The Outcasts' leers made the water colder. Daniel swam nearer, and she felt the brush of something smooth against her back. He had unfurled his wings in the water.

"You would be ill-advised to attempt escape," an Outcast behind Luce droned, as if sensing the stirring of Daniel's wings under the water. "One glance behind you should convince you of our superior numbers, and it only takes one of these." He parted his trench coat to reveal a sheath of silver starshots.

The Outcasts had them surrounded, perched on the stone remains of a sunken Venetian island. They looked haughty, seedy, with their trench coats knotted at their waists, concealing their dirty, toilet paper–thin wings. Luce remembered from the battle in her parents' backyard that the female Outcasts were just as callous and remorseless as the males. That had been only a few days earlier, but it felt like years had passed.

"But if you'd prefer to test us . . ." Lazily, the Outcast nocked an arrow, and Daniel could not completely mask his shudder.

"Silence." One of the Outcasts rose to stand on the buttress. He was not wearing a trench coat, but a long gray robe, and Luce gasped when he pulled back the hood and exposed his pallid face. He was the pale chanting man from the cathedral. He'd been watching her the whole time, hearing everything she said to the priest. He must have followed her here. His colorless lips curled into a smile.

"So," he growled. "She has found her halo."

"This is no business of yours," Daniel shouted, but Luce could hear the desperation in his voice. She still didn't know why, but the Outcasts were intent on making Luce their business. They believed she held some sway in their redemption, their return to Heaven, but their logic eluded her now just as much as it had in her parents' backyard.

"Do not insult us with your lies," the robed Outcast boomed. "We know what you seek, and you know our mission is to stop you."

"You're not thinking clearly," Daniel said. "You're not seeing this for what it is. Even *you* cannot want—"

"Lucifer to rewrite history?" The Outcast's white

eyes bored into the space between him and Luce. "Oh yes, in fact, we would like that very much."

"How can you say that? Everything—the world, our very selves as we know them now—will be annihilated. The entire universe, all consciousness, gone."

"Do you really think our lives these last seven thousand years are something worth preserving?" The leader's eyes narrowed. "Better to wipe us out. Better to erase this blind existence before we begin to fade. Next time . . ." Again he trained his sightless eyes in Luce's direction. She watched them swivel in their sockets, zeroing in on her soul. And it burned. "Next time we will not incur Heaven's wrath in such a senseless way. We will be welcomed back by the Throne. We will play our cards more wisely." His blind gaze lingered on Luce's soul. He smiled. "Next time we will have . . . help."

"You'll have nothing, just as you do now. Step aside, Outcast. This war is bigger than you."

The robed Outcast fingered a starshot and smiled. "It would be so very easy to kill you now."

"A host of angels is already fighting for Lucinda. We will stop Lucifer, and when we do and there is time to deal with pettiness like yourselves, the Outcasts will regret this moment, along with everything you've done since the Fall."

"In the next go-round, the Outcasts will make the

girl our focus from the beginning. We will charm her, as you have done. We will make her believe every word we say, as you have done. We have studied your ways. We know what to do."

"Fools!" Daniel shouted. "You think you'll be any smarter or more valiant next time? You think you'll remember this moment, this conversation, this brilliant plan at all? You'll do nothing but make the same mistakes you made this time. We all will. Only Lucifer will remember his previous errors. And his pursuits serve only his base desires. Surely you recall what his soul looks like," Daniel said pointedly, "even if you see nothing else."

The Outcasts rose on their rotting perches.

"I remember," Luce heard an Outcast behind her say faintly.

"Lucifer was the brightest angel of all," another called, full of nostalgia. "So beautiful, it blinded us."

They were sensitive, Luce realized, about their deformity.

"Cease your equivocation!" A louder voice called over them. The robed Outcast, this scene's leader. "The Outcasts will see again in the next go-round. Vision will lead to wisdom, and wisdom back through the Gates of Heaven. We will be attractive to the Price. She will guide us."

Luce shivered against Daniel.

"Maybe we can *all* get a second chance at redemption." Daniel appealed to them. "If we are able to stop Lucifer . . . there's no reason your kind could not also—"

"No!" The robed Outcast lunged at Daniel from his buttress, his dreary, beat-up wings spreading wide with a crackle like a snapping twig.

Daniel's wings loosened around Luce's waist and the halo was thrust back into her hands as he rose out of the water in self-defense. The robed leader was no match for Daniel, who shot up and threw a right cross.

The Outcast flew backward twenty feet, skimming the water like a stone. He righted himself and returned to his perch on the buttress. With a wave of his pale hand, he cued the rest of his group to rise in a circle in the air.

"You know who she is!" Daniel shouted. "You know what this means for all of us. For once in your existence, do something brave instead of craven."

"How?" the Outcast challenged him. Water streamed from the hem of his robes.

Daniel was breathing hard, eyeing Luce and the golden halo gleaming through the water. His violet eyes looked panicked for a moment—and then he did the last thing Luce would ever have expected.

He looked the robed Outcast deep in his dead white eyes, extended his hand palm up, and said, "Join us."

The Outcast laughed darkly for a long time.

Daniel did not flinch.

"The Outcasts work for no one but themselves."

"You've made that clear. No one is asking you to indenture yourselves. But do not work against the only cause that is right. Seize this chance to save everyone, including yourselves. Join us in the fight against Lucifer."

"It is a trick!" one of the Outcast girls shouted.

"He seeks to deceive you in order to gain his freedom."

"Take the girl!"

Luce gazed in horror at the robed Outcast hovering over her. He drew nearer, his eyes widening hungrily, his white hands trembling as they reached for her. Closer. Closer. She screamed—

But no one heard it, because at that moment, the world *rippled.* The air and light and every particle in the atmosphere seemed to double and split, then folded in on themselves with a crack of thunder.

It was happening again.

Through the thicket of tan trench coats and dirty wings, the sky had turned a dim and smoggy gray, like it had been the last time in the Sword & Cross library, when everything had begun to tremble. Another time-quake. *Lucifer drawing near.*

A tremendous wave crashed over her head. Luce flailed, grasping the halo tight, paddling frantically to keep her head above water.

She saw Daniel's face as a great creaking sounded on their left. His white wings were soaring toward her, but not quickly enough.

The last thing Luce saw before her head dipped under the water seemed to happen in slow motion: The green-gray church spire bowed over in the water, tipping down ever so gently toward her head. Its shadow grew large until with a thud it jerked her down into darkness.

⁂

Luce woke up undulating on a wave: She was on a water bed.

Red reticella lace curtains were drawn over the windows. Gray light slipping through gaps in the intricate lace suggested it was dusk. Luce's head ached and her ankle throbbed. She rolled over in the black silk sheets—and came face to face with a sleepy-eyed girl with a huge mop of blond hair.

The girl moaned and batted heavily shadowed silver eyelids, stretching a slack fist over her head. "Oh," she said, sounding much less surprised to wake next to Luce than Luce felt waking next to her. "How late did we stay out last night?" she slurred in Italian. "That party was *crazy*."

Luce lunged backward and fell out of the bed, sinking into a plush white rug. The room was a cavern, cold and stale-smelling, with dark gray wallpaper and a king-sized sleigh bed on a huge area rug in the center. She had no idea where she was, how she'd gotten there, whose bathrobe she was wearing, who this girl was, or what party the girl thought Luce had been at the night before. Had she somehow fallen into an Announcer? There was a zebra-print footstool by the bed. The clothes she'd left in the gondola were folded neatly on it—the white sweater she'd put on two days earlier at her parents' house, her worn-in jeans, her riding boots leaning against each other to the side. The silver locket with the carved-rose face—she'd tucked it inside her boot just before she and Daniel dove into the water—was resting in a spun glass tray on the night table.

She slipped it back over her head and fumbled into her jeans. The girl in the bed had fallen back asleep, a black silk pillow stuffed over her face, her tangled blond hair spilling out from under it. Luce peeked around the high headboard, finding two empty leather recliners facing a blazing fireplace on the far wall, and a flat-screen TV mounted over it.

Where was Daniel?

She was zipping up her second boot when she heard a voice through the cracked French doors opposite the bed.

"You will not regret this, Daniel."

Before he could respond, Luce's hand was on the

doorknob—and on the other side she found him, seated on a zebra-print love seat in the living room, facing Phil the Outcast.

At the sight of her in the doorway, Daniel rose to his feet. Phil rose, too, standing stiffly beside his chair. Daniel's hands swept across Luce's face, brushing her forehead, which Luce realized was tender and bruised.

"How are you feeling?"

"The halo—"

"We have the halo." Daniel gestured at the enormous gold-edged glass disk resting on the large wooden dining table in the adjacent room. There was an Outcast seated at the table spooning yogurt into his mouth, another leaning in the doorway with his arms crossed over his chest. Both of them were facing Luce, but it was impossible to tell whether they knew they were doing it. She felt on edge around them, felt a chill in the air, but trusted Daniel's calm demeanor.

"What happened to the Outcast you were fighting?" Luce asked, looking for the pale creature in the robe.

"Don't worry about him. It's *you* I'm worried about." He spoke to her as tenderly as if they'd been alone.

She remembered the church spire tilting toward her as the cathedral collapsed underwater. She remembered Daniel's wings casting a shadow over everything as they dipped toward her.

"You took a bad knock on the head. The Outcasts

helped me get you out of the water and brought us here so you could rest."

"How long was I asleep?" Luce asked. It was nightfall. "How much time do we have left—"

"Seven days, Luce," Daniel said quietly. She could hear how keenly he, too, felt the time slipping away from them.

"Well, we shouldn't waste any more time here." She glanced at Phil, who was topping off his and Daniel's glasses from a bottle of something red called Campari.

"You do not like my apartment, Lucinda Price?" Phil said, pretending to look around the postmodernist living room for the first time. The walls were dotted with Jackson Pollock–esque paintings, but it was Phil Luce couldn't stop staring at. His skin was pastier than she remembered, with heavy purple circles around his vacant eyes. She grew cold every time she remembered his tattered wings holding her likeness in the air above her parents' backyard, ready to fly her someplace dark and far away.

"I can't see any of it very well, of course, but I was told it would be decorated in a way that young ladies would find appealing. Who knew I would develop such a taste for mortal flesh after my time with your Nephilim friend Shelby? Did you meet my friend, in the bedroom? She's a sweet girl; they're all so sweet."

"We should go." Luce tugged on Daniel's shirt bossily.

The other Outcasts in the room rose to attention. "Are you sure you cannot stay for a drink?" Phil asked, moving to fill a third glass with the cherry-red liquid, which he couldn't help spilling. Daniel put his hand over the rim, pouring instead from a bottle of sparkling grapefruit soda.

"Sit down, Luce," Daniel said, handing her the glass. "We're not quite ready to leave."

When the two of them sat, the other two Outcasts followed their example. "Your boyfriend is very reasonable," Phil said, kicking his muddy combat boots onto the marble coffee table. "We have agreed that the Outcasts will join you in your efforts to stop the Morning Star."

Luce leaned into Daniel. "Can we talk *alone*?"

"Yes, of course," Phil answered for him, rising stiffly again and nodding to the other Outcasts. "Let us all take a moment." Forming a line behind Phil, the others disappeared behind a swinging wooden door into the apartment's kitchen.

As soon as they were alone, Daniel rested his hands on her knees. "Look, I know they're not your favorite—"

"Daniel, they tried to kidnap me."

"Yes, I know, but that was when they thought"— Daniel paused and stroked her hair, working out a tangle with his fingers—"they thought that presenting you to the Throne would atone for their earlier betrayal. But now the game has changed utterly, partly because of what Lucifer did—and partly because you've come further in breaking the curse than the Outcasts anticipated."

"What?" Luce started. "You think I'm close to breaking the curse?"

"Let's just say you've never been this close before," Daniel said, and something soared inside Luce that she didn't understand. "With the Outcasts' help fighting off our enemies, you can focus on what you need to do."

"The Outcasts' help? But they just ambushed us."

"Phil and I have talked things over. We have an understanding. Listen, Luce"—Daniel took her arm and whispered, though they were the only ones in the room—"the Outcasts are less of a threat with us than against us. They're unpleasant but they're also incapable of lying. We will always know where we stand with them."

"Why do we have to stand with them at all?" Luce leaned back hard against the zebra-print pillow behind her.

"They are armed, Luce. Better equipped and with more warriors than any other faction we will face. The time may come when we need their starshots and their manpower. You don't have to be best friends, but they are excellent bodyguards and ruthless when it comes to their enemies." He leaned back, his gaze settling outside the window, as if something unpleasant had just flown by. "And since they're going to have a horse in this race regardless, it might as well be us."

"What if they still think I'm the price or whatever?"

Daniel gave her a soft, unexpected smile. "I'm certain they still think that. Many do. But only you get to decide how you will fulfill your role in this old story. What we started when we first kissed at Sword & Cross? That awakening in you was only the first step. All those lessons you learned during your time in the Announcers have armed you. The Outcasts can't take that away from you. No one can. And besides"—he grinned—"no one can touch you when I am at your side."

"Daniel?" She took a sip of the grapefruit soda, felt it fizz down her throat. "How will I fulfill my role in this old story?"

"I have no idea," he said, "but I can't wait to find out."

"Neither can I."

The kitchen door swung open and a pale, almost pretty girl's face appeared in the doorway, her blond hair swept back in a severe ponytail. "The Outcasts grow tired of waiting," she sang robotically.

Daniel looked at Luce, who forced a nod.

"You can send them in." Daniel gestured at the girl.

They filed in swiftly, mechanically, all assuming their former positions except for Phil, who drew nearer to

Luce. The yogurt eater's spoon knocked clumsily against the side of his empty plastic container.

"So he has convinced you, too?" Phil asked, perching on the arm of the love seat.

"If Daniel trusts you, I—"

"As I thought," he said. "When the Outcasts stake their allegiance these days, we are fiercely loyal. We understand what is at stake when we make these kinds of . . . choices." He emphasized the last word, nodding unnervingly at Luce. "The choice to ally yourself with a side is very important, don't you think, Lucinda Price?"

"What is he talking about, Daniel?" Luce asked, though she suspected she knew.

"Everyone's fascination these days," Daniel said tiredly. "The near balance between Heaven and Hell."

"After all these millennia, it is nearly complete!" Phil sank back into the love seat opposite Luce and Daniel. He was more animated than Luce had ever seen him before. "With almost every angel allied with one side, dark or light, there is just one who has not chosen"—

One angel who had not chosen.

A flash of memory: stepping through an Announcer to Las Vegas with Shelby and Miles. They'd gone to meet her past-life sister, Vera, and ended up at an IHOP with Arriane, who said that there was going to be a reckoning.

Soon. And in the end, when all the other angels' souls had been accounted for, everything would come down to one essential angel choosing a side.

Luce was certain that the undecided angel was Daniel.

He looked annoyed, waiting for Phil to finish talking.

"And, of course, there are still the Outcasts."

"What do you mean?" Luce said. "The Outcasts haven't chosen a side? I always assumed you were on Lucifer's."

"That is only because you do not like us," Phil said, completely deadpan. "No, the Outcasts do not get to choose." He turned his head as if to look out the window and sighed. "Can you imagine how that feels—"

"You're preaching to the wrong crowd, Phil," Daniel interrupted.

"We should *count*," Phil said, suddenly pleading with Daniel. "All we ask is that we matter in the cosmic balance."

"You don't get to choose," Luce repeated, understanding. "Is that your punishment for indecision?"

The Outcast nodded stiffly. "And the result is that our existences mean nothing in the cosmic balance. Our deaths, too, mean nothing." Phil lowered his head.

"You know this isn't up to me," Daniel said. "And it certainly isn't up to Luce. We're wasting time—"

"Do not be so dismissive, Daniel Grigori," Phil said.

"We all have our goals. Whether or not you admit it, you need us to accomplish yours. We could have joined with the Elders of Zhsmaelim. The one called Miss Sophia Bliss still has her sights trained on you. She is misguided, of course, but who knows—she might succeed where you will fail?"

"Then why didn't you join them?" Luce asked sharply, coming to Daniel's defense. "You had no problem working with Sophia last time when you kidnapped my friend Dawn."

"That was a mistake. At that time we did not know the Elders had murdered the other girl."

"Penn." Luce's voice cracked.

Phil's pale face pinched. "Unforgivable. The Outcasts would never harm an innocent. Much less one with so fine a character, so refined a mind."

Luce looked at Daniel, wanting to convey that perhaps she'd been too quick to judge the Outcasts, but Daniel was scowling at Phil.

"And yet, you met with Miss Sophia yesterday," he said.

The Outcast shook his head.

"Cam showed me the golden invitation," Daniel pressed. "You met with her at the mortal racing track called Churchill Downs to discuss going after Luce."

"Wrong." Phil rose to his feet. He was as tall as Daniel, but sickly and frail. "We met with Lucifer yesterday.

One does not turn down an invitation from the Morning Star. Miss Sophia and her cronies were there, I suppose. The Outcasts sensed their muddy souls, but we are not working with them."

"Wait," Luce said, "you met with Lucifer *yesterday*?" That meant Friday, the day that Luce and the others were at Sword & Cross discussing how to find the relics so they could stop Lucifer from erasing the past. "But we were already back from the Announcers. Lucifer would already have been within the Fall."

"Not necessarily." Daniel explained, "Even though this meeting took place after *you* returned from the Announcers, it still took place in *Lucifer's* past. When he went after you in the guise of that gargoyle, his setting-off point was half a day later, and hundreds of miles away from *your* setting-off point.

The logic made Luce's brain hurt a little, but she was clear on one thing: She distrusted Phil. She turned to him. "So you knew all along that Lucifer was planning to erase the past. Were you going to help him, as you've now pledged to help us?"

"We met with him because we are obliged to come when he calls us. Everyone is, except the Throne, and"— he paused, a thin smile spreading across his lips—"well, I don't know any life force who could resist Lucifer's call." He tilted his head at Luce. "Could you?"

"Enough," Daniel said.

"Besides," Phil said, "he did not want our help. The Morning Star shut us out. He said"—he closed his eyes and, for a moment, looked like a normal teenaged boy, almost cute—"he said he couldn't leave anything else to chance, that it was time to take matters into his own hands. The meeting adjourned abruptly."

"That must have been the moment Lucifer went after you in the Announcers," Daniel said to Luce. She felt queasy, remembering how Bill had found her in the tunnel, so vulnerable, so alone. All those moments she'd been glad to have him at her side, helping her on her quest. He'd almost seemed to like being with her, too, for a while.

Phil's blank eyes fixed on her, as if examining a shift in her soul. Could he sense how flustered she became whenever she thought about all the time she'd spent alone with Bill? Could Daniel sense it?

Phil was not exactly smiling at her, but he did not look as lifeless as usual. "The Outcasts will protect you. We know that your enemies are numerous." He looked at Daniel. "The Scale is also on the move."

Luce glanced at Daniel. "The Scale?"

"They work for Heaven. They're a nuisance, not a threat."

Phil lowered his head again. "The Outcasts believe the Scale may have . . . come unhinged from Heaven."

"What?" Daniel suddenly sounded winded.

"There is a rot among them, the kind that spreads quickly. Did you say you had friends in Vienna?"

"Arriane," Luce gasped. "And Gabbe and Roland. Are they in danger?"

"We have friends in Vienna," Daniel said. "In Avalon as well."

"The Scale is spreading through Vienna."

When Luce spun around to face Daniel, he was unfurling his wings. They burst forth, lighting up the room with their glory. Phil didn't seem to notice or care as he took a sip of the red liqueur. The other Outcasts' empty gazes bored into Daniel's wings with memorized envy.

The french doors to the bedroom opened and the hungover Italian girl Luce had shared the bed with spilled from them, stumbling barefoot into the room. She glanced over at Daniel, rubbed her eyes. "Wow, groovy dream!" she mumbled in Italian before disappearing into the bathroom.

"Enough talking," Daniel said. "If your army is as strong as you say it is, spare a third of your force to drive toward Vienna and protect the three fallen angels you find there. Send another third to Avalon, where you will find Cam and two more fallen."

When Phil nodded, two Outcasts in the living room unfurled their own drab wings and darted out the open window like enormous flies.

"The remaining third of our force falls under my

jurisdiction. We will accompany you to the Mount. Let us take to the air now and I will gather the others on our way."

"Yes," Daniel said quickly. "Ready, Luce?"

"Let's go." She drew her back against Daniel's shoulders so he could wrap her in his arms, leap through the window, and soar into the dark sky over Venice.

FIVE

A THOUSAND KISSES DEEP

They touched down in high mountain desert just before dawn. Light banded the sky near the eastern horizon, haunting pinks and golds dusted with ocher clouds, healing the purple bruise of night.

Daniel set Luce down on a flat rock plateau, too dry and unforgiving to support even the toughest desert scrub. The barren mountainscape stretched out infinitely around them, dropping steeply into darkened valleys here, rising into peaks of colossal tawny boulders resting at impossible angles there. It was cold and windy, and the air was so dry it hurt to swallow. There was scarcely room for Luce and Daniel and the five Outcasts who'd traveled with them to stand on the rock plateau.

Fine sand whipped through Luce's hair as Daniel pulled his wings back in to his sides. "Here we are." He sounded almost reverent.

"Where?" Luce pulled the neck of her white sweater higher to cover her ears from the wind.

"Mount Sinai."

She sucked in a dry, sandy breath, pivoting to get a panoramic view as fine golden light lengthened over the sandstone mountains in the east. "This is where God gave Moses the Ten Commandments?"

"No." Daniel pointed over her shoulder, where a line of doll-sized backpackers were ascending more forgiving terrain a few hundred feet to the south. Their voices carried across the cold, thin desert air. Their soft peals of laughter echoed eerily from the silent mountain summits. A blue plastic water bottle tilted into the sky over someone's head. "*That* is where Moses received the Ten Commandments." He spread his arms and looked at the small circle of rock where they were standing. "This is where some of the angels stood and watched it happen. Gabbe, Arriane, Roland, Cam"—he pointed to one area on the rock, then another, where each of the angels had stood—"a few more."

"What about you?"

He faced her, taking three small steps forward so that their torsos were touching, the tips of their feet overlapping. "Right"—he kissed her—"here."

"What was it like?"

Daniel looked away. "It was the first official covenant with man. Before then, covenants had taken place only between God and the angels. Some of the angels felt betrayed, that it disrupted the natural order of things. Others thought we'd brought it on ourselves, that it was a natural progression."

The violet in his eyes blazed a little brighter for a moment. "The others must be on their way." He turned to face the Outcasts, whose dark silhouettes were outlined by the growing light in the east. "Will you stand guard until they arrive?"

Phil bowed. The other four Outcasts stood behind him, the frayed edges of their soiled wings undulating in the wind.

Daniel drew his left wing across himself and, shielding his body from view, reached inside it with his right hand like a magician reaching into his cape.

"Daniel?" she asked, stepping closer to him. "What's wrong?"

Teeth bared, Daniel shook his head at her. Then he flinched and cried out in pain, which Luce had never witnessed before. Her body tensed.

"Daniel?"

When he relaxed and extended his wing again, he held something white and shimmering in his hand.

"I should have done this sooner," he said.

It looked like a strip of fabric, as smooth as silk but stiffer. It was a foot long and several inches wide, and it quivered in the cold breeze. Luce stared at it. Was that a strip of *wing* that Daniel had torn from himself? She cried out in horror and reached for it without thinking. It was a feather!

To look at Daniel's wings, to be wrapped up in them, was to forget they were made up of individual feathers. Luce had always assumed that their composition was mysterious and otherworldly, the stuff of God's dreams. But then, this was unlike any feather Luce had seen before: broad, densely plumed, alive with the same power that coursed through Daniel.

Between her fingers, it was the softest yet strongest thing Luce had ever touched, and the most beautiful— until her eyes flew to the flow of blood from the spot where Daniel had plucked the feather.

"Why did you do that?" she asked.

Daniel handed the feather to Phil, who tucked it into the lapel of his trench coat without hesitation.

"It is a pennon," Daniel said, glancing at the bloody portion of his wing without concern. "If by chance the others arrive alone, they will know the Outcasts are friends." His eyes followed her own, which were wide with worry, to the bloody region of his wing. "Don't worry about me. I'll heal. Come on—"

"Where are we going?" Luce asked.

"The sun's about to rise," Daniel said, taking a small leather satchel from Phil. "And I figure you must be starving."

Luce hadn't realized it, but she was.

"I thought we could steal a moment before anyone else shows up."

There was a sheer, narrow path from the plateau that led to a small ledge down from where they'd landed. They picked their way down the jagged mountain, hand in hand, and when it was too steep for walking, Daniel coasted, always flying very low to the ground, his wings tucked close to his sides.

"Don't want to alarm the hikers," he explained. "Most places on Earth, people aren't willing to let themselves see miracles, angels. If they catch a glimpse of us flying by, they convince themselves their eyes were playing tricks on them. But in a place like this—"

"People can see miracles," Luce finished for him. "They want to."

"Right. And seeing leads to wonder."

"And wonder leads to—"

"Trouble." Daniel laughed a little.

Luce couldn't help grinning, enjoying that at least for a little while, Daniel was her miracle alone.

They sat down next to each other on the small flat

stretch in the middle of the heart of nowhere, shielded from the wind by a granite boulder and out of sight of everyone but a pale brown partridge picking its way along the scabby rocks. The view when Luce looked past the boulder was life-altering: a ring of mountains, this peak in shadow, this one draped in light, all of them growing brighter with each second that passed as the sun crested over the pink horizon.

Daniel unzipped the satchel and peered inside. He shook his head, laughing.

"What's funny? What's in there?" Luce asked.

"Before we left Venice, I asked Phil to pack a few things from his cupboard. Leave it to a blind Outcast to prepare a nutritious meal." He pulled out a canister of paprika-flavored Pringles, a red bag of Maltesers, a handful of blue-foil-wrapped Baci chocolates, a pack of Daygum, several small bottles of diet soda, and a few sleeves of powdered-espresso packets.

Luce burst out laughing.

"Will this tide you over?" he asked.

Luce snuggled up to him and crunched a few malt balls, watching the eastern sky grow pink, then gold, then baby blue as the sun crested the peaks and valleys in the distance. The light cast strange shadows in the crevices of the mountain. At first she assumed at least some of them were Announcers, but then realized that no—they were simply shadows spun from shifting light.

Luce realized it had been days since she'd seen an Announcer.

Strange. For weeks, months, they'd been appearing before her more and more frequently, until she could barely shift her gaze without seeing one wobbling darkly in a corner, beckoning her. Now they seemed to have disappeared.

"Daniel, what happened to the Announcers?"

He leaned back against the ledge and exhaled deeply before saying, "They are with Lucifer and the host of Heaven. They, too, are part of the Fall."

"What?"

"This has never happened before. The Announcers belong to history. They are the shadows of significant events. They were generated by the Fall and so when Lucifer set this game into motion, they were drawn back there."

Luce tried to picture it: a million trembling shadows surrounding a great dark orb, their tendrils licking the surface of oblivion like sunspots.

"That's why we had to fly here instead of stepping through," she said.

He nodded and bit into a Pringle, more out of the habit of being around mortals than a need to consume food. "The shadows disappeared within moments of our return from the past. This moment we are in right now—these nine days of Lucifer's gambit—this is a limbo time.

It's come unmoored from the rest of history, and if we fail, it will cease to be entirely."

"Where exactly is that? I mean, the Fall."

"Another dimension, no place that I could describe. We were closer to it where I caught you, after you separated from Lucifer, but we were still very far away."

"I never thought I'd say this, but"—she watched the stillness of the everyday shadows on the mountain—"I miss them. The Announcers were my link to my past."

Daniel took her hand and looked deep into her eyes. "The past is important for all the information and wisdom it holds. But you can get lost in it. You've got to learn to keep the knowledge of the past with you as you pursue the present."

"But now that they're gone—"

"Now that they're gone, you can do it on your own."

She shook her head. "How?"

"Let's see," he said. "Do you see that river near the horizon?" He pointed at the barest whisper of blue snaking through the flat plain on the desert floor. It was about as far away as Luce's eyes could see.

"Yes, I think I see it."

"I've lived near here at several different stretches across time, but once, when I lived here a few hundred years ago, I had a camel I named Oded. He was just about the laziest creature ever to walk the Earth. He would pass out when I was in the middle of feeding him, and making it to the closest Bedouin camp for tea was a minor miracle. But when I first met you in that lifetime—"

"Oded broke into a run," Luce said without thinking. "I screamed because I thought he was going to trample me. You said you'd never seen him move like that."

"Yeah, well," Daniel said. "He liked you."

They paused and looked at each other, and Daniel started laughing when Luce's jaw dropped. "I did it!" she cried out. "It was just there, in my memory, a part of me. Like it happened yesterday. It came to me without thinking!"

It was miraculous. All those memories from all those lives that had been lost each time Lucinda died in Daniel's arms were somehow finding their way back to her, the way Luce always found her way back to Daniel.

No. *She* was finding her way to them.

It was like a gate had been left open after Luce's quest through the Announcers. Those memories stayed with her, from Moscow to Helston to Egypt. Now more were becoming available.

She had a sudden, keen sense of who she was—and she wasn't just Luce Price from Thunderbolt, Georgia. She was every girl she'd ever been, an amalgamation of experience, mistakes, achievements, and, above all, love.

She was Lucinda.

"Quick," she said to Daniel. "Can we do another?"

"Okay, how about another desert life? You were living in the Sahara when I found you. Tall and gangly and the fastest runner in your village. I was passing through one day, on my way to visit Roland, and I stopped for the night at the closest spring. All the other men were very distrustful of me, but—"

"But my father paid you three zebra skins for the knife you had in your satchel!"

Daniel grinned. "He drove a hard bargain."

"This is amazing," she said, nearly breathless. How much more did she have in her that she didn't know about? How far back could she go? She pivoted to face him, drawing her knees against her chest and leaning in so that their foreheads were almost touching. "Can you remember everything about our pasts?"

Daniel's eyes softened at the corners. "Sometimes the order of things gets mixed up in my head. I'll admit, I don't remember long stretches of time I've spent alone, but I can remember every first glimpse of your face, every kiss of your lips, every memory I've ever made with you."

Luce didn't wait for Daniel to lean forward and kiss her. Instead, she pressed her lips to his, relishing his moan of surprised pleasure, wanting to cleanse him of any pain he'd ever felt at losing her.

Kissing Daniel was somewhere between exhilaratingly new and unmistakably familiar, like a childhood memory that felt dreamlike until photographic evidence was found in an old box in the attic. Luce felt as if a hangar full of monumental photographs had been discovered, and all those buried moments had been released from their captivity into the recesses of her soul.

She was kissing him now, but strangely she was kissing him *then*. She could almost touch the history of their love, taste its essence on her tongue. Her lips traced Daniel's not just now, but also in another kiss they'd shared, an older kiss, a kiss like this one, with her mouth just there and his arms around her waist like that. He slipped his tongue against her teeth, and that recalled a handful of other kisses, too, every one of them intoxicating. When he passed his hand across her back, she felt a hundred shivers like this one. And when her eyes fluttered open and shut, the sight of him through her tangled lashes seemed a thousand kisses deep.

"Daniel." The flat voice of an Outcast ended Luce's reverie. The pale boy stood over them, looking down from the high rock they'd been leaning against. Through his gray, almost translucent wings, Luce saw a cloud passing in the sky.

"What is it, Vincent?" Daniel said, drawing himself to his feet. He must have known the Outcasts' names from their time together in Heaven before the Fall.

"Forgive me for the interruption," the Outcast said,

lacking the social grace to look away from Luce's burning cheeks. At least he couldn't really see them.

She stood quickly, straightening her sweater, pressing a cold hand to her hot skin.

"Have the others arrived?" Daniel called up.

The Outcast stood motionless above him. "Not exactly."

Daniel's right hand slid around Luce's waist. With one soft *throosh* of his wings, he scaled the fifty feet of vertical rock the way a mortal might take a single step up a flight of stairs. Her stomach lurched downward with the thrill of their soar up.

Setting Luce down first on the rocky plateau, Daniel turned and saw the five Outcasts who'd accompanied them huddled around a sixth figure. Daniel flinched, his wings jerking backward in shock, when he saw the sixth Outcast.

The boy was small, with a slender build and big feet. His head was freshly shaven. He could have been about fourteen if the Outcasts aged in mortal years. Someone had beaten him. Badly.

His face was scraped as if he'd been thrown repeatedly against a brick wall. His lip was bleeding so profusely that shiny blood coated his teeth. At first Luce didn't recognize it as blood, because the Outcast's blood wasn't red. It was pale gray. His blood was the color of ashes.

He was whimpering, whispering something Luce couldn't understand as he lay supine on the rock and let the others tend to him.

They tried to lift him to remove his dirty trench coat, which was slashed in several places and missing one of its sleeves. But the Outcast cried out so violently that even Phil relented, laying the boy back down.

"His wings are broken," Phil said, and Luce realized that, yes, the grimy wings were splayed out unnaturally behind his back. "I don't know how he made it back."

Daniel knelt before the Outcast, shielding the sun from the boy's face. "What happened, Daedalus?" He rested a hand on the Outcast's shoulder, which seemed to soothe the boy.

"It's a trap," Daedalus sputtered hoarsely, spitting ashen blood on his trench coat lapel.

"What is?" Vincent asked.

"Set by whom?" Daniel asked.

"Scale. Want the relic. Waiting in Vienna—for your friends. Large army."

"Army? They're openly fighting angels now?" Daniel shook his head in disbelief. "But they can't have star-shots."

Daedalus's white eyes bulged with pain. "Can't kill us. Only torture—"

"You fought the Scale?" Daniel seemed alarmed and impressed. Luce still didn't understand what the Scale was. She envisioned them vaguely as dark extensions of Heaven thrusting downward into the world. "What happened?"

"Tried to fight. Outnumbered."

"What about the others, Daedalus?" Phil's voice still sounded emotionless, but for the first time Luce could hear something like compassion stirring underneath.

"Franz and Arda"—the boy spoke as if the words themselves caused him pain—"on their way here."

"And Calpurnia?" Phil asked.

Daedalus closed his eyes and shook his head as gently as he could.

"Did they get to the angels?" Daniel asked. "Arriane, Roland, Annabelle? Are they safe?"

The Outcast's eyelids flickered, then shut. Luce had never felt so far away from her friends. If anything happened to Arriane, to Roland, to any of the angels . . .

Phil wedged in next to Daniel, close to the injured boy's head. Daniel inched back to give Phil room. Slowly, Phil drew a long dull silver starshot from the inside of his trench coat.

"No!" Luce shouted, quickly covering her mouth. "You can't—"

"Do not worry, Lucinda Price," Phil said without looking back at her. He reached inside the black leather satchel, which Daniel had brought back up from the ledge, and pulled out a small glass bottle of diet soda.

Using his teeth, he popped the bottle top. It rolled in a long arc before tipping off the surface of the rock. Then, very slowly, Phil inserted the starshot into the bottle's narrow neck.

It sizzled and hissed as it slid into the soda. Phil grimaced as the bottle smoked and steamed in his hands. A sickly sweet scent wafted from it and Luce's eyes widened as the fizzy brown liquid, your basic diet soda, began to swirl and change to a bright iridescent silver color.

Phil withdrew the starshot from the bottle. He dragged the starshot carefully across his lips, as if to clean it, then tucked it back inside his coat. His lips glowed silver for an instant, until he licked them clean.

He nodded at one of the other Outcasts, a girl whose slick blond ponytail reached halfway down her back. Automatically, she reached behind Daedalus's head to lift it a few inches off the rock. Carefully, using one hand to part the boy's bleeding lips, Phil poured the silver liquid down his throat.

His face contorted as he sputtered and coughed, but then everything about Daedalus smoothed out. He began to drink, then to gulp the liquid down, slurping when he reached the bottom of the bottle.

"What is that?" Luce asked.

"There is a chemical compound in the drink," Daniel explained, "a dull poison mortals call aspartame and believe that their scientists invented. But it is an old,

Heavenly substance—a venom, which, when mixed with an antidote contained in the alloy of the starshot, reacts to produce a healing potion for angels. For light ailments such as these."

"He will need to rest now," the blond girl said. "But he will wake refreshed."

"You will forgive us if we have to leave," Daniel said, rising to his feet. His white wings dragged along the rocky surface until he straightened his shoulders and held them aloft. He reached for Luce's hand.

"Go to your friends," Phil said. "Vincent, Olianna, Sanders, and Emmet will accompany you. I will join you with the others when Daedalus is back on his wings."

The four Outcasts stepped forward, bowing their heads before Luce and Daniel as if awaiting a command.

"We will fly the eastern route," Daniel instructed. "North over the Black Sea, then west when we pass Moldova. The wind stream is calmer there."

"What about Gabbe and Molly and Cam?" Luce asked.

Daniel looked at Phil, who looked up from the sleeping Outcast boy. "One of us will stand watch here. If your friends arrive, the Outcasts will send word."

"You have the pennon?" Daniel asked.

Phil pivoted to show the abundant white feather tucked into the buttonhole of his lapel. It glowed and pulsed in the wind, its radiance sharply contrasting with the Outcast's deathly pale skin.

"I hope you have cause to use it." Daniel's words frightened Luce, because they meant he thought the angels in Avalon were in as much danger as the ones in Vienna.

"They need us, Daniel," she said. "Let's go."

Daniel gave her a warm, grateful look. Then, without hesitation, he swept her up into his arms. With the halo tucked under their interlaced fingers, Daniel bent his knees and sprang into the sky.

SIX

FOUND WANTING

It was drizzling in Vienna.

Curtains of mist cloaked the city, making it possible for Daniel and the Outcasts to alight unseen on the eaves of a vast building before night had completely fallen.

Luce saw the splendid copper dome first, glowing sea green against the fog. Daniel set her down before it on a slanted section of the copper roof, which was puddled with rainwater and enclosed by a short marble balustrade.

"Where are we?" she asked, eyeing the dome adorned

with gold tassels, its oval window frames etched with floral designs too high for mortal eyes to see, unless they were in the arms of an angel.

"Hofburg Palace." Daniel stepped over a stone rain gutter and stood at the edge of the roof. His wings brushed the white marble railing, making it look drab. "Home of Viennese emperors, then kings, now presidents."

"Is this where Arriane and the others are?"

"I doubt it," Daniel said. "But it's a pleasant place to get our bearings before we look for them."

A mazelike network of annexes extended beyond the dome to form the rest of the palace. Some of them squared off around shady courtyards ten stories below; others stretched long and formidably straight, farther than the fog would allow Luce's eyes to see. Different portions of the copper roofs shone different shades of green—this one acid, that one almost teal—as if sections of the building had been added over a long period of time, as if they'd rusted during different eras' rains.

The Outcasts spread out around the dome, leaning up against the squat chimneys darkened with soot that punctuated the palace roof, standing before the flagpole that rose from the center bearing the red-and-white-banded Austrian flag. Luce stood at Daniel's side, finding herself between him and a marble statue. It depicted a warrior wearing a knight's helmet and gripping a tall golden spear. They followed the statue's gaze out at the city. Everything smelled like wood smoke and rain.

Beneath the mist and fog, Vienna glittered with the twinkle of a million Christmas lights. It teemed with strange cars and fast-walking pedestrians as accustomed to city life as Luce was not. Mountains stood in the distance and the Danube slung its strong arm around the outskirts of the town. Gazing down with Daniel, Luce felt as if she'd been here before. She couldn't be sure when, but the ever-more-frequent sensation of déjà vu swelled inside her.

She focused on the faint bustle coming from a tented row of Christmas stalls in the circle below the palace, the way the candles flickered in their red and green globed glass lanterns, the way the children chased one another, pulling wooden dogs on wheels. Then it happened: She remembered with a wave of satisfaction that Daniel had once bought her crimson velvet hair ribbons right down there. The memory was simple, joyful, and *hers*.

Lucifer couldn't have it. He could not take it—or any other memory—away. Not from Luce, not from the brilliant, surprising, imperfect world sprawling out below her.

Her body bristled with determination to defeat him, and with the rage of knowing that because of what he was doing, because she had rejected his wishes, all this might disappear.

"What is it?" Daniel laid a hand on her shoulder.

Luce didn't want to say. She didn't want Daniel to know that every time she thought of Lucifer she felt disgusted with herself.

The wind surged around them, parting the mist that lay over the city to reveal an ambling Ferris wheel on the other side of the river. People twirled in its circle as if the world would never end, as if the wheel would spin forever.

"Are you cold?" Daniel draped his white wing around her. The supernatural weight of it felt somehow overbearing, reminding her that her shortcomings as a mortal—and Daniel's concern about them—were slowing them down.

The truth was Luce *was* freezing, and hungry, and tired, but she didn't want Daniel to coddle her. They had important things to do.

"I'm fine."

"Luce, if you're tired or afraid—"

"I said I'm fine, Daniel," she snapped. She didn't mean to and felt sorry immediately.

Through the blurring fog, she could make out horse-drawn carriages carting tourists and the hazy outlines of people tracing out their lives. Just like Luce was struggling to do.

"Have I complained too much since we left Sword & Cross?" she asked.

"No, you've been amazing—"

"I'm not going to die or faint just because it's cold and rainy."

"I know that." Daniel's directness surprised her. "I should have known *you* knew it, too. Generally, mortals are limited by their bodily needs and functions—food, sleep, warmth, shelter, oxygen, nagging fear of mortality, and so on. Because of that, most people wouldn't be prepared to make this journey."

"I've come a long way, Daniel. I *want* to be here. I wouldn't have let you go without me. It was a mutual agreement."

"Good, then listen to me: It is within your power to release yourself from mortal bonds. To be free of them."

"What? I don't need to worry about the cold?"

"Nope."

"Right." She stuffed icy hands into the pockets of her jeans. "And apple strudel?"

"Mind over matter."

A reluctant smile found her face. "Well, we've already established that you can breathe for me."

"Don't underestimate yourself." Daniel smiled back briefly. "This has to do more with you than me. Try it: Tell yourself that you are *not* cold, *not* hungry, *not* tired."

"All right." Luce sighed. "I am not . . ." She'd started to mumble, disbelieving, but then she caught Daniel's eye. Daniel, who believed she could do things she never thought she was capable of, who believed that her will meant the difference between having the halo and letting it slip away. She was holding it in her hands. Proof.

Now he was telling her she had mortal needs only because she thought she did. She decided to give this crazy idea a try. She straightened her shoulders. She projected the words into the misty dusk. "I, Lucinda Price, am *not* cold, *not* hungry, *not* tired."

The wind blew, and the clock tower in the distance struck five—and something lifted off her so that she didn't feel depleted anymore. She felt rested, equipped for whatever the night called for, determined to succeed.

"Nice touch, Lucinda Price," Daniel said. "Five senses transcended at five o'clock."

She reached for his wing, wrapped herself in it, let its warmth spread through her. This time, the weight of his wing welcomed her into a powerful new dimension. "I can do this."

Daniel's lips brushed the top of her head. "I know."

When Luce turned from Daniel, she was surprised to find the Outcasts were no longer hovering, no longer staring at her through dead eyes.

They were gone.

"They've left to seek the Scale," Daniel explained. "Daedalus gave us clues to their whereabouts, but I'll need a better idea of if or where the others are being held so I can distract the Scale long enough for the

Outcasts to rescue them." He sat down on the ledge, his legs straddling a gold-painted statue of an eagle overlooking the city. Luce sank to his side.

"It shouldn't take long, depending on how far away they are. Then maybe half an hour to go through the Scale protocol"—he tilted his head, calculating—"unless they decide to convene a tribunal, which happened the last time they harassed me. I'll find a way to get out of it tonight, postpone it to some other date I won't keep." He took her hand, refocused. "I should be back here by seven at the latest. That's two hours from now."

Luce's hair was wet from the mist, but she followed Daniel's advice and told herself it didn't affect her, and just like that, she no longer noticed it. "Are you worried about the others?"

"The Scale won't hurt them."

"Then why did they hurt Daedalus?"

She pictured Arriane with bloated purple eyes, Roland with broken, bloody teeth. She didn't want to see them looking anything like Daedalus.

"Oh," Daniel said. "The Scale can be fearsome. They relish causing pain, and they may cause our friends some temporary discomfort. But they won't hurt them in any permanent way. They don't kill. That's not their style."

"What is their style, then?" Luce crossed her legs under her on the hard, damp surface of the roof. "You still haven't told me who they are or what we're up against."

"The Scale came into being after the Fall. They're a small group of . . . lesser angels. They were the first to be asked in the Roll Call which side they would stand by, and they chose the Throne."

"There was a roll call?" Luce asked, not sure she'd heard correctly. It sounded more like homeroom than Heaven.

"After the schism in Heaven, all of us were made to choose sides. So, starting with the angels with the smallest dominions, each of us was to be called upon to make an oath of fealty to the Throne." He stared at the mist, and it was as though he could see it all again. "It took ages to call out the angels' names, starting at the lowest ranked and working up. It probably took as long to say our names as it did for Rome to rise and fall. But they didn't make it all the way through the Roll Call before—" Daniel took a ragged breath.

"Before what?"

"Before something happened to make the Throne lose faith in its host of angels . . ."

By now Luce realized that when Daniel's voice trailed off like that, it wasn't because he didn't trust her or because she wouldn't understand, but because despite all the things she'd seen and learned, it still might be too soon for her to know the truth. So she didn't ask— though she was desperate to—what had made the Throne abandon the Roll Call when its highest angels had not yet chosen sides. She let Daniel speak again when he was ready.

"Heaven cast out everyone who had not sided with it. Remember how I told you a few angels never got to choose? They were among the last in the Roll Call, the highest. After the Fall, Heaven was bereft of most of its Archangels." He closed his eyes. "The Scale, who had lucked into seeming loyal, stepped into the breach."

"So because the Scale swore fealty to Heaven first—" Luce said.

"They felt they had a superior amount of honor," Daniel said, finishing her thought. "Since then, they have self-righteously claimed to serve Heaven by acting as celestial parole officers. But the position is self-invented, not ordained. With the Archangels gone after the Fall, the Scale took advantage of a vacuum of power. They carved out a role for themselves, and they convinced the Throne of their importance."

"They lobbied God?"

"More or less. They pledged to restore the fallen to Heaven, to gather back those angels who had strayed, to return them to the fold. They spent a handful of millennia urging us to recommit ourselves to the 'right' side, but somewhere along the way, they gave up trying to change our points of view. Now they mostly just try to prevent us from accomplishing anything."

His steely gaze showed his rage and it made Luce

wonder what could be so bad in Heaven that it kept Daniel in self-exile. Wasn't the peace of Heaven preferable to where he was now, with everyone waiting for him to choose?

Daniel laughed bitterly. "But the angels worth their wings who have returned to Heaven don't need the Scale to get there. Ask Gabbe, ask Arriane. The Scale is a joke. Still, they've had one or two successes."

"But not you?" she asked. "You haven't chosen one side or the other. And so they're after you, aren't they?"

A crowded red tram wound around the paved circle below, then forked up a narrow street.

"They've been after me for years," Daniel said, "planting lies, manufacturing scandals."

"And yet you haven't declared for the Throne. Why haven't you?"

"I've told you. It's not as simple as that," he said.

"But you're clearly not going to side with Lucifer."

"Right, but . . . I can't explain thousands of years' worth of argument in the space of a few minutes. It is complicated by factors beyond my control." He looked away again, out over the city, then down at his hands. "And it's an insult to be asked to choose, an insult for your creator to demand that you reduce the vastness of your love to the tiny, petty confines of a gesture during a Roll Call." He sighed. "I don't know. Maybe I'm too sincere."

"No—" Luce started.

"Anyway, the Scale. They're Heavenly bureaucrats. I think of them as high school principals. Pushing papers and punishing minor transgressions of rules no one cares about or believes in, all in the name of 'morality.'"

Again Luce stared out at the city, which was drawing a dark coat around its shoulders. She thought of the sour-breathed vice-principal at Dover, whose name she couldn't remember, who never had any interest in her side of any story, who had signed her expulsion papers after the fire that killed Trevor. "I've been burned by people like that."

"We all have. They're sticklers for frivolous rules of their own invention, which they deem righteous. None of us like them, but unfortunately the Throne has given them the power to monitor us, to detain us without cause, to convict us of crimes by a jury of their choosing."

Luce shuddered again, this time not because of the cold. "And you think they have Arriane and Roland and Annabelle? Why? Why hold them?"

Daniel sighed. "I *know* they have Arriane and Roland and Annabelle. Their hatred blinds them to the fact that delaying us helps Lucifer." He swallowed hard. "What I fear most is that they also have the relic."

In the distance, four pairs of tattered wings materialized in the fog. Outcasts. As they neared the palace roof, Luce and Daniel rose to greet them.

The Outcasts landed next to Luce, their wings crackling like paper umbrellas as they drew them to their sides. Their faces betrayed no emotion; nothing in their demeanor suggested that their trip had been successful.

"Well?" Daniel asked.

"The Scale have taken control of a place down the river," Vincent announced, pointing in the direction of the Ferris wheel. "The neglected wing of a museum. It is under renovation, covered in scaffolding, so they stake it out unnoticed. It is not equipped with alarms."

"You're certain they're Scale?" Daniel asked quickly.

One of the Outcasts nodded. "We perceived their brands, their gold insignias—the star with seven points for the seven holy virtues painted on their necks."

"What about Roland and Arriane and Annabelle?" Luce asked.

"They are with the Scale. Their wings are bound," Vincent said.

Luce turned away, biting down on her lower lip. How awful it must be for an angel to have her wings restrained. She couldn't bear to think of Arriane without the freedom to flutter her iridescent wings. She couldn't imagine any substance strong enough to contain the power of Roland's marbled wings.

"Well, if we know where they are, let's go rescue them already," she said.

"And the relic?" Daniel said lowly to Vincent.

Luce gaped at him. "Daniel, our friends are in danger."

"Do they have it?" Daniel pressed. He glanced at Luce, put his hand around her waist. "*Everything* is in danger. We will save Arriane and the others, but we have to find that relic, too."

"We do not know about the relic." Vincent shook his head. "The warehouse is heavily guarded, Daniel Grigori. They await your arrival."

Daniel faced the city, his violet eyes casting along the river as if seeking out the warehouse. His wings pulsed. "They won't be waiting long."

"No!" Luce pleaded. "You'll be walking into a trap. What if they take you hostage, the way they've taken the others?"

"The others must have crossed them in some way. As long as I follow their protocol, appeal to their vanity, the Scale will not imprison me," he said. "I'll go alone." He glanced at the Outcasts and added, "Unarmed."

"But the Outcasts are charged with guarding you," Vincent said in his even monotone. "We will follow at a distance and—"

"No." Daniel lifted a hand to stop Vincent. "You will take the warehouse roof. Did you sense Scale there?"

Vincent nodded. "A few. The majority are near the main entrance."

"Good." Daniel nodded. "I'll use their own procedure against them. Once I reach the front doors, the Scale will waste time identifying me, checking me for contraband, anything they can make appear illegal. While I distract them near the entrance, the Outcasts will force your way through the warehouse roof and free Roland, Arriane, and Annabelle. And if you face a member of the Scale up there—"

In unison, the Outcasts held open their trench coats to reveal sheaths of dull silver starshots and compact matching bows.

"You cannot kill them," Daniel warned.

"Please, Daniel Grigori," Vincent begged. "We are all better off without them."

"They are called Scale not only because of their small-minded obsession with rules. They also provide an essential counterbalance to Lucifer's forces. You are quick enough to elude their cloaks. We only need to delay them, and for that a threat will suffice."

"But they only seek to delay *you*," Vincent countered. "All of this delaying will lead to oblivion."

Luce was about to ask where this plan left *her* when Daniel drew her into his arms. "I need you to stay here and guard the relic." They looked at the halo, resting against the base of the warrior statue. It was beaded with rain. "Please don't argue. We can't let the Scale near the relic. You and it will be safest here. Olianna will stay to protect you."

Luce glanced at the Outcast girl, who stared back emptily, her eyes a depthless gray. "Okay, I'll stay here."

"Let us hope the second relic is still at large," he said, arching back his wings. "Once the others have been freed, we can make a plan to find it together."

Luce clenched her fists, closed her eyes, and kissed Daniel, holding him tight for one last moment.

He was gone a second later, his regal wings growing smaller as he soared into the night, the three Outcasts flying alongside him. Soon they all seemed little more than flecks of dust in the clouds.

Olianna hadn't moved. She stood like a trench-coated version of any of the other statues on the roof. She faced Luce with her hands clasped over her chest, the blond hair along her forehead pulled back so tight into its ponytail it looked like it would snap. When she reached inside her trench coat, a harsh scent of sawdust wafted out. When she pulled out and nocked a silver starshot, Luce scrambled a few steps back.

"Do not be afraid, Lucinda Price," Olianna said. "I only want to be prepared to defend you in case an enemy approaches."

Luce tried not to imagine what enemies the blond girl envisioned. She lowered herself to the roof again and sheltered herself from the wind behind the statue of the warrior with the golden spear, more out of habit than need. She adjusted her body so that she could still see the tall brown brick clock tower with the golden face. Five-thirty. She was marking the minutes until Daniel and the other Outcasts came back.

"Do you want to sit down?" she asked Olianna, who lurked directly behind Luce with her arrow at the ready.

"I prefer to stand guard—"

"Yeah, I don't guess you can really *sit* guard," Luce mumbled. "Ha-ha."

A siren wailed from below, a police car speeding through a roundabout. When it passed and the air grew quiet again, Luce didn't know how to fill the silence.

She stared at the clock, squinting as if it would help her see through the fog. Had Daniel reached the warehouse by now? What would Arriane, Roland, and Annabelle do when they saw the Outcasts? Luce realized Daniel hadn't given anyone but Phil a pennon of his wing. How would the angels know to trust the Outcasts? Her shoulders were hunched up around her ears, and her whole body stiffened with the sense of futile frustration. Why was she sitting here, waiting, cracking stupid jokes? She should have an active role in this. After all, it wasn't Luce the Scale wanted. She should be helping rescue her friends or finding the relic instead of sitting here like a distressed damsel, waiting for her knight to return.

"Do you remember me, Lucinda Price?" the Outcast asked so quietly Luce almost didn't hear.

"Why do the Outcasts call us by our full names all of a sudden?" She turned around to find the girl's head tilted down at her, her bow and arrow listing against her shoulder.

"It is a sign of respect, Lucinda Price. We are your allies now. You and Daniel Grigori. Do you remember me?"

Luce thought for a second. "Were you one of the Outcasts fighting the angels in my parents' backyard?"

"No."

"I'm sorry." Luce shrugged. "I don't remember everything about my past. Have we already met?"

The Outcast lifted her head just a bit. "We knew one another before."

"When?"

The girl shrugged, her shoulders rising delicately, and Luce suddenly realized she was pretty. "Just before. It is hard to explain."

"What isn't?" Luce swiveled back around, not in the mood to decode another cryptic conversation. She stuffed her freezing hands inside the sleeves of her white sweater and watched the traffic moving up and down the slick roads, the tiny cars wedged into slanted spaces on crooked alleys, people in long dark coats marching over illuminated bridges, carrying groceries home to their families.

Luce felt painfully lonely. Was her family thinking of her? Did they picture her in the cramped dorm room she'd slept in at Sword & Cross? Was Callie back at Dover by now? Would she be huddled on the cold window seat of her room, letting her dark-red fingernails dry, chatting on the phone about her weird Thanksgiving trip to see some friend who wasn't Luce?

A dark cloud drifted past the clock, rendering it invisible as it struck six. Daniel had been gone an hour that felt like a year. Luce watched the church bells ringing, watched the hands of the great old clock, and she let her memory drift back to her lives spent before the invention of linear time, when time meant seasons, the planting and the harvest.

After the sixth gong of the clock came another—closer, and Luce spun around just in time to see Olianna slump forward to her knees. She fell and landed heavily in Luce's arms. Luce turned the ragged angel over and touched the Outcast's face.

Olianna was unconscious. The sound Luce had heard was the Outcast being hit in the head.

Before Luce stood an enormous black-cloaked figure. His face was craggy with wrinkles and looked impossibly old, layers of skin drooping under his dull blue eyes and below his protruding chin, beneath a mouthful of crooked black-and-yellow teeth. In his huge right hand was the flagpole he must have used as a weapon. The Austrian flag hung from the end of the pole, fluttering softly against the surface of the roof.

Luce shot to her feet, feeling her fists rise even as she

wondered what good they'd be against this enormous fiend.

His wings were a very pale blue, just a shade away from white. Even though his body towered over her, his wings were small and dense, spanning only a little farther than his arms could reach.

Something small and golden was pinned to the front of the man's cloak: a feather—a marbled gold-black feather. Luce knew whose wing it had come from. But why would Roland have given this creature a pennon from his wings?

He wouldn't have. This feather was bent and severed and missing some of its matter near the quill. Its point was maroon with blood, and instead of standing upright like the brilliant plume Daniel had given to Phil, this feather seemed to have withered and faded when it was attached to the gruesome angel's black cloak.

A trick.

"Who are you?" Luce asked, falling to her knees. "What do you want?"

"Show some respect." The angel's throat convulsed as if he meant to bark, but his voice came out warbled and faint and old.

"Earn my respect," Luce said. "And I'll give it to you."

He gave her half an evil smirk and dropped his head low. Then he pulled down the cloak to expose the back of his neck. Luce blinked in the dim light. His neck bore a painted brand, which shimmered gold in the glow of streetlights mingled with the moon. She counted seven points on the star.

He was one of the Scale.

"Recognize me now?"

"Is this how the Throne's enforcers work? Bludgeoning innocent angels?"

"No Outcast is innocent. Nor is anyone else, for that matter, until they are proven to be so."

"You've proven yourself innocent of any honor, striking a girl from behind."

"Insolence." He wrinkled his nose at her. "Won't get you far with me."

"That's exactly where I want to be." Luce's eyes darted to Olianna, to her pale hand and the starshot clenched in its grip.

"But it's not where you will stay," the Scale said haltingly, as if having to force himself to commit to their illogical banter.

Luce snatched at the starshot as the Scale lurched for her. But the angel was much faster and stronger than he looked. He wrested the starshot from her hands, knocked her onto her back against the stone roof with one strong slap across the face. He held the arrow tip of the starshot up close to Luce's heart.

They can't kill mortals. They can't kill mortals, she

kept repeating in her head. But Luce remembered Bill's bargain with her: She had one immortal part of her that *could* be killed. Her soul. And she would not part with that, not after everything she'd been through, not when the end was so near.

She raised her leg, preparing to kick him like she'd seen in kung fu movies, when suddenly he pitched the arrow and its bow straight over the edge of the roof. Luce jerked her head to the side, her cheek pressing against the cold stone, and watched the weapon twirl through the air on its way into the twinkling Christmas lights of the Vienna streets.

The Scale angel rubbed his hands on his cloak. "Filthy things." Then he grabbed Luce roughly by the shoulders and yanked her to her feet.

He kicked the Outcast aside—Olianna moaned but did not stir—and there, under her thin, trench-coated body, was the golden halo.

"Thought I might find this here," the Scale angel said, snatching it up and thrusting it under the folds of his cloak.

"No!" She plunged her hands into the dark place where she'd seen the halo disappear, but the angel slapped her a second time across the face, sending her backward, her hair swinging over the edge of the roof.

She clutched her face. Her nose was bleeding.

"You are more dangerous than they think," he

croaked. "We were told you were a whiner, not courageous. I'd better bind you up before we fly."

The angel quickly slipped off his cloak and dropped it over her head like a curtain, blinding Luce for a long, horrible moment. Then the Vienna night—and the angel—were visible again. Luce noticed that beneath the cloak he'd been wearing, the Scale wore another, precisely like the one he'd removed and fastened around Luce. He bent down, and with the pull of a string, Luce's cloak constricted around her like a straitjacket. When she kicked, convulsed, she felt the cloak become tighter.

She let out a scream. "Daniel!"

"He won't hear you," the angel chuckled mirthlessly as he stuffed her under one arm and moved toward the edge of the roof. "He wouldn't hear you if you screamed forever."

SEVEN

KNOT ANGELS

The cloak was paralyzing.

The more Luce moved, the more it constricted around her. Its rough fabric was secured with a strange rope that pinched her skin and held her body rigidly. When Luce writhed against it, the rope responded, cinching tighter around her shoulders, squeezing her ribs until she could barely breathe.

The Scale angel held Luce under his bony arm as he scraped through the night sky. With her face buried in the fetid waist of the regenerated cloak the angel wore, she could see nothing, could only feel wind whipping across the surface of her miserable mildewed cocoon. All she could hear was wind-howl, punctuated by the beating of stiff wings.

Where was he taking her? How would she get word to Daniel? They did *not* have time for this!

After a while the wind stopped, but the Scale angel didn't land.

He and Luce hovered in the air.

Then the angel let out a roar. "Trespasser!" he bellowed.

Luce felt the two of them dropping, but she could see only the darkness of the folds of her captor's cloak, which muffled her cries of terror—until the sound of breaking glass halted even those.

Thin, razor-like shards sliced through her constricting cloak, through the fabric of her jeans. Her legs stung like they'd been cut in a thousand places.

When the Scale angel's feet slammed in a landing, Luce shuddered with the impact. He dropped her roughly, and she landed on her hip bone and shoulder. She rolled a couple of feet, then stopped. She saw that she was near a long wooden workman's table piled high with fragments of faded cloth and porcelain. She squirmed under its temporary shelter, almost succeeding at preventing her cloak from constricting more tightly around her. It had begun to close around her trachea.

But at least now she could see.

She was in a cold, cavernous room. The floor beneath her was a lacquered mosaic made of triangular gray and red tiles. The walls were a gleaming mustard-colored marble, as were the thick square pillars in the center of the room. She briefly studied a long row of frosted skylights that spanned the vast ceiling forty feet above. The roof was pocked by open craters of broken glass, revealing dark-gray vistas of cloudy night on the other side. That must have been where she and the angel crashed through.

And this must be the museum wing the Scale had overtaken, the one Vincent had told Daniel about on the copper roof. That meant Daniel must be just outside— and Arriane and Annabelle and Roland should be somewhere inside! Her heart soared, then sank.

Their wings were bound, the Outcasts had said. Were they in the same shape she was in? She hated that she had made it here and couldn't even help them, hated that she had to move to save them but that moving put her life in peril. There was perhaps nothing worse than not being able to *move*.

The Scale angel's muddy black boots appeared before her. Luce peered up at his towering figure. He bent down, smelling like rotting mothballs, his dull eyes leering. His black-gloved hand reached for her—

Then the Scale angel's hand fell limply—as if he had been knocked out. He lunged forward, crashing heavily into the workman's table, pushing it back, exposing Luce. The severed sculpture head that had apparently struck the Scale rolled eerily to rest on the floor near Luce's face, seeming to stare into Luce's eyes.

As Luce rolled back under the table, more blue wings blurred in her peripheral vision. More Scale. Four of them flew in loose formation toward a recessed alcove about halfway up the wall . . . where Luce now saw Emmet standing, brandishing a long silver saw.

Emmet must have thrown the head that had saved her from the Scale! He was the trespasser whose entrance through the ceiling had enraged her kidnapper. Luce had never thought she'd be so happy to see an Outcast.

Emmet was surrounded by sculptures on platforms and pedestals, some shrouded, some scaffolded, one newly beheaded—and by four impossibly old Scale angels, hovering closer to him in the air, cloaks extended, like shabby vampires. These stiff black cloaks seemed to be their only weapon, their only tool, and Luce knew well it was a brutal one. Her pained breathing was evidence of that.

She suppressed a gasp as Emmet pulled a starshot from a quiver beneath his trench coat and held it out in front of him. Daniel had made the Outcasts promise not to kill the Scale!

The Scale in the air backed slowly away from Emmet,

hissing, "Vile! Vile!" so loudly that it caused Luce's captor to stir on the table above her. Then the Outcast did something that amazed everybody in the room. He aimed the starshot at himself. Luce had seen Daniel suicidal in Tibet, so she knew something about that emotion's desperate atmosphere, the defeated body language that accompanied a gesture so extreme. But Emmet seemed as confident and defiant as ever as he looked from one leathery Scale face to another.

The Scale became emboldened by Emmet's strange behavior. They hovered ever closer, blocking the thin Outcast from Luce's view with the slow intensity of vultures approaching a carcass on a desert highway. Where were the other Outcasts? Where was Phil? Had the Scale already done away with them?

What sounded like thick and heavy fabric being torn echoed loudly through the room. The Scale hovered motionlessly, their broad, overlapping cloaks like the gaping mouth of an Announcer that led somewhere terrible and sad. Then a slicing sound cut through the air, followed by another tearing sound—and then the four Scale angels spun like rag dolls toward Luce, their jaws slack, their eyes open, their cloaks mutilated and ripped open to expose black hearts and black lungs twitching spastically, streaming pale blue blood.

Daniel had told the Outcasts they could not use their starshots to *kill* the Scale, but he had not said the Outcasts could not hurt them.

The four Scale angels fell to the floor in a clump like puppets whose strings had been snipped. Luce looked up from where they lay, struggling to breathe, to the alcove, where Emmet was wiping black Scale blood from the fletchings of his starshot. Luce had never heard of anyone using the butt end of a starshot as a weapon—and apparently neither had the Scale.

"Is Lucinda here?" Luce heard Phil call out. She looked up to see his face glowing through a crater in the roof.

"Here!" Luce shouted up to him, unable to keep herself from lunging as she did so, causing her cloak to cinch even more tightly around her throat. When she grimaced sharply, the cloak tightened a little more.

A huge leg drooped over the edge of the table, its black boot swinging into Luce's face, striking her flush on the nose, bringing tears of pain to her eyes. Her captor was awake! This realization, coupled with the sudden pain that half blinded her, caused Luce to push back more deeply under the table's shelter. When she did so, her cloak closed all the way around her neck, pinching her trachea completely shut. She panicked, gasped uselessly for air, writhing now that it didn't matter if the cloak constricted any more—

Then she remembered how she'd discovered in Venice that she could hold her breath for longer than she'd thought possible. And Daniel had just told her she could will herself to overcome mortal limitations anytime she wanted. So she did it; she just did it; she willed herself to stay alive.

But that didn't stop her captor from knocking the sheltering workman's table aside, sending pottery and the severed limbs of ancient sculptures flying.

"You look . . . uncomfortable." He grinned, revealing blood-slick teeth, and extended a black-gloved hand toward the hem of Luce's cloak.

But the Scale angel froze when a starshot fletching burst through the place where, only a moment before, his right eye had been. Blue blood jetted from the emptied socket, down onto Luce's cloak. He cried out, staggered wildly around the room, arms flailing, the backward starshot protruding from his wizened face.

Pale hands appeared before her, then the sleeves of a ratty tan trench coat, followed by a shaven blond head. Phil's face betrayed no feeling as he dropped to his knees to face her.

"There you are, Lucinda Price." He gripped the collar of the binding black cloak and lifted Luce up. "I had returned to the palace to check on you."

He set her atop a nearby table. She immediately fell over, not able to hold herself upright. Emmet righted her with as little emotion as his colleague had.

At last she could afford to take a longer view. In front of her, three shallow stairs led down to an expansive main chamber. In its center, a red velvet rope sectioned off a towering statue of a lion. It was reared up on two feet, teeth bared toward the sky mid-roar. Its mane was chipped and yellowed.

Blue-gray wings coated the floor of the restoration wing, reminding Luce of a locust-covered parking lot she'd seen one summer after a Georgia rainstorm. The Scale weren't dead—they had not vanished into starshot dust—but so many of them were unconscious the Outcasts could barely tread without crunching their wings. Phil and Emmet had been busy, incapacitating at least fifty of the Scale. Their short blue wings twitched occasionally, but their bodies did not move.

All six Outcasts—Phil, Vincent, Emmet, Sanders, the other Outcast girl, whose name Luce did not know, even Daedalus with his bandaged face—were still on their feet, brushing pieces of tissue and bone from their blue-splattered trench coats.

The blond girl, the one who'd helped nurse Daedalus back to health, grabbed a barely breathing female Scale angel by the hair. The old hag's moldy blue wings trembled as the blond Outcast battered the Scale's head against a marble pillar. She shrieked the first four or five times her head struck the stone. Then the shrieks petered out and her bulged eyes rolled back in her head.

Phil struggled with the black straitjacket fastened around Luce. His quick fingers made up for his lack of sight. An unconscious Scale angel fell from somewhere above her, his battered cheek coming to rest between her neck and shoulder. She felt hot blood trickle onto her neck. She squeezed her eyes shut and shuddered.

Phil kicked the angel off the table, sending him into Luce's one-eyed captor, who still staggered clumsily around the room, groaning, "Why me? I do everything right."

"He has the halo—" Luce started.

But Phil's attention jerked back to the sickly mass of Scale angel wings, where a portly Scale with hair like a Tibetan monk's had risen and now advanced on Daedalus from behind. A coarse black cloak hung over the Outcast's head, ready to drop.

"I will be right back, Lucinda Price." Phil left Luce in her binds on the table and nocked a starshot in his bow. In an instant, he had shoved himself between Daedalus and the Scale angel.

"Drop the cloak, Zaban." Phil looked as fierce as he had when he'd first appeared in Luce's parents' backyard. Luce was surprised to realize they knew each other by name, but of course, they must have once all lived in Heaven together. That was hard to imagine now.

Zaban had watery blue eyes and bluish lips. He looked almost gleeful at finding the starshot pointed at him. He slung the cloak over his shoulder and turned to face Phil, freeing Daedalus to pick up a spindly Scale angel by the feet. He swung the old angel around in a circle three times, then sent him crashing through the eastern window, out into a tower of scaffolding below.

"Threatening to shoot me, are you, Phillip?" Zaban's eyes were on the starshot. "You want to tip the balance toward Lucifer? Why doesn't that surprise me?"

Phil bristled. "You don't matter enough for your death to tip the balance."

"At least we count for *something*. All together, our lives make a difference in the balance. Justice always makes a difference. You Outcasts"—he smiled in mock pity—"stand for nothing. That is what makes you worthless."

That was enough for Phil. There was something about this Scale he couldn't endure. With a grunt he loosed the arrow toward Zaban's heart.

"I stand opposed to you," he muttered, and waited for the blue-winged geezer to vanish.

Luce waited for the vanishing, too. She'd seen it happen before. But the arrow glanced off Zaban's cloak and clattered to the floor.

"How did you—?" Phil asked.

Zaban laughed and pulled something from a hidden breast pocket in his cloak. Luce leaned forward, eager to see how Zaban had protected himself. But she leaned too far and slid off the table. She landed on the floor on her face.

No one noticed. They were staring at the small book Zaban had produced from his cloak. Propping herself up slightly, Luce saw it was bound in leather, the same shade of blue as Scale angel wings. It was bound with a knotted golden cord. It looked like a Bible, the kind Civil War soldiers used to stuff in their breast pockets in the hope the books would protect their hearts.

This book had done just that.

Luce squinted to read its title, squirming a few inches closer on the floor. She was still too far away.

In a single movement, Phil retrieved his starshot and swatted the book out of Zaban's hand. By a stroke of luck, it landed a few feet away from Luce. She wriggled again, knowing she couldn't pick it up, not the way the cloak was binding her. Still, she had to know what its pages contained. It seemed familiar, as if she'd seen it long, long before. She read the golden letters on its spine.

A Record of the Fallen

Now Zaban ran for it, stopping short of Luce, who lay exposed in the center of the floor. He glared at her and pocketed the book.

"No, no," he said. "*You* don't get to look at this. You

don't get to see all that's been accomplished by Scale wings. Nor what's left to do to achieve the ultimate harmonious balance. Not when you've spent all this time too busy to take note of us, to take note of justice, selfishly falling in and out of love."

Though Luce hated the Scale, if there was a record of the fallen, she burned to know whose names were on those pages, to see where Daniel's name was tallied now. This was what the fallen kept talking about. A single angel who would tip the scale.

But before Zaban could hurtle any more criticism at Luce, a pair of brilliant white wings filled her vision— an angel descending through the largest hole in the skylights.

Daniel touched down in front of her and eyed the cloak imprisoning her. He studied her constricted neck. His muscles strained through his T-shirt as he tried to tear the cloak away.

Out of the corner of her eye, she saw Phil lift a small pickax from a nearby table and slice it across Zaban's chest. The Scale angel swerved, trying to spin out of range. The blade connected with his arm. The blow was so powerful it severed Zaban's hand at the wrist. Sickened, Luce watched the pale, slack fist thump to the floor. Aside from the blue blood streaming from it, it could have belonged to one of the ravaged statues.

"Tie that on with one of your knots," Phil taunted as

Zaban fumbled after his missing appendage among the battered, unconscious bodies of his sect.

"Is it hurting you?" Daniel tore at the knots binding Luce.

"No." She willed it to be true. It almost was.

When brute force didn't work, Daniel tried approaching the cloak more strategically. "I had the loose end just a moment ago," he muttered. "Now it's riddled up inside the cloak." His fingers inched across her body, feeling close and far away.

Luce wished that her hands, over any other part of her body, were free so she could touch Daniel right now, soothe his anxiety. She trusted him to free her. She trusted him to do anything.

What could she do to help him? She closed her eyes and drifted back to the lifetime in Tahiti. Daniel had been a sailor. He had taught her dozens of knots in their quiet afternoons on the beach. She remembered now: the alpine butterfly, which made a long loop in the middle of a rope with two lobed wings on either side, good for carrying extra weight on a line. Or the lover's knot, which looked simple, heart-shaped, but could only be untied using four hands at once; each one had to loop a strand through a different portion of the heart's core.

The cloak was so tight Luce could not move a muscle. His fingers trolled the collar, tightening it further. Daniel cursed at how it pinched her neck.

"I can't," he finally cried out. "The Scale straitjacket is composed of infinite knots. Only one of them can unbind it. Who did this to you?"

Luce jerked her head toward the blue-winged angel howling to himself, staggering in a corner by a marble faun. The starshot fletching still protruded from his eye. She wanted to tell Daniel how her captor had taken out Olianna with a flagpole, then bound her up and brought her here.

But she could not even speak. The cloak was too tight.

By then, Phil had the whining angel in his grasp, gripped by the collar of his blood-wet cloak. He slapped the Scale three times before the Scale ceased his self-pitying moans and pulled back his blue wings in alarm. Luce saw that a thick ring of dried blue blood had formed around the place where the starshot fletching protruded from his socket.

"Unbind her, Barach," Daniel ordered, recognizing Luce's captor immediately, making Luce wonder how well they knew each other.

"Not likely." Barach leaned away and spat a stream of blue blood and a couple of sharp and tiny teeth out onto the floor.

In a flash, Phil had a starshot trained between the angel's eyes. "Daniel Grigori instructed you to unbind her. You will oblige."

Barach flinched, eyeing the starshot with disdain. "Vile. Vile!"

A dark shadow fell over Phil's body.

Hazily, Luce processed the sight of another Scale angel, the craggy old hag with moldy blue wings. She must have roused herself after she'd been knocked out. Now she came at Phil with the same pickax he'd used on Zaban—

But then the Scale angel vanished into dust.

Ten feet behind her, Vincent stood with an empty bow in hand. He nodded at Phil, then turned back to scour the carpet of blue wings for movement.

Daniel turned to Phil and muttered, "We need to be careful about how many we take out. The Scale do matter in the balance. A little."

"Unfortunate," Phil said, strange envy in his voice. "We will keep the killing to a minimum, Daniel Grigori. But we would prefer to kill all of them." He raised his voice for Barach's ears. "Welcome to the realm of sightlessness. The Outcasts are more powerful than you think. I would kill you without a second thought, without a first one, even. However, I will ask again: Unbind her."

Barach stood for a long moment, as if weighing his options, blinking his one remaining wrinkled old eyelid.

"Unbind her! She cannot breathe!" Daniel roared.

Barach growled and approached Luce. His age-spotted hands worked out a series of knots that neither Phil nor Daniel had been able to find. Luce felt no relief in her neck, though. Not until he began to whisper something, very low, under his rancid breath.

Lack of oxygen had made her feel faint, but the words tunneled into her foggy mind. They were an ancient form of Hebrew. Luce didn't know how she knew the language, but she did.

"And Heaven wept to see the sins of her children."

The words were almost unintelligible. Daniel and Phil had not even heard them. Luce couldn't be sure she'd heard them right—but then, they were familiar. Where had she heard them before?

The memory came to her faster than she would have liked: a different member of the Scale, sweeping Luce in a different body into an older cloak than this one. It had happened a very long time ago. She'd been through all this before, bound up and then released.

In that lifetime, Luce had gotten her hands on something she wasn't supposed to see. A book, tied up with a complicated knot.

A Record of the Fallen.

What was she doing with it? What did she want to see?

The same thing she wanted to see now. The names of

the angels who had yet to choose. But she hadn't been permitted to read the book then, either.

Long before, Luce had held the book in her hands, and without knowing how, she had nearly untied its knot. Then came the moment when the Scale caught her and bound her in the cloak. She had watched his blue wings shudder with intensity as the angel tied and retied the book. Making sure her impure fingers hadn't damaged it, he had said. She heard him whisper those words—the same strange words—just before he shed a tear over the book.

The gold thread had unraveled like magic.

She looked up at the craggy old angel now and watched a silvery tear slide from his eye down the maze of his cheek. He looked truly moved, but in a patronizing sort of way, like he pitied the fate of her soul. The tear landed on the cloak, and the knots mysteriously unknotted.

She gasped for air. Daniel yanked the cloak the rest of the way off her. She swung her arms around him. Freedom.

She was still embracing Daniel when Barach leaned in close to her ear. "You'll never succeed."

"Silence, fiend," Daniel commanded.

But Luce wanted to know what Barach meant. "Why not?"

"You are not the one!" Barach said.

"Silence!" Daniel shouted.

"Never, never, never. Not in a million years," the angel chanted, rubbing his sandpaper cheek against Luce's—right before Phil loosed the arrow into his heart.

EIGHT

HOW HEAVEN WEPT

Something thudded at their feet.

"The halo!" Luce gasped.

Daniel swooped down and snatched the golden relic from the ground. He marveled at it, shaking his head. Somehow it had remained when the Scale angel and his strange, regenerating clothes had disappeared.

"I am sorry for taking his life, Daniel Grigori," Phil said. "But I could not tolerate Barach's lies any longer."

"It was beginning to grate on me, too," Daniel said. "Just be careful with the others."

"Take this," Phil said, sliding the black satchel off his shoulder and handing it to Daniel. "Conceal it from the Scale. They are hungry for it." When Daniel opened the satchel, Luce saw his book, *The Book of the Watchers,* tucked inside.

Phil zipped it up and left the bag with Daniel. "I will now return to stand guard. The wounded Scale could rouse at any moment."

"You've done well against the Scale," Daniel said, sounding impressed. "But—"

"We know," Phil said. "There will be more. Did you encounter many outside the museum?"

"Their numbers are legion," Daniel said.

"If you would let us use the starshots freely, we could secure your escape—"

"No. I don't want to disturb balance to that extent. No more killing unless in absolute self-defense. We'll just have to hurry and get out of here before the Scale reinforcements arrive. Go now, guard the windows and the doors. I will be with you in a moment."

Phil nodded, turned, and was gone, wading among the carpet of blue wings.

As soon as they were alone, Daniel's hands searched Luce's body. "Are you hurt?"

She looked down at herself, rubbed her neck. She

was bleeding. The skylight's glass had sliced through her jeans in a few places, but none of the wounds looked fatal. Following Daniel's earlier advice, she told herself, *It doesn't hurt you.* The stinging eased.

"I'm fine," she said quickly. "What happened to you?"

"Precisely what we wanted to happen. I held off the majority of the Scale while the Outcasts found this way in." He closed his eyes. "Only I never meant for you to get hurt. I'm sorry, Luce, I shouldn't have left you—"

"I'm fine, Daniel, and the halo is safe. What about the other angels? How many more Scale are there?"

"Daniel Grigori!" Phil's shout rang out across the lofty room.

Luce and Daniel crossed the wing quickly, stepping over blue Scale wings to the arched threshold of the room. Then Luce stopped short.

A man in a navy blue uniform lay facedown on the tile floor. Red blood pooled around his head—red mortal blood.

"I—I killed him," Daedalus stammered, holding a heavy iron helmet in his hand and looking scared. The visor of the helmet was slick with blood. "He rushed in through the doorway and I thought he was Scale. I thought I would just knock him out. But he was a mortal man."

A mop and bucket on wheels lay tipped over behind

the body. They had killed a janitor. Until then, in some ways, the fight against the Scale hadn't seemed real. It was brutal and senseless, and yes, two Scale members had been killed—but it had been separate from the mortal world. Luce felt sick watching the blood seep into the grooves of the tile floor, but she couldn't tear her eyes away.

Daniel rubbed his jaw. "You made a mistake, Daedalus. You did well to guard the door from intruders. The next one who comes in will be Scale." He scanned the room. "Where are the fallen angels?"

"What about him?" Luce stared at the dead man on the floor. His shoes were freshly shined. He wore a thin gold wedding band. "He was just a janitor coming in to see about the noise. Now he's *dead*."

Daniel took Luce by the shoulders and pressed his forehead to hers. His breath came short and hot. "His soul has sped to peace and joy. And many more will be lost if we don't find our friends, get the relic, and get out of here." He squeezed her shoulders, then released her too quickly. She choked back a cry for the dead man, swallowed hard, and turned to look at Phil.

"Where are they?"

Phil pointed a pale finger skyward.

Dangling from a thick crossbeam near the shattered skylight were three black burlap pods. One of them bulged and swayed, like something trying to be born.

"Arriane!" Luce shouted.

The same sack bulged again, more violently this time.

"You will never free them in time," a voice warbled from the ground. A Scale member with a fish face rose up on his elbows. "More Scale are on the way. We will bind you all in the Cloaks of the Just and handle Lucifer ourselves—"

A bronze shield thrown like a Frisbee by Phil nicked off a piece of the Scale's scalp, sent him back into the pile of blue wings.

Phil turned to Daniel. "If you do need Scale assistance to unbind your friends, we'll have more luck while their force is small."

Daniel's eyes burned violet as he flew around the wing, moving from one scaffolded restoration station to another, then to a wide marble table that looked like one of the museum restorers' workstations. It was stacked with paperwork and tools—mostly useless after that night—which Daniel dug through with intense scrutiny, flinging aside an empty water bottle, a stack of plastic binders, a faded picture in a frame. Finally, his hands seized a long, heavy-duty scalpel.

"Take this," he told Luce, sliding Phil's heavy satchel across her shoulder. She held it close at her side and held her breath as Daniel arched back his wings and lifted off the ground.

She watched him rise effortlessly, magically, and

wondered how it was that his wings could make every-thing in the dim museum glow. When Daniel finally reached the ceiling, he drew the scalpel cleanly along the rafter, slicing through the rope from which each of the three black pods hung. They slipped into his arms with-out a sound, and Daniel's wings beat once as he carried the whole mass easily back to the floor.

Daniel laid the black pods side by side on a bare stretch of floor. Hurrying over to him, Luce could see each of the three angels' faces poking out of the top. Their bodies were bound up in the same type of rigid black cloak that had kept Luce breathlessly constricted. But the angels had also been gagged with a strip of black burlap cloth. Even as she watched, the gags seemed to slither through the mouths of her friends. Arriane writhed and strained and grew redder in the face and looked so furious Luce thought she would explode.

Phil glanced at the struggling forms on the ground. He lifted one up under the arms. The Scale angel blinked, in a daze. "Would you like the Outcasts to se-lect a Scale volunteer to help you unbind your friends, Daniel Grigori?"

"We will never reveal the secrets of our knots!" the Scale angel came to enough to hiss. "We would rather die."

"We would rather you die, too," Vincent said, ap-proaching their circle with a starshot in either hand, drawing one to the throat of the Scale angel who had spoken.

"Vincent, hold your fire," Phil instructed.

Daniel was already kneeling over the first black cloak—Roland's—working his fingers over the invisible knots. "I can't find the ends."

"Perhaps a starshot would slice it," Phil suggested, holding out a silver arrow. "Like a Gordian knot."

"That won't work. The knots are blessed with an occult charm. We may need the Scale."

"Wait!" Luce dropped to her knees next to Roland. He lay still, but his eyes told Luce everything about how powerless he felt. Nothing should restrict a soul like Roland's. Through this cloak she could see none of the class and elegance that made the fallen angel who he was—whether he was out-fencing all the Nephilim at Shoreline, spinning records at a Sword & Cross party, or stepping through Announcers more deftly than anyone she knew. That the Scale had done this to her friend infuriated Luce to the point of tears.

Tears.

That was it.

The Hebrew words came back to her. Her traveling had given her a gift for languages. She closed her eyes and, in her memory, watched the golden thread fall off the book. She remembered Barach's chapped lips self-righteously mouthing the words—

And Luce said them now to Roland, not knowing what they meant, only hoping they could help.

"And Heaven wept to see the sins of her children."

Roland's eyes widened. The knots slithered loose. The cloak dropped to his sides and the gag in his mouth slid off, too.

He gasped for air, rolled to his knees, stood up and shot out his golden wings with stunning force. The first thing he did was clap Luce on the shoulder.

"Thank you, Lucinda. I owe you a solid for a solid thousand years."

Roland was back—but blood pooled from the place where Barach had ripped that false pennon from his wings.

Daniel reached for Luce's hand, pulling her toward the other two bound angels. He had watched and learned from Luce. He went to work on Annabelle, while Luce knelt before Arriane. Arriane could not stay still. The cloak was cinched so tightly around her that Luce almost cringed to look at her.

Their eyes locked. Arriane made a noise that Luce took to mean she was glad to see Luce's face. Luce's eyes watered as she remembered her first day at Sword & Cross, when she'd seen Arriane endure electroshock therapy. The ultra-cool angel had seemed so fragile then, and though Luce had barely known the girl, she'd felt an urge to protect Arriane, they way you did with old friends. That urge had only strengthened over time.

A hot tear slipped down her cheek and landed in the center of Arriane's chest. Luce whispered the Hebrew words, hearing Daniel whisper them to Annabelle at the same time. She glanced at him. His cheeks were wet.

All at once the knots loosened, then unraveled completely. The angels were free by Luce's and Daniel's hands—and hearts.

A gust was generated by the release of Arriane's awesome iridescent wings, followed by a gentler breeze from Annabelle's lustrous silver ones. The room was almost silent in the moments before both girls' gags came off. Arriane also had a piece of duct tape over her mouth; she'd probably been the reason the others had been gagged in the first place. Daniel grabbed a corner of the tape and ripped it off quickly with a *cricccck*.

"Hot damn! It's good to be free!" Arriane shouted, dabbing the swollen red square of skin around her mouth with her fingers. "Three cheers for the knot master, Lucinda!" Her voice had its sparkle, but her eyes were dotted with tears. She noticed Luce notice, and wiped them quickly away.

She paced around the wing-strewn floor, making different taunting faces at each of the unconscious Scale, lunging like she was about to hit them. Her denim overalls were torn almost to shreds, her hair was wild and greasy, and she had a bruise the shape of Australia on her left cheekbone. The bottom tips of her iridescent wings were bent and dragging on the littered floor.

"Arriane," Luce whispered. "You're hurt."

"Aw shucks, kid, don't worry 'bout me." Arriane offered a lopsided grin. "I'm feeling sprightly enough to kick some scaly old Scale ass!" She looked around the room. "'Cept it looks like the Outcasts beat me to it."

Annabelle rose more slowly than Arriane, spreading, then flexing her muscular silver wings, stretching her long limbs like a ballerina. But when she looked up at Luce and Arriane, she smiled and cocked her head. "There must be something we can do to pay them back."

Arriane's wings fluttered and she lifted a few feet off the ground, flying around the museum wing in great circles, scanning the wreckage. "I'll think of something—"

"Arriane," Roland warned, looking up from a whispered conversation he'd been having with Daniel.

"Whaa?" Arriane pouted. "You never let me have any fun anymore, Ro."

"We don't have time for fun," Daniel told her.

"These fossils tortured us for hours," Annabelle called from the top of the lion's head. "We might as well return the favor."

"No," Roland said. "Enough priceless damage has been done. We should spend our energy finding the second relic."

"At least let us make sure they stay down while we do that," Annabelle said.

Roland looked at Daniel, who nodded.

With a smile, Annabelle flitted to a table against the back wall of the warehouse. She turned on a faucet, humming to herself. She poured what Luce assumed must be plaster of Paris or some other casting agent into a bucket and started adding water.

"Arriane," she said with bravado. "A hand, please."

"Yes, ma'am." Arriane took the first bucket from Annabelle and flew over the semiconscious Scale, smiling sweetly. Slowly, she began to pour the wet slurry over their heads. It slopped down their sides and gathered in a pool between their bodies. A few of them struggled against the thickening mixture, which was hardening quickly into a kind of artificial quicksand. Luce recognized the genius of the plan. In a few moments, when it dried, they would be stuck in their sprawled positions in rocklike plaster.

"This is not wise!" one of the Scale burbled through the wet plaster.

"We're making you monuments to Justice!" Annabelle shouted.

"You know, I think I prefer the Scale when they're plastered." Arriane laughed, betraying more than a tinge of vengeful glee.

The girls kept pouring bucket after bucket—a full

bucket over each of the threatening angels' heads, until their voices did not carry anymore—until the Outcasts had no need to stand over the Scale with their starshots.

Daniel and Roland stood apart from the group, arguing in hushed voices. Luce stared at Arriane's purple bruise, at the blood on Roland's wings, at the gash in Annabelle's shoulder.

Then she had an idea.

She reached inside the satchel and pulled out three small bottles of diet soda and a handful of starshots in their silver sheath. She twisted off the caps.

Quickly, she dipped a starshot into each one, holding the bottles as they boiled and steamed, letting the brown liquid inside turn to silver. Finally, she rose from the corner where she'd been crouched and was pleased to find a Chinese porcelain tray that had somehow survived the battle.

"Here, everyone," she said.

Daniel and Roland stopped talking.

Arriane stopped dousing the Scale with wet plaster.

Annabelle alighted on the lion statue's mane again.

None of them said anything, but all of them looked impressed as they claimed their bottles, clinked each other's in celebration, and drank.

Unlike the Outcast Daedalus, the angels didn't have to close their eyes and go to sleep after they'd downed the transformed soda. Maybe because they weren't as badly beaten, or maybe because this higher form of angel had a higher tolerance. Still, the drink calmed them.

As a final gesture, Roland clapped his hands, igniting a powerful flame between them. He threw waves of heat toward the plastered Scale, glazing their plaster coating, making it harder to escape than their cloaks had been.

When he was finished, Roland, Arriane, Annabelle, and Luce sat down on one of the tall tables facing Daniel.

Daniel reached for the satchel and unzipped it to show the others the halo.

Arriane gasped in awe and reached out to touch it.

"You found it." Annabelle winked at Luce. "Proper!"

"What about the second relic?" Daniel asked. "Did you get it? Did the Scale take it from you?"

Annabelle shook her head. "We never found it."

"We sure fooled them," Arriane said, narrowing her eyes in the direction of the Scale. "They thought they could beat it out of us."

"Your book is too vague, Daniel," Roland said. "We came to Vienna looking for a list."

"The desiderata," Daniel said. "I know."

"But that was *all* we knew. In the hours between our arrival and our capture by the Scale, we went to seven different city archives and found nothing. It was foolish. We attracted too much attention."

"It's my fault," Daniel muttered. "I should have uncovered more when I wrote that book centuries ago. I was too impulsive and impatient in that era. Now I can't recall what led me to the desideratum, or precisely what it says."

Roland shrugged. "It might not have mattered anyway. The city was a minefield by the time we arrived. If we'd had the desideratum, they would have only taken it away. They would have destroyed it, the way they've caused the destruction of this art."

"Most of these pieces were forgeries anyway," Daniel said, making Luce feel a little less guilty about what they'd done to the museum. "And for now the Outcasts can handle the Scale. The rest of us must hurry to find the desideratum. You say you went inside the Hofburg Library?"

Roland nodded.

"What about the university library?"

"Um, yeah," Annabelle said, "and we probably shouldn't show our faces there anytime soon. Arriane destroyed several very valuable parchment scrolls in their Special Collections—"

"Hey," Arriane snapped, indignant. "I glued them back together!"

A thunder of footfalls sounded in the hallway and all heads shot toward the open archway. At least twenty more Scale were attempting to fly into the room, but the Outcasts held them at the doorway with their starshots.

One of them spotted the halo in Daniel's hand and gasped. "They have stolen the first relic."

"And they are working together! Angels and demons and"—narrowed eyes fell on Luce—"those who do not know their place, all working together for an impure cause. The Throne does not endorse this. You will never find the desideratum!"

"*Desideratum,*" Luce said, faintly recalling a long boring lesson in her Latin class at Dover. "That's . . . singular." She spun around to face Daniel. "You said *desiderata* a moment ago. That's plural."

"Desired thing," Daniel whispered. His violet eyes began to pulse, and soon his entire being seemed to be glowing—a smile of recognition spread across his face. "It's just one thing. That's right."

Then the deep gong of a church tower clock sounded somewhere in the distance.

It was midnight.

Lucifer was another day closer. Six days to go.

"Daniel Grigori," Phil shouted over the bells, "we cannot hold them forever. You and your angels must go."

"We're leaving," Daniel called back. "Thank you." He faced the angels. "We will visit every library, every archive in this city until—"

Roland looked doubtful. "There must be hundreds of libraries in Vienna."

"And maybe let's try not to be so destructive in them?" Annabelle suggested, tilting her head at Arriane. "Mortals care about their pasts, too."

Yes, Luce thought, mortals cared very much about their pasts. Memories of her past lives were coming to her more frequently. She couldn't stop or slow them. As the angels readied their wings to fly, Luce stood still, debilitated by the most intense flashback.

Crimson hair ribbons. Daniel and the Christmas market. A slushy rainstorm and she hadn't had a coat. The last time she'd been in Vienna . . . there had been more to that story . . . something else . . . a doorbell—

"Daniel." Luce gripped his shoulder. "What about the library you took me to? Remember?" She closed her eyes. She wasn't thinking so much as feeling her way through a memory buried shallowly in her brain. "We came to Vienna for the weekend . . . I don't remember when, but we went to see Mozart conduct *The Magic Flute* . . . at the Theater an der Wien? You wanted to see this friend of yours who worked at some old library, his name was—"

She broke off, because when she opened her eyes, the others were staring at her, incredulous. No one, least of all Luce, had expected *her* to be the one to know where they would find the desideratum.

Daniel recovered first. He flashed her a funny smile Luce knew was full of pride. But Arriane, Roland, and Annabelle continued to gape at her as if they'd suddenly learned she spoke Chinese. Which, come to think of it, she did.

Arriane wiggled a finger around inside her ear. "Do I need to ease up on the psychedelics, or did LP just recall one of her past lives unprompted at the most crucial juncture ever?"

"You're a genius," Daniel said, leaning forward and kissing her deeply.

Luce blushed and leaned in to extend the kiss a little longer, but then heard a cough.

"Seriously, you two," Annabelle said. "There will be time enough for snogs if we pull this off."

"I'd say 'get a room' but I'm afraid we'd never see you again," Arriane added, which caused them all to laugh.

When Luce opened her eyes, Daniel had spread his wings wide. The tips brushed away broken bits of plaster and blocked the Scale angels from view. Slung over his shoulder was the black leather satchel with the halo.

The Outcasts gathered the scattered starshots back into their silver sheaths. "Wingspeed, Daniel Grigori."

"To you as well." Daniel nodded at Phil. He spun

Luce around so her back was pressed to his chest and his arms fit snugly around her waist. They clasped hands over her heart.

"The Foundation Library," Daniel said to the other angels. "Follow me, I know exactly where it is."

NINE

THE DESIDERATUM

Fog engulfed the angels. They flew back over the river, four pairs of wings making a tremendous *throosh* each time they beat. They stayed low enough to the ground that the muted orange glow of the sodium lamps looked like airport runway lights. But this flight did not land.

Daniel was tense. Luce could feel it running all through his body: in both his arms around her waist, in his shoulders aligned with hers, even in the manner that his broad wings beat above them. She knew how he felt;

she was as anxious to get to the Foundation Library as Daniel's grip suggested he was.

Only a few landmarks cut through the fog. There was the towering spire of the massive Gothic church, and there the darkened Ferris wheel, its empty red cabins swaying in the night. There was the green copper dome of the palace where they'd landed when they first arrived in Vienna.

But wait—they'd passed the palace already. Maybe half an hour earlier. Luce had tried to look for Olianna, whom the Scale angel had knocked unconscious. She hadn't seen her on the roof then, and she didn't see her now.

Why were they circling? Were they lost?

"Daniel?"

He didn't answer.

Church bells rang in the distance. It was their fourth ringing since Luce, Daniel, and the others had taken off through the shattered skylight at the museum. They'd been flying for a long time. Could it really be three o'clock in the morning?

"Where *is* it?" Daniel muttered under his breath, banking to the left, following the groove of the river, then breaking from it to trace a broad avenue lined with darkened department stores. Luce had seen this street already, too. They were flying in circles.

"I thought you said you knew exactly where it was!"

Arriane dipped out of the formation they'd been flying in—Daniel and Luce at the front, with Roland, Arriane, and Annabelle forming a tight triangle behind them—and swooped down about ten feet below Daniel and Luce, close enough to talk. Her hair was wild and frizzy and her iridescent wings flickered in and out of the fog.

"I *do* know where it is," Daniel said. "At least, I know where it *was*."

"You've got a circuitous sense of direction, Daniel."

"Arriane." Roland used the warning tone he reserved for those too frequent occasions when Arriane went too far. "Let him concentrate."

"Yeah yeah yeah." Arriane rolled her eyes. "Better return to 'formation.'" Arriane beat her wings the way some girls batted their eyelashes, flashed a peace sign with her fingers, and fell back.

"Okay, so where *was* the library?" Luce asked.

Daniel sighed, drew in his wings slightly, and dropped fifty feet straight down. Cold wind blasted Luce in the face. Her stomach surged up as they plummeted, then settled when Daniel stopped abruptly, as if he'd landed on an invisible tightrope, over a residential street.

It was quiet and empty and dark, just two long stretches of stone town houses spanning either side. Shutters were drawn for the night. Tiny cars rested in narrow angled spaces on the street. Young urban oak trees punctuated the cobbled sidewalk that ran along the small, well-maintained front yards.

The other angels hovered on either side of Daniel and Luce, about twenty feet above street level.

"This is where it was," Daniel said. "It was *here*. Six blocks from the river, just west of Türkenschanzpark. I swear it was. None of this"—he waved his hand at the stretch of indistinguishable stone town houses below— "was here."

Annabelle frowned and hugged her knees to her chest, her silver wings beating softly to keep her aloft. Her crossed ankles revealed hot-pink striped socks peeking out below her jeans. "Do you think it was destroyed?"

"If it was," Daniel said, "I have no idea how to recover it."

"We're screwed," Arriane said, kicking a cloud in frustration. She glared at its wispy tendrils, which ambled eastward, unaffected. "That's never as satisfying as I think it's going to be."

"Maybe we go to Avalon," Roland suggested. "See if Cam's group has had any more luck."

"We need all three relics," Daniel said.

Luce pivoted slightly in Daniel's arms to face him. "It's just a hitch. Think about what we had to go through in Venice. But we got the halo. We'll get the desideratum, too. That's all that matters. When was the last time any of us were at this library, two hundred years ago? Of course things are going to change. It doesn't mean we give up. We'll just have to . . . just have to—"

Everyone was looking at her. But Luce didn't know what to do. She only knew that they couldn't give up.

"The kid's right," Arriane said. "We don't give up. We—"

Arriane broke off when her wings began to rattle.

Then Annabelle yelped. Her body tossed in the air as her wings shuddered, too. Daniel's hands shook against Luce as the foggy night sky morphed into that peculiar gray—the color of a rainstorm on the horizon—that Luce now recognized as the color of a timequake.

Lucifer.

She could almost hear the hiss of his voice, feel his breath against her neck.

Luce's teeth chattered, but she felt it deeper, too, in her core, raw and turbulent, as if everything inside her were being wound up like a chain.

The buildings below shimmered. Lampposts doubled. The very atoms of the air seemed to fracture. Luce wondered what the quake was doing to the townspeople below, dreaming in their beds. Could they feel this? If not, she envied them.

She tried to call Daniel's name but the sound of her voice was warped, as if she were underwater. She closed her eyes but that made her feel nauseated. She opened them and tried to focus on the solid white buildings, quaking in their foundations until they became abstract blurs of white.

Then Luce saw that one structure stayed still, as if it were invulnerable to the fluctuations of the cosmos. It was a small brown building, a house, in the center of the shuddering white street.

It hadn't been there a second before. It appeared as though through a waterfall and was visible only for a moment, before it doubled and shimmered and disappeared back into the expansive row of modern, monochrome town houses.

But for a moment, the house had been there, one fixed thing in all-consuming chaos, both apart from and a part of the Viennese street.

The timequake shuddered to a stop and the world around Luce and the angels stilled. It was never quieter than in those moments right after a quake in time.

"Did you see that?" Roland shouted, gleeful.

Annabelle shook out her wings, smoothing the tips with her fingers. "I'm still recovering from that latest violation. I *hate* those things."

"Me too." Luce shuddered. "I saw something, Roland. A brown house. Was that it? The Foundation Library?"

"Yes." Daniel flew in a tight circle over the place where Luce had seen the house, zeroing in.

"Maybe those booty-quakes *are* good for something," Arriane said.

"Where did the house go?" Luce asked.

"It's still there. It's just not here," Daniel said.

"I've heard legends about these things." Roland ran his fingers through his thick gold-black dreads. "But I never really thought they were possible."

"What things?" Luce squinted to try to see the brown building again. But the row of modern town houses stayed put. The only movement on the street was bare tree branches leaning in the wind.

"It's called a Patina," Daniel said. "It's a way of bending reality around a unit of time and space—"

"It's a rearrangement of reality in order to secret something away," Roland added, flying to Daniel's side and peering down as if he could still see the house.

"So while this street exists in a continuous line through one reality"—Annabelle waved at the town houses—"beneath it lays another, independent realm, where this road leads to our Foundation Library."

"Patinas are the boundary between realities," Arriane said, thumbs tucked into her overall suspenders. "A laser light show only *special* folks can see."

"You guys seem to know a lot about these things," Luce said.

"Yeah," Arriane scoffed, looking as if she'd like to kick another cloud. "'Cept how to get through one."

Daniel nodded. "Very few entities are powerful enough to create Patinas, and those that can guard them closely. The library is here. But Arriane's right. We'll need to figure out the way in."

"I heard you need an Announcer to get through one," Arriane said.

"Cosmic legend." Annabelle shook her head. "Every Patina is different. Access is entirely up to the creator. They program the code."

"I once heard Cam tell a story at a party about how he accessed a Patina," Roland said. "Or was that a story about a party that he threw in a Patina?"

"Luce!" Daniel said suddenly, making all of them startle in midair. "It's you. It was always you."

Luce shrugged. "Always me what?"

"You're the one who always rang the bell. You're the one who had entry to the library. You just need to ring the bell."

Luce looked at the empty street, the fog tinting everything around them brown. "What are you talking about? What bell?"

"Close your eyes," Daniel said. "Remember it. Pass into the past and find the bellpull—"

Luce was already there, back at the library the last time she'd been in Vienna with Daniel. Her feet were firmly on the ground. It was raining and her hair splayed all across her face. Her crimson hair ribbons were soaked, but she didn't care. She was looking for something. There was a short path up the courtyard, then a dark alcove outside the library. It had been cold outside, and a fire blazed within. There, in the musty corner near the door, was a woven cord embroidered with white peonies hanging from a substantial silver bell.

She reached into the air and pulled.

The angels gasped. Luce opened her eyes.

There, in the center of the north side of the street, the row of contemporary town houses was interrupted at its midpoint by a single small brown house. A curl of smoke rose from its chimney. The only light—aside from the angels' wings—was the dim yellow glow of a lamp on the sill of the house's front window.

The angels landed softly on the empty street and Daniel's grip around Luce softened. He kissed her hand. "You remembered. Well done."

The brown house was only one story high, while the surrounding town houses had three levels, so you could see behind the house to parallel streets lined with more modern white stone town houses. The house was an anomaly: Luce studied its thatched roof, the gabled gate at the edge of a weed-ridden lawn, the arched wooden asymmetrical front door, all of which made the house look as if it belonged in the Middle Ages.

Luce took a step toward the house and found herself on a sidewalk. Her eyes fell on the large bronze placard pressed into the packed-mud walls. It was a historical marker, which read in big carved letters THE FOUNDATION LIBRARY, EST. 1233.

Luce looked around at the otherwise mundane street. There were recycling bins filled with plastic water bottles, tiny European cars parallel parked so closely that their bumpers were touching, shallow potholes in the road. "So we're on a real street in Vienna—"

"Exactly," Daniel said. "If it were daytime, you would see the neighbors, but they wouldn't see you."

"Are Patinas common?" Luce asked. "Was there one over the cabin I slept in on the island back in Georgia?"

"They are highly uncommon. Precious, really." Daniel shook his head. "That cabin was just the most secluded safe haven we could find on such short notice."

"A poor man's Patina," Arriane said.

"I.e., Mr. Cole's summerhouse," Roland added. Mr. Cole was a teacher at Sword & Cross. He was mortal, but he'd been a friend to the angels since they'd arrived at the school, and was covering for Luce now that she'd left. It was thanks to Mr. Cole that her parents weren't more worried than usual about her.

"How are they made?" Luce asked.

Daniel shook his head. "No one knows that except the Patina's artist. And there are very few of those. You remember my friend Dr. Otto?"

She nodded. The doctor's name had been on the tip of her tongue.

"He lived here for several hundred years—and even he didn't know how this Patina got here." Daniel studied the building. "I don't know who the librarian is now."

"Let's go," Roland said. "If the desideratum is here, we need to find it and get out of Vienna before the Scale regroup and track us down."

He slid open the latch on the gate and held it aside for the others to pass. The pebble path leading to the brown house was overgrown with wild purple freesia and tangled white orchids filling the air with their sweet scent.

The group reached the heavy wooden door with its arched top and flat iron knocker, and Luce grabbed Daniel's hand. Annabelle rapped on the door.

No answer.

Then Luce looked up and saw a bellpull, woven with the same stitches as the one she'd rung in the air. She glanced at Daniel. He nodded.

She pulled and the door creaked slowly open, as if the house itself had been expecting them. They peered into a candlelit hallway so long Luce couldn't see where it ended. The interior was far bigger than its exterior suggested; its ceilings were low and curved, like a railroad tunnel through a mountain. Everything was made of a lovely soft-pink brick.

The other angels deferred to Daniel and Luce, the only two who had been there before. Daniel crossed the threshold into the hallway first, holding Luce's hand. "Hello?" he called out.

Candlelight flickered on the bricks as the other angels entered and Roland shut the door behind them. As they walked, Luce was conscious of how quiet the hallway was, of the echoing thumps their shoes made on the smooth stone floor.

She paused at the first open doorway on the left side of the hall as a memory flooded her mind. "Here," she said, pointing inside the room. It was dark but for the yellow glow of a lamp on the windowsill, the same light they'd seen from the outside of the house. "Wasn't this Dr. Otto's office?"

It was too dark to see clearly, but Luce remembered a fire blazing cheerily in a hearth on the far side of the room. In her memory the fireplace had been bordered by a dozen bookshelves crammed with the leather spines of Dr. Otto's library. Hadn't her past self propped her wool-stockinged feet on the footrest near the fire and read Book IV of *Gulliver's Travels*? And hadn't the doctor's freely flowing cider made the whole room smell like apples, cloves, and cinnamon?

"You're right." Daniel took a glowing candelabra from its brick alcove in the hallway and held it inside to give the room more light. But the grate over the fireplace was shut, as was the antique wooden secretary in the corner, and even in the warm candlelight, the air seemed cold and stale. The shelves were sagging and distressed by the weight of the books, which were covered with a mist of dust. The window, which had once looked out on a busy residential street, had its dark green shades drawn, giving the room a bleak sense of abandonment.

"No wonder he hasn't answered any of my letters," Daniel said. "It looks as if the doctor has moved on."

Luce moved toward the bookshelves and dragged her finger across a dusty spine. "Do you think one of these books might contain the desired thing we're looking for?" Luce asked, pulling one from the shelf: *Canzoniere* by Petrarch, typeset in Gothic font. "I'm sure Dr. Otto wouldn't mind us taking a look around if it could help us find the desi—"

She stopped speaking. She'd heard something—the soft croon of a woman's voice.

The angels eyed one another as another sound reached them in the dark library. Now, in addition to the haunting song, came the clopping sound of shoes and the jangle of a cart being wheeled. Daniel moved to the open doorway and Luce followed, cautiously peering into the hallway.

A dark shadow stretched toward them. Candles flickered in the pink stone alcoves of the curved, tunnellike hallway, distorting the shadow, making its arms look wraithlike and impossibly long.

The shadow's owner, a thin woman in a gray pencil skirt, a mustard-colored cardigan, and very high black heels, walked toward them, pushing a fancy silver tea tray on wheels. Her fiery red hair was pulled up in a chignon. Elegant golden hoops glittered in her ears. Something about the way she walked, the way she carried herself, seemed familiar.

As the woman crooned her wordless melody, she lifted her head slightly, casting her profile in shadow against the wall. The curve of the nose, the upward swoop of the chin, the short jut of the brow bone— all gave Luce the feeling of déjà vu. She searched her past for other lives where she might have known this woman.

Suddenly, the blood drained from Luce's face. All the hair dye in the world couldn't fool her.

The woman pushing the tea cart was Miss Sophia Bliss.

Before she knew it, Luce had her hands around a cold brass fire poker resting in a stand by the library door. She raised it like a weapon, jaw clenched and heart hammering, and barreled into the hallway.

"Luce!" Daniel called.

"Dee?" Arriane shouted.

"Yes, dear?" the woman said, a second before she

noticed Luce charging at her. She jumped just as Daniel's arm engulfed Luce, holding back her lunge.

"What are you doing?" Daniel whispered.

"She's—she's—" Luce struggled against Daniel, feeling his grasp burn her waist. This woman had murdered Penn. She'd tried to kill Luce. Why didn't anyone else want to kill her?

Arriane and Annabelle ran to Miss Sophia and tackled her in a double hug.

Luce blinked.

Annabelle kissed the woman's pale cheeks. "I haven't seen you since the Peasants' Revolt in Nottingham . . . when was that, the 1380s?"

"Surely it hasn't been that long," the woman said politely, her voice lilting in the same kindly-librarian way it had early on at Sword & Cross, when she had tricked Luce into liking her. "Lovely time."

"I haven't seen you in a while, either," Luce said hotly. She jerked away from Daniel and raised the fire poker again, wishing it were something more deadly. "Not since you murdered my friend—"

"Oh dear." The woman did not flinch. She watched Luce coming at her and tapped a slender finger to her lips. "There must be some confusion."

Roland stepped forward, separating Luce from Miss Sophia. "It's just that you look like someone else." His calm hand on her shoulder made Luce pause.

"What do you mean?" the woman said.

"Oh, of course!" Daniel gave Luce a sad smile. "You thought she was—we should have told you that trans-eternals often look alike."

"You mean she's not Miss Sophia?"

"Sophia Bliss?" The woman looked as if she'd just bitten into something sour. "That bitch is still around? I was sure someone would have put her out of her misery by now." She wrinkled her tiny nose and shrugged at Luce. "She is my sister, so I can only display a small percentage of the rage I have accumulated over the years toward that disgusting bag."

Luce laughed nervously. The fire poker slipped from her hand and clattered to the floor. She studied the older woman, finding similarities to Miss Sophia—a face that seemed old and young at the same time—and differences. Compared to Sophia's black eyes, this woman's small eyes looked almost golden, emphasized by the matching yellow shade of her cardigan.

The scene with the fire poker had embarrassed Luce. She leaned back against the curved brick wall and sank to the ground, feeling empty, unsure whether she was relieved not to have to face Miss Sophia again. "I'm sorry."

"Don't worry, dear," the woman said brightly. "The day I encounter Sophia again, I'll grab the nearest heavy object and bludgeon her myself."

Arriane flung out a hand to help Luce up, pulling her so hard her feet shot off the ground. "Dee's an old friend. And a first-class party animal, might I add. Got the metabolism of a donkey. She almost brought the Crusades to a grinding halt the night she seduced Saladin."

"Oh, nonsense!" Dee said, flapping a hand dismissively.

"She's the best storyteller, too," Annabelle added. "Or she was before she dropped off the face of the earth. Where've you been hiding, woman?"

The woman drew a deep breath and her golden eyes dampened. "Actually, I fell in love."

"Oh, Dee!" Annabelle crooned, clasping the woman's hand. "How wonderful."

"Otto Z. Otto." The woman sniffed. "May he rest . . ."

"Dr. Otto," Daniel said, stepping out of the doorway. "You knew Dr. Otto?"

"Backwards and forwards." The mysterious lady sniffed.

"Oops, my manners!" Arriane said. "We must do introductions. Daniel, Roland, I don't think you've ever officially met our friend Dee—"

"What a pleasure. I am Paulina Serenity Bisenger." The woman smiled, dabbed her damp eyes with a lace handkerchief, and extended a hand first to Daniel, then to Roland.

"Ms. Bisenger," Roland said, "may I ask why the girls call you Dee?"

"Just an old nickname, love," the woman said, offering the kind of cryptic smile that was Roland's specialty. When she turned to Luce, her golden eyes lit up.

"Ah, Lucinda." Instead of holding out her hand, Dee opened her arms for a hug, but Luce felt funny about accepting it. "I apologize for the unfortunate resemblance that gave you such a fright. I must say that my sister looks like me; I do *not* look like *her*. But you and I have known each other so well over many lifetimes, so very many years, I forget that you might not remember. It was to me that you entrusted your darkest secrets—your love of Daniel, your fears for your future, your confusing feelings about Cam." Luce flushed, but the woman didn't notice. "And it was to you that I entrusted the very reasons for my existence, as well as the key to everything you seek. You were the one innocent I knew I could always rely upon to do what needed to be done."

"I—I'm sorry I don't remember," Luce stammered, and she was. "Are you an angel?"

"Transeternal, dear."

"They're technically mortals," Daniel explained, "but they can live for hundreds, even thousands of years. They have long worked closely with angels."

"It all started with Great-Granddaddy Methuselah," Dee said proudly. "He invented prayer. He did!"

"How did he do that?" Luce asked.

"Well, in the old days, when mortals wanted something, they just *wished* for it in a scattershot manner. Granddaddy was the first to appeal to God directly, and—here's the genius part—he asked for a message confirming that he had been heard. God responded with an angel, and the messenger angel was born. It was Gabbe, I think, who carved out the airspace between Heaven and Earth so mortal prayers could flow more freely. Granddaddy loved Gabbe, he loved the angels, and he taught all his kin to love them, too. Oh, but that was many years ago."

"Why do transeternals live so long?" Luce asked.

"Because we are enlightened. For our family history with messenger angels, and the fact that we are able to receive an angel's glory without being overcome, as many mortals are, we were rewarded with an extended life span. We liaise between angels and other mortals, so that the world can always feel a sense of angelic guardianship. We can be killed at any time, of course, but short of assassinations and freak accidents, a transeternal will live on until the end of days. The twenty-four of us who remain are the last surviving descendants of Methuselah. We used to be exemplary people, but I'm ashamed to say we are in decline. You've heard of the Elders of Zhsmaelim?"

The mention of Miss Sophia's evil clan sent a chill through Luce's body.

"All transeternals," Dee said. "The Elders *began* nobly. There was a time when I was involved with them myself. Of course, the good ones all defected"—she glanced at Luce and frowned—"not long after your friend Penn was murdered. Sophia has always had a cruel streak. Now it's become ambitious." She paused, taking out a white handkerchief to polish a corner of the silver tea cart. "Such dark things to speak of on our reunion. There is a bright spot, though: You remembered how to travel through my Patina." Dee beamed at Luce. "Exemplary work."

"*You* made that Patina?" Arriane asked. "I had no idea you could do that!"

Dee raised an eyebrow, the faintest smile on her lips. "A woman can't reveal *all* her secrets, lest she be taken advantage of. Can she, girls?" She paused. "Well, now that we're all friends again, what brings you to the Foundation? I was just about to sit down for my predawn jasmine tea. You really must join me, I always make too much."

She stepped aside to reveal the silver tray packed with a tall silver teapot, china plates of tiny crustless cucumber sandwiches, fluffy scones with golden raisins, and a crystal bowl brimming with clotted cream and cherries. Luce's stomach flopped at the sight of the food.

"So you've been expecting us," Annabelle said, counting the teacups with her finger.

Dee smiled, turned around, and took up wheeling the cart down the hallway again. Luce and the angels jogged to keep up as Dee's heels clicked along, forking right into a large room made of the same pink brick. There were a bright fire in the corner, a polished oak dining table that could have seated sixty, and a huge chandelier made of a petrified tree trunk and decorated with hundreds of sparkling crystal candlesticks.

The table was already set with fine china for far more guests than they had in their party. Dee set about filling the teacups with steaming amber-colored tea. "Very casual here, just take a seat wherever you like."

After a few purposeful looks from Daniel, Arriane finally stepped forward and touched Dee—who was scooping a mound of cream into a goblet and topping it with fruit—lightly on the back.

"Actually, Dee, we can't stay for tea. We're in a bit of a hurry. See—"

Daniel stepped forward. "Has the news reached you about Lucifer? He is attempting to erase the past by carrying the host of angels forward from the time of the Fall to the present."

"That would explain the shuddering," Dee murmured, filling another teacup.

"You can feel the timequakes, too?" Luce asked.

Dee nodded. "But most mortals can't, in case you were wondering."

"We've come because we need to track down the original location of the Fall," Daniel said, "the place where Lucifer and the host of Heaven will appear. We have to stop him."

Dee looked strangely undeterred from her tea service, continuing to divvy up the cucumber sandwiches. The angels waited for her to respond. A log in the fire splintered, cracked, and tumbled from the grate.

"And all because a boy loved a girl," she said at last. "Quite disturbing. Really brings out the worst in all the old enemies, doesn't it? Scale coming unhinged, Elders killing innocents. So much unpleasantness. As if all you fallen angels didn't have enough to bother with. I say, you must be awfully tired." She gave Luce a reassuring smile and gestured again for them to sit down.

Roland pulled out the chair at the head of the table for Dee and sat down in the seat to her left. "Maybe you can help us." He motioned for the others to join him. Annabelle and Arriane sat beside him, and Luce and Daniel sat across the table. Luce slid her hand over Daniel's, twining her fingers around his.

Dee passed the cups of tea around the table. After a clattering of china and spoons stirring sugar into tea, Luce cleared her throat. "We're going to stop Lucifer, Dee."

"I should hope so."

Daniel grasped Luce's fingers. "Right now we're

searching for three objects that tell the early history of the fallen. When brought together, they should reveal the original location of the Fall."

Dee sipped her tea. "Clever boy. Had any luck?"

Daniel produced the leather satchel and unzipped it to reveal the gold-and-glass halo. An eternity had passed since Luce dove into the sunken church to pry it from the statue's head.

Dee's forehead wrinkled. "Yes, I remember that. The angel Semihazah created it, didn't he? Even in prehistory, he had a biting aesthetic. No written texts for him to satirize, so he made this as a sort of commentary on the silly ways mortal artists try to capture angelic glow. Amusing, isn't it? Imagine bearing a hideous . . . basketball hoop on your head. Two points and all of that."

"Dee." Arriane reached into the satchel and pulled out Daniel's book, then thumbed through it until she found the notation in the margin about the desideratum. "We came to Vienna to find this"—she pointed—"the desired thing. But we're running out of time and we don't know what it is or where to find it."

"How splendid. You've come to the right place."

"I knew it!" Arriane crowed. She leaned back into her chair and slapped Annabelle, who was politely nibbling at a scone, on the back. "As soon as I saw you, I knew we'd be okay. You have the desideratum, don't you?"

"No, dear." Dee shook her head.

"Then . . . what?" Daniel asked.

"I *am* the desideratum." She beamed. "I've been waiting such a long time to be called into service."

TEN

STARSHOT IN THE DUST

"*You're* the desideratum?" Luce's cucumber sandwich fell from her fingers and bounced off her teacup, leaving a glob of mayonnaise on the lace-embroidered table-cloth.

Dee beamed at them. There was an almost impish gleam in her golden eyes that made her look more like a teenager than a woman many hundreds of years old. As she pinned a shiny strand of red hair back into her chignon and poured everyone more tea, it was hard to fathom that this elegant, vibrant creature was also, in fact, an artifact.

"That's how you got the nickname Dee, isn't it?" Luce asked.

"Yes." Dee looked pleased. She winked at Roland.

"Then you know where the site of the Fall is?"

The question brought everyone to attention. Annabelle sat straighter, elongating her long neck. Arriane did the opposite, slumping lower in her chair, elbows on the table, chin resting on clasped hands. Roland leaned forward, tucking his dreads behind one shoulder. Daniel clenched Luce's hand. Was Dee the answer to every question they had?

She shook her head.

"I can help you discover where the Fall took place." Dee set her teacup down in its saucer. "The answer is within me, but I am unable to express it in any way that I or you can understand. Not until all of the pieces are in place."

"What do you mean, 'in place'?" Luce asked. "How will we know when that happens?"

Dee walked over to the fireplace and used a poker to return the fallen log to its place inside. "You will know. We will all know."

"But you at least know where the third artifact is?" Roland passed around a plate of sliced lemons after dropping one into his tea.

"Indeed I do."

"Our friends," Roland said, "Cam, Gabbe, and Molly, have gone to Avalon to search for it. If you could help them locate—"

"You know as well as I that the angels must locate each artifact on their own, Sir Sparks."

"I thought you'd say that." He leaned back in his chair, eyeing Dee. "Please, call me Roland."

"And I thought you'd ask. Roland." She smiled. "I'm glad you did. It makes me feel as if you trust me to help you defeat Lucifer." She tilted her head at Luce. "Trust is important, don't you think, Lucinda?"

Luce looked around the table at the fallen angels she'd first met at Sword & Cross, epochs earlier. "I do."

She had once had a very different kind of conversation with Miss Sophia, who had described trust as a careless pursuit, *a good way to get oneself killed.* It was eerie how much the two resembled each other in body, while the words produced by their dissimilar souls differed so completely.

Dee reached for the halo in the center of the table. "May I?"

Daniel handed over the piece, which Luce knew from personal experience was very heavy. In Dee's hands, it seemed to weigh nothing.

Her slender arms were barely long enough to wrap around its gold circumference, but Dee cradled the halo like a child. Her reflection peered back dimly in the glass.

"Another reunion," she said softly, to herself. When Dee looked up, Luce couldn't tell whether she was content or sad. "It will be wonderful when the third artifact is in your possession."

"From your mouth to God's ears," Arriane said, pouring something from a fat silver flask into her tea.

"That's great-granddaddy's route!" Dee said with a smile.

Everyone laughed, a little nervously.

"Speaking of the third artifact"—Dee looked down at a thin gold watch buried among her tangle of pearl bracelets—"did someone mention you all were rather in a hurry to move on?"

There was a clamor of teacups jostling back into their saucers, chairs being pushed back, and wings whooshing open around the table. Suddenly, the massive dining hall seemed smaller and brighter and Luce felt the familiar tingle run through her body when she saw Daniel's broad wings unfurled.

Dee caught her eye. "Lovely, isn't it?"

Instead of blushing at being caught staring at Daniel, Luce just smiled, for Dee was on their side. "Every time."

"Where to, Cap'n?" Arriane asked Daniel, tucking scones into the pockets of her overalls.

"Back to Mount Sinai, right?" Luce said. "Isn't that

where we agreed Cam and the others are supposed to meet us?"

Daniel glanced toward the door. His forehead wrinkled in agitation. "Actually, I didn't want to mention this until we'd found the second artifact, but . . ."

"Come on, Grigori," Roland said. "Let's have it."

"Before we left the warehouse," Daniel said, "Phil told me that he received a message from one of the Outcasts who he'd sent to Avignon. Cam's group was intercepted—"

"Scale?" Dee asked. "Still harboring fantasies of their importance in the cosmic balance?"

"We can't be sure," Daniel said, "though it does seem likely. We will set a course for the Pont Saint Bénézet in Avignon." He glanced at Annabelle, whose face turned a shade of scarlet.

"What?" she cried. "Why there?"

"My marginalia in *The Book of the Watchers* suggest it is the approximate location of the third artifact. It should have been Cam, Gabbe, and Molly's first stop."

Annabelle looked away and didn't say anything else. The mood turned serious as the group filed out of the dining room. Luce felt tense with worry for Cam and Molly, imagining them bound up in black Scale cloaks like Arriane and Annabelle.

Angel wings rustled along the narrow brick walls as

they walked back down the endless hallway. When they reached the curved wooden doorway leading back outside, Dee swung open an iron circle covering the peephole and peered out.

"Hmmm." She let the peephole swing shut.

"What is it?" Luce asked, but by then, Dee had already opened up the door and was gesturing for everyone to leave the peculiar brown house, whose soul was so much richer than its exterior suggested.

Luce went first and stood on the porch—which was really just a heap of frost-kissed straw—to wait for the others. The angels poured out of the doorway one at a time—Daniel arching his white wings back as he exited chest out, Annabelle tucking her thick silver wings fast to her sides, Roland bundling his golden marble wings around the front of his body like an invincible shield, and Arriane plowing through recklessly, cursing an unnoticed candle by the doorway that singed a tip of wing.

Afterward, all the angels stood together on the lawn and flexed their wings, glad to be out in the crisp air again.

Luce noticed the darkness. She was certain that when they'd entered the Foundation, the sun had not been far from rising. The church bells had chimed once more, announcing four o'clock, and the sky had been grasping for the precious gold of dawn.

Had they been inside with Dee for just an hour? Why was the sky now a dark, dead-of-night blue?

Lights were on in the white stone town houses. People passed behind the windows, frying eggs, pouring cups of coffee. Men with briefcases and women in smart suits walked out their front doors and, without ever once glancing at the congregation of angels in the middle of the street, got into cars and drove away, toward what Luce assumed was work.

She remembered Daniel had explained that Viennese people could not see them when they were inside the Patina. They didn't see the brown house at all. Luce watched a woman in a black terry cloth bathrobe and a plastic rain bonnet walk groggily toward them with her small furry dog. Her property bordered the overgrown pebble path that led to the front door of the Foundation. The woman and her dog stepped onto the path.

And disappeared.

Luce gasped, but then Daniel pointed behind her, to the other side of the Foundation's lawn. She spun around. Forty feet away, where the pebble path ended and the modern sidewalk picked up once again, the woman and her dog reappeared. The dog yapped hysterically, but the woman walked on as if nothing had disturbed her morning routine.

It was strange, Luce realized, that the angels' whole mission was to keep her life that way. So that nothing happened to erase this woman's world, so that she never even noticed how much danger she'd been in.

But while the people on the street might not have noticed Luce or the angels, they certainly did notice the sky. The woman with the dog kept glancing up at it worriedly, and most of the people leaving their houses wore slickers and carried umbrellas.

"Is it going to rain?" Luce had flown through pockets of rain with Daniel, warm showers that left them refreshed and exhilarated . . . but this sky was ominous, nearly black.

"No," Dee said. "It isn't going to rain. That's the Scale."

"What?" Luce's head shot up. She squinted at the sky, horrified when it shifted and pitched. Storm clouds didn't move like that.

"The sky is dark with their wings." Arriane shuddered. "And their cloaks."

No.

Luce stared at the sky until it began to make sense. With a feeling akin to vertigo, she made out an undulating mass of blue-gray wings. They were smeared across the sky, thick as a coat of paint, blocking out the rising sun. The beats of the short, brutish wings buzzed like a swarm of hornets. Her heart clenched as she tried to count them. It was impossible. How many hundreds hovered in the multitude above?

"We're under siege," Daniel said.

"They're so close," Luce said, flinching as the sky roiled. "Can they see us?"

"Not exactly, but they know we're here," Dee said nonchalantly as a small group of Scale swooped lower, low enough for them to see their shriveled, bloodthirsty faces. Cold eyes trolled the space where Luce and the others were gathered, but when it came to the Patina, Scale seemed to be about as blind as the Outcasts.

"My Patina surrounds us, the way a tea cozy surrounds a pot, forming a protective barrier. The Scale can't see or travel through it." Dee managed a smile at Luce. "It only answers to the ringing of a certain kind of soul, one innocent of its own potential."

Daniel's wings pulsed beside her. "They're gathering more brethren all the time. We need some way to get out of here, and we need to hurry."

"I do not intend to be bound in one of their broke-neck burkas," Dee said. "No one takes me in my own house!"

"I like the way she talks," Annabelle said sideways to Luce.

"Follow me!" Dee shouted, breaking into a run along a gated alley. They jogged behind her through an unexpected pumpkin patch, around an ornate and dilapidated gazebo, and into an expansive and lushly green backyard.

Roland's chin tilted toward the sky. It was darker now, denser with wings.

"What's the plan?"

"Well, for starters"—Dee wandered over to stand under a mottled oak tree in the center of the garden—"the library must be destroyed."

Luce gasped. "Why?"

"Simple mechanics. This Patina has always encompassed the library, so with the library it must stay. In order to move past the Scale, we'll have to open the Patina, thereby exposing the Foundation, and I do not intend to leave it for their indiscriminating wings to root through." Her hand patted Luce's stricken face. "Don't worry, dear, I've already donated the valuable volumes in the collection—to the Vatican, mostly, though some went to the Huntington, and to an unsuspecting little town in Arkansas. No one will miss this place. I'm the last librarian here, and frankly, I don't plan to return after this mission."

"I still don't understand how we get past them." Daniel's gaze stayed fixed on the swirling blue-black sky.

"I will have to produce a second Patina, surrounding only our bodies, guaranteeing us safe passage. Then I will open this one and let the Scale flow in."

"I think I'm smelling what you're cooking," Arriane said, climbing up a branch like a monkey to sit nestled in the oak tree.

"The Foundation will be sacrificed"—Dee frowned—"but at least the Scale will make nice kindling."

"Hold on, how does the library get sacrificed?" Roland crossed his arms over his chest and looked down at Dee.

"I was hoping you could help with that, Roland," Dee said, eyes twinkling. "You're rather good at starting fires, aren't you?"

Roland raised his eyebrows, but Dee had already turned around. Facing the tree trunk, she reached for a knot in its bark, pulled it like a secret doorknob, and opened the trunk to a hollowed chamber. Inside, the wood was polished, the chamber about the size of a small locker. Dee's arm dipped in and pulled out a long golden key.

"That's how you open the Patina?" Luce asked, surprised that it required so physical a key.

"Well, this is how I unlock it so that it can be manipulated for our needs."

"When you open it, if there's a fire," Luce said, remembering the way the woman walking her dog had blinked out of existence for a moment while she crossed the Foundation's front lawn, "what will happen to the houses, to the people on the street?"

"Funny thing about the Patina," Dee said, kneeling down and rooting around in the garden for something. "The way it sits on the border between realities past and present, we can be here, and not here, in the present, and also elsewhere. It's a place where everything we imagine about time and space comes together materially." She lifted up the fronds of an oversized fern, then dug in the dirt with her hands. "No mortals outside will be affected, but if the Scale are as ravenous as we all know they are, as soon as I open this Patina, they'll swoop right toward us. For one tense moment, they will join us in the elsewhere reality when the Foundation Library stood on this street."

"And we'll fly out, enclosed in the second Patina," Daniel guessed.

"Precisely," Dee said. "Then we have only to close this one around them. Just as they can't get in now, they won't be able to get out then. And while we soar on safely to lovely, ancient Avignon, the library will go up in smoke, with the Scale trapped inside."

"It's brilliant," Daniel said. "The Scale will still technically be alive, so our action won't tip the Heavenly balance, but they'll be—"

"Burn marks of the past, sealed off, out of our way. Right. Everybody on board?" Dee's face lit up. "Ah, *there* it is!"

As Luce and the angels stood over her, Dee brushed the dirt off a collared hole that had been buried in the garden. She closed her eyes, held the key close to her heart, and whispered a blessing:

"Light surround us, love enfold us, shelter us, Patina, from the evil that must come."

Carefully, she fit the key into the lock. Her wrist shook with the force required to turn the key, but finally, it creaked a quarter turn to the right. Dee exhaled heavily and rose to her feet, wiping her hands on her skirt.

"Here we go."

She raised her arms above her head and then, very slowly, very purposefully, brought them down toward her heart. Luce waited for the earth to shift, for anything to happen, but for a moment, nothing seemed to have changed.

Then, as the space around them grew pin-drop quiet, Luce heard an almost inaudible swishing sound, like bare palms being rubbed together. The air seemed to slightly warp, making everything—the brown house, the row of Viennese town houses surrounding it, even the blue wings of the Scale above—waver. Colors bent, melted. It was like standing inside the cloudy haze that rises from flowing gasoline.

As before, Luce could both see and not see the Patina. Its amorphous boundary was visible one moment—with the iridescent transparency of a soap bubble—then it disappeared. But she could *feel* it molding around the small space in the garden where she and the others stood, emanating warmth and the feeling of being embraced by something powerfully protective.

No one spoke, silenced by the wonder of Dee.

Luce studied the old woman, who was humming so intensely she almost seemed to buzz. Luce was surprised when she sensed the inner Patina was complete. Something that hadn't felt whole a moment before now did. Dee nodded, her hands at her heart as if in prayer. "We are in the Patina within the Patina. We are in the heart of safety and security. When I open the outer rim to the Scale, trust that security and remain calm. No harm can come to you."

She whispered the words again—*Light surround us, love enfold us, shelter us, Patina, from the evil that must come*—and Luce found herself murmuring along. Daniel's voice chimed in, too.

Then there was a hole, like a gust of cold air entering a warm room. They shuffled closer together, wings pressing up against each other, Luce in the center. They watched the shifting sky.

A savage shriek came from high above, and a thousand others joined in. The Scale could see it now.

They swarmed toward the hole.

The opening was mostly invisible to Luce, but it must have been directly over the chimney of the brown house. That was where the Scale headed, like winged ants attacking a drop of fallen jam. They thudded to the roof, to the grass, to the eaves of the house. Their cloaks rippled with the impact of rough landings. Their eyes trolled the property—both sensing and not sensing Luce, Dee, and the angels.

Luce held her breath, did not make a sound.

The Scale kept coming. Soon the yard bristled with their stiff blue wings. They surrounded Dee's inner Patina, casting glances hungry as wolves' directly at the place where the prey they sought were hiding. But the Scale could not see the angels, the girl, and the transeternal safe inside.

"Where are they?" one of them snarled, his cloak tangling in a sea of blue wings as he pushed through the crowd of his brethren. "They're here somewhere."

"Prepare to fly fast and hard to Avignon," Dee whispered, standing stiffly as a Scale angel with a birthmark splashed across his face leaned in near the limits of their Patina and sniffed like a pig seeking slop.

Arriane's wings were trembling and Luce knew she was thinking of what the Scale had done to her. Luce reached for her friend's hand.

"Roland, how about that mighty conflagration?" Daniel said through pursed lips.

"You got it." Roland interlaced his fingers and furrowed his brow, then gave one hard glance at the brown house. There was a great blast, like a detonating bomb, and the Foundation Library exploded. Scale were sent shrieking into the Patina sky, their cloaks engulfed in fingerlike flames.

Roland waved his hand, and the hole where the library had stood became a volcano spewing flames and lava rivers through the lawn. The oak tree caught fire. Flames spread through its branches as if they were matches in a box. Luce was sweating and dizzy from the heat searing through the Patina, but even as the Scale were blown back by repercussive shock waves, the group inside Dee's small Patina did not burn.

Dee shouted, "Let's fly!" just as a tornado of hot, flame-laden air swirled through the yard, swallowing a hundred Scale and lifting them into its blazing core, carouseling them across the lawn.

"Ready, Luce?" Daniel's arms wrapped around her just as Roland's wrapped tight around Dee. Smoke ricocheted off the walls on the outside of the Patina, but Luce was having a hard time breathing through her sore, bruised neck.

Then Daniel lifted her off the ground. They flew straight up. Out of the corners of her eyes, Luce saw Roland's marbled wings on the right, Annabelle and Arriane on the left. All the angels' wings were beating so fast and hard that they wove a pure blinding brightness, straight up out of the fire and into clear blue air.

But the Patina was still open. The Scale who could still fly had some sense that they were being tricked, trapped. They tried to rise out of the blaze, but Roland sent another wave of flame washing down onto them, thrusting them back into the burning earth, singeing off their crinkled skin until they were skeletons with wings.

"Just another moment . . ." Dee's fingertips and steady gaze manipulated the boundaries of the Patina. Luce studied Dee, then the mess of burning Scale. She imagined the Patina cinching at the top like a cloak around a neck, sealing the Scale inside, choking them out.

"All done," Dee shouted as Roland took her higher through the air.

Luce looked down, beneath her and Daniel's feet, as the ground sped away from them. She saw the ugly fire blink, then shiver, and then disappear, swallowed into a smoking hidden elsewhere. The street they left below was white, and modern, and full of people who had never sensed anything at all.

⋇⋇

The ground was miles beneath them when Luce stopped envisioning Scale wings cooking in red flames. There was no use looking back. She could only look ahead toward the next relic, toward Cam, Gabbe, and Molly, toward Avignon.

Through gaps in the thin sheets of clouds, the terrain became rocky, dark gray, and mountainous. The winter air grew colder, sharper, and the ceaseless beat of angel wings shattered the quiet at the edges of the atmosphere.

About an hour into the flight, Roland's marbled wings came into view a few feet below Luce and Daniel. He carried Dee the same way Daniel carried Luce: shoulders lined up with hers, one arm wrapped over her chest, the other around her waist. Like Luce, Dee crossed her legs at the ankles, and her stiletto heels dangled precariously so high above the ground. Roland's dark muscles encasing Dee's frail, older frame made the pair look almost comical as they came into and out of focus, rippling through the clouds. But the thrilled sparkle in Dee's eyes made her seem much younger than she was. Strands of her red hair whipped across her cheek, and her scent—cold cream and roses—perfumed the air through which they flew.

"Well, I think the coast is clear," Dee said.

Luce felt the air around her warble. Her body tensed in preparation for another timequake. But this time, it wasn't Lucifer's encroaching Fall causing the ripple. It was Dee, withdrawing the second Patina. A hazy boundary moved closer to Luce's skin, then passed through her, making her shiver with an untraceable pleasure. Then it retracted until it was a tiny orb of light around Dee. She closed her eyes and, a moment later, absorbed the Patina into her skin. It was mostly invisible—and was one of the most beautiful things Luce had ever seen.

Dee smiled and beckoned Luce nearer with a little

wave. The two angels carrying them tilted their wings upward so that the ladies could talk.

Dee cupped a hand over her mouth and called to Luce over the wind. "So tell me, dear, how did you two meet?"

Luce felt Daniel's shoulder shudder behind her with a chuckle. It was a normal question to ask two people in a happy relationship; why did it make Luce miserable?

Because the answer was needlessly complicated.

Because she didn't even know the answer.

She pressed a hand to the locket at her neck. It bobbed against her skin as Daniel's wings beat another strong stroke. "Well, we went to the same school, and I . . ."

"Oh, Lucinda!" Dee was laughing. "I was teasing. I merely wondered whether you had uncovered the story behind your *original* meeting."

"No, Dee," Daniel said firmly. "She has not learned that yet—"

"I've asked, but he won't tell me." Luce eyed the vertiginous drop below, feeling as far away from the truth of that first meeting as she was from the towns over which they were flying. "It drives me crazy that I don't know."

"All in good time, dear," Dee said calmly, staring straight ahead at the curved horizon. "I take it you have tapped into at least *some* of your earlier memories?"

Luce nodded.

"Brilliant. I'll settle for the tale of the earliest romance you can recall. Go on, dear. Humor an old lady. It'll help us pass the time to Avignon, like Canterbury pilgrims."

A memory flashed before Luce's eyes: the cold, damp tomb she'd been locked in with Daniel in Egypt, the way his lips had pressed against hers, their bodies against each other, as though they were the last two people in the world. . . .

But they hadn't been alone. Bill had been there, too. He'd been there waiting, watching, wanting her soul to die inside a dank Egyptian tomb.

Luce snapped her eyes open, returning to the present, where his red eyes could not find her. "I'm tired," she said.

"Rest," Daniel said softly.

"No, I'm tired of being punished simply because I love you, Daniel. I don't want anything to do with Lucifer, with Scale and Outcasts and whatever other sides there are. I'm not a pawn; I'm a person. And I've had enough."

Daniel wrapped his hand over Luce's and squeezed.

Dee and Roland both looked as if they wanted to reach out and do the same.

"You've changed, dear," Dee said.

"Since when?"

"Since before. I've never heard you talk like that. Have you, Daniel?"

Daniel was quiet for a moment. Finally, over the

sounds of wind and the flapping of the angels' wings against thin air, he said, "No. But I'm glad she can now."

"And why not? It's a trans-dimensional tragedy what you kids have been through. But this is a girl with tenacity, a girl with muscles, a girl who once told me she would never cut her hair, even though she was cursed—your words, dear—by snarls and tangles, a magnet for briars, because that hair was a part of her, indelibly tied to her soul."

Luce squinted at the old woman. "What are you talking about?"

Dee tilted her head at Luce and pursed her plump lips.

Luce stared at her hard, at her golden eyes and fine red hair, at the delicate way she hummed as they flew. And it hit her.

"I remember you!"

"Lovely," Dee said, "I remember you, too!"

"Didn't I live in a hut on an open plain?"

Dee nodded.

"And we *did* talk about my hair! I'd—I'd run through a patch of nettles diving after something on a hunt . . . was it a fox?"

"You were quite the tomboy. Braver than some of the men on the prairie, actually."

"And you," Luce said, "you spent hours picking them out of my hair."

"I was your favorite auntie, figuratively speaking. You used to say the devil cursed you with such thick hair. A trifle dramatic, but you *were* only sixteen—and not far off from the truth, as only sixteen-year-olds can be."

"You said a curse is only a curse if I allowed myself to be cursed by it. You said . . . I had it in my power to free myself of any curse—that curses were preludes to blessings. . . ."

Dee winked.

"Then you told me to cut it off. My hair."

"That's right. But you wouldn't."

"No." Luce closed her eyes as the cool mist of a cloud washed over her, its condensation tickling her skin. She was suddenly inexplicably sad. "I wouldn't. I wasn't ready to."

"Well," Dee said. "I certainly like how you've styled your hair since you've come to your senses!"

"Look." Daniel pointed to where the cloud floor fell away like a cliff. "We're here."

They descended into Avignon. The sky above the town was clear, with no clouds to interrupt their view. The sun cast shadows of the angels' wings onto the small medieval village of stone buildings bordered by verdant pastures of farmland. Cows loafed below them. A tractor threaded through land.

They banked left and flew over a horse stable, breathing in the dank stench of hay and manure. They swooped low over a cathedral made from the same tawny stone as most of the buildings in the town. Tourists sipped coffees in a cheerful café. The town glowed golden in the midday sun.

The startled sense of arriving so quickly mingled with the feeling of time slipping through Luce's fingers. They had been searching for the relics for four and a half days. Half the time before Lucifer's Fall would be upon them was up.

"That's where we're going." Daniel pointed to a bridge on the outskirts that did not extend fully across the shimmering river winding through the town. It was as if half the bridge had crumbled into the water. "Pont Saint Bénézet."

"What happened to it?" Luce asked.

Daniel glanced over his shoulder. "Remember how quiet Annabelle got when I mentioned we were coming here? She inspired the boy who built that bridge in the Middle Ages in the time when the popes lived here and not in Rome. He noticed her flying across the Rhône one day when she didn't think anyone could see her. He built the bridge to follow her to the other side."

"When did it collapse?"

"Slowly, over time, one arch would fall into the river. Then another. Arriane says the boy—his name was Bénézet—had a vision for angels, but not for architecture. Annabelle loved him. She stayed in Avignon as his muse until he died. He never married, kept apart from the rest of Avignon society. The town thought he was crazy."

Luce tried not to compare her relationship with Daniel to what Annabelle had had with Bénézet, but it was hard not to. What kind of a relationship could an angel and a mortal *really* have? Once all this was over, if they beat Lucifer . . . then what? Would she and Daniel go back to Georgia and be like any other couple, going out for ice cream on Fridays after a movie? Or would the whole town think she was crazy, like Bénézet?

Was it all just hopeless? What would become of them in the end? Would their love vanish like a medieval bridge's arches?

The idea of sharing a normal life with an angel was what was crazy. She sensed that in every moment Daniel *flew* her through the sky. And yet she loved him more each day.

They landed on the bank of the river under the shade of a weeping willow tree, sending a flock of agitated ducks flapping into the water. In broad daylight, the angels folded in their wings. Luce stood behind Daniel to watch the intricate process as his retracted into his skin. They drew in from the center first, making a series of soft snaps as layers of muscle folded on empyreal feathers. Last came Daniel's thin, nearly translucent wing tips, which glowed as they disappeared inside his body, leaving no trace on his specially tailored T-shirt.

They walked to the empty bridge, like any other tourists interested in architecture. Annabelle walked much more stiffly than normal, and Luce saw Arriane reach out and touch her hand. The sun was bright and the air smelled like lavender and river water. The bridge was made of big white stones, held up by long arches underneath. There was a small stone chapel with a single tower attached along one side near the entrance of the bridge. It held a sign that read CHAPELLE DE SAINT NICOLAS. Luce wondered where the real tourists were.

The chapel was coated with a fine, silvery dust.

They walked the bridge silently, but Luce noticed that Annabelle wasn't the only one upset. Daniel and Roland were trembling, keeping well clear of the entrance to the chapel, and Luce remembered they were forbidden to enter a sanctuary of God.

Dee ran her fingers over the narrow brass railing with a heavy sigh. "We are too late."

"This isn't—" Luce touched the dust. It was insubstantial and light, with a hint of silver shimmer, like the dust that had covered her parents' backyard. "You mean—"

"Angels have died here." Roland's voice was a monotone as he stared into the river.

"B-but," Luce stammered, "we don't know whether Gabbe and Cam and Molly even made it here."

"This used to be a beautiful place," Annabelle said. "Now they've marred it forever. *Je m'excuse,* Bénézet."

That was when Arriane held up a quivering silver feather. "Gabbe's pennon. Intact, so it must have been taken by her own hand. Perhaps to give to an Outcast who didn't get it before . . ." She looked away, holding the feather to her chest.

"But I thought the Scale didn't kill angels," Luce said.

"They don't." Daniel bent down and wiped away some of the dust that was mounded like snow at his feet.

Something was buried underneath it.

His fingers found a dusty silver starshot. He wiped it on his shirt and Luce shivered each time his fingers drew near the deadly dull tip. At last, he held it out for the others to examine. It was branded with an ornate letter Z.

"The Elders," Arriane whispered.

"*They* are happy to kill angels," Daniel said softly. "In fact, there's nothing they'd rather do."

There was a sharp crack.

Luce whipped around, expecting . . . she didn't know what. Scale? Elders?

Dee shook out her fist, rubbing red knuckles with her other hand. Then Luce saw: The wooden door to the chapel was smashed in the center. Dee must have punched it. No one else thought it was remarkable that such a tiny woman could cause so much damage.

"You all right there, Dee?" Arriane called out.

"Sophia has no business here." Her voice quaked with rage. "What Lucifer is doing is beyond the compass of the Elders' concern. And yet she could ruin everything for you angels. I could kill her."

"Promise?" Roland asked.

Daniel slipped the starshot into the satchel and clasped it shut. "However this battle ended, it must have begun over the third relic. Someone found it."

"A war of resources," Dee said.

Luce flinched. "And someone died for it."

"We don't know what happened, Luce," Daniel said. "And we won't know until we stand before the Elders. We need to track them down."

"How?" Roland asked.

"Maybe they went to Sinai to stake us out," Annabelle suggested.

Daniel shook his head and paced. "They don't know to go to Sinai—unless they tortured the location out of one of our angels." He stopped and looked away.

"No," Dee said, looking around their circle on the bridge. "The Elders have their own agenda. They're greedy. They want a larger stake in all of this. They want to be remembered, like their forefathers. If they die, they want to go as martyrs." She paused. "And what is the most self-indulgent location to stage your own martyrdom?"

The angels shifted their weight. Daniel scanned the pale pink western sky. Annabelle ran her long nails through her hair. Arriane hugged her arms around her chest and stared hard at the ground, at a loss for sarcastic words. Luce seemed to be the only one who didn't know what Dee was talking about. Finally, Roland's voice echoed ominously across the crumbling bridge:

"Golgotha. Place of skulls."

ELEVEN

VIA DOLOROSA

As the angels banked right over the southern coast of France, Luce watched the dark waves roll below them, washing up along the distant shore. She did some math in her head:

At midnight, it would be Tuesday, December 1. Five days had passed since she'd returned from the Announcers, which meant they were past the midpoint of the nine-day period over which the angels fell to Earth. Lucifer and all their earlier selves were more than halfway through the Fall.

They had two of the three relics, but they didn't know what the third was, didn't know how to read them once they got them all together. Worse, in the process of locating the relics, they'd gained more enemies. And it looked like they had lost their friends.

Dust from the Pont Saint Bénézet was under Luce's fingernails. What if it was Cam? In a handful of days, Luce had gone from being wary about Cam's involvement in their mission to feeling despondent at the thought of losing him. Cam was fierce and dark and unpredictable and intimidating and not the guy that Luce was meant to be with—but that didn't mean she didn't care about him, didn't care *for* him in a certain way.

And Gabbe. The Southern beauty who always knew the right thing to say and do. From the moment Luce met Gabbe at Sword & Cross, the angel had done nothing but look out for her. Now Luce wanted to look out for Gabbe.

Molly Zane had also gone to Avignon with Cam and Gabbe. Luce had feared, then hated Molly—until the other morning, when Luce had come in through the bedroom window at her parents' house to find Molly covering for her in bed. It was a solid favor. Even Callie liked spending time with Molly. Had the demon changed? Had Luce?

The rhythmic beats of Daniel's wings across the starry sky lulled Luce into a deep state of relaxation, but she did not want to sleep. She wanted to focus on what might greet them when they arrived at Golgotha, to brace herself for what was coming.

"What's on your mind?" Daniel asked. His voice was low and intimate in the frantic wind they were flying through. Annabelle and Arriane flew in front of them and a little bit below. Their wings, dark silver and iridescent, spread wide over the green boot of Italy.

Luce touched the silver locket around her neck. "I'm afraid."

Daniel squeezed her tight. "You're so brave, Luce."

"I feel stronger than I ever have before, and I'm proud of all the memories I can access on my own, especially if they can help us stop Lucifer"—she paused, glancing down at her dusty fingernails—"but I'm still afraid of what we're flying toward now."

"I won't let Sophia get anywhere near you."

"It's not what she might do to me, Daniel. It's what she may have already done to people I care about. That bridge, all that dust—"

"I hope as much as you do that Cam and Gabbe and Molly are unharmed." His wings gave one great beat and Luce felt her body rise above a swollen rain cloud. "But angels can die, Lucinda."

"I know that, Daniel."

"Of course you do. And you know how dangerous this is. Every angel who joins our struggle to stop Lucifer knows it, too. By joining us, they acknowledge that our mission is more important than any single angel's soul."

Luce closed her eyes. *A single angel's soul.*

There it was again. The idea she'd first heard Arriane speak about in the Vegas IHOP. One powerful angel to tip the scales. One choice to determine the outcome of a fight that had lasted for millennia.

When she opened her eyes, the moon was bathed in soft white light as it rose over the dark landscape below.

"The forces of Heaven and Hell," she began, "are they really in balance against each other right now?"

Daniel was quiet. She felt his chest rise against her and then fall. His wings beat a bit more swiftly, but he didn't answer.

"You know?" Luce pressed on. "The same number of demons on one side and the same number of angels on the other?"

Wind whipped against her.

Finally, Daniel said, "Yes, though it's not that simple. It's not a matter of a thousand here versus a thousand there. Different players matter more than others. The Outcasts carry no weight. You heard Phil lamenting that. The Scale are almost negligible—though you'd never know that from the way they carry on about their importance." He paused. "One of the Archangels? They are worth a thousand lesser angels."

"Is it still true that there's one important angel who has yet to choose a side?"

A pause. "Yes, that is still true."

She'd already begged him to choose once, on the rooftop at Shoreline. They were in the middle of an argument and the time hadn't been right. But their bond was stronger now. Surely if he knew how much she supported him, that she'd stand by him and love him no matter what, it would help him finally make up his mind. "What if you just went ahead and . . . chose?"

"No—"

"But, Daniel, you could stop this! You could tip the scales, and no one else would have to die, and—"

"I mean no, it's not that easy." She heard him sigh and knew, even without looking, the precise shade his eyes would be glowing now: a deep, wild lupine violet. "It's not that easy anymore," he repeated.

"Why not?"

"Because this present no longer matters. We're in a pocket of time that may cease to exist. So choosing now wouldn't mean a thing, not until this nine-day glitch is fixed. We still have to stop him. Either Lucifer gets his way and erases the past five or six millennia and we all begin again—"

"Or we succeed," Luce said automatically.

"If that happens," Daniel said, "we'll reassess how the ranks are aligned."

Twenty feet below them, Arriane was flying in slow, trancelike loop-the-loops, as if to pass the time. Annabelle flew into one of the rain showers that the angels usually avoided. She came out on the other side with her wings damp and her pink hair plastered to the sides of her face without even seeming to notice. Roland was somewhere behind them, probably deep in his own thoughts as he carried Dee in his arms. Everyone seemed weary, distracted.

"But *when* we succeed, couldn't you . . ."

"Choose Heaven?" Daniel said. "No. I made my choice a very long time ago, almost at the Beginning."

"But I thought—"

"I chose you, Lucinda."

Luce swept her hand over Daniel's as the tar-dark sea beneath them washed up onto a swath of desert. The landscape was far below, but it reminded her of the terrain around Sinai: rocky cliffs interrupted by the green scrub of an occasional tree. She didn't understand why Daniel had to choose between Heaven and love.

All she'd ever wanted was his love—but at what price? Was their love worth the erasure of the world and all its stories? Could Daniel have prevented this threat if he'd chosen Heaven long before?

And would he have returned there, where he belonged, had his love for Luce not led him astray?

As if he were reading her mind, Daniel said, "We put our faith in love."

Roland caught up to them. His wings angled and his body pivoted to face Daniel and Luce. In his arms, Dee's red hair was flying and her cheeks were aglow. She gestured for the two of them to come close. Daniel's wings gave one full, graceful beat, and they shot through a cloud to hover at Roland and Dee's side. Roland whistled and Arriane and Annabelle doubled back, closing an iridescent circle in the dark sky.

"It's nearly four o'clock in the morning in Jerusalem," Dee said. "That means we can expect the majority of mortals to be asleep or otherwise out of the way for perhaps another hour. If Sophia has your friends, she's probably planning . . . well, we should hurry, dears."

"You know where they'll be?" Daniel asked.

Dee thought for a moment. "Before I defected from the Elders, the plan was always to reconvene at the Church of the Holy Sepulchre. It was built on the slope of Golgotha, in the Christian Quarter of the Old City."

The group glided toward the hallowed ground. They were a column of glowing wings. The clear sky was navy, sprinkled with stars, and the white stones of distant buildings below shone an eerie acid blue. Though the land seemed naturally dry, dusty, the earth was studded with thick palm trees and groves of olive trees.

They swooped over the most expansive cemetery Luce had ever seen, built on a gradual slope facing the Old City of Jerusalem.

The city itself was dark and sleepy, tucked in moonlight and surrounded by a tall stone partition. The formidable Dome of the Rock mosque sat high on a hill, its golden dome gleaming even in darkness. It was at a distance from the rest of the crammed city, set off by long flights of stone stairs and tall gates at every entrance. Beyond the old walls, a few modern high-rise buildings cut out a distant skyline, but within the Old City, the structures were much older, smaller, crafting a maze of narrow cobbled alleys best navigated by foot.

They alighted on the rampart of a tall gate marking the entrance to the city.

"This is the New Gate," Dee explained. "It's the closest entrance to the Christian Quarter, where the church is."

By the time they had filed down the worn stairs from the top of the gate, the angels had retracted their wings into their shoulders. The cobbled street narrowed as Dee brandished a small red plastic flashlight and led them onward toward the church. Most of the stone storefronts had been fitted with metal doors that slid up and down like the door on Luce's parents' garage. The doors were all closed now, padlocked along the street through which Luce walked next to Daniel, holding his hand and hoping for the best.

The deeper into the city they went, the more the buildings seemed to press in on either side of them. They passed under the striped tented awnings of empty Arab markets, under long stone arches and dim corridors. The air smelled like roasted lamb, then incense, then laundry soap. Azalea vines climbed the walls, searching for water.

The neighborhood was silent but for the angels' steps and a coyote yowling in the hills. They passed a shuttered Laundromat, its sign posted in Arabic, then a flower shop with Hebrew stickers plastered across its windows.

Everywhere Luce looked, narrow walkways forked off from the street: through an open wooden gate here, up a short flight of stairs there. Dee seemed to be counting the doorways they passed, wagging her finger as they walked. At one point she snapped her fingers, ducked under a weathered wooden arch, turned a corner, and disappeared. Luce and the angels glanced at each other quickly, then followed her: down several steps, around a damp and darkened corner, up a few more steps, and suddenly, they were on the roof of another building, looking down at another cramped street.

"There it is." Dee nodded grimly.

The church towered over everything nearby. It was built of pale, smooth stones and stood easily five stories, taller at its pair of slender steeples. At its center, an enormous blue dome looked like a blanket of midnight sky wrapped around a stone. Giant bricks formed large arches along the façade, marking places for massive wooden doors on the first story and arched stained-glass windows higher up. A ladder leaned on a brick ledge outside a third-story window, reaching up for nothing.

Portions of the church's façade were crumbling and black with age, while others looked recently restored. On either side, two long stone arms branched forward from the church, forming a border around a flat cobbled plaza. Just behind the church, a tall white minaret stabbed the sky.

"Wow," Luce heard herself say as she and the angels descended another surprising flight of stairs to enter the plaza.

The angels approached the heavy double doors that towered over them, forty feet high at least. They were painted green and flanked by three plain stone pillars on either side. Luce's eye was drawn to the ornate frieze between the doors and the arches above them—and above that, the gleaming golden cross puncturing the sky. The building was quiet, somber, alive with spiritual electricity.

"In we go, then," Dee said.

"We can't go in there," Roland said, moving away from the church.

"Oh, yes," Dee said, "the incendiary business. You think you can't go in because it's a sanctuary of God—"

"It's *the* sanctuary of God," Roland said. "I don't want to be the guy who takes this place down."

"Only it isn't a sanctuary of God," Dee said simply. "Quite the opposite. This is the place where Jesus suffered and died. Therefore it has never been a sanctuary as far as the Throne is concerned, and that's the only opinion that really matters. A sanctuary is a safe haven, a refuge from harm. Mortals step within these walls to pray, in their infinitely morbid way, but as far as your curse is concerned, you will not be affected." Dee paused. "Which is good, because Sophia and your friends are inside."

"How do you know?" Luce asked.

She heard footsteps on stone on the east side of the courtyard. Dee squinted down the narrow street.

Daniel grabbed Luce's waist so swiftly she fell into him. Turning a corner beneath a street sign that read VIA DOLOROSA, two elderly nuns strained under the weight of a large wooden cross. They wore simple navy habits, thick, sensible sandals, and beaded rosaries around their necks.

Luce relaxed at the sight of the old believers, whose

average age seemed to be eighty-five. She started to move toward the women, obeying an instinct to assist the elderly with a heavy load, but Daniel's grasp on Luce's waist did not loosen as the nuns approached the great doors of the church with excruciating slowness. It seemed impossible that the nuns would not have seen the group of angels twenty feet away—they were the only other souls in the plaza—but the struggling sisters never so much as glanced in the angels' direction.

"A little early for the Sisters of the Stations of the Cross to be out, isn't it?" Roland whispered to Daniel.

Dee straightened her skirt and pinned a rebellious strand of hair behind her ear. "I had hoped it wouldn't come to this, but we'll simply have to kill them."

"What?" Luce glanced at one of the feeble, sun-weathered women. Her gray eyes sat like pebbles in the deep folds of her face. "You want to kill those nuns?"

Dee frowned. "Those aren't nuns, dear. They are Elders and they must be disposed of, or they will dispose of us."

"I'm disposed to say they already look disposed of." Arriane shifted her weight from side to side. "Apparently Jerusalem recycles."

Maybe Arriane's voice found the nuns and startled them, or maybe they were waiting to arrive at precisely the right location, but at that moment, as they reached the church doors, they stopped and turned so that the long beam of their cross pointed across the plaza, toward the angels, like a cannon.

"Time, she is a-wasting, angels," Dee said through tight lips.

The pebble-eyed nun bared veiny gums at the angels and fumbled with something on the base of the beam. Daniel shoved the satchel into Luce's hands, then positioned her behind Dee. The older woman didn't cover Luce exactly—the top of her head came only as high as Luce's chin—but Luce got the idea and ducked. The angels unleashed their wings with brutish speed as they fanned out on both sides—Arriane and Annabelle veering left, Roland and Daniel diving right.

The giant cross was not a pilgrim's penitential burden. It was an enormous crossbow, filled with starshots meant to kill everybody there.

There was no time for this to register with Luce. One of the nuns released the first shot; it sizzled through the air, heading for Luce's face. The silver arrow grew larger in Luce's vision as it swirled closer in the air.

Then Dee jumped.

The tiny woman spread her arms open wide. The starshot's dull tip collided with the center of her chest. Dee grunted as the arrow—harmless to mortals, Luce knew—glanced off her tiny body and clattered to the ground, leaving the transeternal sore but unharmed.

"Presidia, you fool," Dee shouted at the nun, dragging the arrow backward with her high heel. Luce leaned down to pick it up and slipped it inside the satchel. "You know that won't hurt me! Now you've annoyed my friends." She gestured broadly at the angels darting forward to disarm the costumed Elders.

"Stand down, defector!" Presidia replied. "We require the girl! Surrender her and we will—"

But Presidia never finished. Arriane was at the Elder's back in a flash, brushing the veil from her head, taking her white hair in her fists.

"Because I respect my Elders," Arriane hissed through her clenched teeth, "I feel I must prevent them from embarrassing themselves." Then she lifted off the ground, still holding Presidia by the hair. The Elder kicked the air as if pedaling an invisible bicycle. Arriane pivoted and slammed the old woman's body into the cornice of the church's façade with such force it left an indentation when she collapsed in a twisted heap, hands and legs sticking out at grisly angles.

The other incognito Elder had dropped the cannon-cross and was trying to escape, running hard for an alley that opened into the opposite corner of the plaza. Annabelle took up the cross and became a javelin thrower, rearing back like a tightening coil, springing to release the heavy wooden *T*.

The cross arced through the air and speared the

fleeing Elder in her sloping spine. She fell forward and convulsed, impaled by the replica of an ancient instrument of execution.

The courtyard fell quiet. Instinctively, everyone turned to look at Luce.

"She's okay!" Dee called, raising Luce's hand in the air as if the two of them had just won a relay race.

"Daniel!" Luce pointed at a flash of white disappearing behind Daniel's back, into the church. As the double doors slowly shut, an elderly monk they hadn't noticed could be heard ascending the staircase inside.

"Follow him," Dee shouted, stepping over Presidia's mangled corpse.

Luce and Dee ran to catch up to the others. When they entered the church, it was dark and silent. Roland pointed toward a flight of stone steps in the corner. They opened into a small stone archway, which led to a longer staircase. The space was too cramped for the angels to spread their wings, so they picked their way up the steep steps as quickly as they could.

"The Elder will lead us to Sophia," Daniel whispered as they ducked under the stone archway to the darkened staircase. "If she has the others—if she has the relic—"

Dee laid a firm hand on Daniel's arm. "She must not know of Luce's presence. You must prevent the Elder from reaching Sophia."

Daniel's eyes flickered back at Luce, then up to Roland, who nodded swiftly, rocketing up the stairs as if he had run through old stone fortresses before.

Barely two minutes later, he was waiting for them at the top of the cramped staircase. The Elder lay dead on the floor, lips blue, eyes glassy and wet. Behind Roland, an open doorway curved sharply to the left. Someone on that landing was singing what sounded like a hymn.

Luce shivered.

Daniel motioned for them to stay back as he peered past the edge of the curved stairway. From where she stood, pressed against a stone wall, Luce could see a small portion of the chapel beyond the landing. The walls were painted with elaborate frescos, lit by dozens of small tin lamps suspended by beaded chains from the vaulted ceiling. There was a small room with a mosaic of the crucifixion spanning the entire western wall. Beyond this was a row of highly decorated vaulted columns several feet wide, portioning off a second, larger chapel that was hard to see from here. Between the two chapels, a large gilded shrine to Mary was covered in flower bouquets and half-burned sacramental candles.

Daniel cocked his head. A flash of red swished past one of the columns.

A woman in a long scarlet robe.

She was bending over an altar made from a great marble slab adorned with a white lace sheet. Something lay on that altar, but Luce could not tell what it was.

The woman was frail but attractive, with short gray hair cut in a fashionable bob. Her robe was cinched at the waist with a colorful woven belt. She lit a candle at the front of the altar. The flowing sleeves of her robe slipped up her arms as she genuflected, exposing wrists adorned with stacks and stacks of pearl bracelets.

Miss Sophia.

Luce pushed off Daniel to climb one step higher, desperate for a better view. The wide columns obstructed the majority of the chapel, but when Daniel helped her go just a little farther up the stairs, she could see more. There were not one but three altars in the room, not one but three scarlet-robed women ritually lighting candles all around them. Luce didn't recognize the other two.

Sophia looked older, more tired than she had behind her librarian's desk. Luce wondered briefly if it was because she had gone from surrounding herself with teenagers to running with beings who hadn't been teenagers in several hundred years. That night, Sophia's face was painted, lips like blood. The robe she wore was dusty and dark with rings of sweat. Hers had been the chanting voice. When she started up again in a language that sounded like Latin but wasn't, Luce's whole body clenched. She remembered it.

This was the ritual that Miss Sophia had performed on Luce the last night she'd been at Sword & Cross.

Miss Sophia had been just about to murder her when Daniel came crashing through the ceiling.

"Pass me the rope, Vivina," Miss Sophia said. They were so consumed with their dark ritual that they did not sense the angels crouched along the stairs outside the chapel. "Gabrielle looks a little too comfy. I'd like to bind her throat."

Gabbe.

"There is no more," Vivina said. "I had to double bind Cambriel here. He was squirming. Ooh, he still is."

"Oh my God," Luce whispered. Cam and Gabbe were there. She assumed the presence of a third robed lady meant Molly was there, too.

"God has nothing to do with this," Dee said under her breath. "And Sophia is too crazy to know it."

"Why are the fallen being so quiet?" Luce whispered. "Why don't they resist?"

"They must not realize that this place is *not* a sanctuary of God," Daniel said. "They must be in shock— I know I would be—and Sophia must be using it to her advantage. She knows they're worried that anything they do or say might make the church erupt into flames."

"I know how they feel," Luce whispered. "We have to stop her." She started for the door, emboldened by the fresh memory of the Elders they'd destroyed outside, by the power of the angels behind her, by Daniel's love, by the knowledge of the two relics they had already discovered. But a hand clamped her shoulder, drawing her back into the corridor.

"All of you stay here," Dee whispered, making eye contact with each of the angels to ensure they understood. "If they see you, they will know Luce is with you. Wait here." She pointed to the columns, thick enough for three angels to hide behind. "I know how to handle my sister."

Without another word, Dee strode into the chapel, her heels slapping the black-and-white tile floor.

"I'd say you've been given quite enough rope, Sophia," Dee said.

"Who's there?" Vivina yelped, startled in mid-genuflection.

Dee crossed her arms over her chest as she walked around the altars, clucking in mock disapproval of the Elders' work. "Very shoddy dressing. Leave it to Sophia to bring her B game to a sacrifice with cosmic and eternal implications."

Luce was desperate to study the reaction on Miss Sophia's face, but Daniel held her back. There were a scraping sound, a melodramatic gasp, and a cruel soft cackle.

"Ah yes," Miss Sophia said. "My tramp sister returns, just in time to witness my finest hour. This will trump your overrated piano recital!"

"You're really very dumb."

"Because I don't have the recommended brand of rope?" Sophia snorted.

"Forget the rope, dope," Dee said. "You're dumb in many dozens of ways, not the least of which is thinking you might get away with this."

"Do not condescend to her!" hissed the third Elder.

"There's really no other way to approach her," Dee instantly replied.

"Thank you, Lyrica, but I can handle Paulina," Sophia said without looking away from Dee. "Or what do you have people call you now? Pee?"

"You know very well it is Dee. You only wish you knew why."

"Ah yes, *Dee*. Biiiiiig difference. Well, let us enjoy our brief reunion as best we can."

"Let them go, Sophia."

"Let them go?" Sophia cackled. "But I want them dead." Her voice rose and Luce pictured her hand sweeping over the angels bound upon the altars. "I want *her* dead most of all!"

Luce couldn't even gasp. She knew whom the librarian meant.

"It won't stop Lucifer from erasing your existence." Dee's voice sounded almost sad.

"Well, you know what Daddy always used to say: 'We're all Hell-bound, anyway.' Might as well try to get what we want while we're on this Earth. Where is she, Dee?" Sophia spat. "Where is the mewling child Lucinda?"

"I wouldn't know." Dee's voice was smooth. "But I have come to keep you from finding out."

Now Daniel let Luce press a little closer to the first chapel's entrance.

"I hate you!" Sophia shouted, pouncing on Dee. Roland turned to look at Daniel, asking with his eyes if they should interfere. Daniel seemed confident in the desideratum's abilities. He shook his head once.

Sophia's assistant Elders watched from their altars as the two sisters rolled across the floor, moving out of, then back into Luce's view. Dee on top, then Sophia, then Dee on top again.

Dee's hands found Sophia's neck and squeezed. The old Sword & Cross librarian's face glowed red as her hands strained against Dee's chest and she struggled to survive.

Slowly, Sophia worked her knee up until it pressed deeply into her sister's stomach to push her back. Dee's arms were fully extended, reaching to keep their hold on Sophia's neck. She gazed down at her sister's rage-distorted face, her eyes on fire with hatred.

"Your heart turned black, Sophia," Dee said, her voice soft with something like nostalgia. "It was like a light went off. No one could turn the light back on. We could only try to stop you from running over us in the dark." Then she released Sophia, allowed her to draw a huge and panicked breath into her lungs.

"You betrayed me," Sophia gasped as Dee took her sister's collar in her hands, closed her eyes, and moved to slam Sophia's skull against the tiles of the mosaic floor.

But instead there came a long shriek as Dee was launched into the air. Sophia had kicked her with a force Luce had forgotten the old woman possessed. She leaped to her feet. She was sweating and red in the face, her hair white and wild, as she ran to where Dee had come to rest several feet away. Luce rose on her toes and winced when she saw Dee's eyes were closed.

"Ha!" Sophia returned to the altars and reached beneath the one binding Cam. She pulled out a sheath of starshots.

Back in the alcove Roland glanced at Daniel again. This time Daniel nodded.

In an instant, Arriane, Annabelle, and Roland flew from their hiding places into the room. Roland drove toward Miss Sophia, but at the last instant, she ducked and deftly avoided him. His wing slapped her across the face, but she had eluded his grasp.

In the face of angel wings, the two other Elders cowered, shrinking in panicked fear. Annabelle held them back while Arriane flicked open a Swiss Army knife from her pocket—the pink one, the same one Luce had used to cut the girl's hair months earlier—and sawed at the ropes binding Gabbe to the altar.

"Stop or I'll kill him!" Sophia shouted at the angels as she tore out a fistful of arrows and leaped on Cam. Straddling him, she raised the silver shafts above his head.

His dark hair was matted and greasy. His hands were pale and trembling. Miss Sophia studied these details with a smirk.

"I do so love to see an angel *die*." She cackled, holding the starshots high. "And such an arrogant one to kill." She looked back down at Cam. "His death will be a beautiful thing to behold."

"Go ahead." Cam's voice came for the first time, low and even. Luce nearly cried out when she heard him mutter: "I never asked for a happy ending."

Luce had watched Sophia kill Penn with her bare hands and no remorse. It would not happen again. *"No!"* Luce shouted, struggling to break free from Daniel's grip and dragging him with her into the chapel.

Slowly Miss Sophia craned her body around toward Luce and Daniel, clutching her fistful of starshots. Her eyes gleamed silver and her thin lips curled in a ghastly smile as Luce tugged Daniel forward, pulling against his relentless grip.

"We have to stop her, Daniel!"

"No, Luce, it's too dangerous."

"Oh, there you are, dear." Miss Sophia beamed. "And Daniel Grigori! How nice. I've been waiting for you." Then she winked and whipped the starshots over her head in a dense cluster aimed straight at Daniel and Luce.

TWELVE

UNHOLY WATER

It happened in the broken fraction of a second:

Roland tackled Miss Sophia, knocking her to the ground. But he was half a heartbeat too late.

Five silver starshots sailed silently across the empty space of the chapel. The cluster of them loosened as they flew, seeming to hang in midair for a moment on their path toward Luce and Daniel.

Daniel.

Luce pressed herself back against Daniel's chest. He

had the opposite instinct: His arms pulled tight against her and dragged her down hard against the floor.

Two great pairs of wings crossed the space in front of Luce, erupting from left and right. One was a radiant coppery gold, the other the purest silvery white. They filled the air before her and Daniel like enormous feathered screens—and then were gone in the blink of an eye.

Something whizzed by her left ear. She turned and saw a single starshot ricochet off the gray stone wall and clatter to the floor. The other starshots were gone.

A fine iridescent grit settled around Luce.

Squinting through the mist of dust, she took in the room: Daniel crouching beside her. A roused Dee struggling atop a writhing Miss Sophia. Annabelle standing above the other Elders, who lay lifeless on the floor. Arriane holding an empty length of rope and her Swiss Army knife in trembling hands. Cam, still bound on the altar, stunned.

Gabbe and Molly, just freed from their altars by Arriane—

Disappeared.

And Luce's and Daniel's bodies covered in a film of dust.

No.

"Gabbe . . . Molly—" Luce got to her knees. She held out her hands, examining them as if she'd never seen hands before. Candlelight played off her skin, turning the dust a soft, shimmery gold, then a bright glittering silver as she flipped her hands to gaze at her palms. "No no no no no no no no."

She looked back, locking eyes with Daniel. His face was ashen, his eyes burning with such a concentrated violet it was hard to hold their gaze.

That became harder still when her vision blurred with tears.

"Why did they—?"

For a moment, everything was still.

Then an animal's roar rent the room.

Cam forced his right leg free from the ropes that had bound it, ripping his ankle raw in the process. He strained to free his wrists, bellowed as he tore his right hand loose from his bonds, shredding the wing that had been pinned with an iron post and dislocating his shoulder. His arm swung in a gruesomely distended way from his shoulder, as if it had nearly been ripped off.

He leaped from the altar onto Sophia, pushing Dee aside. The force knocked all three of them to the ground. Cam landed on top of Sophia, pinning her on her side, seeking to crush her with his weight. She let out a tortured howl, pulled her arms weakly before her face as Cam's hands reached for her neck.

"Strangling is the most intimate way to kill someone," Cam said, as if teaching Violence 101. "Now let's see the beauty of your death."

But Miss Sophia's struggle was ugly. Gargles and grunts bubbled from her throat. Cam's fingers tightened, slammed her head with brutal thumps against the floor, again and again and again. Blood began to trickle from the old woman's mouth, darker than her lipstick.

Daniel's hand touched Luce's chin, turned her to face him. He gripped her shoulders. They locked eyes again, searching for a way to tune out Sophia's wet groans.

"Gabbe and Molly knew what they were doing," Daniel whispered.

"They knew they were going to be killed?" Luce said.

Behind them, Sophia whimpered, sounding almost like she'd accepted that this was how she'd die.

"They knew that stopping Lucifer is more important than an individual life," Daniel said. "More than anything else that has happened, let this convince you of how urgent our task is here."

The silence around them was loud. No more bloody coughs came from Miss Sophia. Luce didn't have to look to know what it meant.

An arm encircled her waist. A familiar mop of black hair rested on her shoulder. "Come on," Arriane said, "let's get you two cleaned up."

Daniel handed Luce over to Arriane and Annabelle. "You girls go ahead."

Luce followed the angels numbly. They walked Luce to the back of the chapel, opening several closets until they found what they were looking for: a small black lacquered door that opened onto a circular, windowless room.

Annabelle lit a candelabra on a tiled table near the door, then lit another one in a stone alcove. The red-brick room was the size of a large pantry and had no furniture but a raised, eight-sided baptismal bath. Inside, the bath was made with green-and-blue mosaics; outside it was marble carved with a wraparound frieze of angels descending to Earth.

Luce felt miserable and dead inside. Even the baptismal pool seemed to mock her. Here she was—the girl whose cursed soul was somehow important, up for grabs because she'd never been baptized as a child—about to wash away the dust of two dead angels. Was saving Luce and Daniel worth their souls? How could it be? This "baptism" broke Luce's already broken heart a little more.

"Don't worry," Arriane said, reading her mind. "This won't count."

Annabelle found a sink in the corner of the room, behind the baptismal font. She poured bucket after large wooden bucket of steaming hot water into the tub. Arriane stood next to Luce, not looking at her, just holding her hand. When the bath was full and refracting a deep blue-green from the tiles, Annabelle and Arriane hoisted Luce above the surface of the water. She was still wearing her sweater and jeans. They hadn't thought to undress her, but then they noticed her boots.

"Whoops," Annabelle said softly, unzipping them one at a time and tossing them aside. Arriane lifted the silver locket over Luce's head and slipped it inside a boot. Their wings fluttered as they lifted off the ground to lower Luce into the warm water.

Luce closed her eyes, slipped her head beneath the water, stayed a while. If she shed a tear, she wouldn't feel it if she stayed submerged. She didn't want to feel. It was like Penn had died all over again, fresh pain exposing old pain that still felt fresh to Luce.

After what seemed like a long time, she felt hands slip under her arms to pull her upright in the bath. The surface of the water was a film of gray dust. It didn't shimmer anymore.

Luce didn't take her eyes off it until Annabelle started tugging her sweater up over her head. She felt it lift off her, followed by the T-shirt she'd been wearing underneath. She fumbled with the button on her jeans. How many days had she worn these clothes? It was strange to be free of them, like slipping off a layer of skin and looking at it on the floor.

She ran a hand through her wet hair to wipe it from her face. She hadn't realized how grimy it was. Then she sat on the bench at the back of the tub, leaned against the side, and started shivering. Annabelle added more hot water to the pool, but it did nothing to stop Luce's tremors.

"If I'd just stayed out in the hallway like Dee told me to—"

"Then Cam would be dead," Arriane said. "Or someone else. Sophia and her clan were going to make dust one way or another tonight. The rest of us knew that going into this, but you didn't." She sighed. "So coming out and trying to save Cam? That took serious guts, Luce."

"But *Gabbe*—"

"Knew what she was doing."

"That's what Daniel said. But why would she sacrifice herself to save—"

"Because she's gambling on Daniel and you and the rest of us succeeding." Arriane rested her chin on her arm on the edge of the tub. She trailed a finger in the water, breaking up the dust. "But knowing that doesn't make it any easier. We all loved her very much."

"She can't really be gone."

"She *is* gone. Gone from the highest altar in creation."

"What?" That wasn't what Luce meant. She meant that Gabbe was her friend.

Arriane's brow furrowed. "Gabbe was the highest of the Archangels—you didn't know? Her soul was worth . . . I don't even know how many others. It was worth a lot."

Luce had never before considered how her friends

were ranked in Heaven, but now she thought about the times Gabbe had looked out for her, taken care of her, brought her food or clothes or advice. She'd been Luce's kind, celestial mother. "What does her death mean?"

"Way back when, Lucifer was ranked first," Annabelle said. After a pause, she glanced at Luce, registered her shock. "He was right there, next to all the action. Then he rebelled and Gabbe moved up."

"Though being ranked next to the Throne is a mixed blessing," Arriane murmured. "Ask your buddy ol' pal Bill."

Luce wanted to ask who came after Gabbe, but something stopped her. Maybe it had once been Daniel, but his place in Heaven was in jeopardy because he kept on choosing Luce.

"What about Molly?" Luce finally asked. "Does her death . . . cancel out Gabbe's? In terms of the balance between Heaven and Hell?" She felt callous talking about her friends as commodities—but she also knew, right now, the answer mattered.

"Molly was important, too, though a little lower in the ranks," Annabelle said. "This was before the Fall, of course, when she sided with Lucifer's host. I know we're not supposed to speak ill of the dusted, but Molly really used to bug me. So much negativity."

Luce nodded guiltily.

"But something changed in her recently. It's like she

woke up." She glanced at Luce. "To answer your question, the balance between Heaven and Hell can still be struck. We'll just have to see how things play out. A lot of things that matter now become irrelevant if Lucifer succeeds."

Luce looked toward Arriane, who'd disappeared behind the door and sneezed three times in a row. "Hello, mothballs!" When she emerged, she was holding a white towel and an oversized checked bathrobe. "It'll have to do for now. We'll find you a change of clothes before we leave Jerusalem."

When Luce didn't move from the tub, Arriane clucked her tongue like she was coaxing a horse out of its stable and held the towel out for Luce to step into. She stood up, feeling like a kid as Arriane engulfed her in the towel and dried her off. The towel was thin and coarse, but the robe that followed was thick and warm.

"We need to skedaddle before the tourist cavalry arrives," said Arriane, gathering Luce's boots.

By the time they left the baptismal room and walked back into the chapel, the sun had risen, and it cast colorful rays of light through the stained-glass depiction of the Ascension in the window.

Beneath the window lay the bodies of Miss Sophia and the two other Elders, bound together.

When the girls crossed to the front of the larger chapel, Cam, Roland, and Daniel were sitting on the center altar, talking softly. Cam was drinking the last of the starshot colas from Phil's black leather satchel. Luce could actually *see* his bloody ankle scab over and then the scab begin to flake away. He swallowed the last drop and rotated his shoulder back into its socket with a snap.

The boys looked up to see Luce standing between Annabelle and Arriane. All three of them hopped off the altar, but Cam stepped toward Luce first.

She stood very still as he approached. Her heart was beating fast.

His skin was pale, making the green of his eyes look like emeralds. There were sweat along his hairline and a small scratch near his left eye. His wing tips had stopped bleeding and had been bandaged with some kind of fancy gauze.

He smiled at her. Took her hands. His were warm and alive and there had been a moment when Luce thought she might never see him again, never see his eyes shine, never watch his golden wings unfurl, never hear the way his voice rose when he made a dark joke . . . and though she loved Daniel more than anything else, more than she ever thought possible, Luce could not bear to lose Cam. That was what had sent her bounding into the room. "Thank you," he said.

Luce felt her lips quiver and her eyes burn. Before she knew what she was doing, she fell into Cam's arms, felt his hands wrap around her back. When his chin rested on the top of her head, she began to weep.

He let her cry. Held her close. He whispered, "You're so brave."

Then Cam's arms shifted and his chest pulled lightly away. For a second, she felt cold and exposed, but then another chest, another pair of arms replaced Cam's. And she knew without opening her eyes that it was Daniel. No other body in the universe fit hers so well.

"Mind if I cut in?" he asked softly.

"Daniel—" She clenched her fists and squeezed her arms around him, wanting to squeeze away the pain.

"Shhh." He held her like that for what might have been hours, rocking her slightly, cradling her in his wings until her tears had tapered off and the weight in her heart had eased enough that she could breathe without sniffling.

"When an angel dies," she said against his shoulder, "does she go to Heaven?"

"No," he said. "There is nothing for an angel after death."

"How can that be?"

"The Throne never anticipated that any angel would rebel, much less that the fallen angel Azazel would spend centuries over a fire in a deep Greek cave, developing a weapon to kill angels."

Her chest shuddered again. "But—"

"Shhh," he whispered. "Grief can choke you. It's dangerous, something else you have to beat."

She took a deep breath and pulled back enough to see his face. Her eyes felt swollen and exhausted, and Daniel's shirt was soaked with her tears, like she'd baptized him with her sorrow.

Beyond Daniel's shoulder, resting on the altar where Gabbe had been bound, something silver gleamed. It was an enormous goblet, as big around as a punch bowl, but oblong in shape and made of hammered silver.

"Is that it?" Was this the relic that had cost her friends their lives?

Cam walked over to it, picked it up. "We uncovered it at the base of the Pont Saint Bénézet right before the Elders overtook us." He shook his head. "I do hope this spittoon is worth it."

"Where's Dee?" Luce looked around for the person most likely to know the significance of the relic.

"She's downstairs." Daniel explained, "The church opened to the public a little while ago, so Dee went down to build a small Patina to cloak the corpses of the Elders. Now she's at the base of the stairs with a sign that says this 'wing' is closed for reconstruction."

"And it worked?" Annabelle asked, impressed.

"No one's gotten past her yet. Religious tourists aren't football hooligans," Cam smirked. "Storm the prayer pillows!"

"How can you joke right now?" Luce asked.

"How can I not?" Cam countered darkly. "Would you prefer I cried?"

A rap sounded at the window on the other side of the chapel. The angels stiffened as Cam went to open the pane next to the stained glass. His jaw clenched. "Ready the starshots!"

"Cam, wait!" Daniel cried. "Don't shoot."

Cam paused. A moment later, a boy in a tan trench coat slipped through the open window. As soon as he was on his feet, Phil raised his shaved blond head and fixed his dead white eyes on Cam.

Cam snarled. "You're lost, Outcast."

"They're with us now, Cam." Daniel pointed to the pennon from his own wing tucked into Phil's lapel.

Cam swallowed, crossed his arms over his chest. "Apologies. I did not know that." He cleared his throat, adding, "That explains why the Outcasts we saw on the bridge in Avignon were fighting the Elders when we arrived. They never had a chance to explain before all of them were—"

"Killed," Phil said. "Yes. The Outcasts sacrificed themselves for your cause."

"The universe is everyone's cause," Daniel said, and Phil gave a curt nod.

Luce hung her head. All that dust on the bridge. It hadn't occurred to her that it could have been Outcasts'.

She'd been too worried about Gabbe and Molly and Cam.

"These last few days have dealt a heavy blow to the Outcasts," Phil said. His voice betrayed a shade of sorrow. "Many were captured in Vienna at the hands of Scale. Many more fell to Elders in Avignon. Four of us remain. May I show them in?"

"Of course," Daniel said.

Phil held out a hand toward the window and three more tan trench coats slipped through the open pane: a girl Luce didn't recognize, who Phil introduced as Phresia; Vincent, one of the Outcasts who'd stood guard for Luce and Daniel at Mount Sinai; and Olianna, the pale girl from the palace rooftop in Vienna. Luce flashed her a smile she knew the Outcast girl could not see. But Luce hoped Olianna could sense it, because Luce was glad to see her recovered. All the Outcasts looked like siblings, modest and attractive, alarmingly pale.

Phil pointed at the dead Elders under the window. "It looks as if you need some assistance with the disposal of these corpses. May the Outcasts take them off your hands?"

Daniel let out a surprised laugh. "Please."

"Just make sure you don't pay this geriatric roadkill any respect," Cam added.

"Phresia." Phil nodded at the girl, who dropped to her knees before the bodies, slung them over her shoulders, unfurled her mud-brown wings, and shot through the window. Luce watched her cross the sky, carrying away the last glimpse of Miss Sophia that Luce would ever see.

"What's in the duffel bag?" Cam pointed to the navy blue canvas bag strapped over Vincent's shoulders.

Phil motioned for Vincent to drop the duffel bag on the center altar. It landed with a heavy *thwump*. "In Venice, Daniel Grigori asked me whether I had any food for Lucinda Price. I have been regretting that all I had to offer was cheap unhealthful snacks, the kind of foods my Italian model friends prefer. This time, I asked a mortal Israeli girl what sort of things she liked to eat. She led me to a something called a falafel stand." Phil shrugged and his voice lilted in a question at the end.

"Are you saying I'm looking at a solid brick of falafel?" Roland raised a doubtful eyebrow at Vincent's bulging bag.

"Oh no," Vincent said. "The Outcasts also purchased hummus, pita, pickles, a container of something called tabbouleh, cucumber salad, and fresh pomegranate juice. Are you hungry, Lucinda Price?"

It was an absurd amount of delicious food. Somehow it felt wrong to eat on the altars, so they spread out a smorgasbord on the floor and everyone—Outcast, angel, mortal—tucked in. The mood was somber, but the food was filling and hot and exactly what all of them seemed to need. Luce showed Olianna and Vincent how to make a falafel sandwich; Cam even asked Phil to pass him the hummus. At some point, Arriane flew out the window to find Luce some new clothes. She returned with a faded pair of jeans, a white V-neck T-shirt, and a cool Israeli army flak jacket with a patch depicting an orange-and-yellow flame.

"Had to kiss a soldier for this," she said, but her voice didn't have the same showy lightness it would have if she'd been performing for Gabbe and Molly, too.

When none of them could eat any more, Dee appeared in the doorway. She greeted the Outcasts politely and rested a hand on Daniel's shoulder. "Do you have the relic, dear?"

Before Daniel could answer, Dee's eyes found the goblet. She lifted it and twirled it in her hands, examining it carefully from all sides. "The Silver Pennon," she whispered. "Hello, old friend."

"I take it she knows what to do with that thing," Cam said.

"She knows," Luce answered.

Dee pointed to a brass plate that had been welded into one of the broad sides of the goblet and muttered something under her breath, as if she were reading. She ran her fingers across a hammered image there. Luce inched forward for a better look. The illustration looked like angel wings in free fall.

At last, Dee looked up to face them with a strange expression on her face. "Well, now it all makes sense."

"What makes sense?" Luce asked.

"My life. My purpose. Where we need to go. What we need to do. It's time."

"Time for what?" Luce asked. They'd gathered all the artifacts now, but she didn't understand any better what they had left to do.

"Time for my final act, dear," Dee said warmly. "Don't worry, I'll walk you through it, step by step."

"To Mount Sinai?" Daniel rose from the floor and helped Luce to her feet.

"Close." Dee shut her eyes and took a deep breath, as if to draw the memory from within her lungs. "There's a pair of trees in the mountains about a mile above Saint Catherine's Monastery. I'd like for us to convene there. It is called the *Qayom Malak*."

"*Qayom Malak . . . Qayom Malak,*" Daniel repeated. The words sounded like *kayome malaka*. "That's in my book." He unzipped the satchel and flipped through some pages, muttering under his breath. At last, he held it out for Dee to see. Luce stepped forward to take a look. At the bottom of the page, about a hundred pages in, Daniel's finger pointed at a faded note scribbled in a language Luce didn't recognize. Next to the note he had written the same group of letters three times:

QYWM' ML'K'. QYWM' ML'K'. QYWM' ML'K'.

"Well done, Daniel." Dee smiled. "You knew it all along. Though *Qayom Malak* is much easier for modern tongues to pronounce than—" She made a string of complicated guttural noises Luce couldn't have replicated.

"I never knew what it meant," Daniel said.

Dee looked out the open window, at the holy city's afternoon sky. "Soon you will, my boy. Very soon you will."

THIRTEEN

THE EXCAVATION

Throosh of wingbeats overhead.

Tendrils of ambling cloud sliding over skin.

Luce was soaring across darkness, deep in the drug-like tunnel of another flight. She was weightless as the wind.

A single star hung in the center of a navy sky, miles above the belt of rainbow light near the horizon.

Twinkling lights on darkened ground seemed impossibly far away. Luce was in another world, ascending into infinity, lit up by the glow of brilliant silver wings.

They beat again, thrusting forward, then back, carrying her higher . . . higher. . . .

The world was quiet up here, like she had it all to herself.

Higher . . . higher . . .

No matter how high, she was always canopied by the warm silver winglight overhead.

She reached for Daniel, as if to share this peace, to caress his hand where it always rested, clasped around her waist.

Her hand met her own bare skin. His hand wasn't there.

Daniel wasn't there.

There were only Luce's body, and a darkening horizon, and a single distant star.

She jolted from her sleep. Aloft, awake, she found Daniel's hands again—one holding her waist, the other higher, draped across her chest. Right where they always were.

It was late afternoon—not nighttime. She and Daniel and the others climbed a ladder of puffy white clouds that obscured the stars.

Just a dream.

A dream in which *Luce* had been the one flying. Everybody had these dreams. You were supposed to wake up just before you hit the ground. But Luce, who flew in real life every day, had awakened when she realized she was flying under her own power. Why hadn't she looked up then, to see what her wings looked like, to see if they were glorious and proud?

She closed her eyes, wanting to return to that simpler sky, where Lucifer wasn't thundering toward them, where Gabbe and Molly weren't gone.

"I don't know if I can do this," Daniel said.

Her eyes shot open, back to reality. Below, the red granite peaks of the Sinai Peninsula were so jagged they looked like they were made of shards of broken glass.

"What is it you can't do?" Luce asked. "Find the location of the Fall? Dee's going to help us, Daniel. I think she knows exactly how to find it."

"Sure," he said, unconvinced. "Dee's great. We're lucky to have her. But even if we find the Fall site, I don't know how we're going to stop Lucifer. And if we can't"— his chest heaved against her back—"I can't go through another seven thousand years of losing you."

Throughout her lives, Luce had seen Daniel brooding, frustrated, worried, passionate, brooding again, tender, diffident, desperately sad. But she had never heard him sound defeated. The dull surrender in his tone cut into her, sudden and deep, the way a starshot sliced through angel flesh.

"You won't have to do that."

"I keep picturing what we're looking at if Lucifer succeeds." He fell back slightly from the formation they were flying in—Cam and Dee taking the lead, Arriane,

Roland, and Annabelle just behind, the Outcasts fanned out around them all. "It's too much, Luce. This is why angels choose sides, why people join teams. It costs too much not to; it weighs too heavily to soldier on alone."

There was a time when Luce would have turned instinctively inward, made insecure by Daniel's doubt, as if it suggested a weakness in their relationship. But now she was armed with the lessons from their past. She knew, when Daniel was too tired to remember, the measure of his love.

"I don't want to go through it all again. All that time without you, always waiting, my foolish optimism that someday it would be different—"

"Your optimism was justified! Look at me. Look at us! This *is* different. I know it is, Daniel. I saw us in Helston and Tibet and Tahiti. We were in love, sure, but it was nothing like what we have now."

They'd dropped back farther, out of earshot of the others. They were just Luce and Daniel, two lovers talking in the sky. "I'm still here," she said. "I'm here because you believed in us. You believed in me."

"I did—I do believe in you."

"I believe in you, too." She heard a smile enter her voice. "I always have."

They were *not* going to fail.

※ ※

They descended into a dust storm.

It hung over the desert like a vast duvet, as if enormous hands had tossed the Sahara into the air. Within the thick, tawny haze, the angels and their surroundings merged into indistinction: ground was overlapped with whirling sand; horizon was erased by great pulsating sheets of brown. Everything looked pixilated, bathed in dusty static, like white noise rusted, a foreshadowing of what would come if Lucifer got his way.

Sand filled Luce's nose and mouth. It reached beneath her clothes and scratched her skin. It was far harsher than the velvety dust left behind by Gabbe's and Molly's deaths, a bleak reminder of something more beautiful and worse.

Luce lost all sense of her surroundings. She had no idea how close they were to landing until her feet brushed the invisible rocky ground. She sensed that there were great rocks, maybe mountains, to their left, but she couldn't see more than a few feet in front of her. Only the glow of the angels' wings, dulled by waves of sand and wind, signaled where the others were.

When Daniel released her on the uneven rock, Luce tugged her Israeli army jacket up around her ears to block her face from the sting of the sand. They had gathered in a circle, the angels' wings generating a halo of light on a rocky path at the foothills of a mountain: Phil and the remaining three Outcasts, Arriane, Annabelle,

Cam and Roland, Luce and Daniel, and Dee standing in the center of them all, as calmly as a museum docent giving a tour.

"Don't worry, it's often like this in the afternoon!" Dee shouted over a wind so rough it tossed the angels' wings. She used her hand like a visor, placing it sideways on her brow. "This will all blow over soon! Once we reach the location of the *Qayom Malak,* we will bring all three relics together. They will tell us the true story of the Fall."

"Exactly where *is* the *Qayom Malak*?" Daniel shouted.

"We're going to have to climb that mountain." Dee pointed behind her at the barely visible promontory whose foothills had been the angels' landing place. What little Luce could see of the mountain looked unfathomably sheer.

"You mean fly, right?" Arriane clicked the heels of her black sneakers together. "Never been much of a 'climber.'"

Dee shook her head. She reached for the duffel bag Phil was holding, unzipped it, and pulled out a pair of sturdy brown hiking boots. "I'm glad the rest of you are already wearing sensible shoes." She kicked off her pointy high heels, tossed them into the bag, and began lacing up the boots. "It's no picnic of a hike, but in these conditions, the path to the *Qayom Malak* is really best navigated by foot. You can use your wings for balance against the winds."

"Why don't we wait out the sandstorm?" Luce suggested, her eyes tearing in the dusty wind.

"No, dear." Dee slipped the black strap of the duffel bag back over Phil's narrow shoulder. "There's no time. It must be now."

So they formed a line behind Dee, trusting her to navigate again. Daniel's hand found Luce's. He still seemed morose after their conversation, but his grip on her hand never slackened.

"Well, so long, it's been good to know ya!" Arriane joked as the others began to climb.

"If you seek me, ask the dust," Cam said in reply.

Dee's route led them up into the mountains, along a rocky path that grew narrow and steeper. It was strewn with jagged rocks Luce couldn't see until she'd tripped on them. The sinking sun looked like the moon, its light diminished and pale behind the clogged curtain of air.

She was coughing, gagging on dust, her throat still sore from the battle in Vienna. She zigzagged left and right, never seeing where she went, only sensing it was always vaguely up. She focused on Dee's yellow cardigan, which rippled like a flag on the old woman's little body. Always, Luce held on to Daniel's hand.

Here and there the dust storm snagged around a boulder, creating a brief pocket of visibility. In one of those moments, Luce spotted a pale green speck in the distance. It sat along a path hundreds of feet above them and equally as far to the right from where they stood. That dash of muted color was the only thing breaking the rhythm of the barren sepia landscape for miles. Luce stared at it as if it were a mirage until Dee's hand brushed her shoulder.

"That's our destination, dear. Good to keep your eyes on the prize."

Then the storm wrested itself free from the boulder's angles, dust swirled, and the green speck was gone. The world became a mass of grainy bullets once again.

Images of Bill seemed to form in the swirling sand: the way he'd cackled at their first meeting, changing from an imposter Daniel to a toad; his inscrutable expression when she'd met Shakespeare at the Globe. The images helped Luce right herself when she stumbled on the path. She would not stop until she beat the devil.

Images of Gabbe and Molly drove Luce forward, too. The flashes of their wings in two great gold and silver arcs played out again before Luce's eyes.

You're not tired, she told herself. *You're not hungry.*

At last they felt their way around a tall boulder shaped like an arrowhead, its tip pointed to the sky. Dee gestured for them to huddle against the up-mountain face of the arrowhead, and there, finally, the wind died down.

Dusk had fallen. The mountains wore a darkening

silver dress. They stood on a mesa about the size of Luce's living room at home. Except for a small gap where the path had dropped them off, the small round expanse was bordered on all sides by sheer, curving russet cliffs of rock, forming a space that could have served as a natural amphitheater. It shielded them from more than merely wind: Even if there hadn't been a sandstorm, most of the mesa would have been hidden by the arrowhead boulder and the high surrounding rocks.

Here, no one coming up the path could see them. Pursuing Scale would have to luck into flying directly over them. This enclosed steppe was a kind of sanctuary.

"I'd like to say I'm on a natural high," Cam said.

"This hike would have *ruined* John Denver," Roland agreed.

Ghosts of rivers left winding veins in the dust-encrusted ground. The craggy mouth of a cave opened at the base of the rock wall to the left of the arrowhead boulder.

On the far side of the mesa, slightly to the right of where they stood, a rockslide had come to rest against the sheer curving wall of stone. The pile was made of boulders that varied in size from small as a snowball to bigger than a refrigerator. Lichen grew between cracks in the rocks, seeming to hold the boulders together on the slope.

A pale-leafed olive tree and a dwarf fig tree strained

to grow diagonally around the boulders on the slope. This must have been the green speck Luce had seen at a distance from below. Dee had said it was their destination, but Luce couldn't believe they'd climbed all that way through the long expanse of writhing dust.

Everybody's wings looked like they belonged to Outcasts, brown and battered, emitting the dullest glow. The actual Outcasts' wings looked even more fragile than normal, like cobwebs. Dee used a wind-stretched sweater sleeve to wipe the dust from her face. She ran red-nail-polished fingers through wild red hair. Somehow the old lady still looked elegant. Luce didn't want to consider what she looked like.

"Never a dull moment!" Dee's voice trailed behind her as she disappeared into the cave.

They followed her inside, stopping a few feet in, where the dusky light withered into darkness. Luce leaned against a cold reddish-brown sandstone wall next to Daniel. His head nearly skimmed the low ceiling. All the angels had to tuck their wings down to accommodate the tightness of the cave.

Luce heard a scraping sound, and then Dee's shadow stretched into the lit portion at the entrance of the cave. She pushed a large wooden chest toward them with the toe of her hiking boot.

Cam and Roland rushed to help her, the muted amber glow of their dusty wings altering the darkness of the space. Each lifted a corner of the chest and they carried it to a natural alcove in the cave that Dee's gestures indicated. At her approving nod, they set it down against the cave wall.

"Thank you, gentlemen." Dee ran her fingers along the brass edge of the trunk. "It seems like only yesterday I had this carted up here. Though it must have been nearly two hundred years ago." Her face furrowed into a small frown of nostalgia. "Oh, well, a person's life is but a day. Gabbe helped me, though because of the dust storms, she never recalled the exact location. That was an angel who knew the value of advance preparation. She knew this day would come."

Dee slipped an elegant silver key from the pocket of her cardigan and twisted it in the chest's lock. As the old thing creaked open, Luce edged forward, expecting something magical—or at least historic—to be revealed. Instead, Dee tossed out six standard-issue army canteens, three small bronze lanterns, a heavy stack of blankets and towels, and an armful of crowbars, pickaxes, and shovels.

"Drink up if you need to. Lucinda first." She distributed the canteens, which were filled with cold, delicious water. Luce inhaled the contents of her canteen and wiped her mouth on the back of her hand. When she licked her lips, they were prickly with dry sand.

"That's better, isn't it?" Dee smiled. She slid open a

box of matches and lit a candle in each one of the lanterns. Light flickered off the walls, generating dramatic shadows as the angels bent over, pivoted, brushed each other off.

Arriane and Annabelle scrubbed at their wings with the dry towels. Daniel, Roland, and Cam preferred to shake the sand out of theirs, beating them against the rocks until the soft *sssss* sound of sand falling on the stone floor faded. The Outcasts seemed content to stay dirty. Soon the cave was brightly lit with an angelic glow, as if someone had started a bonfire.

"What now?" Roland asked, pouring the sand out of one of his leather boots.

Dee had moved to the mouth of the cave, her back to the others. She walked to the flat stone expanse outside, then waited for them to follow.

They gathered in a small half circle, facing the sloping pile of boulders and the struggling olive and fig trees.

"We need to go *inside*," Dee said.

"Inside where?" Luce turned around to look behind her. The cave they'd just walked out of was the only "inside" option Luce could see. Out here, there was only the flat floor of the mesa and the rockslide against the cliff wall.

"Sanctuaries are built on top of sanctuaries are built on top of sanctuaries," Dee said. "The first one on Earth used to stand right here under this slope of fallen rock.

Inside it, the final piece of the fallens' early history is encoded. This is the *Qayom Malak*. After the first sanctuary was destroyed, several others followed in its place, but the *Qayom Malak* always remained within them."

"You mean that mortals have used the *Qayom Malak*, too?" Luce asked.

"Without much thought or understanding. Over the years it grew more and more misunderstood by each new group to build their temple here. For many, this site has been considered unlucky"—she glanced at Arriane, who shifted her weight—"but that is no one's fault. It was a long time ago. Tonight, we unearth what once was lost."

"You mean the knowledge of our Fall?" Roland paced the perimeter of the slope of rocks. "That's what the *Qayom Malak* will tell us?"

Dee smiled cryptically. "The words are Aramaic. They mean . . . well, it's better if you just see for yourselves."

Beside them, Arriane was chewing noisily on a strand of her hair, her hands stuffed deep into the pockets of her overalls, her wings stiff and unmoving. She stared at the fig and olive trees, as if in a trance.

Luce noticed now what was strange about the trees. The reason they seemed to grow diagonally out of the stone was that their trunks lay buried deep beneath the boulders.

"The trees," she said.

"Yes, once they were fully exposed." Dee bent down to caress the withering green leaves of the little fig tree. "As was the *Qayom Malak*." She rose and patted the heap of boulders. "This whole mesa was once much larger. A lovely, vibrant place at times, though that's hard to imagine now."

"What happened to it?" Luce asked. "How was the sanctuary destroyed?"

"The most recent one was covered up by this rockslide. That was about seven hundred years ago, after a particularly severe earthquake. But even before that, the list of calamities to occur here was unprecedented— flood, fire, murder, war, explosions." She paused, peering into the pile of boulders as if it were a mass of crystal balls. "Still, the only part that matters endures. At least I hope it does. And that's why we need to go inside."

Cam ambled over to one of the larger boulders, leaned against it with his arms crossed. "I excel at many things, Dee, not the least of which is rock. But passing *through* rock isn't one of my gifts."

Dee clapped her hands. "That is precisely why I packed the shovels all those years ago. We'll have to clear the rocks aside," Dee said. "We seek what lies within."

"You're saying we're going to excavate the *Qayom Malak*?" Annabelle asked, biting pink fingernails.

Dee touched a mossy patch at the center of the

mound of boulders spilled long before from the cliffs. "I'd start here if I were you!"

When they realized that Dee was serious about dismantling the tower of boulders, Roland distributed the tools Dee had flung out of the wooden chest. They set to work.

"As you clear, make sure you leave this area free." Dee gestured to the open space between the rockslide and the head of the trail that had brought them there. She marked off an area of about ten square feet. "We're going to need it."

Luce took a pickax and tapped it uncertainly against the rock.

"Do you know what it looks like?" she said to Daniel, whose crowbar was wedged around a rock behind the fig tree. "How will we recognize the *Qayom Malak* when we find it?"

"There's no illustration in my book for this." Daniel split the rock easily with a tilt of his hand. The muscles of his arms trembled as he lifted the boulder halves, each the size of a large suitcase. He tossed them behind him, careful not to let them land inside the area Dee had marked off. "We'll just have to trust that Dee remembers."

Luce stepped into the open space where the boulder Daniel moved aside had been. The rest of the olive and fig trees were now exposed, down to their trunks. They had been nearly flattened by the tons of fallen rock. Her gaze flew around the gigantic pile of rocks they'd have to clear. It was easily twenty feet high. Could anything have withstood the might of this landslide?

"Don't worry," Dee called out, as if reading Luce's mind. "It's in there somewhere, tucked away as safely as your first memory of love."

The Outcasts had flown to the top of the slope. Phil showed the others where to cast the boulders they'd already chipped away, and they slammed them back into the face of the slope, causing the compounded rock to fracture and slide down the sides.

"Hey! I see some really old yellow brick." Annabelle's wings fluttered above the rockslide's highest point, where it edged up against the mountain's sheer, vertical walls. She heaved away some debris with her shovel. "I think it might be a wall of the sanctuary."

"A wall, dear? Very good," Dee said. "There should be three more of them, the way walls often go. Keep digging." She was distracted, pacing the flat square of rock she'd marked off near the trailhead, not noticing the progress of the dig. She seemed to be counting something. Her gaze was fixed on the mesa floor. Luce watched Dee for a few moments and saw that the old lady was counting her steps, as if blocking a play.

She looked up, caught Luce's eye. "Come with me."

Luce glanced at Daniel, at his sweat-glistening skin. He was busy with a large, unwieldy boulder. She turned and followed Dee into the mouth of the cave.

Dee's lantern wobbled strobe-like into the dark recesses. The cave was infinitely darker and colder without the glow of angel wings. Dee rummaged for a few moments in her chest.

"Where is that bloody broom?" Dee asked.

Luce crouched over Dee, holding up another lantern to help light her search. She reached into the enormous trunk and her hands brushed the rough straw of a broom. "Here."

"Wonderful. Always the last place you look, especially when you can't see." Dee slung the broom over her shoulder. "I want to show you something while the others continue with the excavation."

They walked back out onto the mesa, into the echoing of metal striking stone. Dee stopped at the edge of the rockslide, facing the space she'd asked the angels to leave clear. She began to drag the broom in brisk straight lines. Luce had thought the mesa was all made of the same flat red rock, but as Dee brushed and swept and brushed and swept, Luce noticed there was a shallow marble platform underneath. And a pattern was emerging: Pale yellow stone alternated with white rocks to form an intricate, inlaid design.

Eventually Luce recognized a symbol: one long line

of yellow stone, edged by white descending diagonal lines of decreasing length.

Luce crouched down to run her fingers along the stone. It looked like an arrowhead, pointing away from the top of the mountain, back down in the direction from which the angels had arrived.

"This is the Arrowhead Slab," Dee said. "Once everything is ready, we will use it as a kind of stage. Cam crafted the mosaic many years ago, though I doubt that he remembers. He's been through so much since then. Heartbreak is its own form of amnesia."

"You know about the woman who broke Cam's heart?" Luce whispered, remembering that Daniel had told her never to mention it.

Dee frowned, nodded, and pointed to the yellow arrow in the marble tiles. "What do you think of the design?"

"I think it's beautiful," Luce said.

"I do, too," Dee said. "I have a similar one tattooed over my heart."

Smiling, Dee unbuttoned the top two buttons of her cardigan to reveal a yellow camisole. She drew the neckline down a couple of inches, exposing the pale skin of her chest. At last, she pointed to a black tattoo over her breast. It was precisely the same shape as the lines in the stone on the ground.

"What does it mean?" Luce asked.

Dee patted the tattoo and pulled her camisole back up. "I can't wait to tell you"—she smiled, pivoting to face the slope of rock behind them—"but first things first. Look how well they're doing!"

The angels and Outcasts had cleared away a portion of the exterior of the rockslide. The right angle of two old brick walls rose several feet out of the debris. They were badly damaged, unintended windows smashed into existence here and there. The roof was gone. Some of the bricks were blackened by a long-forgotten fire. Others looked moldy, as if recovering from a prehistoric flood. But the rectangular shape of the former temple was starting to become clear.

"Dee," Roland called, waving the woman over to the northern wall to inspect his progress.

Luce returned to Daniel's side. In the time she'd been with Dee, he'd cleared a heaping pile of rock and stacked it neatly to the right of the slope. She felt bad that she was barely helping. She lifted the pickax again.

They worked for hours. It was well after midnight by the time they'd cleared half the slope. Dee's lanterns lit the mesa, but Luce liked staying close to Daniel, using the unique glow of his wings to see. Her jaw ached from the tension in her face. Her shoulders were sore and her eyes stung. But she didn't stop. She didn't complain.

She kept hacking. She took a swing at a square of pink stone exposed by a boulder Daniel had just removed, expecting her ax to glance off solid rock. Instead, she sliced into something soft. Luce dropped her ax and burrowed with her hands into this surprisingly claylike patch. She'd reached a layer of sandstone so crumbly it fell apart at the touch of a finger. She moved the lantern closer to get a better look as she tore away large chunks. Underneath several inches of sandstone she felt something smooth and hard. "I found something!"

The others circled around as Luce wiped her hands on her jeans and used her fingers to brush clean a square tile about two feet in diameter. Once, it must have been completely painted, but all that was visible now was a thin outline of a man with a halo orbiting his head.

"Is this it?" she asked, excited.

Dee's shoulder brushed against Luce's. She touched the tile with her thumb. "I'm afraid not, dear. This is just a depiction of our friend Jesus. We have to go further back than him."

"Further back?" Luce asked.

"All the way inside." Dee knocked on the tile. "This is the façade of the most recent sanctuary, a medieval monastery for particularly antisocial monks. We must dig down to the original structure, behind this wall."

She noticed Luce's hesitation. "Don't be afraid to destroy ancient iconography," Dee said. "It must be done to get to what's *really* old." She looked at the sky, as if searching for the sun, but it had long before sunk below the flat drop of horizon behind them. The stars were out. "Oh dear. Time ticks on, doesn't it? Keep going! You're doing fine!"

Finally, Phil stepped forward with his crowbar and bashed through the Jesus tile. It left a hole, and the space behind it was hollow and dark and smelled strange and musty and old.

The Outcasts leaped on the busted tile, widening the crevice so they could dig deeper inside. They were hard workers, efficient in their destruction. They found that without a roof over the sanctuary, the rockslide had filled the interior, as well. The Outcasts took turns tearing the wall away and casting aside the boulders flowing out from the structure.

Arriane stood away from the group, in a darkened corner of the enclosed plateau, kicking a pile of rocks as if trying to start a lawn mower. Luce walked over to her.

"Hey," Luce said. "You okay?"

Arriane looked up, thumbing the straps of her overalls. A crazy smile flashed across her face. "Remember when we had detention together? They made us clean up the cemetery at Sword & Cross? We got paired together, scrubbing that angel?"

"Of course." Luce had been miserable that day—chewed out by Molly, anxious about and infatuated with Daniel, and, come to think of it, unsure whether Arriane liked her or was simply taking pity on her.

"That was fun, wasn't it?" Arriane's voice sounded distant. "I'm always going to remember that."

"Arriane," Luce said, "that's not what you're really thinking about right now, is it? What is it about this place that's making you hide over here?"

Arriane stood with her feet balanced on her shovel and swayed back and forth. She watched the Outcasts and the other angels unearthing a tall interior column from the rocks.

Finally, Arriane closed her eyes and blurted out, "I'm the reason this sanctuary doesn't exist anymore. I'm the reason it's bad luck."

"But—Dee said it wasn't anyone's fault. What happened?"

"After the Fall," she said, "I was getting my strength back, looking for shelter, for a way to mend my wings. I hadn't yet returned to the Throne. I didn't even know how to do that. I didn't remember what I was. I was alone and I saw this place and I—"

"You wandered into the sanctuary that used to be here," Luce said, remembering what Daniel had told her about the reason fallen angels didn't go near churches. They had all been edgy at the Church of the Holy Sepulchre. They wouldn't go near the chapel on Pont Saint Bénézet.

"I didn't know!" Arriane's chest shuddered when she inhaled.

"Of course you didn't." Luce put her arm around Arriane's side. She was skin and bones and wings. The angel rested her head on Luce's shoulder. "Did it blow up?"

Arriane nodded. "The way you do . . . no"—she corrected herself—"the way you *used* to in your other lives. Poof. The whole thing up in flames. Only, this wasn't—sorry for saying this—like, all beautifully tragic or romantic. This was bleak and black and *absolute*. Like a door slamming in my face. That's when I knew that I was really kicked out of Heaven." She turned to Luce, her wide blue eyes more innocent than Luce could ever remember seeing them. "I never meant to leave. It was an accident, a lot of us just got swept up in . . . someone else's battle."

She shrugged and a corner of her mouth curved mischievously. "Maybe I got too used to being a reject. Kinda suits me, though, don't you think?" She made a pistol with her fingers and fired it in Cam's direction. "I guess I don't mind running around with this pack of outlaws." Then Arriane's face changed, any trace of whimsy disappearing. She gripped Luce by the shoulders and whispered, "That's it."

"What?" Luce spun around.

The angels and the Outcasts had cleared away several tons of stone. They were now standing where the pile of rocks had stood. It had taken until just before dawn. Around them rose the inner sanctuary Dee had promised they would find. The old, elegant lady was as good as her word.

Only two frail walls were left, forming a right angle, but the gray tile border on the floor suggested an original design that spanned roughly twenty square feet. Large solid marble bricks made up the bases of the walls, where smaller crumbling sandstone bricks had once held up a roof. Weathered friezes decorated portions of the structure—winged creatures so old and worn they almost blended back into the stone. An ancient fire had scorched portions of the flared decorative cornices near the tops of the walls.

The now completely uncovered fig and olive trees marked the barrier between Dee's broom-swept Arrowhead Slab and the excavated sanctuary. The two missing walls left the rest of the structure exposed to Luce's imagination, which pictured ancient pilgrims kneeling to pray here. It was clear where they would kneel:

Four Ionic marble columns with fluted bases and scrolled caps had been built around a raised platform in the center of the tile. And on that platform stood a giant rectangular altar built of pale tan stone.

It looked familiar, but unlike anything Luce had ever seen before. It was caked with dirt and rocks and Luce could make out the shadow of a decoration carved on top: two stone angels facing each other, each the size of a large doll. They'd once been painted with gold, it seemed, but now only flecks of their former sheen remained. The carved angels kneeled in prayer, heads down, halo-free, with their beautifully detailed wings arched forward so that the top edges were touching.

"Yes." Dee took a deep breath. "That's it. *Qayom Malak*. It means 'the Overseer of the Angels.' Or, as I like to call it, 'the Angels' Aide.' It holds a secret no soul has ever deciphered: the key to where the fallen fell to Earth. Do you remember it, Arriane?"

"I think so." Arriane seemed nervous as she stepped toward the sculpture. When she reached the platform, she stood still for a long time before the kneeling angels. Then she kneeled herself. She touched their wings, the place where the two angels connected. She shivered. "I only saw it for a second before—"

"Yes," Dee said. "You were blasted out of the sanctuary. The force of the explosion caused the first avalanche that buried the *Qayom Malak,* but the fig and olive trees remained exposed, a beacon for the other sanctuaries that were built in the coming years. The Christians were here, the Greeks, the Jews, the Moors. Their sanctuaries fell, too, to avalanche, fire, to scandal or fear, creating a nearly impenetrable wall around the *Qayom Malak*. You needed me to help you find it again. And you couldn't find me until you *really* needed me."

"What happens now?" Cam asked. "Don't tell me we have to pray."

Dee's eyes never left the *Qayom Malak,* even as she tossed Cam the towel draped over her shoulder. "Oh, it's far worse, Cam. Now you've got to clean. Polish the angels, especially their wings. Polish them until they shine. We are going to need the moonlight to shine on them in precisely the right way."

FOURTEEN

AIR APPARENT

Boom.

It sounded like thunder, the brewing of a dark tornado. Luce jumped awake inside the cave, where she'd fallen asleep on Daniel's shoulder. She hadn't meant to doze off, but Dee had insisted on resting before explaining the purpose of the *Qayom Malak*. Stirred from sleep now, Luce had the feeling that many precious hours had passed. She was sweating in her flannel sleeping bag. The silver locket felt hot against her chest.

Daniel was lying very still, his eyes fixed on the mouth of the cave. The rumbling stopped.

Luce propped herself up on her elbows, noticed Dee across from her, asleep in the fetal position, stirring slightly, her red hair loose and messy. To Dee's left lay the Outcasts' empty sleeping bags; the strange creatures stood alert, huddled at the back of the small space, their drab wings overlapping. To her right, Annabelle and Arriane were asleep, or at least resting, their silver wings entwined uninhibitedly, like sisters.

The cave was calm. Luce must have dreamed the rumbling. She was still tired.

When she rolled over, nestling her back into Daniel's chest so that he was cradling her with his right wing, her eyelids fluttered shut. Then they flew open.

She was face to face with Cam.

He was inches away, on his side, head propped on his hand, green eyes holding hers as if they were both in a trance. He opened his mouth as if to say something—

BOOM.

The room trembled like a leaf. For an instant, the air seemed to take on a strange transparency. Cam's body shimmered, both there and somehow *not* there, his very existence seeming to flicker.

"Timequake," Daniel said.

"A big mother," Cam agreed.

Luce sprang upright, gaping at her own body in the

sleeping bag, at Daniel's hand on her knee, at Arriane, whose muffled voice called out, "I'wuzznt me," until Annabelle's wing slapped her awake. All of them were *flickering* before each other's eyes. Solidly present one moment, as insubstantial as ghosts the next.

The timequake had jarred loose a dimension in which they weren't even *there*.

The cave around them shuddered. Sand sifted down from the walls. But unlike those of Luce and her friends, the physical properties of the red rock remained fixed, as if to prove that only people—souls—were at risk of being erased.

"The *Qayom Malak!*" Phil said. "A rockslide would bury it again."

Luce watched, queasy, as the Outcast's pale wings flickered when he scrambled wildly toward the mouth of the cave.

"This is a seismic shift in reality, Phillip, not an earthquake," Dee called, stopping Phil. Her voice sounded like someone was turning her volume up and down. "I appreciate your concern, but we'll just have to ride this one out."

And then there was one last great boom, a long, terrible rumbling during which Luce couldn't see *any* of them, and then they were back, solid, *real* again. There was a sudden hush around everything, so absolute that Luce heard her heart pounding in her chest.

"There, now," Dee said. "The worst of it is over."

"Is everyone okay?" Daniel asked.

"Yes, dear, we're fine," Dee said. "Though that was most unpleasant." She rose and walked, her voice trailing behind her. "At least it was one of the last seismic shifts anyone ever has to experience."

Sharing glances, the others followed her outside.

"What do you mean?" Luce asked. "Is Lucifer that close already?" Her brain scrambled to count sunrise, sunset, sunrise, sunset. They blurred together, one long stream of frenzy and panic and wings across the sky.

It had been morning when Luce fell asleep. . . .

They stopped in front of the *Qayom Malak*. Luce stood on the Arrowhead Slab, facing the two angels in the sculpture. Roland and Cam soared into the sky and hovered about fifty feet in the air. They gazed across the horizon, dipped close together to speak quietly. Their enormous wings blocked the sun—which Luce noticed sat troublingly low on the horizon.

"It is now the evening of the sixth day since Lucifer began his solitary Fall," Dee said softly.

"We slept all day?" Luce asked, horrified. "We wasted so much time—"

"Nothing was wasted," Dee said. "I have a very big night tonight. Come to think of it, you do, too. You'll soon be glad you had your rest."

"Let's get it on before another shift hits, before we

have to fight off any Scale," Cam said as he and Roland touched down on the ground again. Their wings jostled lightly from the force of their landings.

"Cam is right. We don't have any time to waste." Daniel produced the black satchel, which contained the halo Luce had stolen from the sunken church in Venice. Then he slung over the duffel bag, which bulged at the center, where he'd zipped the round cup of the Silver Pennon. He placed both bags, unzipped, before Dee, so that all three artifacts sat in a row.

Dee didn't move.

"Dee?" Daniel asked. "What do we have to do?"

Dee didn't answer.

Roland stepped forward, touching her back. "Cam and I saw signs of more Scale on the horizon. They don't know our location yet, but they aren't far away. It would be best if we hurried."

Dee frowned. "I'm afraid that is impossible."

"But you said—" Luce broke off as Dee stared at her placidly. "The tattoo. The symbol on the ground—"

"I would be happy to *explain*," Dee said, "but there will be no hurrying the deed itself."

She glanced around the circle of angels, Outcasts, and Luce. When she was sure she had all their attention, she began. "As we know, the early history of the fallen was never written down. Although you may not remember very clearly"—her gaze swept over the angels—"you recorded your first days on Earth in *things*. To this day, the essential elements of your prehistoric lore are encoded in the fabric of different artifacts. Artifacts that are, to the naked eye, something else altogether."

Dee reached for the halo and held it up to the sunlight. "You see"—she ran her finger along a series of cracks in the glass that Luce hadn't noticed before—"this glass halo is also a lens." She held it up for them to look through. Behind it, her face was slightly distorted by the convex curve of the glass, making her golden eyes look huge.

She put the halo down, moved to the duffel bag, and removed the Silver Pennon. It shone in the day's last rays of sunlight as she ran her hand softly across its interior. "And this goblet"—she pointed to the illustration hammered into the silver, the wings Luce had noticed in Jerusalem—"bears a record of the exodus from the Fall site, the first diaspora of angels. To return to your first home on Earth, you first must fill this goblet." She paused, staring deeply inside the Silver Pennon. "When it is filled, we will empty it on the Slab's intricate tiled floor, which contains imagery of how the world once was."

"When the goblet is filled?" Luce repeated. "Filled with what?"

"First things first." Dee walked to the edge of the stone platform and brushed away a bit of grit. Then she bowed to place the goblet directly on top of the yellow symbol in the stone. "I believe this goes here."

Luce stood rapt beside Daniel as they watched Dee pace slowly up and down the platform. Finally, she picked up the halo again and carried it to the *Qayom Malak*. At some point, she had changed out of her hiking boots, back into her stilettos, and her heels clicked on the marble. Her unkempt hair swished down to her waist. She took a deep, luxurious breath and let it out.

With both hands, she raised the halo over her head, whispered a few words of prayer, and then, very carefully, lowered the halo directly into the circle of air carved out by the sculpture of the praying angels' touching wings. It fit like a ring on a finger.

"I did *not* see that coming," Arriane muttered to Luce.

Neither had Luce—although she was certain that the woman was engaged in something powerfully sacred.

When she spun around to face Luce and the angels, Dee looked as if she were going to say something. Instead, she sank to her knees and lay down on her back at the foot of the *Qayom Malak*. Daniel lurched toward her, ready to help, but she waved him away. The toes of her shoes rested on the base of the *Qayom Malak;* her slender arms stretched over her head so that her fingertips grazed the Silver Pennon. Her body spanned the distance precisely.

She closed her eyes and lay still for several minutes.

Just when Luce was beginning to wonder whether Dee had fallen asleep, Dee said, "It's a good thing I stopped growing two thousand years ago."

She stood up then, taking a hand from Roland, and dusted herself off.

"Everything is in order. When the moon hits right about there." She pointed toward the eastern sky, just above where the rocks tapered off.

"The moon?" Cam gave Daniel a glance.

"Yes, the moon. It needs to shine through precisely here." Dee tapped the center of the halo's glass, where a jagged crack became more visible than it had been minutes earlier. "If I know the moon, which I do—after all these years, one does develop an intimate relationship with one's companions—it should fall precisely where we need it to at the stroke of midnight tonight. Fitting, really, since midnight is my favorite time of day. The witching hour—"

"What happens then?" Luce asked. "At midnight, when the moon is where it needs to be?"

Dee slowed her pace and cupped her hand against Luce's cheek. "Everything, dear."

"And what do we do in the meantime?" Daniel asked.

Dee reached into her cardigan pocket and revealed a large gold pocket watch. "A few things remain to be done."

They followed Dee's instructions down to the smallest detail. Each of the artifacts was swept, polished, dusted by several pairs of hands. It was well into the night before Luce was able to visualize what Dee had in mind for the ceremony.

"Two more lanterns, please," Dee instructed. "That will make three, one for each of the relics." It was strange the way Dee referred to the relics as if she were not one of them. Even stranger was the way she buzzed around the enclosed plateau, like a hostess preparing for a dinner party, making sure everything was just right.

The quartet of Outcasts lit the lanterns ritualistically, their shaven heads orbiting the expanse of rock like planets. The first light illuminated the *Qayom Malak*.

The second lantern shone on the Silver Pennon, which still sat where Dee had placed it, atop the golden arrow on the Slab, at a distance of Dee's height exactly— a scant five feet—from the *Qayom Malak*. Earlier, the angels had arranged a half-moon arc of flat-topped boulders like benches on the left and right sides of the Slab so that it resembled a stage. This made the space look even more like an amphitheater as Annabelle dusted the boulders like an usher preparing seats for an imminent audience.

"What will Dee do with all this?" Luce whispered to Daniel.

Daniel's violet eyes were heavy with something he

couldn't voice, and before Luce could beg him to try, Dee's hands found their way to Luce's shoulders.

"Please don these robes. I find that ceremonial costumes help to maintain focus on the task at hand. Daniel, I think this should fit you." She pressed a heavy brown cloak into his arms. "And here's one for graceful Arriane." She passed it to the angel. "That leaves you, Luce. There are smaller robes at the bottom of my chest over there. Take my lantern and help yourself." Luce took the lantern and started to lead Daniel toward the cave where they had slept the night before, but Dee gripped Daniel's arm.

"A word?"

Daniel nodded for Luce to go on alone, so she did, wondering what Dee didn't want to say in front of her. She slipped the lantern's handle over her forearm, its light swinging as she walked toward the mouth of the cave.

She eased open the stiff lid of the chest and reached inside. A long brown robe was the only thing in it. She picked it up. It was made of heavy wool, thick as a peacoat and musty, like tobacco. When Luce held it up against her body, it looked about three feet too long. Now she was even more curious about why Dee had sent her away. She set the lantern on the ground and clumsily pulled the robe over her head.

"Need some help?"

Cam had entered the cave as quietly as a cloud. Standing behind her, he gathered a fold of the cloak's material and cinched it under the garment's woven belt. He knotted it in place so that the hem ended at Luce's ankles perfectly, as if the cloak had been made for her.

She turned around to face him. Lantern light flickered on his face. He stood very still, in the way that only Cam could.

Luce slid her thumb along the belt he'd knotted. "Thanks," she said, moving back toward the entrance of the cave.

"Luce, wait—"

She stopped. Cam looked down at the toe of his boot, kicking the edge of the chest. Luce stared at it, too. She was wondering how she hadn't heard him come into the cave, how they'd ended up alone.

"You still don't believe I'm on your side."

"It doesn't matter now, Cam." Her throat felt impossibly tight.

"*Listen.*" Cam took a step toward her so that there were only inches between them. She thought he was going to grab her, but he didn't. He didn't even try to touch her; he just stayed very still and close. "Things used to be different. Look at me." She did, nervously. "I may wear Lucifer's gold on my wings now, but it wasn't always like that. You knew me before I went that way, Lucinda, and you and I were friends."

"Well, like you said, things change."

Cam let out a frustrated groan. "It is *impossible* to apologize to a girl with such a conveniently selective memory. Allow me to venture a guess: As you awaken to your true self, you're unpacking all sorts of sumptuous memories in which you and Daniel fall in love, and Daniel says this beautiful phrase, and Daniel turns and broods toward silken silhouettes caressing the tender tips of stars on the horizon—"

"Why shouldn't I? We belong to each other. Daniel is my everything. And you're—"

"What does he say about me?" Cam's eyes narrowed.

Luce cracked her knuckles and thought about the way, early on at Sword & Cross, Daniel's hand had swept over hers to stop the mindless habit. His touch had been familiar from the beginning.

"He says he trusts you."

A pause followed that Luce refused to fill. She wanted to leave. What if Daniel looked over and saw her in this dim cave with Cam? They were arguing, but Daniel wouldn't be able to tell that from a distance. What did they look like, she and Cam? When she looked up, his eyes were clear, green, and profoundly sad.

"*Do you* trust me?" he asked.

"Why does this matter right now—"

His eyes shot open, wild and excited. "*Everything matters right now.* This is the showtime for which all other shows have been warm-ups. And in order for you to do what you need to do, you can't see me as the enemy. You have no idea what you've gotten into."

"What are you talking about?"

"Luce." It was Dee's voice. She and Daniel were standing at the mouth of the cave. Dee was the only one smiling. "We're ready for you!"

"Me?"

"You."

Luce was suddenly frightened. "What do I have to do?"

"Why don't you come and see?"

Dee's hand was extended but Luce found it difficult to move. She glanced at Cam but he was looking at Daniel. Daniel was still looking at her, his eyes burning the hungry way they did when he was about to sweep her into his arms and kiss her deeply. But he didn't move and that turned the ten feet of space between them into two thousand miles.

"Have I done something wrong?" she asked.

"You're about to do something wonderful," Dee said, still holding out her hand. "Let us not waste time we do not have."

Luce took her hand and it felt so cold that it scared her. She studied Dee, who looked paler, more fragile, older than she had at the library in Vienna. But somehow, underneath her withered skin and prominent bones, something still shone bright and effervescent from within her.

"Do I look all right, dear? You're staring."

"Of course," Luce said. "It's just—"

"My soul? It's glowing, isn't it?"

Luce nodded.

"Good."

Cam and Daniel did not speak as they brushed past each other, Cam striding into the suddenly windy wilderness outside, Daniel circling behind Luce to carry the lantern.

"Dee?" Luce turned to the woman, whose freezing hand she was trying to warm with her own. "I don't want to go out there. I'm afraid and I don't know why."

"That is as it should be. But this cup cannot pass you."

"Can someone please tell me what is going on?"

"Yes," Dee said, giving Luce's hand a firm but supportive forward tug. "Just as soon as we're outside."

As they rounded the arrowhead-shaped boulder that partly shielded the entrance to the small cave, the cold wind bore into them unforgivingly. Luce staggered back, shielding her face from the sudden spray of sand with her free hand. Dee and Daniel made her press on past the head of the trail they'd climbed the night before, where they were most exposed to the wind.

Luce found that the peaks around the rest of the mesa

formed barriers to the swirling, gritty gusts, allowing her to hear and see again. Though she could hear the daily dust storm howl beyond the plateau, everything within its curved rock walls seemed suddenly too quiet and too clear.

Two lanterns glowed on the marble Slab—one before the *Qayom Malak,* one behind the Silver Pennon. Both lights attracted swirls of gnats that bounced off the small glass panes, strangely calming Luce. At least she was still in a world where light attracted bugs. She was still in a world she knew.

The lantern illuminated the two golden angels bowing toward each other in prayer. Its light touched the edges of the heavy, cracked glass halo, which Dee had returned to its rightful place, cradled by the angels' wings.

On the cliffs towering over the plateau, four Outcasts perched on ledges, each pale warrior watching a different cardinal direction. The Outcasts' wings, tucked to their sides, were barely visible, but the edges of Daniel's lantern light revealed the starshots in each of their silver bows, as if they expected the Scale's arrival at any moment.

The four fallen angels Luce knew best occupied the stone seats around the ceremonially placed relics. Arriane and Annabelle sat on one side, backs straight, their wings concealed. On the other side sat Cam and Roland— with one empty seat between them.

Was it for Luce or Daniel?

"Good, everyone's here except the moon." Dee looked up at the eastern sky. "Five more minutes. Daniel, will you take a seat?"

Daniel handed Dee the lantern and walked across the marble slab. He stood before the *Qayom Malak*. Luce wanted to go to him, but before she could even lean in his direction, Dee's grip tightened around her hand. "Stay with me, honey."

Daniel sat down between Roland and Cam and turned his expressionless gaze to Luce.

"Allow me to explain." Dee's calm, clear voice echoed off the red-rock walls, and all the angels straightened in attention. "As I told you earlier, we require the moon to make an appearance, and now, in a moment, she will visit us above this peak. She will grin down through the lens of the Halo. We are fortunate the sky is clear tonight, with nothing to obscure the shadows of her lovely craters as they join with the cracks in the Halo's glass.

"Together, these elements will project the outlines of continents and lines of countries, which, in concert with the carvings on the Slab, will comprise the Map of the Simulacrum Terra Prima. Right here." She pointed to an empty space on the marble step, where she'd lain earlier, measuring the distance between the *Qayom Malak* and the Silver Pennon. "You will see a representation of the way the world was when you angels fell to Earth. Yes"— she inhaled—"just another moment. There."

The crown of the moon rose above the rocky crag that jutted out behind the *Qayom Malak*. And even though the moon was pale white and waning, at the moment, it shone as brilliantly as dawn. The angels, the Outcasts, Luce, and Dee stood quietly for several minutes, watching the moon climb, watching it cast a little light and then a little more through the translucent surface of the halo. The marble slab beyond it was blank, then clouded; then, all at once, the projection was clear and focused and real. It projected lines, intersections—*continents*—borders, lands, and seas.

It looked half complete. Some lines trailed off into nothing; some boundaries never closed. But it was clearly a map of the Earth, Luce thought, as it would have looked when Daniel fell for her. It stirred something in the deepest recesses of her memory. It looked familiar.

"Do you see the yellow stone at the center there?" Dee asked.

Luce squinted to see a tile of the same slightly darker yellow stone as the one where the goblet had been placed. "That is us, right here in the middle of everything."

"Like an arrow saying, 'You Are Here,'" Luce said.

"That's right, dear." Dee turned to Luce. "And now, my Lucinda, have you figured out your role in this ceremony yet?"

Luce squirmed. What did they want from her? This was their story, not hers. After all this commotion, she was just another girl, swept up in the promise of love. Daniel had found her on Earth after his fall from grace; someone should ask him what was going on. "I'm sorry. I don't know."

"I'll give you a hint," Dee said. "Do you see the spot where angels fell marked on this map?"

Luce sighed, eager to get to the point. "No."

"It was ordained many millennia ago that this location on this map could only be revealed in blood. The blood that courses through our veins knows far more than we do. Look closely. See the grooves along the marble? They are the lines to close the boundaries of the angelico-prelapsarian Earth. They shall become clear once the blood is shed and poured. The blood will pool in one vitally important place. The knowledge, my dear, is in the blood."

"The site of the Fall," one of the angels said reverently. It was Arriane or Annabelle, Luce couldn't tell which.

"Somewhat like a treasure map in an adventure story, the impact point—that's the site of the Fall—will be marked with a five-pointed star of blood. Now . . ."

Dee was talking but Luce could no longer hear what she was saying. So this was what it was going to take to stop Lucifer. This was what Cam meant she had to do. This was why Daniel wouldn't look at her. Her throat felt like it was stuffed with cotton. When she opened her mouth, her voice sounded like she was speaking underwater. "You need"—she swallowed in pain—"my blood."

Dee choked on her laugh and pressed a cold hand to Luce's hot cheek. "Good heavens, no, child! You keep yours. I'm going to give you mine."

"What?"

"That's right. As I am passing out of this world, you will fill the Silver Pennon with my blood. You will pour it into this depression just east of the golden arrow marker"—she indicated a dent at the left of the goblet, then fanned her hands out dramatically toward the map—"and watch it follow the grooves here and there and here and there until you find the star. Then you will know where to meet Lucifer and thwart his plan."

Luce cracked her knuckles. How could Dee speak about her own death so casually? "Why would you do this?"

"Why, it's what I was created for. Angels were made to adore and I have a purpose, too." Then, from the deep pocket of her brown cloak, Dee withdrew a long silver dagger.

"But that's—"

The dagger Miss Sophia had used to kill Penn. The one she'd had in Jerusalem when she bound up the fallen angels.

"Yes. I picked this up in Golgotha," Dee said, admiring the craftsmanship of the blade. It shone as if freshly sharpened. "Dark history, this knife. It's time it was put to some *good* use, dear." She held out the knife, its blade flat on her open palm, its hilt pointing toward Luce. "It would mean a lot to me if you would be the one to spill my blood, dear. Not only because you *are* dear to me, but also because it *must* be you."

"Me?"

"Yes, you. You must kill me, Lucinda."

FIFTEEN

THE GIFT

"I can't!"

"You can," Dee said. "And you will. No one else can do it."

"Why?"

Dee looked over her shoulder in Daniel's direction. He was still seated, looking at Luce, but he didn't seem to see her. None of the angels rose to help her.

Dee spoke in a whisper. "If you are, as you say you are, fully resolved to break your curse—"

"You know I am."

"Then you must use my blood to break it."

No. How could her curse be bound up in someone else's blood? Dee had brought them up here to the *Qayom Malak* to reveal the site of the angels' Fall. That was her role as the desideratum. It didn't have anything to do with Luce's curse.

Did it?

Break the curse. Of course Luce wanted to; it was all she wanted.

Could she break it, right here, right now? How would she live with herself if she killed Dee? Luce looked to the old woman, who took her by the hands.

"Don't you want to know the truth of your original life?"

"Of course I do. But why would killing you reveal my past?"

"It will reveal all kinds of things."

"I don't understand."

"Oh dear." Dee sighed, looking past Luce at the others. "These angels have done well to keep you safe—but they have also protected you into complacency. The time has come for you to awaken, Lucinda, and to awaken, you must *act.*"

Luce turned away. The look in Dee's golden eyes was too pleading, too intense. "I've seen enough death."

A single angel rose in the darkness from the circle

they'd formed around the *Qayom Malak*. "If she can't do it, she can't do it."

"Shut *up,* Cam," Arriane said. "Sit down."

Cam stepped forward, approaching Luce. His narrow frame cast its shadow across the Slab. "We've taken it this far. You can't say we haven't given it every kind of shot." He turned to face the others. "But maybe she just can't. There is only so much you can ask a person to do. She wouldn't be the first filly anybody lost a fortune on. So what if she happens to be the last?"

His tone did not match his words, and neither did his eyes, which said with desperate sincerity, *You can do this. You have to.*

Luce weighed the dagger in her hand. She'd seen its blade slice the life out of Penn. She had felt it sting her flesh when Sophia tried to murder her in the chapel at Sword & Cross. The only reason Luce wasn't dead now was that Daniel had crashed through the roseate window to save her. The only reason she bore no scar was Gabbe's healing touch. They'd saved her life for this moment. So that she could take another's.

Dee perceived how far away fear had carried Luce. She motioned for Cam to sit down. "Perhaps it would be better, dear, if you didn't think of this as taking my life. You would be giving me the greatest gift, Lucinda. Can't you see that I'm ready to move on?" She pressed her lips together in a smile. "I know it's hard to understand, but there comes a time in a mortal body's journey when it seeks to die in the most advantageous way it can. They used to call it a 'good death.' It is time for me to go, and if you give me the gift of this *very* good death, I promise you won't regret it."

With tears stinging her eyes, Luce looked past Dee. "Dan—"

"I can't help you, Luce." Daniel spoke before she'd even finished saying his name. "You must do this alone."

Roland rose from his seat and examined the map. He looked east at the moon. "If it were done when it is done, then it would be well it were done quickly."

"There isn't much time," Dee interpreted, resting a frail hand on Luce's shoulder.

Luce's hands were shaking, sweating on the heavy silver hilt of the dagger, making it difficult to hold. Behind Dee she could see the Slab with its half-drawn map, and beyond the map, the *Qayom Malak,* in which the glass halo was secured. The Silver Pennon sat at Dee's feet.

Luce had been through a sacrifice before: in Chichén Itzá, when she'd cleaved to her past self Ix Cuat. The ritual made no sense to Luce. Why did something dear have to die so other dear things could live? Didn't whoever made these rules think they deserved an explanation? It was like Abraham's being asked to sacrifice Isaac. Had God created love to make pain feel even worse?

"Will you do this for me?" Dee asked.

Break the curse.

"Will you do it for yourself?"

Luce held the knife between her open palms. "What do I do?"

"I'll guide you through it." Dee's left hand closed around Luce's right, which closed around the dagger. The hilt was slick with the sweat on her palms.

With her right hand free, Dee unbound her cloak and slipped it off, standing before Luce in a long white tunic. Her upper chest was bare, revealing her arrowhead tattoo.

Luce whimpered at the sight of it.

"Please don't worry, dear. I'm a special breed, and this moment has always been my destiny. One quick thrust of the blade into my heart should release me."

It was what Luce needed to hear. The dagger trembled as Dee guided it toward the tattoo on her chest. The old woman could steady Luce only so much, though; Luce knew that soon she would have to hold the blade alone.

"You're doing fine."

"Wait!" Luce cried as the blade pricked Dee's flesh. A red dot of blood bloomed on her skin, just above the hem of the tunic. "What will happen to you when you die?"

Dee smiled so peacefully that Luce had no doubt it

was for her benefit. "Why, dear, I shall slip into the masterpiece."

"You'll go to Heaven, won't you?"

"Lucinda, let's not talk of—"

"Please. I can't send you out of this life unless I know what your next one will look like. Will I see you again? Do you just go away like an angel?"

"Oh no, my death will be a secret life, like sleep," Dee said. "Better than sleep, actually, because for once I shall be able to dream. In life, transeternals never dream. I shall dream of Dr. Otto. It's been so long since I have seen my love, Lucinda. Surely you can understand?"

Luce wanted to weep. She understood. Of course she understood that much.

Trembling ever harder, she drew the knife back over the tattoo on Dee's breast. The old woman gave her hands the softest squeeze. "Bless you, child. Bless you abundantly. Hurry up, now." Dee looked anxiously at the sky, blinking at the moon. "In you go."

Luce grunted as she plunged the knife into the old woman's chest. The blade ground through flesh and bone and muscle—and then it was inside her beautiful heart, up to the hilt. Luce's and Dee's faces were almost touching. The clouds their breaths made mingled in the air.

Dee gritted her teeth and gripped Luce's hand as she gave the blade a sharp twist to the left. Her gold eyes widened, then froze in pain or shock. Luce wanted to look away but couldn't. She searched for the scream inside her.

"Expel the blade," Dee whispered. "Pour my blood into the Silver Pennon."

Wincing, Luce yanked the dagger out. She felt something deep inside Dee rip apart. The wound was a yawning black cavern. Blood streamed to its surface. It was terrifying to see Dee's gold eyes go cloudy. The lady fell in a heap on the moonlit plateau.

In the distance, the shriek of a Scale rang out. All the angels looked above.

"Luce, we need you to move quickly," Daniel said, his forced calmness sparking more alarm in her than open panic would.

Luce still held the dagger in her hands. It was slick and red and dripping with transeternal blood. She tossed it to the ground. It landed with a tinny clank that made her furious because it sounded like a toy instead of the mighty weapon that had killed two souls Luce loved.

She wiped her bloody hands on her cloak. She gasped for air. She would have fallen to her knees if Daniel hadn't caught her.

"I'm sorry, Luce." He kissed her, his eyes beaming their old tenderness.

"For what?"

"That I couldn't help you do it."

"Why couldn't you?"

"You did what none of us could do. You did it on your own." Taking her by the shoulders, Daniel turned Luce toward the sight she did not want to see.

"No. Please, don't make me—"

"Look," Daniel said.

Dee was sitting up, cradling the Silver Pennon in her arms so that its rim pressed against her breast. Blood poured from her heart freely, surging with each powerful beat, as if it were not blood but something magical and strange from another world. Luce supposed it was. Dee's eyes were closed but she was beaming, her face lifted, lit up by the moon. She didn't look like she had ever been in any pain.

When the goblet was filled, Luce stepped forward, bending down to take it and place it back on the yellow arrow on the Slab. When she wrested the Silver Pennon from Dee, the old woman tried to stand. Her bloody hands pressed into the ground to prop her up. Her knees trembled as she struggled to one foot, then the other. She slouched forward, her body convulsing slightly, as she took the black cloak in her hands. She was trying to drape it back over her shoulders, Luce realized, so that her wound would be covered. Arriane stepped forward to help her, but it didn't matter. Fresh blood flooded through the cloak.

Dee's gold eyes were paler, her skin almost translucent.

Everything about her seemed muted and soft, as if she were already someplace else. A new sob rose in Luce's chest as Dee took a halting step toward her.

"Dee!" Luce closed the gap between them, holding out her arms to catch the dying woman. Her body felt like a shard of what she'd been before Luce had taken the dagger in her hands.

"Shhh," Dee cooed. "I only wanted to thank you, dear. And to give you this small parting gift." She reached inside her cloak. When she withdrew her hand, her thumb was dark with blood. "The gift of self-knowledge. You must remember how to dream what you already know. Now it's time for me to sleep and for you to wake up."

Dee's eyes swept over Luce's face, and it seemed like she could see everything there was to see about her—all her past and all her future. Finally, she daubed the center of Luce's forehead with her bloody thumb.

"Enjoy it, dear."

Then she hit the ground.

"Dee!" Luce lunged for her, but the old woman was dead. *"No!"*

Behind Luce, Daniel clasped her shoulders with his hands, giving her all the strength he could. It wasn't enough. It couldn't bring Dee back or change the fact that Luce had killed her. Nothing could.

Tears blurred Luce's eyes. Wind swept in from the west and whistled off the curving cliffs, bringing with it another shriek of Scale. It felt like every inch of the world was in chaos, and nothing would ever settle down. She reached up and touched the bloody thumbprint on her forehead—

White light blazed around her. Her insides seared with heat. She staggered, holding her arms out in front of her and swaying as her body filled with . . .

Light.

"Luce?" Daniel's voice sounded far away.

Was she dying?

She felt suddenly galvanized, as if the thumbprint on her forehead were an ignition switch and Dee had launched her soul.

"Is this another timequake?" she asked, though the sky was not gray but a brilliant white. So bright she couldn't see Daniel or any of the other angels around her on the slab.

"No." Roland's voice. "It's her."

"It's you, Luce." Daniel's voice trembled.

Her feet skimmed the stone as her body rose in a splendor of weightlessness. For a moment, the world hummed with incandescent harmony.

Now it's time for you to wake up.

The air before Luce seemed to sputter, turning from white to blurry gray. Then deep in the distance came the vision of Bill's cackling face. His black wings spread wider than the sky, wider than a thousand galaxies, filling her mind, filling every crevice in the universe, engulfing Luce with infinite fury.

This time I will win.

His voice like shards of glass dragging across bare skin. How close was he now?

Luce's feet slammed into the mesa floor. The light was gone.

She fell to her knees, landing next to Dee, who had come to rest on her side, one arm slung out to cradle her head, her long red hair spilling out like blood. Her eyes were closed, her face serene, so unlike the face that had been haunting Luce for the past week. She tried to stand, but she felt clumsy.

Daniel dropped to his knees at her side. Sitting next to her on the Slab, he took her in his arms. The smell of his hair and the touch of his hands soothed her. He whispered, "I'm here, Luce, it's okay."

She didn't want to tell him she kept seeing Bill. She wanted to go back to that light. She touched the thumbprint on her forehead and nothing happened. Dee's blood was dry.

Daniel was staring at her, lips tight. He brushed the hair out of her eyes and pressed his palm to her forehead. "You're burning up."

"I'm fine." She did feel feverish, but there was no time to worry about that. She staggered to her feet and looked up at the moon.

It was directly overhead, in the center of the sky. This was the moment Dee had told them to wait for, the moment her death would become worthwhile.

"Luce. Daniel." Roland's voice. "You'd better look at this."

He held the goblet at an angle and was tipping the last of Dee's blood into the depression at the base of the map. When Luce and Daniel filed in next to the others, the blood had already flowed into most of the marble's broken lines. Though Dee had said that the Earth was different back at the time of the angels' Fall, the map before them looked increasingly similar to a contemporary map of the Earth.

South America was nearer to bumping against Africa. The northeast corner of North America nudged more closely to Europe, but mostly it was the same. There was the slip of water where the Gulf of Suez parted mainland Egypt from the Sinai Peninsula, and in the middle of the peninsula was the yellow stone marking the plateau where they were right now. To the north was the Mediterranean, dimpled with a thousand tiny islands—and on the other side of its narrow belt, at the point where Asia reached for Europe, was a shallow pool of blood sharpening slowly into a star.

Luce heard Daniel swallow at her side. The angels all looked stupefied as Dee's blood filled out the points of the star, indicating modern Turkey—more specifically—

"Troy," Daniel said finally, shaking his head in amazement. "Who would have guessed . . ."

"*There* again," Roland said, his tone conveying a tortured history with the city.

"I always got the sense that place was doomed." Arriane shivered. "But I—"

"Never knew why," Annabelle finished.

"Cam?" Daniel said, and the others looked away from the map to eye the demon.

"I'll go," Cam said quickly. "I'm fine."

"Then that's it," Daniel said as if he couldn't believe it. "Phillip," he called, looking upward.

Phil and his three Outcasts rose from their perches on the cliff peaks overhead.

"Alert the others."

What others? Who else was left by now? Luce thought.

"What will I tell them?" Phil asked.

"Tell them we know the site of the Fall, that we're leaving now for Troy."

"No." Luce's voice halted the Outcasts' movement. "We can't leave yet. What about Dee?"

⁂

In the end, it was no surprise that Dee had taken care of everything, down to the details for her memorial. Annabelle found them tucked into a slat on the roof of the creaky wooden trunk, which, as Dee's letter explained, flipped over to form a catafalque. The sun was low in the sky by the time they began to make her memorial. It was the end of the seventh day; Dee's letter assured them this wouldn't be a waste of their time.

Roland, Cam, and Daniel carried the catafalque to the center of the marble platform. They covered the map completely so that when the Scale descended there, they would see a funeral, not the site of the angels' Fall.

Annabelle and Arriane carried Dee's body behind the catafalque. They laid her carefully on its center, so that her heart was directly above the star of her blood. Luce remembered that Dee had said that sanctuaries were built on top of sanctuaries. Her body would form a sanctuary for the map it hid.

Cam draped Dee's cloak over her body, but he left her face exposed to the sky. In her final resting place, Dee, their desideratum, looked small but mighty. She looked at peace. Luce wanted to believe Dee was wandering through dreams with Dr. Otto.

"She wants Luce to be the one to bless her," Annabelle read from the letter.

Daniel squeezed her hand, as if to say, *Are you okay?*

Luce had never done anything like this before. She waited to feel awkward, guilty for speaking at the funeral for someone she had slain, but in those emotions' place sat a sense of honor and awe.

She stepped up to the catafalque. She gave herself a few moments to gather her thoughts.

"Dee was our desideratum," she began. "But she was more than one desired thing."

She took a breath and realized she wasn't blessing just
Dee, but also Gabbe and Molly, whose bodies were air—
and Penn, whose funeral she hadn't been able to attend.
It was all too much. Her vision swirled and the words
vanished and all she knew was that Dee had smeared sac-
rificial blood on Luce's forehead.

It was Dee's gift to Luce.

*You must remember how to dream what you already
know.*

Blood thrummed at her temples. Her head and her
heart were ablaze with heat, her hands icy as she wove
them through Dee's.

"Something's happening." Luce held her face in her
hands, her hair spilling down around her. She closed
her eyes and found bright white light on the backs of her
eyelids.

"Luce—"

When she opened her eyes, the angels had flung off
their cloaks and unfurled their wings. The mesa was
flooded with light. A great mass of Scale shrieked somewhere just above her.

"What's happening?" She shielded her eyes.

"We need to hurry, Daniel," Roland shouted from
above. Had the other angels already taken off? What was
the source of the light?

Daniel's arms wrapped around her waist. He held
her tightly. It felt good but she was still afraid.

"I'm here with you, Lucinda. I love you, no matter what."

She knew that her feet were drifting from the ground, that her body was taking flight. She knew she was with Daniel. But she was barely aware of their transit through the burning sky, barely aware of anything beyond the strange new pulsing in her soul.

SIXTEEN

APOCALYPSE

Somewhere along the way it started raining.

Raindrops pattered on Daniel's wings. Thunder rolled in the sky before them. Lightning ripped through the night. Luce had been sleeping, or in a heavy state of something similar to sleep, because when the storm came, she stirred to a dreamy half-awareness.

The headwind was brutal and incessant, flattening Luce against Daniel's body. The angels flew through it at a tremendous speed, every wingbeat thrusting them across whole cities, mountain ranges. They flew over clouds that looked like giant icebergs, passing them in the blink of an eye.

Luce didn't know where they were or how long they'd been traveling. She didn't feel like asking.

It was dark again. How much time remained? She couldn't remember. Counting seemed impossible, though Luce had once loved to solve complex calculus proofs. She almost laughed at the thought of sitting at a wooden desk in calculus, chewing on an eraser, next to twenty mortal kids. Had that ever really happened to her?

The temperature dropped. The rain intensified as the angels flew into a gale that stretched farther than her eye could see. Now the raindrops pelting Daniel's wings sounded like hail hitting icy snow.

The weather came sideways and upward. Luce's clothes were drenched. She felt hot one moment, frozen the next. Daniel's hands, encircling her body, rubbed goose bumps from her arms. She watched water streaming off the toes of her black boots toward the ground, thousands of feet below.

Visions appeared in the darkness through the storm. She saw Dee letting down red hair that swirled around her body. The old lady was whispering, *Break the curse.* Her hair became bloody tendrils, enclosing her like mummy wrap, then like a caterpillar's cocoon . . . until the body became a massive column of thick and dripping blood.

Through the mist, a golden light grew brighter. Cam's wings sharpened in the space between Luce's feet and the speck of land she had been watching.

"Is this it?" Cam shouted through the wind.

"I don't know," Daniel said.

"How *will* we know?"

"We just will."

"Daniel. The time—"

"Don't rush me. We have to get her to the right place."

"Is she asleep?"

"She's feverish. I don't know. Shhh."

A grunt of frustration accompanied the fading of Cam's glow back into the mist.

Luce's eyelids flickered. *Was* she asleep? The sky did seem to be raining nightmares. Now she saw Miss Sophia, her black eyes gleaming in the light reflected from the raindrops. She raised her dagger, and her pearl bracelets rattled as she brought the knife into Luce's heart. Her words—*Trust is a careless pursuit*—echoed again and again in Luce's mind until she wanted to scream. Then the vision of Miss Sophia flickered and swirled, darkening into the gargoyle who Luce *had* trusted, so carelessly.

Little Bill, who'd posed as a friend, all the while hiding something vast and terrifying. Maybe that was what friendship was to the devil: love always tinged with evil.

The gargoyle's body was a husk for forces darkly powerful.

In her vision, Bill bared rotten black fangs and exhaled clouds of rust. He roared, but silently, a silence that was worse than anything he ever could have said, because her imagination filled the void. He consumed her plane of vision as Lucifer, as Evil, as the End.

She snapped open her eyes. She clasped her hands over Daniel's arms around her as they flew through the endless storm.

You're not afraid, she vowed silently in the rain. It was the hardest of the things she'd had to convince herself of on this journey.

When you face him again, you will not be afraid.

※ ※

"Guys," Arriane said, appearing on the right side of Daniel's wings. "Look."

The clouds thinned as they drove onward. Below them was a valley, a broad stretch of rocky farmland that met a narrow strait of sea on its west side. A huge wooden horse stood absurdly in the barren landscape, a monument to a shadowed past. Luce could make out stony ruins near the horse, a Roman theater, a contemporary parking lot.

The angels flew on. The valley spread out below, dark but for a single light in the distance: an electric lamp that shone through the window of a tiny hut in the center of the slope.

"Fly toward the house," Daniel called to the others.

Luce had been watching a line of goats drift across the sodden fields, gathering in a grove of apricot trees. Her stomach lurched as Daniel swooped suddenly down. When they touched the ground, Luce and the angels were about a quarter of a mile from the white hut.

"Let's go inside." Daniel took her hand. "They'll be waiting for us."

Luce walked next to Daniel through the rain, her dark hair splayed across her face, her borrowed coat drenched with what felt like a thousand pounds of raindrops.

They were trudging up a winding muddy path when a large drop of water clung to Luce's eyelashes and dripped inside her eye. When she rubbed it away and blinked, the Earth had utterly changed.

An image flashed before her eyes, a long-forgotten memory returning to life:

The wet ground beneath her feet had gone from green to singed black in one place, ashen gray in another. The valley surrounding them was pocked with deep, smoking craters. Luce smelled carnage, roasted flesh and rot so thick and sharp it burned her nostrils and clung to the roof of her mouth. Craters sizzled, sounding like rattlesnakes, as she walked past. Dust—angel dust—was everywhere. It floated through the air, coated the ground and rocks, fell like snowflakes on her face.

Something silver was in her peripheral vision. It looked like broken pieces of a mirror, except that it was phosphorescent—shimmering, almost alive. Luce dropped Daniel's hand, fell to her knees, and crawled along the muddy ground toward the broken silver glass.

She didn't know why she did this. She only knew she had to touch it.

She reached for a large piece, groaning with the effort. She had her hand firmly around it—

And then she blinked and came up with nothing but a fistful of soft mud.

She looked up at Daniel, her eyes filled with tears. "What's happening?"

He glanced at Arriane. "Get Luce inside."

She felt herself being lifted by the arms. "You'll be okay, kiddo," Arriane said. "Promise."

The dark wood door of the hut opened and a warm light poured out from within. Peering out at the wet angels was the calm, collected face of Steven Filmore, Luce's favorite teacher from Shoreline.

"Glad you could make it," Daniel said.

"Same to you." Steven's voice was steady and professorial, just as Luce remembered. Somehow it was reassuring.

"Is she all right?" Steven asked.

No. She was losing it.

"Yes." Daniel's confidence took Luce by surprise.

"What happened to her neck?"

"We ran into some Scale in Vienna."

Luce was hallucinating. She was not all right. Trembling, she met Steven's eyes. They were steady, comforting.

You are all right. You have to be. For Daniel.

Steven held open the door and led them inside. The small hut had a dirt floor and straw roof, a heap of blankets and rugs in one corner, a crude cooking stove near the fire, and a square of four rocking chairs in the center of the room.

Standing in front of the chairs was Francesca—Steven's wife and the other Nephilim teacher at Shoreline. Phil and the other three Outcasts stood alert along the opposite wall of the hut. Annabelle, Roland, Arriane, Daniel, and Luce all crammed into the firelit warmth of the house.

"What now, Daniel?" Francesca asked, all business.

"Nothing," Daniel said quickly. "Nothing yet."

Why not? Here they were on the fields of Troy, near the place where Lucifer was expected to land. They'd raced here to stop him. Why go through everything they'd gone through this week just to sit around in a cabin and wait?

"Daniel," Luce said. "I could use some explanation."

But Daniel only looked to Steven.

"Please have a seat." Steven steered Luce to one of the rocking chairs. She sank into it, and nodded thanks when he handed her a metal cup of spicy Turkish apple tea. He gestured around at the hut. "It isn't much, but it keeps the rain and most of the wind out, and you know what they say—"

"Location, location, location," Roland finished, leaning on the arm of the rocking chair where Arriane had curled up across from Luce.

Annabelle looked around at the rain wailing on the window, at the cramped room. "So *this* is the Fall site? I mean, I can kind of feel it, but I don't know if that's because I'm trying so hard. This is *weird*."

Steven was polishing his glasses on his fisherman's sweater. He slipped them back onto his nose, resuming his professorial tone. "The Fall site is very large, Annabelle. Think of the space required for one hundred and fifty million, eight hundred and twenty-seven thousand, eight hundred and sixty-one—"

"You mean one hundred and fifty million, eight hundred and twenty-seven thousand, *seven hundred and forty-six*—" Francesca interrupted.

"Of course, there are discrepancies." Steven always humored his beautiful, combative wife. "The point is many angels fell, so the impact site is vast." He glanced, very quickly, at Luce. "But yes, you are sitting in a portion of the place where the angels fell to Earth."

"We followed the old broad's map," Cam said, poking

at the fire in the stove. It had burned down to cinders, but his touch brought it roaring back to life. "But I still wonder how we know for sure that this is it. There's not much time left. How do we *know*?"

Because I'm seeing visions of it, Luce's mind suddenly screamed. *Because somehow, I was there.*

"I'm glad you asked." Francesca spread a scroll of parchment on the floor between the rocking chairs. "The Nephilim library at Shoreline has one map of the Fall site. The map was drawn at so close a range that until someone could determine a geographical location, it could have been anywhere."

"It might as well have been an ant farm," Steven added. "We've been awaiting Daniel's signal since Luce came back through the Announcers, tracking your progress, trying to stay within reach for when you needed us."

"The Outcasts found us at our winter home in Cairo just after midnight." Francesca drew her shoulders together, as if she were warding off a shudder. "Luckily, this one had your pennon or we might have—"

"His name is Phillip. The Outcasts are with us now," Daniel said.

It was strange that Phil had posed as a student at Shoreline for months and Francesca didn't recognize him. Then again, the snobbish angel teacher paid attention only to the "gifted" students at the school.

"I'd hoped you would be able to make it in time," Daniel said. "How were things at Shoreline when you left?"

"Not good," Francesca said. "Worse for you, I'm sure, but still, not good for us. The Scale came through Shoreline on Monday."

Daniel's jaw clenched. "No."

"Miles and Shelby," Luce gasped. "Are they okay?"

"Your friends are all fine. They couldn't find anything to charge us with—"

"That's right," Steven said proudly. "My wife runs a tight ship. Above reproach."

"Still," Francesca said. "The students were very alarmed. Some of our biggest donors pulled their children from the school." She paused. "I hope this is worth it."

Arriane shot to her feet. "You bet your bangles it will be worth it."

Roland stood up quickly and tugged Arriane back to her seat. Steven took Francesca's arm and pulled her over to the window. Soon everyone was whispering and Luce didn't have enough strength to hear more than Arriane's loud "I got her big donation right here."

Out the window, the slenderest band of russet light hugged the mountains. Luce stared at it, her stomach knotted, knowing it marked the sunrise of the eighth day, the last full day before—

Daniel's hand was on her shoulder, warm and strong. "How are you doing, there?"

"I'm fine." She sat up straighter, feigning alertness. "What do we need to do next?"

"Sleep."

She straightened her shoulders. "No, I'm not tired. The sun's rising, and Lucifer—"

Daniel leaned over the rocking chair and kissed her forehead. "It will go better if you're rested."

Francesca looked up from her conversation with Steven. "Do you think that's a good idea?"

"If she's tired, she needs to sleep. A few hours won't hurt. We're already here."

"But I'm *not* tired," she protested, though it was obvious she was lying.

Francesca swallowed. "I guess you're right. It's either going to happen or it's not."

"What does she mean?" Luce asked Daniel.

"Nothing," he said softly. Then, turning to Francesca, he said very quietly, "It's *going* to happen." He lifted Luce enough so he could slide into the rocking chair beside her. He wrapped his arms around her waist. The last things she felt were his kiss on her temple and his whisper in her ear. "Let her have one last sleep."

⁂

"Are you ready?"

Luce stood beside Daniel in a fallow plot of farmland

outside the white hut. Mist rose from the soil, and the sky was the sharp blue color of a heavy storm's wake. There was snow in the hills to the east, but the sloping plains of the valley exuded springlike warmth. Flowers bloomed on the fringes of the field. Butterflies were everywhere, white and pink and gold.

"Yes."

Luce had been awake only an instant when she felt Daniel lift her from the rocking chair and out the door of the quiet hut. He must have held her in his arms all night.

"Wait," she said. "Ready for what?"

The others were watching her, gathered in a circle as if they had been waiting, the angels and Outcasts all with their wings extended.

A cloud of storks crossed the sky, their black-tipped wings spread wide as palm fronds. Their flight darkened the sun for a moment, casting shadows on the angels' wings, before the birds moved on.

"Tell me who I am," Daniel said plainly.

He was the only angel with his wings concealed inside his clothes. He stepped away from her, rolled back his shoulders, closed his eyes, and released his wings.

They unfurled swiftly, with supreme elegance, blooming out on either side of him and sending back a gust of wind that swayed the boughs of the apricot trees.

Daniel's wings towered over his body, radiant and wondrous, making him look unfathomably beautiful. He

shone like a sun—not only his wings, his whole body—
and even more than that. What the angels called their
glory radiated from Daniel. Luce couldn't take her eyes
off him.

"You're an angel."

He opened his violet eyes.

"Tell me more."

"You're—you're Daniel Grigori," Luce continued.
"You're the angel who has loved me for thousands of
years. You're the boy I've loved back from the moment—
no, from *every* moment I first saw you." She watched the
sun play off the whiteness of his wings, yearned to feel
them wrap around her. "You are the soul that fits into
mine."

"Good," Daniel said. "Now, tell me who *you* are."

"Well . . . I'm Lucinda Price. I'm the girl you fall in
love with."

There was a tense stillness all around them. All the
angels seemed to hold their breath.

Daniel's violet eyes filled with tears. He whispered:
"More."

"Isn't that enough?"

He shook his head.

"Daniel?"

"Lucinda."

The way he said her name—so gravely—made her
stomach ache. What did he want from her?

She blinked, and it sounded like a thunderbolt—and then the Trojan plain went black like it had the night before. The earth was marred by crooked fissures. Smoking craters stood where the field had been. Dust and ash and death were everywhere. The trees were on fire along the horizon, and a foul belch of rot rolled in on the wind. It was as if her soul had been hurled millennia back in time. There was no snow in the mountains, no tidy white hut before her, no circle of angels' worried faces.

But there was Daniel.

His wings shone through the dusty air. His bare skin was perfect, dewy, pink. His eyes glowed with the same intoxicating violet, but he wasn't looking at her. He was looking at the sky. He didn't seem to know that Luce was next to him.

Before she could follow his gaze upward, the world began to swirl. The scent on the air changed from rot to arid dust. She was back in Egypt, in the dark tomb where she'd been locked away and almost lost her soul. That scene played out before her eyes: the starshot warm inside her dress, the panic clear on her past face, the kiss that brought her back—and Bill flitting around the pharaoh's sarcophagus, already forming his most ambitious scheme. Her ears rang with his craggy laughter.

And then the laughter was gone. The vision of Egypt morphed into another: A Lucinda from an even more distant past lay prone in a field of high flowers. She wore a deerskin dress and held a daisy over her face, picking off the petals one by one. The last one wobbled in the wind and she thought, *He loves me.* The sun was blinding until something crossed before it. Daniel's face, his eyes brimming violet love, his blond hair sculpting a halo from the rays of the sun.

He smiled.

Then his face disappeared. A new vision, another life: the heat of a bonfire on her skin, desire burning in her chest. There were strange, loud music; people laughing; friends and family all around. Luce saw herself with Daniel, dancing wildly around the flames. She could feel the rhythms of the movements deep within her, even as the music faded and the flames licking the sky shifted from hot red to silvery softness—

A waterfall. A long, lush drop of icy water down a limestone cliff. Luce was underneath it, parting a cloud of water lilies with her strokes. Her long, wet hair gathered around her shoulders as she rose above the water, then dipped below. She came up on the other side of the waterfall's torrent, in a humid stone lagoon. And there was Daniel, waiting as if he'd been waiting for her all his life.

He dove from a rock, splashing her when his body struck the water. He swam toward her, drawing her to him, one arm around her back and the other cradled under her knees. She laced her hands around his neck and let him kiss her. She closed her eyes—

Boom.

The thunderbolt again. Luce was back on the smoking Trojan plain. But this time, she was trapped in one of the craters, her body pinned beneath a boulder. She couldn't move her left arm or leg. She struggled, crying out, seeing spots of red and shards of something that looked like a broken mirror. Her head swirled with the most intense pain she had ever felt.

"Help!"

And then: Daniel hovering over her, his violet eyes roving her body in unblinking horror. *"What happened to you?"*

Luce didn't know the answer—didn't know where she was or how she had gotten there. The Lucinda of her memory didn't even recognize Daniel. But she did.

Suddenly, she realized that this was the very first time she and Daniel had met on Earth. This was the moment she'd been begging for, the moment Daniel would never talk about.

Neither recognized the other. They were already, instantly, in love.

How could *this* be the place of their first meeting? This plagued dark landscape reeked of filth and death. Her past self looked beaten, bloodied—like she had been shattered into a thousand pieces.

Like she had fallen from an unfathomable height.

Luce glanced at the sky. Something was there—a mass of infinitesimal sparks, as though Heaven had been electrocuted and shock waves would ripple from it for the rest of time.

Except the sparks were drawing nearer. Dark forms limned with light tumbled from an infinity above. There must have been a million of them gathered in a chaotic, amorphous band across the sky, dark and light, suspended and falling simultaneously, as if beyond the reach of gravity.

Had Luce been up there? She felt almost as if she had.

Then she realized something: *Those were the angels. This was the Fall.*

The memory of witnessing their fall to Earth agonized Luce. It was like watching all the stars fall out of the night sky.

The farther they fell, the looser their aimless formation became. Single entities became visible, autonomous. She couldn't imagine any of her angels, her friends, ever looking like this. More lost and out of control than the most destitute mortal on the worst day of his life. Was Arriane among them? Was Cam?

Her gaze traced one orb of light directly overhead. It grew larger and brighter as it approached.

Daniel looked up, too. Luce realized he didn't recognize the falling forms, either. His impact on Earth had shuddered through him so thoroughly that it had erased his memory of who he was, where he'd come from, how magnificent he used to be. He watched the sky with raw terror in his eyes.

A smattering of falling angels were hundreds of feet above their heads one second . . . then close enough that Luce could make out the strange, dark bodies within their vessels of light. The bodies did not move but seemed undeniably alive.

Closer they fell, bearing down on Luce until she screamed—and the great mass of dark and light crashed into the field beside her.

An explosion of fire and black smoke knocked Daniel out of Luce's sight. More were coming. Over a million more were coming. They would pummel the Earth and every living thing on it to a pulp. Luce ducked and shielded her eyes and opened her mouth to scream again.

But the sound that came out was no scream—

Because the memory had shifted into something even further back. Further back than the Fall?

Luce was no longer in the field of smoking craters and meteoric angels.

She was standing in a landscape of pure light. Any terror in her voice did not belong here, could not have *existed* in this place, which she knew and did not know. She had a sense of where she was, but it couldn't possibly be real.

Streaming from her soul was a strong, rich chord of music so beautiful that it turned everything around her white. The crater was gone. The Earth was gone. Her body was—

She didn't know. She couldn't see it. She couldn't see anything but this fantastic silver-tinged white glow. The brightness unfolded like a package until Luce could make out a vast white meadow spread out before her. Splendid groves of white trees lined either side of the field.

In the distance was a rippling silver ledge. Luce sensed it was important. Then she saw that there were seven more of them, forming a grand arch in the air around something so bright Luce couldn't stand to look at it.

She focused on the ledge, the third one from the left. She could not wrest her gaze from it. Why?

Because . . . Her memory reeled back. . . . Because—

This ledge belonged to her.

Long before, she used to sit here, next to . . . whom? It seemed to matter.

Her vision swirled and faded and the silver ledge dissolved. The remaining whiteness focused, separating into shapes, into—

Faces. Bodies. Wings. A backdrop of blue sky.

This was not a memory. She was back in the present, her real and final life. Around her stood her teachers Francesca and Steven; her allies the Outcasts; her friends Roland, Arriane, Annabelle, and Cam. And her love, Daniel. She stared at each one of them and she found them so beautiful. They were watching her with dumb joy on their faces. They were also crying.

The gift of self-knowledge, Dee had told her. *You must remember how to dream what you already know.*

All this had been within her the whole time, in every instant of her every life. Yet only now did Luce feel awake beyond her capacity to imagine what it meant to be awake. A light wind blew across her skin and she could *feel* the distant sea carried on it from the Mediterranean, telling her she was still in Troy. Her vision, too, was clearer than it had ever been before. She saw brilliant dots of pigment making up the wings of a passing golden butterfly. She breathed in the cold air, filling her lungs, smelling the zinc in the loamy soil that would make it fertile in the spring.

"I was there," she whispered. "I was in—"

Heaven.

But she couldn't say it. She knew too much to deny it—and yet not enough to speak the words. Daniel. He would help her.

Go on, his eyes were pleading.

Where did she begin? She touched the locket with the picture taken when she and Daniel had lived in Milan.

"When I visited my past life in Helston," she began, "I learned that our love ran deeper than who we were in any single lifetime—"

"Yes," Daniel said. "Our love transcends everything."

"And . . . when I visited Tibet, I learned that a single touch or kiss was not the trigger to my curse."

"Not touch." Roland's voice. He was smiling, standing next to Daniel with his hands clasped behind his back. "Not touch but self-awareness. A level you weren't ready for—until now."

"Yes." Luce touched her forehead. There was more, so much more. "Versailles." She began to speak more quickly. "I was condemned to marry a man I didn't love. And your kiss released me, and my death was glorious because we would always find each other again. Forever."

"Together forever, whatever the weather," Arriane chimed in, swiping damp eyes on Roland's shirtsleeve.

By now Luce's throat felt so tight it was difficult to speak. But it was no longer sore. "I didn't realize until London that your curse was so much worse than mine," she said to Daniel. "What you had to go through, losing me—"

"It never mattered," Annabelle murmured, her wings buzzing so much that her feet were inches off the ground. "He would always wait for you."

"Chichén Itzá." Luce closed her eyes. "I learned that an angel's glory could be deadly to mortals."

"Yes," Steven said. "But you're still here."

"Keep going, Luce." Francesca's voice was more encouraging than it had ever been at Shoreline.

"Ancient China." She paused. This one's significance was different from the others. "You showed me that our love was more important than any arbitrary war."

No one spoke. Daniel gave the faintest nod.

And that was when Luce understood not just who she was—but what it all added up to. There was another lifetime from her voyage through the Announcers that Luce felt she had to mention. She took a breath.

Don't think of Bill, she told herself. *You are not afraid.*

"When I was locked in the tomb in Egypt, I knew once and for all that I would always choose your love."

That was when the angels dropped to one knee, gazing up at her expectantly—all of them except Daniel. His eyes glowed the most potent shade of violet she had ever seen. He reached for her, but before his hands met hers:

"Auugh!" Luce cried out as a sharp pain sliced through her back. Her body convulsed with a foreign, piercing sensation. Her eyes teared. Her ears rang. She thought she might be sick from the pain. But slowly, it localized, from an acute agony all over her back, into two small sections at the tops of her shoulder blades.

Was she bleeding? She reached back, over her shoulder. The wound felt tender and raw, and also as if something were being drawn out from within her. It didn't hurt, but it was bewildering. Panicked, she whirled her head around but she could see nothing, could only hear the sound of skin sliding and being stretched, the *thrrrrrp* that sounded like new muscles were being generated.

Then came a sudden feeling of heaviness, as if weights had been strapped around her shoulders.

And then—in her peripheral vision, vast billowing whiteness on either side of her as a collective gasp rose from the angels' lips.

"Oh, Lucinda," Daniel whispered, his hand covering his mouth.

It was this easy: She spread her wings.

They were luminous, buoyant, impossibly light, made of the finest, most reflective empyrean matter. From tip to tip, her wingspan was maybe thirty feet, but they felt vast, endless. She felt no more pain. When her fingers curled around the base of them behind her shoulders, they were several inches thick and plush. They were silver, yet not silver, like the surface of a mirror. They were inconceivable; they were inevitable.

They were her wings.

They contained every ounce of strength and empowerment she had amassed over the millennia she had lived. And at the slightest whim of a thought, her wings began to beat.

Her first thought: *I can do anything now.*

Wordlessly, she and Daniel reached for one another's hands. Their wings' top edges arched forward in a kind of kiss, like the angels' wings on the *Qayom Malak*. They were crying and laughing, and soon, they were kissing.

"So?" he asked.

She was stunned and amazed—and happier than she'd ever been before. It couldn't possibly be real, she thought—unless she spoke the truth aloud, with Daniel and the rest of the fallen angels there to witness.

"I'm Lucinda," she said. "I'm your angel."

SEVENTEEN

THE INVENTION OF LOVE

Flying was like swimming, and Luce was good at both.

Her feet lifted off the ground. It took no thought or preparation. Her wings beat with sudden intuition. Wind hummed against the fibers of her wings, carrying her in the gauzy pink sky. Aloft, she felt the weight of her body, especially in her feet, but overpowering that was a new, unimaginable buoyancy. She slid over low tiers of clouds, causing the slightest disruption, like a breeze passing through a chime.

She gazed from one wing tip to the other, examining their silver-pearl luster, in awe of all her changes. It was as if the rest of her body deferred to her wings now. They responded at the first inkling of desire with elegant strokes that generated tremendous velocity. They flattened like an airfoil to glide solely on momentum, then pulled back into a heart shape behind her shoulders as she swizzled straight into the air.

Her first flight.

Except . . . it wasn't. What Luce knew now, as keenly as her wings knew how to fly, was that there had been a monumental *before*. Before Lucinda Price, before her soul had ever seen the curving Earth. For all the lives on Earth she'd witnessed in the Announcers, all the bodies she had inhabited, Luce had barely scratched the surface of who she was, who she had been. There was a history older than history during which she'd beat these wings.

She could see the others watching her from the ground. Daniel's face shone with tears. He had known this all along. He had waited for her. She wanted to reach him, wanted him to soar up and fly with her—but then, suddenly, she couldn't see him anymore.

The light gave way to the total darkness . . .

Of another memory crashing through.

She closed her eyes and surrendered to it, letting it carry her back. Somehow she knew that this was the earliest memory, the moment at the furthest reaches of her soul. Lucinda had been there from the beginning of the beginning.

The Bible had left this part out:

Before there was light, there were angels. One moment, darkness; the next, the warm feeling of being coaxed out of inexistence by a gentle, magnificent hand.

God created the Heavenly host of angels—all three hundred and eighteen million of them—in a single, brilliant moment. Lucinda was there, and Daniel, and Roland and Annabelle and Cam—and millions more, all perfect, all glorious, all designed to adore their Creator.

Their bodies were made of the same substance that composed the firmament of heaven. They were not flesh and blood, but empyreal matter, the stuff of light itself—strong, indestructible, beautiful to behold. Their shoulders, arms, and legs shimmered into being, foreshadowing the shapes mortals would take upon their own creation. The angels all discovered their wings simultaneously, each pair slightly different, reflecting the soul of its possessor.

As early as the angels' genesis, Lucinda's wings were bright reflective silver, the color of starlight. They had shone in their singular glory since the dawn of the dawn of time.

Creation occurred at the speed of God's will, but it unfolded in Luce's memory like a story, another of God's earliest creations, a by-product of time. One moment there was nothing; then Heaven was replete with angels. In those days, Heaven was limitless, its ground covered by cloudsoil, a soft white substance like misty cloud that covered the angels' feet and wing tips when they walked along the ground.

There were endless tiers in Heaven, each level teeming with alcoves and winding paths fanning out in all directions under a honey-colored sky. The air was perfumed with nectar welling in delicate white flowers springing up in delightful groves. Their round blooms dotted all of Heaven's nooks and crannies, looking something like ancestors of white peonies.

Orchards of silver trees bore the most delicious fruits that had ever existed. The angels feasted and gave thanks for their first and only home. Their voices joined together in praise of their Creator, forming a blended sound that in humans' throats would later be known as harmony.

A meadow rolled into existence, dividing the orchard in two. And when everything else in Heaven was complete, God placed a stunning Throne at the head of the meadow. It pulsed with divine light.

"Come before me," God commanded, settling into the deep seat with deserved satisfaction. "Henceforth you will know me as the Throne."

The angels gathered on the plain of Heaven and approached the Throne in gladness. They flowed naturally into a single line, ranking themselves instantly and forevermore. By the time they neared the edge of the meadow, Lucinda remembered that she could not clearly see the Throne. It shone too brightly for angels' eyes to withstand. She also remembered that she had once been the third angel in line—the third angel closest to God.

One, two, three.

Her wings stretched and thickened with the honor.

In the air over the Throne, eight ledges made of rippled silver hung in an arch, like a canopy sheltering the Throne. God called the first eight angels in the line to fill these seats and become the Throne's Archangels. Lucinda took her place on the third seat from the left. It fit her body precisely, having been created just for her. This was where she belonged. Adoration poured from her soul, flowing to God.

It was perfect.

It did not last.

God had more plans for the universe. Another memory filled Lucinda, causing her to shiver.

God left the angels.

All was joyful in the Meadow, and then the Throne became empty. God walked past the thresholds of Heaven, went away to create the stars and the Earth and the moon.

Man and woman hovered near the brink of existence.

Heaven dimmed when God left it. Lucinda felt cold

and useless. It was then, she remembered, that the angels began to see one another differently, to notice the variations in color among their wings. Some began to gossip that God had wearied of them and their harmonizing songs of praise. Some said that humans would soon take the angels' place.

Lucinda remembered reclining in her silver seat next to the Throne. She remembered noticing how simple and dull it looked without God's animating presence. She tried to adore her Creator from afar, but she couldn't replace her loneliness. Adoration in God's presence was what she had been designed for and all she felt now was a hole. What could she do?

She looked down from her chair and saw an angel roaming the cloudsoil. He looked lethargic, melancholy. He seemed to feel her gaze on him and looked up. When their eyes met, he smiled. She remembered how beautiful he'd been before God had gone away. . . .

They did not think. They reached for one another. Their souls entwined.

Daniel, Luce thought. But she couldn't be sure. The Meadow had been dim and her memory was foggy. . . .

Was this the moment of their first connection?

Flash.

The Meadow was bright white again. Time had passed; God had returned. The Throne blazed with sublime glory. Lucinda no longer sat upon her rippling silver chair beside the Throne. She was crammed into the Meadow with the full host of angels, being asked to choose something.

The Roll Call. Lucinda had been there, too. Of course she had. She felt hot and nervous without knowing why. Her body flushed the way it used to when she was inside a past self and on the brink of dying. She could not still her trembling wings.

She had chosen—

Her stomach dropped. The air felt thin. She was . . . falling. Luce blinked and saw the sun clipping the mountains and she knew that she was back in the present, back in Troy. And falling from the sky, twenty feet . . . forty. Her arms flailed, as if she were a mere girl again, as if she couldn't fly.

She spread her wings, but it was too late.

She landed with a soft thump in Daniel's arms. Her friends surrounded her on the grassy plain. Everything was just as it had been before: flat-topped cedar trees around a muddy, fallow farm; abandoned hut in the middle of barren expanse; purple hills; butterflies. Faces of fallen angels watching over her, filled with concern.

"Are you all right?" Daniel asked.

Her heart was still racing. Why couldn't she remember what had happened at the Roll Call? Maybe it wouldn't help them stop Lucifer, but Luce desperately wanted to know.

"I came so close," she said. "I almost understood what happened."

Daniel set her softly on the ground and kissed her. "You will get there, Luce. I know you will."

It was dusk on the eighth day of their journey. As the sun slipped over the Dardanelles, casting gold light on the sloping fallow fields, Luce wished there was a way to draw it backward.

What if one day wasn't enough time?

Luce hunched and unhunched her shoulders. She wasn't used to the weight of her wings, light as rose petals in the sky, but heavy as lead curtains when her feet were on the ground.

When her wings first unfurled, they'd torn through her T-shirt and the khaki army jacket. The clothes lay on the grass in shreds, strange proof. Annabelle had quickly emerged from the hut with an extra T-shirt. It was electric blue with a silk-screened image of Marlene Dietrich on the chest, subtle wing slits tailored into the back.

"Instead of thinking of all that you don't yet remember," Francesca said, "recognize what you *have* come to know."

"Well." Luce paced the meadow, feeling the new sensation of her wings bobbing behind her. "I know that the curse prevented me from knowing my true nature as an angel, caused me to die whenever I began to approach a memory of my past. That's why none of you could tell me who I was."

"You had to walk that lonesome valley by yourself," Cam said.

"And the reason it took you until this lifetime was also part of your curse," Daniel said.

"This time I was raised without one specific religion, without a single set of rules determining my destiny, which allows me to"—Luce paused, thinking back to the Roll Call—"choose for myself."

"Not everyone has that luxury." Phil spoke up from the line of Outcasts.

"That's why the Outcasts wanted me?" she asked, knowing suddenly it was true. "But haven't I already chosen Daniel? I couldn't remember before, but when Dee gave me her gift of knowledge, it seemed like"—she reached for Daniel—"the choice was always already there inside of me."

"You know who you are now, Luce," Daniel said. "You know what matters to you. Nothing should be beyond your grasp."

Daniel's words seeped into her. This was what she was now—it was what she *always* had been.

Her gaze moved to where the Outcasts stood at a distance from the group. Luce didn't know how much they could have seen of her transformation, whether their blind eyes could perceive a soul's metamorphosis. She watched for a sign in Olianna, the female Outcast who'd guarded Luce on the rooftop in Vienna. But as she stared at Olianna, she realized Olianna had also . . . changed.

"I remember you," Luce said, walking closer to the thin blond girl with the cavernous white eyes. She knew her, from Heaven. "Olianna, you were one of the Twelve Angels of the Zodiac. You ruled over Leo."

Olianna took a deep, shuddering breath and nodded. "Yes."

"And you, Phresia. You were a Luminary." Luce closed her eyes, remembering. "Weren't you one of the Four who emanated from Divine Will? I remember your wings. They were"—she halted, feeling her expression darken at the sight of the drab brown wings the girl bore now—"exceptional."

Phresia straightened her slumped shoulders, raised her pale gaunt face. "No one has truly seen me in ages."

Vincent, the youngest-looking of the Outcasts, stepped forward. "And me, Lucinda Price? Do you remember me?"

Luce reached out and touched the boy's shoulder, remembering how deathly sick he'd looked after the Scale had tortured him. Then she remembered something deeper than that. "You are Vincent, Angel of the North Wind."

Vincent's blind eyes clouded, as if his soul wanted to cry but his body refused.

"Phil," Luce said, gazing finally at the Outcast she'd

feared so much when he came for her in her parents' backyard. His lips were taut and white, nervous. "One of Monday's Angels, weren't you? Instilled with the Powers of the Moon."

"Thank you, Lucinda Price." Phil bowed haltingly, but graciously. "The Outcasts confess, we were wrong to try to take you away from your soul mate and your obligations. But we knew, as you have just proven, that you alone could see us for who we used to be. And that you alone could restore us to our glory."

"Yes," she said. "I can see you."

"The Outcasts can see you, too," Phil said. "You are radiant."

"Yes, she is."

Daniel.

She turned to him. His blond hair and violet eyes, the strong cut of his shoulders, the full lips that had brought her back to life a thousand times. They had loved each other even longer than Luce had realized. Their love had been strong since the early days of Heaven. Their relationship spanned the entire story of existence. She knew where she'd first met Daniel on Earth—right here, on the singed fields of Troy while the angels were falling— but there was an earlier story. A different beginning to their love.

When? How had it happened?

She searched for the answer in his eyes—but she

knew she wouldn't find it there. She had to look back in her own soul. She closed her eyes.

The memories came easier now, as if her spreading wings had sent a web of fissures breaking through the wall between the girl Lucinda and the angel she had been before. Whatever separated her from her past was fragile now, as thin and brittle as an eggshell.

Flash.

Back on the Meadow, astride her silver ledge, aching for God to return. Luce was looking down at the fair-haired angel, the one she'd already remembered reaching for. She remembered his slow, sad steps on the cloudsoil. The crown of his head before he looked up. Heaven was quiet then. Luce and the angel were alone for a rare moment, away from the harmony of others.

He turned to look up at Lucinda. He had a square face, wavy amber hair, and blue eyes the color of ice. They crinkled when he smiled at her. She did not recognize him.

No, that wasn't it—she recognized him, knew him. Long before, Lucinda had *loved* this angel.

But he wasn't Daniel.

Without knowing why, Luce wanted to spin away from this memory, to pretend she hadn't seen it, to blink back and be with Daniel on the rocky plains of Troy. But her soul was welded to the scene. She could not turn away from this angel who was not Daniel.

He reached for her. Their wings entwined. He whispered in her ear:

"Our love is endless. There can be nothing else."

No.

At last, she jolted herself from the memory. Back at Troy. Out of breath. Her eyes must have betrayed her. She felt wild and panicked.

"What did you see?" Annabelle whispered.

Luce's mouth opened but no words came.

I betrayed him. Whoever he was. There was someone before Daniel, and I—

"It's not over yet." Finally, she found her voice. "The curse. Even though I know who I am and I know that I choose Daniel, there's something else, isn't there? Someone else. He's the one who cursed me."

Daniel ran his fingers very lightly over the shining border of her wings. She shivered, because every touch against her wings burned with the passion of a deep kiss and ignited something deep inside her. Finally she knew the pleasure she brought to him when she let her hands glide over his. "You have come so very far, Lucinda. But there is still a ways to go. Search your past. You already know what you are looking for. Find it."

She closed her eyes, searching again through millennia of fraught memories.

The Earth drew away beneath her feet. A maze of colors blurred around her, and her heart hammered in her chest, and everything went white.

Heaven again.

It was bright with God's return to the Throne. The sky shone the color of an opal. The cloudsoil was thick that day, tufts of white reaching nearly to the angels' waists. Those towering white spires to the right were trees in the Grove of Life; the silvery blossoms in full bloom to the left would soon bear the fruits of the Orchard of Knowledge. The trees were taller now. They'd had time to grow since Luce's last recollection.

She was back in the Meadow, in the center of a great, flickering congregation of light. The angels in Heaven were gathered before the Throne, which was restored to a brightness so intense Lucinda cringed to look at it.

The silver ledge that had once been Lucifer's had now been moved to the far end of the Meadow. It had been lowered to an insulting level by the Throne. Between Lucifer and the Throne the rest of the angels were united in a single mass—but soon, Lucinda realized, they would be partitioned off to one side or the other.

She was back at the Roll Call. This time she would force herself to remember how it went.

Every son and every daughter of Heaven would be asked to choose a side. God or Lucifer. Good or . . . no, he wasn't evil.

Evil didn't exist yet.

Crowded together like that, every angel was stunning, distinct but somehow indistinguishable from the next. There was Daniel, in the center, the purest glow she would ever know. In her memory, Lucinda was moving toward him.

Moving from where?

Daniel's voice filled her ears: *Search your past.*

She hadn't looked at Lucifer yet. She didn't want to.

Look where you do not want to look.

When she turned to the far end of the Meadow, she saw the light around Lucifer. It was splendid and ostentatious, as if he sought to compete with everything in the Meadow—the Orchard, the Heavenly hum, the Throne itself. Lucinda had to focus hard to see him clearly.

He was . . . lovely. Amber hair spilled down his shoulders in shiny waves. His body seemed grander, defined by muscle no mortal would ever achieve. His cold blue eyes were mesmerizing.

Lucinda couldn't take her eyes off him. Then, between bars of the Heavenly hum, she heard it. Though she didn't remember learning the song, she knew the words and would always know them, the way mortals carried nursery rhymes through their lives.

Of all the pairs the Throne endorsed
None rose to burn as bright
As Lucifer, the Morning Star,
And Lucinda, his Evening Light

The lines echoed in her head, drawing memory to them, recollection raining down with every word.

Lucinda, his Evening Light?

Lucinda's soul crawled, sickened, toward a realization. Lucifer had written this song. It was a part of his design.

She was . . . had she been *Lucifer's* lover?

The moment she wondered whether that horror was possible, Luce knew it was the oldest, coldest truth. She had been wrong about everything. Her first love had been Lucifer, and Lucifer had been hers. Even their names were paired. Once, they had been soul mates. She felt twisted, foreign to herself, as if she'd awakened to realize she had killed someone in her sleep.

Across the Meadow, Lucinda and Lucifer locked eyes at the Roll Call. Hers widened in disbelief as his crinkled up in an inscrutable smile.

Flash.

A memory inside a memory. Luce tunneled even further through the darkness, to the place where she most loathed to go.

Lucifer held her, his wings caressing hers, creating unmentionable pleasure, openly, there on her silver seat around the empty Throne.

Our love is endless. There can be nothing else.

When he kissed her, Lucinda and Lucifer became the first beings to experiment with affection beyond God.

The kisses had been strange and wonderful and Lucinda had wanted more, but she feared what the other angels would think of Lucifer's kisses on her. She worried that his kiss would look like a brand on her lips. Most of all, she feared God would know when God returned and resumed the title of the Throne.

"Say you adore me," Lucifer begged.

"Adoration is for God," Lucinda replied.

"It doesn't have to be," Lucifer whispered. "Imagine how strong we'd be if we could openly declare our love before the Throne, you adoring me, me adoring you. The Throne is only one—united in love, we could be greater."

"What's the difference between love and adoration?" Lucinda asked.

"Love is taking the adoration you feel for God and giving it to somebody actually *here*."

"But I don't want to be greater than God."

Lucifer's face darkened at her words. He spun away from her, rage taking root in his soul. Lucinda sensed a strange change within him, but it was so foreign she didn't recognize it. She began to fear him. He seemed to fear nothing, except her ever leaving him. He taught her the song about the greatness of their union. He made her sing it constantly, until Lucinda saw herself as Lucifer's Evening Light. He told Lucinda this was love.

Luce writhed with the pain of the memory. It went on and on like that with Lucifer. With every interaction, every caress of Lucinda's wings, he grew more possessive, more envious of her adoration of the Throne, telling Lucinda that if she truly loved him, Lucifer would be enough.

There was one day she remembered during that dark period: She'd been weeping in the Meadow, up to her neck in cloudsoil, wanting to sink away from everything. An angel's shadow hovered over her.

"Leave me alone!" she had cried.

But the wing that draped over hers did the opposite. It cradled her. The angel seemed to know what she needed better than she knew herself. Slowly, Lucinda lifted her head. The angel's eyes were violet.

"Daniel." She knew him as the sixth Archangel, charged with watching over lost souls. "Why have you come to me?"

"Because I have been watching you." Daniel stared and Luce knew that before then, no one had ever seen an angel cry. Lucinda's tears were the first. "What is happening to you?"

For a long time she searched for the words. "I feel like I'm losing my light."

The story poured out of her, and Daniel let it come. No one had listened to Lucinda in a very long time.

When she finished, Daniel's eyes were wet with tears.

"What you call love does not sound very beautiful," he said slowly. "Think of the way we adore the Throne. That adoration makes us the best versions of ourselves. We feel encouraged to go further with our instincts, not to change ourselves for love. If I were yours and you were mine, I would want you to be exactly as you are. I would never eclipse you with my desires."

Lucinda took Daniel's warm, strong hand. Maybe Lucifer had discovered love, but this angel seemed to understand how to build it into something wonderful.

Suddenly, Lucinda was kissing Daniel, showing him how it was done, needing for the first time to give her soul entirely to another. They held each other, Daniel's and Lucinda's souls glowing brighter, two halves made better as a whole.

Flash.

Of course, Lucifer came back to her. The rage within him had swelled so much that he was twice as tall as her. They had once stood eye to eye. "I can stand the yoke no longer. Will you come before the Throne with me and declare your sole allegiance to our love?"

"Lucifer, wait—" Lucinda wanted to tell him about Daniel, but he wouldn't have heard her anyway.

"It is a lie for me to play adoring angel when I have you and require nothing more. Let us make plans, Lucinda, you and I. Let us scheme for glory."

"How is that love?" she had cried. "You adore your

dreams, your ambition. You taught me how to love, but I cannot love a soul so dark it eats up others' light."

He did not believe her, or he pretended not to hear her, because Lucifer soon challenged the Throne to gather all the souls in the Meadow for the Roll Call. He'd held Lucinda in his grip when he made the challenge, but when he started to speak, he was distracted and she was able to slip away. She walked into the Meadow, wandered among bright souls. She saw the one she'd been seeking all along.

※ ※

Lucifer bellowed at the angels:

"A line has been drawn in the cloudsoil of the Meadow. Now you are all free to choose. I offer you equality, an existence without an authority's arbitrary rankings."

Luce knew he meant that she was only free to follow him. Lucifer might have thought he loved her, but what he loved was controlling her with a dark, destructive fascination. It was as if Lucifer thought Lucinda was an aspect of him.

She huddled next to Daniel in the Meadow, basking in the warmth of a burgeoning love that was pure and sustaining, as Daniel's name rang out across the Meadow. He had been called. He rose above the riot of angelic light and said with calm self-possession, "With respect, I will not do this. I will not choose Lucifer's side, nor will I choose the side of Heaven."

A roar went up from the vast camps of angels, from those who stood beside the Throne, from Lucifer most of all. Lucinda had been stunned.

"Instead, I choose *love*," Daniel went on. "I choose love and leave you to your war. You're wrong to bring this upon us," Daniel said to Lucifer.

Then, to the Throne: "All that is good in Heaven and on Earth is made of love. Maybe that wasn't your plan when you created the universe—maybe love was just one aspect of a complicated and brutal world. But love was the best thing you made, and it has become the only thing worth saving. This war is not just. This war is not good. Love is the only thing worth fighting for."

The Meadow fell silent after Daniel's words. Most of the angels looked dumbfounded, as if they did not understand what Daniel meant.

It had not been Lucinda's turn. The angels' names were called by the celestial secretaries according to their rank, and Lucinda was one of a handful of angels higher than Daniel. It didn't matter. They were a team. She rose to his side in the Meadow.

"There should never have to be a choice between love and You," Lucinda declared to the Throne. "Maybe one day You will find a way to reconcile adoration and the true love You have made us capable of. But if forced to choose, I must stand beside my love. I choose Daniel and will choose him forevermore."

Then Luce remembered the hardest thing she'd ever had to do. She turned to Lucifer, her first love. Without being honest with him, none of this would count. "You showed me the power of love, and for that I will always be grateful. But love ranks a distant third for you, far behind your pride and rage. You have begun a fight you can never win."

"I am doing all of this for you!" Lucifer shouted.

It was his first great lie, the universe's first great lie.

Arm in arm with Daniel in the center of the Meadow, Lucinda had made the only possible choice. Her fear paled in comparison to her love.

But she never could have anticipated the curse. Luce remembered now that the punishment had come from both sides. That was what had made the curse so binding: Both the Throne and Lucifer—out of jealousy or spite or a loveless view of justice—had sealed Daniel and Lucinda's fate for many thousands of years.

In the silence of the Meadow, a strange thing happened: *Another* Daniel soared up next to Lucinda and Daniel. He was an Anachronism—the Daniel she had met at Shoreline, the angel Luce Price knew and loved.

"I come here to beg clemency," Daniel's twinning spoke. "If we must be punished—and, my Master, I do not question your decision—please at least remember that one of the great features of Your power is Your mercy, which is mysterious and large and humbles us all."

At the time Lucinda had not understood this—but in Luce's memory, finally, everything made sense. He had given Luce the gift of a loophole in the curse, so that someday in the distant future, she could liberate their love.

The last thing she remembered was clutching Daniel tightly when the cloudsoil boiled black. The ground dropped out from under them and the angels began their fugue, their Fall. Daniel had slipped from her reach. Her body had fixed into immobility. She lost him. She lost all memory. She lost herself.

Until now.

When Luce opened her eyes, night had fallen. The air was so cool her arms were trembling. The others huddled around her, so quiet she could hear crickets whistling in the grass. She didn't want to look at anyone.

"It was because of me," she said. "All this time I thought they were punishing you, Daniel, but the punishment was for me." She paused. "Am I the reason Lucifer revolted?"

"No, Luce." Cam gave her a sad smile. "Maybe you were the inspiration, but inspiration is an excuse for doing something you already want to do. Lucifer was look-ing for an entrance into evil. He would have found another way."

"But I betrayed him."

"No," Daniel said. "He betrayed you. He betrayed all of us."

"Without his rebellion, would we have fallen in love?"

Daniel smiled. "I like to think we would have found a way. Now, finally, we have a chance to put all of this behind us. We have a chance to stop Lucifer, to break the curse and love each other the way we always wanted to. We can make all these years of suffering worthwhile."

"Look," Steven said, pointing at the sky.

The stars were out in droves. One, far in the dis-tance, was particularly bright. It flickered, then seemed to go out altogether before returning even brighter than before.

"That's them, isn't it?" she said. "The Fall?"

"Yes," Francesca said. "That's it. It looks just like the old texts say it would."

"It was just"—Luce furrowed her brow, squinting—"I can only see it when I—"

"Concentrate," Cam ordered.

"What's happening to it?" Luce asked.

"It is coming into being in this world," Daniel said. "It wasn't the physical transit from Heaven to Earth that took nine days. It was the shift from a Heavenly realm to an Earthly one. When we landed here, our bodies were . . . different. We became different. That took time."

"Now time is taking us," Roland said, looking at the golden pocket watch that Dee must have given him before she died.

"Then it is time for us to go," Daniel said to Luce.

"Up there?"

"Yes, we must soar up to meet them. We will fly right up to the limits of the Fall, and then you—"

"I have to stop him?"

"Yes."

She closed her eyes, thought back to the way Lucifer had looked at her in the Meadow. He looked like he wanted to crush every speck of tenderness there was. "I think I know how."

"I told you she would say that!" Arriane whooped.

Daniel pulled her close. "Are you sure?"

She kissed him, never surer. "I just got my wings back, Daniel. I'm not going to let Lucifer take them away."

So Luce and Daniel said goodbye to their friends, reached for each other's hands, and took off into the night. They flew upward forever, through the thinnest outer skin of the atmosphere, through a film of light at the edge of space.

The moon became enormous, shone like a noontime sun. They passed through hazy clouded galaxies and by other moons with other crater-shadowed faces and strange planets glowing with red gas and striped rings of light.

No amount of flying tired Luce. She began to understand how Daniel could go for days without rest; she was not hungry or thirsty. She was not cold in the frozen night.

At last, at the edge of nothing, in the darkest pocket of the universe, they reached the perimeter. They saw the black web of Lucifer's Announcer, wobbling between dimensions. Inside it was the Fall.

Daniel hovered at her side, his wings brushing hers, transmitting strength. "You will have to pass through the Announcer first. Don't get hung up there. Move through until you find him in the Fall."

"I have to go in alone, don't I?"

"I would follow you to the ends of the Earth and beyond. But you're the only one who can do this," Daniel said. He took her hand and kissed her fingers, her palm. He was shaking. "I'll be here."

Their lips met one last time.

"I love you, Luce," Daniel said. "I will love you always, whether or not Lucifer succeeds—"

"No, don't say that," Luce said. "He won't—"

"But if he does," Daniel continued, "I want you to

know that I would do it all again. I will choose you every time."

A calmness came over Luce. She would not fail him. She would not fail herself.

"I won't be long."

She squeezed his hand and turned away and plunged through darkness, into Lucifer's Announcer.

EIGHTEEN

CATCH A FALLING STAR

The darkness was total.

Luce had only ever traveled through her own Announcers, which were cool and damp, even peaceful. The entrance to Lucifer's was stale, hot, filled with acrid smoke—and deafening. Phlegmy pleas for mercy and jagged radiating sobs permeated its inner wall.

Luce's wings bristled—a sensation she'd never experienced—as she realized that the devil's Announcers were outposts of Hell.

It's just a passage, she told herself. *It's like any other Announcer, a portal to pass through to another place and time.*

She pushed forward, gagging on smoke. The ground was spiked with something she didn't recognize until she stumbled to her knees and felt the excruciation of glass shards in the hands Daniel had just released.

Don't get hung up there, he had told her. *Move through until you find him.*

She took a deep breath, righted herself, remembered what she was. She spread her wings and the Announcer flooded with light. Now Luce could see how horrible it was—every smoldering surface covered by protruding shards of glass of different colors, semi-human forms dead or dying in sticky pools on the floor, and, worst of all, an overwhelming sense of loss.

Luce looked down at her bleeding hands, vicious little triangles of brown glass sticking out of her palms. In an instant they were healed. She gritted her teeth and flew, her body penetrating the Announcer's inner wall, deep into the belly of Lucifer's stolen Fall.

It was vast. That was the first thing. Vast enough to be its own universe, and eerily silent. The Fall was so bright with the light of falling angels that Luce could hardly see. Somehow, she could feel them—all around, her sisters and her brothers, more than a hundred million of Heaven's host, decorating the sky like paintings.

They hung suspended, frozen in space and time, each one entombed in a different orb of light.

That was how she'd fallen, too. She remembered it now, painfully. Those nine days had contained nine hundred eternities. And yet, still as the falling angels were, Luce saw now that they were changing all the time. Their forms took on a strange, inchoate translucence. Here and there light flashed on the underside of a pair of wings. An arm hazily flickered into being, then became indistinct again. This was what Daniel had meant about the shift that occurred within the Fall—souls metamorphosing from the way they had been in the Heavenly realm to the way they would be in the Earthly realm.

The angels were shedding their angelic purity, entering the incarnations they would wear on Earth.

Luce drew near the nearest angel. She recognized him: Tzadkiel, the angel of Divine Justice, her brother and her friend. She had not seen his soul in ages. He didn't see her now, and he couldn't have responded if he had.

The light within him warbled, causing Tzadkiel's essence to shimmer like a gem in muddy water. It coalesced into a blurry face Luce didn't recognize. It looked grotesque—crudely formed eyes, half-realized lips. It wasn't him, but as soon as the angels hit the unforgiving soil of Earth, it would be.

The farther she waded into the suspended sea of

souls, the heavier she felt. Luce recognized all of them—
Saraquel, Alat, Muriel, Chayo. She realized with horror
that when her wings drew near enough, she could *hear*
each angel's falling thoughts.

Who will take care of us? Whom will we adore?

I can't feel my wings.

I miss my orchards. Will there be orchards in Hell?

I am sorry. I am so sorry.

It was too painful to remain near any of them for
longer than a single thought. Luce pushed on, direction-
less, overwhelmed, until a bright, familiar light attracted
her.

Gabbe.

Even in unformed transition, Gabbe was gorgeous.
Her white wings folded like rose petals around her fo-
cusing features; the dark drape of her eyelashes made
her look peaceful and steady.

Luce pressed up against Gabbe's silvery orb of light.
For a moment, she considered that there might be a
bright side to Lucifer's Fall: Gabbe would return.

Then the light within Gabbe flickered and Luce heard
the falling angel think.

*Move on. Lucinda. Please move on. Dream what you
already know.*

Luce thought of Daniel, waiting on the other side.
She thought of Lu Xin, the girl she'd been during the
ancient Shang dynasty in China. She had killed a king,

dressed in his general's clothes, and readied herself for a war that wasn't hers to fight—all because of her love for Daniel.

Luce had recognized her soul inside Lu Xin from the moment she saw her. She could find herself here, too, even with bright souls shining all around her like city lights flung up in the air. She would find herself within the Fall.

That, she knew suddenly, was where she would find Lucifer.

She closed her eyes, beat her wings lightly, asked her soul to guide her to herself. She moved through millions, sliding over glowing tidal waves of angels. It took a small eternity. For nine days she and her friends had been racing time, thinking only of how to find the Fall. Now that they had found it, how long would it take Luce to locate the soul she needed, the needle in this haystack made of angels changing forms? How much time was left?

Then, in a galaxy of frozen angels, Luce froze.

Someone was singing.

It was a love song so beautiful it made her wings quiver.

She came to rest behind the fixed white orb of a falling angel called Ezekiel, and listened:

"My sea has found a shore. . . . My burning has found a flame. . . ."

Her soul swelled with a long-forgotten memory. She

peered around Ezekiel, the Angel of the Clouds, to see who was singing in the clearing.

It was a boy, cradling a girl in his arms, his serenading voice soft and sweet as honey.

The slow rocking of his arms was the only motion in the entire frozen Fall.

Then Luce realized that girl was not simply a girl. She was a half-formed orb of light surrounding an angel in metamorphosis. She was the soul that used to be Lucinda.

The boy looked up, sensing a presence. He had a square face, wavy amber hair, and eyes the color of ice, radiant with dumb love.

But he was not a boy. He was an angel so devastatingly beautiful that Luce's body clenched with a loneliness she didn't want to remember.

He was Lucifer.

This was how he used to look in Heaven. But he was mobile, fully formed, unlike the millions of angels surrounding him—which assured Luce he was the demon of the present, the one who had cast his Announcer around the Fall to incite its second link with Earth. His own falling soul could be anywhere in here, just as paralyzed as the rest of them had been when the Throne cast them out of Heaven.

Luce had been right about her soul's leading her to Lucifer. After he had set this Fall in motion, he must have dipped inside here through his own Announcer.

And spent the past nine days doing what? Singing lul-
labies and rocking back and forth while the world hung
in the balance and armies of angels raced around the
world to stop him?

Her wings burned. She knew this was all he'd done,
because she knew that he loved her, that he still wanted
her. Her betrayal of Lucifer was what this was all about.

"Who's there?" he called.

Luce moved forward. She had not come here to hide
from him. Besides, he had already sensed her soul's glow
behind Ezekiel. She heard the vexed recognition in his
voice.

"Oh. It's you." He raised his arms slightly, holding
out Luce's falling self. "Have you met my love? I think
you'd find her"—Lucifer looked above him, searching
for a word—"refreshing."

Luce edged closer, drawn equally to the radiant angel
who had broken her heart and the strange, half-formed
version of herself. This was the angel who would become
the girl Luce had been on Earth. She watched her own
face flicker into being inside the light in Lucifer's arms.
Then it was gone.

She considered cleaving to this strange creature. She
knew that she could do it: reach out and take possession
of her oldest body, feel her stomach drop as she joined
with her past, blink and find herself in Lucifer's arms, in
falling Lucinda's mind, as she had done so many times
before.

But she didn't need to do that anymore. Bill had taught Luce how to cleave before she had known who she truly was, before she'd had access to the memories she did now. She didn't have to cleave to her falling soul for help with what to say to Lucifer. Luce already knew the whole story.

She folded her hands in front of her. She thought of Daniel on the other side of the Announcer.

"The love you feel is not returned, Lucifer."

He offered Luce a bright, defiant smile. "Do you have any idea how rare a moment like this is?"

Without thinking, Luce found herself drawing nearer.

"The two of you, together at once? The one who cannot leave me"—he caressed the metamorphosing body in his arms and looked up—"and the one who doesn't know how to stay away."

"She and I share the same soul," Luce said. "And neither one of us loves you anymore."

"And they say *my* heart has hardened!" Lucifer grimaced, all sweetness gone. His voice plunged downward through the registers, deeper than anything Luce had ever heard. "You disappointed me in Egypt. You shouldn't have done that, and you shouldn't be here now. I deposited you in the outer realm so that you could not interfere."

His figure changed: the youthful, lovely face shriveled into wrinkles that splintered down his body in long, craggy seams. Mighty wings burst from behind his shoulders. Claws shot from his fingers, long and curled and yellow. Luce winced as they dug into her falling half-formed body in his grip.

His eyes glowed from icy blue to red like molten lead and he swelled to ten times the size he'd been. Luce knew this was because he was indulging the rage he had subdued in order to appear as his lovely, former self. He seemed to fill all empty space, shrinking the expanse of suspended angels in an instant.

Luce flew up to his eye level and sighed.

"You might as well stop there," she said.

"Built up a tolerance, have you?"

Luce shook her head and extended her wings as wide as they would go. They stretched to lengths that still astonished her.

"I know who I am, Lucifer. I know what I can do. Neither of us is constrained by mortal bounds. I could become horrific, too. But what's the point?"

Steam rose off Lucifer's head as he studied Luce's wings. "Your wings always were breathtaking," he said. "But don't get used to them. Time's almost up and then—and then—"

He was watching her face for fear or agitation. She knew how he worked, where he drew his energy and power from. His grainy muscles flexed, and Luce watched the light of her falling body flicker, agitated but immobile, defenseless in his arms. It was like witnessing a loved one in grave danger, but Luce would not reveal that it bothered her.

"I am not afraid of you."

His grunt was a cloud of mucus and smoke. "You will be, as you have been before, as you really are now. Fear is the only way to greet the devil."

The swelling stopped. His eyes cooled back to their startling ice blue. His muscles relaxed into the sleek figure that had once made him the most gorgeous among Heaven's host. There was a shimmer to his pale skin that Luce hadn't remembered until now.

He was more beautiful even than Daniel.

Luce let herself remember. She had *loved* him. He had been her first true love. She had given him her whole heart. And Lucifer had loved her, too.

When his gaze fell on her, the entire history of their relationship played across his handsome face: the fire of their early romance, his desperate yearning to possess her, the anguish of love he'd said had inspired his rebellion against the Throne.

Her mind knew it was Great Deceiver's first great lie—but her heart felt something different, in part because she knew Lucifer had come to believe his lie. It had a secret, spreading power, like a flood nobody saw.

She couldn't help it: She softened. Lucifer's eyes bore the same tenderness that Daniel's did when he looked at her. She felt her eyes begin to return this tenderness to Lucifer.

He *still* loved her—and every moment that he didn't have her hurt him deeply. That was why he'd spent the past nine days with a shadow of her soul, why he'd sought to reset the entire universe to have her back.

"Oh, Lucifer," she said. "I'm sorry."

"You see?" He laughed. "You *are* afraid of me. You're afraid of what I make you feel. You don't want to remember—"

"No, it's not—"

From a hidden sheath behind his back, Lucifer produced a long silver starshot. He rolled it between his fingers, humming a tune Luce recognized. She shivered. It was the hymn he'd written, pairing the two of them together. *Lucinda, his Evening Light.*

She watched the starshot gleam. "What are you doing?"

"*You* loved me. You were mine. Those of us who understand eternity know what true love means. Love never dies. That's why I know that when we hit the ground, when everything starts over, you will make the right choice. You will choose me instead of him, and we will rule together. We will be together"—he looked up at her—"or else—"

Then Lucifer came at her with the starshot.

"Yes!" Luce shouted. "I loved you once!"

He froze, the dull deadly weapon poised above her breast, her earlier soul dangling from the crook of his arm.

"But it was longer ago than you recall," she said. "You appreciate eternity, but you don't appreciate how in a moment eternity can change. I did not love you when we fell."

"Lies." He lowered the starshot closer. "You've loved me more recently than you think. Even just last week, in your Announcers, thinking you loved another—we were wonderful together. Remember nesting in the passion fruit tree in Tahiti? We had earlier moments, too. I expect you've been remembering those." He stepped away from her, studied her reaction.

"I taught you everything you think you know about love! We were supposed to rule together. You promised to follow me. You deceived *me*." His eyes pleaded with her, conflagrations of pain and rage. "Imagine how lonely it was, in a Hell of my own making, stranded at the altar, the greatest fool of all time, enduring seven thousand years of agony."

"Stop," she whispered. "You have to stop loving me. Because I stopped loving you."

"Because of *Daniel Grigori*, who isn't a tenth of the angel I am, even at my worst? It's ridiculous! You know that I have always been more radiant, more talented. You were there when I invented love. I made it out of nothing, out of mere . . . *adoration*!" Lucifer frowned as he said the word, as if it made him nauseated.

"And you don't even know the half. Without you, I went on to invent evil, the other end of the spectrum, the necessary balance. I inspired Dante! Milton! You should see the underworld. I took the Throne's ideas and improved them. You can do whatever you want! You've missed out on *everything.*"

"I missed nothing."

"Oh, darling"—he reached for her, his soft hand caressing her cheek—"surely you can't believe that. I could give you the greatest kingdom never known—we work hard, then we party. Even the Throne offered you the benefits of eternal peace! And what have you chosen? Daniel. What has that haircut ever done?"

Luce brushed his hand away. "He has captured my heart. He loves me for who I am, not what I can bring to him."

He smirked. "You always were a sucker for acknowledgment. Baby, that's your Achilles' heel."

She glanced at the glowing, still souls around them, millions of them, stretching thousands of miles into the distance, accidental eavesdroppers on the truth about the universe's first romantic love.

"I thought that what I felt for you was right," Luce said. "I loved you until it hurt me, until our love was consumed by your pride and rage. The thing you called

love made me disappear. So I had to stop loving you."
She paused. "Our adoration never diminished the
Throne, but your love diminished me. I never meant to
hurt you. I only meant to stop you from hurting me."

"Then stop hurting me!" he pleaded, stretching out
arms that Luce remembered encircling her, feeling like
home. "You can learn to love me again. It is the only way
to stop my pain. Choose me now, again, for always."

"No," she said. "It's really over, Lucifer." She motioned toward the other angels falling around them. "It
was over before any of this even happened. I never promised to rule with you outside of Heaven. You projected
that dream onto me, like I was another one of your blank
slates. You will accomplish nothing by dropping *this* Lucinda to Earth. She will not return your love."

"She might." He gazed down at the angel in his arms.
He tried to kiss her, but the light surrounding Lucinda's
falling self blocked his lips from touching her skin.

"I am sorry for the pain I caused you," Luce said. "I
was . . . young. I got . . . swept up. I played with fire. I
shouldn't have. Please, Lucifer. Let us go."

"Oh." He nuzzled his face into the body in his arms.
"I ache."

"You will ache less if you accept that what we shared
is in the past. Things are not the way they were. If you
love me, you must find it in your soul to let me go on as
I must."

Lucifer took a long look at Luce. His expression darkened, then turned quizzical, as if he was considering an idea. He looked away for a moment, blinked, and when he looked at Luce again, she thought he could see her as she truly was: the angel who'd become a girl, who'd lived through millennia, who'd grown more and more certain of her destiny, who had found her way back to becoming an angel once again. "You . . . deserve more," Lucifer whispered.

"More than Daniel?" Luce shook her head. "I don't want anything more than him."

"I mean you deserve more than all this suffering. I'm not blind to what you've been through. I've been watching. At times, your pain has caused me a kind of joy. I mean, you know me." Lucifer smiled sadly. "But even my brand of joy is always edged with guilt. If I could do away with guilt, you'd *really* see something big."

"Free me from my suffering. Stop the Fall, Lucifer. It is within your power."

He staggered toward her. His eyes filled with tears. The devil shook his head. "Tell me how a guy, with a decent job, loses a—"

"ENOUGH!"

The voice brought everything to a halt. The rotation of the sun, the inner consciousness of three hundred and eighteen million angels, even the velocity of the plummeting Fall itself *simply stopped.*

It was the voice that had created the universe: layered and rich, as if millions of versions of it spoke in unison.

Enough.

The Throne's command ripped through Luce. It consumed her. Light flooded her vision, obscuring Lucifer, her falling self, the whole world with brightness. Her soul buzzed with unspeakable electricity as a weight fell from her, zipped into the distance.

The Fall.

It was gone. Luce had been thrust out of it with a single word and a jolt that made her feel inside out. She was moving across a great void, toward an unknown destination, faster than the speed of light multiplied by the speed of sound.

She was moving at Godspeed.

NINETEEN

LUCINDA'S PRICE

Nothing but white.

Luce sensed she and Lucifer had returned to Troy, but she couldn't be sure. The world was too bright, ivory on fire. It blazed in total silence.

At first the light was everything. It was white hot, blinding.

Then, slowly, it began to fade.

The scene before Luce sharpened: The lessening light allowed the field, the slender cypress trees, the goats grazing on blond straw, the angels around her to come into focus. This light's brilliance seemed to have a texture, like feathers brushing her skin. Its power made her humble and afraid.

It faded further, seemed to shrink, condensing as it drew in on itself. Everything dimmed, lost its color as the light pulled away. It gathered into a brilliant sphere, a tiny glowing orb, brightest at its core, hovering ten feet from the ground. It pulsed and flickered as its rays took shape. They stretched, glittering like pulled sugar, into a head, a torso, legs, arms. Hands.

A nose.

A mouth.

Until the light became a person.

A woman.

The Throne in human form.

Long before, Luce had been a favorite of the Throne—she knew that now, knew it in the fabric of her soul—yet Luce had never really *known* the Throne at all. No being was capable of that kind of knowledge.

It was the way of things, the nature of divinity. To describe her was to reduce her. So here, now, even though she looked very much like a queen in a flowing white robe, the Throne was still the Throne—which meant that she was *everything*. Luce couldn't stop staring.

She was staggeringly beautiful, her hair spun silver

and gold. Her eyes, blue like a crystal ocean, exuded the power to see everything, everywhere. As the Throne gazed across the Trojan plains, Luce thought she recognized a flash of her own face in God's expression—determined, the way Luce Price's jaw clenched when she'd made up her mind. She'd seen it in her reflection a thousand times before.

And when God's face shifted to take in the audience before her, her expression changed into something else. It looked like Daniel's devotion; it captured that particular light in his eyes. Now, in the slack, open way she held her hands, Luce recognized her mother's selflessness—and now she saw the proud smile that belonged only to Penn.

Except Luce saw now that it *didn't* belong to Penn. Every fleeting trace of life found its origin in the force standing before Luce. She could see how the whole world—mortals and angels alike—had been created in the Throne's mercurial image.

An ivory chair appeared at one edge of the plain. The chair was made of an otherworldly substance Luce knew she had seen before: the same material as in the silver staff with the curled spiral tip that the Throne held in her left hand.

When the Throne took her seat, Annabelle, Arriane, and Francesca rushed to come before her, falling on their knees in adoration. The Throne's smile shone down on them, casting rainbows of light on their wings. The angels hummed together in harmonious delight.

Arriane raised her glowing face, beating her wings to rise to address the Throne. Her voice burst out in glorious song. "Gabbe's gone."

"Yes," the Throne hummed back, though of course the Throne already knew this. It was a ritual of commiseration rather than a sharing of information. Luce remembered that this was the purpose for which the Throne had created speech and song; it was meant to be another way of feeling, another wing to brush up against your friend's.

Then Arriane's and Annabelle's feet skimmed the ground and they fluttered up above the Throne. They hovered there, facing Luce and the rest of their friends, gazing adoringly at their Creator. Their formation looked strange—somehow incomplete—until Luce realized something:

The ledges.

Arriane and Annabelle were taking their old places as Archangels. In Heaven's Meadow, the rippled silver ledges had once formed an arch over the head of the Throne. They were back where they belonged: Arriane just to the right of the Throne's shoulders, and Annabelle only inches off the ground near the Throne's right hand.

Bright gaps shone in the space around the Throne.

Luce remembered which ledge Cam used to fly to, which was Roland's, and which one belonged to Daniel. She caught flashes of Molly's place before the Throne, and Steven's, too—though they were not Archangels, but angels who adored happily from the Meadow.

At last, she saw Lucifer's and her places, their matching silver ledges on the Throne's left side. Her wings tingled. It was all so clear.

The other fallen angels—Roland, Cam, Steven, Daniel, and Lucifer—did not step forward to adore the Throne. Luce felt torn. Adoring the Throne came naturally; it was what Lucinda was made for. But somehow she couldn't move. The Throne looked neither disappointed nor surprised.

"Where is the Fall, Lucifer?" The voice made Luce want to fall on her knees and pray.

"Only God can tell," Lucifer growled. "It doesn't matter. Perhaps I didn't want it after all."

The Throne twirled her silver staff in her hands, worrying a muddy recess into the soil where its end met the earth. A vine of silver-white lilies sprang up, lashing in a spiral around the staff. The Throne didn't seem to notice; she fixed her blue eyes on Lucifer until his blue eyes twitched up to lock with hers.

"I believe the first two statements," the Throne said, "and soon you will be convinced of the last. My indulgence has very famous limits."

Lucifer started to speak, but the Throne's gaze passed from him, and he kicked the earth in frustration. It opened up beneath him, lava bubbling and cooling on the ground, a personal volcano.

With the slightest gesture of her hand, the Throne brought them back to attention. "We must deal with the curse of Lucinda and Daniel," she said.

Luce swallowed hard, feeling terror edge along her stomach.

But the Throne's phosphorescent eyes were kind when she tucked a silver-gold strand of hair behind her ear, leaned back in her throne, and surveyed the gathering before her. "As you know, the time has come for me to again ask these two a question."

Everyone quieted, even the wind.

"Lucinda, we'll begin with you."

Luce nodded. The calmness of her wings juxtaposed her pounding heart. It was a strangely mortal sensation, reminding her of being called before the principal at school. She approached the Throne, head bowed.

"You have paid your debt of suffering over these past six-odd millennia—"

"It wasn't only suffering," Luce said. "There were difficult times, but"—she looked around her at the friends she'd made, at Daniel, even at Lucifer—"there was a lot of beauty, too."

The Throne gave Luce a curious smile. "You have

also met the conditions of discovering your nature without help—of being true to yourself. Would you say that you have come to know your soul?"

"Yes," Luce said. "Deeply."

"You are now more fully Lucinda than you ever have been. Any decision you make bears not just the knowledge you bring to it as an angel, but also the weight of seven thousand years of life lessons in every state of human being."

"I am humbled by my responsibility," she said, using words that didn't sound anything like Luce Price, but, she realized, sounded everything like Lucinda, her true soul.

"You may have heard it said that in this lifetime, your soul is 'up for grabs'?"

"Yes. I've heard that."

"And you may have heard something about a balance between the angels of Heaven and the forces of Lucifer?"

Luce nodded slowly.

"And so the question falls to you once more: Will it be Heaven, or will it be Hell? You have learned your lessons and are now four hundred lives the wiser, so we ask you again: Where do you wish to spend eternity? If it is to be Heaven, allow me to say that we will welcome you home and see that the transition is made easy." God cast her eyes on Lucifer, but Luce didn't follow suit. "If Hell is your choice, I hazard to guess that Lucifer will accept you?"

Lucifer did not respond. Luce heard heavy shuffling behind her. She swiveled around to see the backs of his wings twisted into a knot.

It had not been easy inside the Fall to tell Lucifer she did not love him, would not choose him. It felt impossible to say the same thing to the Throne. Luce stood before the power that created her and had never felt more like a child.

"Lucinda?" The Throne's stare bore down on her. "It falls to you to tip the scale."

The conversation she'd had with Arriane in the Vegas IHOP came back to her again: *In the end, it was going to come down to one powerful angel choosing a side. When that happenned, the scale would finally tip.*

"It falls to *me*?"

The Throne nodded as if Luce should have known this all along. "The last time you refused to choose."

"No, that isn't true," Luce said. "I chose love! Just now, you asked whether I knew my soul, and I do. I must stay true to who I am and place love highest of all."

Daniel reached for her hand. "We chose love then and we will make the same choice today."

"And if you curse us for it now," Luce said, "the outcome will be the same. We found each other over and over for seven thousand years. You are all witnesses. We will do it again."

"Lucifer?" the Throne asked. "What do you say to this?"

He looked at Luce with blazing eyes, his pain obvious to everyone there. "I say we will all regret this moment forever. It is the wrong choice, and a selfish one."

"There is always some regret when we accept that love has moved away from us." The even voice came from the Throne. "But I will take your response as a small display of mercy and acquiescence, which offers the universe some hope. Lucinda and Daniel have made their choice clear and I hold us both to our vows made at the Roll Call. Their love is out of our hands. So be it. But it will come at a price." She shifted her gaze back to Luce and Daniel. "Are you prepared to pay the ultimate sacrifice for your love?"

Daniel shook his head. "If I have Lucinda, and Lucinda has me, there is no such thing as sacrifice."

Lucifer cackled, soaring off his feet and hovering in the air above Luce and Daniel. "So, we could rob everything from you—your wings, your strength, your *immortality*? And still you'd choose your *love*?"

From the corner of her eye, Luce caught a glimpse of Arriane. Her wings were folded behind her. Her hands were stuffed inside the pockets of her overalls. She nodded smugly, lips pursed in satisfaction, as if to say, *Hell yeah, they would.*

"Yes." Luce and Daniel spoke as one.

"Fine," the Throne responded. "But understand:

There is a price. You may have each other, but you may have nothing else. If you choose love once and for all, you must give up your angelic natures. You will be born again, made anew as mortals."

Mortals?

Daniel, her angel, reborn as a mortal?

All these nights she'd lain wondering what would become of her and Daniel's love at the end of these nine days. Now the Throne's decision reminded her of Bill's suggestion that Luce kill her reincarnating soul in Egypt.

Even then, she'd considered living out her mortal life and leaving Daniel to his own. There would be no more pain from another lost love. She'd almost been able to do it. What had stopped her was the thought of losing Daniel. But this time . . .

She could have him, really have him, for a long time. Everything would be different. He would be at her side.

"If you accept"—the Throne's voice rose above Lucifer's raspy chortle—"you won't remember what you once were, and I cannot guarantee that you will meet during your lifetime on Earth. You will live and you will die, just as any other mortal in creation. The powers of Heaven that have always drawn you to each other will pull away. No angel will cross your path." She gave a warning look to the angels, Luce and Daniel's friends. "No friendly hand will appear in darkest night to guide you. You will be truly on your own."

A soft sound escaped Daniel's lips. She turned to him and took his hand. So they would be mortals, wandering the Earth in search of their other half, just like everyone else. It sounded like a beautiful proposition.

From just behind them Cam said, "Mortality is the most romantic story ever told. Just one chance to do everything you should. Then, magically, you move on."

But Daniel looked crestfallen.

"What is it?" Luce whispered. "You don't want to?"

"You only just got back your wings."

"Which is exactly why I know I can be happy without them. As long as I have you. You're the one who'd really be giving them up. Are you sure it's what *you* want?"

Daniel lowered his face to hers, his lips close, soft. "Always."

Tears welled in Luce's eyes as Daniel turned back to face the Throne.

"We accept."

Around them, the glow of wings grew very bright, until the whole field hummed with light. And Luce felt the other angels—their dear and precious friends—move from wild anticipation into shock.

"Very well," the Throne almost whispered, her expression inscrutable.

"Wait!" Luce shouted. There was one more thing. "We—we accept on one condition."

Daniel stirred beside her, watching Luce from the corner of his eye, but he didn't interrupt.

"What is your condition?" the Throne boomed, resoundingly unaccustomed to negotiation.

"Take the Outcasts back into the fold of Heaven," she said before her confidence failed. "They have proven themselves worthy. If there was room enough to take me back into your Meadow, there is room enough for the Outcasts."

The Throne looked at the Outcasts, who were silent and glowing dimly. "This is unorthodox but, at its core, a selfless request. You shall have it." Slowly, she extended one of her arms. "Outcasts, step forward if you would enter Heaven once again."

The four Outcasts strode to stand before the Throne with more purpose than Luce had ever before seen them possess. Then, with a single nod, the Throne restored their wings.

They lengthened.

Thickened.

Their tattered brown color drained to become a brilliant white.

And then the Outcasts smiled. Luce had never seen one smile before, and they were beautiful.

At the end of their metamorphoses, the Outcasts' eyes bulged as their irises bloomed back into sight. They could see again.

Even Lucifer looked impressed. He muttered, "Only Lucinda could pull that off."

"It is a miracle!" Olianna hugged her wings around her body to admire them.

"That's her job," Luce said.

The Outcasts returned to their old positions of adoration around the Throne.

"Yes." The Throne closed her eyes to accept their adoration. "I believe that's better after all."

Finally, the Throne raised her staff in the air and pointed it at Luce and Daniel. "It is time to say goodbye."

"Already?" Luce didn't mean to let the word slip.

"Make your farewells."

The former Outcasts swept Luce with gratitude and hugs, binding her and Daniel in their arms. When they pulled away, Francesca and Steven stood before them, arms linked, gorgeous, beaming.

"We always knew you could do it." Steven winked at Luce. "Didn't we, Francesca?"

Francesca nodded. "I was hard on you, but you proved yourself to be one of the most impressive souls I have ever had the pleasure of instructing. You are an enigma, Luce. Keep it up."

Steven shook Daniel's hand and Francesca kissed their cheeks before they backed away.

"Thank you," Luce said. "Take care of each other. And take care of Shelby and Miles, too."

Then angels were all around them, the old crew who'd formed at Sword & Cross and hundreds of other places before that.

Arriane, Roland, Cam, and Annabelle. They'd saved Luce more times than she could ever say.

"This is hard." Luce folded herself into Roland's arms.

"Oh, come on. You already saved the world." He laughed. "Now go save your relationship."

"Don't listen to Dr. Phil!" Arriane squealed. "Don't ever leave us!" She was trying to laugh but it wasn't working. Rebellious tears streamed down her face. She didn't wipe them away; she just held on tight to Annabelle's hand. "Okay, fine, *go!*"

"We'll be thinking of you," Annabelle said. "Always."

"I'll be thinking of you, too." Luce had to believe it was true. Otherwise, if she was really going to forget *all this,* she couldn't bear to leave them.

But the angels smiled sadly, knowing she had to forget them.

That left Cam, who was standing close to Daniel, their arms clapped around each other's shoulders. "You pulled it off, brother."

"Course I did." Daniel played at being haughty, but it came off as love. "Thanks to you."

Cam took Luce's hand. His eyes were bright green, the first color that had ever stood out to her in the grim, dreary world of Sword & Cross.

He tilted his head and swallowed, considering his words carefully.

He drew her close, and for a moment, she thought he was going to kiss her. Her heart pounded as his lips by-passed hers and came to a stop, whispering in her ear: "Don't let him flip you off next time."

"You know I won't." She laughed.

"Ah, Daniel, a mere shadow of a true bad boy." He pressed his hand to his heart and raised an eyebrow at her. "Make sure he treats you well. You deserve the best of everything there is."

For once, she didn't want to let go of his hand. "What will you do?"

"When you're ruined, there's so much to choose from. Everything opens up." He looked past her into the distant desert clouds. "I'll play my role. I know it well. I know goodbye."

He winked at Luce, nodded one final time at Daniel, then rolled back his shoulders, spread his tremendous golden wings, and vanished into the roiling sky.

Everyone watched until Cam's wings were a fleck of far-off gold. When Luce lowered her eyes, they fell on Lucifer. His skin had its lovely shimmer, but his eyes were glacial. He said nothing, and it seemed he would have held her in his gaze forever if she hadn't turned away.

She had done all she could for him. His pain was not her problem anymore.

The voice boomed from the Throne. "One more goodbye."

Together, Luce and Daniel turned to acknowledge the Throne, but the second their eyes fell upon it, the stately figure of the woman blazed into white-hot glory, and they had to shield their eyes.

The Throne was indiscernible again, a gathering of light too brilliant to be gazed upon by angels.

"Hey, guys." Arriane sniffed. "I think she meant for you two to say goodbye to each other."

"Oh," Luce said, turning to Daniel, suddenly panicked. "Right now? We have to—"

He took her hand. His wings brushed hers. He kissed the centers of her cheeks.

"I'm afraid," she whispered.

"What did I tell you?"

She sifted through the million exchanges she and Daniel had ever shared—the good, the sad, the ugly. One rose above the clouds of her mind.

She was shaking. "That you will always find me."

"Yes. Always. No matter what."

"Daniel—"

"I can't wait to make you the love of my mortal life."

"But you won't know me. You won't remember. Everything will be different."

He wiped away her tear with his thumb. "And you think that will stop me?"

She closed her eyes. "I love you too much to say goodbye."

"It isn't goodbye." He gave her one last angelic kiss and embraced her so tightly she could hear his steady heartbeat, overlapping her own. "It's until we meet again."

TWENTY

PERFECT STRANGERS

Seventeen Years Later

Luce clipped her dorm room key card between her teeth, craned her neck to swipe it through the lock, waited for the small electric click, and opened the door with her hip.

Her hands were full: Her collapsible yellow laundry basket was heaped with clothes, most of which had shrunk during their first dryer cycle away from home. She dumped the clothes onto her narrow bottom bunk, amazed she'd found a way to wear so many different things in so short a span of time. The whole week of freshman orientation at Emerald College had passed in a disconcerting blur.

Nora, her new roommate, the first person outside Luce's family to see her wearing her retainer (but it was cool because Nora had one, too), was sitting in the windowsill, painting her nails and talking on the phone.

She was always painting her nails and talking on the phone. She had a whole bookshelf devoted to nail polish bottles and had already given Luce two pedicures in the week they'd known each other.

"I'm telling you, Luce isn't like that." Nora waved excitedly at Luce, who leaned against the bed frame, eavesdropping. "She's never even kissed a guy. Okay, once—Lu, what was that shrimpy kid's name, from summer camp, the one you were telling me about—"

"Jeremy?" Luce wrinkled her nose.

"*Jeremy,* but it was, like, truth or dare or something. Child's play. So yeah—"

"Nora," Luce said. "Is this really something you need to share with . . . who are you even talking to?"

"Just Jordan and Hailey." She stared at Luce. "We're on speaker. Wave!"

Nora pointed out the window at the dusky autumn evening. Their dorm was a pretty U-shaped white brick building with a small courtyard in the middle where everyone hung out all the time. But that wasn't where Nora was pointing. Directly across from Luce and Nora's third-floor window was another third-floor window. The pane was up, tan legs dangled out, and two girls' arms appeared, waving.

"Hi, Luce!" one of them shouted.

Jordan, the spunky strawberry blond from Atlanta, and Hailey, petite and always giggling, with thick black hair that fell in dark cascades around her face. They seemed nice, but why were they discussing all the boys Luce had never kissed?

College was so weird.

Before Luce had driven the nineteen hundred miles up to Emerald College with her parents a week earlier, she could have named each time she'd been outside Texas—once for a family vacation to Pikes Peak in Colorado, twice for regional championship swim meets in Tennessee and Oklahoma (the second year, she beat her own personal best in freestyle and took home a blue ribbon for the team), and the yearly holiday visits to her grandparents' house in Baltimore.

Moving to Connecticut to go to college was a *huge* deal for Luce. Most of her friends from Plano Senior High were going to Texas schools. But Luce had always had the feeling that there was something waiting for her way out in the world, that she had to leave home to find it.

Her parents supported her—especially when she got

that partial scholarship for her butterfly stroke. She'd packed her whole life into one oversized red duffel bag and filled a few boxes with sentimental favorites she couldn't part with: the Statue of Liberty paperweight her dad had brought her back from New York; a picture of her mom with a bad haircut when she was Luce's age; the stuffed pug that reminded her of the family dog, Mozart. The cloth along the bucket back seats of her battered Jeep was frayed, and it smelled like cherry Popsicles, and that was comforting to Luce. So was the view of the back of her parents' heads as her father drove the speed limit for four long days up the East Coast, stopping from time to time to read historical markers and take a tour at a pretzel factory in northwestern Delaware.

There had been one moment when Luce thought about turning back. They were already two days' drive from home, somewhere in Georgia, and her dad's "shortcut" from their motel to the highway took them out along the coast, where the road got pebbly and the air started to stink from all the skunk grass. They were barely a third of the way up to school and already Luce missed the house she'd grown up in. She missed her dog, the kitchen where her mom made yeast rolls, and the way, in late summer, her father's rosebushes grew up around her windowsill, filling her room with their soft scent and the promise of fresh-cut bouquets.

And that was when Luce and her parents drove past

a long winding driveway with a high, foreboding gate that looked electrified, like a prison. A sign outside the gate read in bold black letters SWORD & CROSS REFORM SCHOOL.

"That's a little ominous," her mother chirped from the front seat, looking up from her home-remodeling magazine. "Glad you're not going to school there, Luce!"

"Yeah," she said, "me too." She turned and watched out the back window until the gates disappeared into the winding woods. Then, before she knew it, they were crossing into South Carolina, closer to Connecticut and her new life at Emerald College with every revolution of the Jeep's new tires.

Then she was there, in her dorm room, and her parents were all the way back home in Texas. Luce didn't want her mom to worry, but the truth was she was desperately homesick.

Nora was great—it wasn't that. They'd been friends since the moment Luce walked into the room and saw her new roommate tacking up a poster of Albert Finney and Audrey Hepburn from *Two for the Road*. The bond cemented when the girls tried to make popcorn in the seedy dorm kitchen at two in the morning the first night and succeeded only in setting off the fire alarm, sending everyone outside in their pajamas. The whole week of orientation, Nora had gone out of her way to include Luce in every one of her many plans. She'd gone to a fancy prep school before Emerald, so she walked into college orientation already assimilated to life inside a dorm. It didn't seem weird to her that there were boys living next door, that the online campus radio station was the *only* acceptable way to listen to music, that you had to swipe a card to do anything around here, that class papers would have to be a whopping four pages long.

Nora had all these friends from Dover Prep, and she seemed to make twelve more every day—like Jordan and Hailey, still dangling and waving through their window. Luce wanted to keep up, but she had spent her whole life in a sleepy nook of Texas. Things were slower there, and now she realized that she liked it that way. She found herself pining for things she'd always said she hated at home, like country music and gas station fried chicken on a stick.

But she'd come to school up here to find herself, for her life to finally begin. She kept having to tell herself that.

"Jordan was just saying their next-door neighbor thinks you're cute." Nora gave Luce's wavy waist-length dark hair a tug. "But he's a player, so I was making it clear that you, dear, are a lady. You wanna go over there in a few and pre-party before that other party I told you about tonight?"

"Sure." Luce popped the top on the Coke she'd

bought at the vending machine near the powder-detergent-strewn laundry stations.

"I thought you were bringing me a diet?"

"I did." Luce reached into her laundry basket for the can she'd bought for Nora. "Sorry, I must have left it downstairs. I'll run and get it. Be right back."

"Pas de prob," Nora said, practicing her French. "But hurry. Hailey says there's a varsity soccer team infiltration on their side of the hall. Soccer boys equal good parties. We should head over there soon. Gotta go," she said into the phone. "No, I'm wearing the black shirt. Luce is wearing yellow—or, are you gonna change? Either way . . ."

Luce waved to Nora that she'd be right back and ducked out of the room. She took the stairs two at a time, winding down the floors of the dorm until she stood on the tattered maroon carpet at the entrance to the basement, which everyone on campus called the Pit, a term that made Luce think of peaches.

At the window looking out into the courtyard, Luce paused. A car full of boys was stopped in the circular drive of the dorm. As they climbed out, laughing and shoving each other, Luce saw they all had Emerald Varsity Soccer shirts on. Luce recognized one of them. His name was Max and he'd been in a couple of Luce's orientation sessions that week. He was seriously cute—blond hair, big white smile, typical prep-school-boy look (which she recognized now, after Nora had drawn her a diagram the other day at lunch). She'd never talked to Max, not even when they were teamed up with a few other kids on the campus scavenger hunt. But maybe if he was going to be at the party that night . . .

All the boys getting out of that car were really cute, which for Luce equaled intimidating. She didn't like the thought of being the one shy girl in Jordan and Hailey's room upstairs.

But she did like the thought of being at the party. What else was she supposed to do? Hide in her dorm room because she was nervous? She was obviously going to go.

She jogged down the final flight of stairs to the basement. It was getting close to sunset, so the laundry room had emptied, giving it a lonely glow. Sunset was the time you wore the things you'd washed and dried. There was just one girl in crazy thigh-high striped kneesocks, savagely scrubbing a stain from a tie-dyed pair of jeans as if all her future hopes and dreams depended on the stain's removal. And a boy, sitting atop a loud and shaking dryer, tossing a coin in the air and catching it in his palm.

"Heads or tails?" he asked when she walked in. He had a square face, wavy amber hair, big blue eyes, and a tiny gold chain around his neck.

"Heads." Luce shrugged and gave a little laugh.

He flipped the coin, caught it, and flipped it over

into his palm, and Luce saw that it wasn't a quarter. It was old, really old, a dusty golden color with faded writing in another language's script. The boy raised an eyebrow at her. "You win. I don't know what you won yet, but that's probably up to you."

She twirled around, searching for the diet soda she'd left down there. Then she saw it about an inch from the boy's right knee. "This isn't yours, is it?" she asked.

He didn't answer; he just stared at her with icy blue eyes, which she saw now suggested a profound sadness that didn't seem possible in someone his age.

"I left it down here earlier. It's for my friend. My roommate. Nora," Luce said, reaching for the can. This boy was strange, intense. She was blabbering. "I'll see you later."

"One more time?" he asked.

She turned around in the doorway. He meant the coin game. "Oh. Heads."

He flipped. The coin seemed to hover in the air. He caught it without looking, flipped it over, and opened his palm. "You win again," he sang in a voice eerily identical to that of Hank Williams, a favorite old singer of Luce's dad.

Back upstairs, Luce tossed Nora the Coke. "Have you met the crazy coin-toss guy in the laundry room?"

"Luce." Nora squinted. "When I run out of underwear, I buy new underwear. I am hoping to make it to

Thanksgiving without having to do laundry. Are you ready? Soccer boys are waiting, hoping to score. We are their goal, but we must remind them they can't use their hands."

She took Luce by the elbow and steered her out of the room.

"Now, if you meet a boy named Max, I suggest avoidance. I went to Dover with him, and I'm positive he'll be on the soccer team. He will seem cute and very charming. But he has the biggest bitch of a girlfriend back home. Well, she thinks she's his girlfriend"—Nora murmured behind her hand—"and she got rejected from Emerald and is ferociously bitter about it. She's got spies everywhere."

"Got it." Luce laughed, frowning inside. "Stay away from Max."

"What's your type, anyway? I mean, I know you've moved on from gangly old Jeremy."

"Nora." Luce gave her a little shove. "You are not allowed to bring him up all the time. That was late-night roommate private conversation. What happens in pajamas stays in pajamas."

"You're totally right." Nora nodded, putting up her hands in surrender. "Some things are sacred. I respect that. Okay. If you had to describe your dream kiss in five words or less . . ."

They were walking around the second bend of the

U-shaped dorm. In a moment, they would turn the corner and approach the end of the hall, called the Caboose, where Jordan and Hailey's room was. Luce leaned against the wall and sighed.

"I'm not embarrassed about having, you know, no experience," Luce said quietly—these walls were thin. "It's just, do you ever feel like *nothing* has happened to you? Like you know you have a destiny, but all you've seen of life so far is unexceptional? I want my life to be different. I want to feel that it's begun. I'm waiting for *that* kiss. But sometimes I feel like I could wait forever and nothing would ever change."

"I'm in a hurry, too." Nora's eyes had gone a little fuzzy. "I know what you mean—but you do have at least a little control. Especially when you stick with me. We can make things happen. Our first semester's barely even started, kid."

Nora was eager to get to the party, and Luce wanted to go; she really did. But she was talking about that indescribable thing that was bigger than having a good time at a party. She was talking about a destiny that Luce felt like she had as much control over as the outcome of a coin toss—something that was and wasn't really in her hands.

"You okay?" Nora tilted her head at Luce. A short auburn curl flopped down over her eye.

"Yeah." Luce nodded nonchalantly. "I'm good."

They went to the party—which was just a bunch of open dorm room doors and freshmen walking into and out of them. Everyone had plastic cups filled with this super-sweet red punch that seemed to replenish itself automatically. Jordan DJ'ed from her iPod, shouting "Holla!" every now and then. The music was good. Her sweet next-door neighbor David Franklin ordered pizza, which Hailey improved by adding fresh oregano from the herb garden she'd brought from home and installed in the corner by the window. These were good people, and Luce was glad to know them.

Luce met twenty students in thirty minutes and most of them were boys who leaned in and put their hands on the small of her back when she introduced herself, as if they couldn't hear her otherwise, as if touching made her voice clearer. She realized she was keeping an eye out for the coin-toss guy from the laundry room.

Three cups of punch and two slices of amazing thin-crust pepperoni pizza later, Luce had been officially introduced to and then spent the next ten minutes trying to avoid Max. Nora was right: He was good-looking, but way too flirtatious for someone with a crazy girlfriend back home. She and Nora and Jordan were crammed on Jordan's bed, whispering ratings for all the boys there in between fits of giggles, when Luce decided that she'd had a little too much mystery punch. She left the party and slipped down the stairs, seeking quiet air.

The night was cool and dry, nothing like Texas. This breeze refreshed her skin. There were a few stars out and a few kids in the courtyard, but no one Luce knew, so she felt free to sit down on one of the stone benches between two stout peony bushes. They were her favorite flowers. She'd taken it as a good omen when she saw the grounds around her dorm were blooming with them, even at the end of August. She fingered the deeply lobed petals of one of the full white blossoms and leaned forward to breathe in its soft nectar.

"Hello."

She jumped. With her nose buried in a flower, she hadn't seen him approach. Now a pair of ragged Converse sneakers was standing right in front of her. Her eyes traveled up: faded jeans, a black T-shirt, a thin red scarf tied loosely around his neck. Her heart picked up and she didn't know why; she hadn't even seen his face— short golden hair . . . obscenely soft-looking lips . . . eyes so gorgeous that Luce sucked in her breath.

"I'm sorry," he said. "I didn't mean to scare you."

What color were his eyes?

"That's not why I gasped. I mean . . ." The flower fell from her hand, three petals landing on the boy's shoes.

Say something.

He loves me. He loves me not. He loves me.

Not that!

It was physically impossible to say anything. Not only was this guy the most incredible thing Luce had ever seen in all her life, he'd walked up to her and introduced himself. The way he was looking at her made Luce feel as if she were the only other person in the courtyard. As if she were the only other person on Earth. And she was blowing it.

Instinctively, she reached up to touch her necklace—and found her neck was bare. That was strange. She always wore the silver locket her mother had given her on her eighteenth birthday. It was a family heirloom, containing an old picture of her grandmother, looking very much like Luce, taken right around the time she'd met the man who would become her grandfather. Had she forgotten to put it on that morning?

The boy tilted his head in a kind of smile.

Oh no. She'd been staring at him this whole time. He raised his hand as if to give a little wave. But he didn't wave. His fingers hovered in the air. And her heart started pounding, because all of a sudden, she had no idea what this stranger would do. He could do anything. A friendly gesture was just one possibility. He could flip her off. She probably deserved to be flipped off for staring at him like a crazy stalker. That was ridiculous. She was being ridiculous.

He waved, as if to say, *Hello in there*. "I'm Daniel."

When he smiled, she saw that his eyes were beautifully

gray with just a hint of—was that violet? Oh God, she was going to fall in love with a guy with purple eyes. What would Nora say?

"Luce," she finally managed. "Lucinda."

"Cool." He smiled again. "Like Lucinda Williams. The singer."

"How did you know that?" No one ever guessed Lucinda Williams. "My parents met at a Lucinda Williams concert in Austin. Texas," she added. "Where I'm from."

"*Essence* is my favorite of her albums. I listened to it for half the drive out here from California. Texas, eh? Big adjustment coming to Emerald?"

"Total culture shock." It felt like the most honest thing she'd said all week.

"You get used to it. I did after two years, anyway." He reached out and touched her shoulder when he noticed her panicked expression. "I'm kidding. You look much more adaptable than I am. I'll see you next week and you'll be completely settled in, wearing a sweatshirt with a big 'E' on it."

She was looking at his hand on her arm. But more than that, she was experiencing a thousand tiny explosions inside her, like the finale of a fireworks show on the Fourth of July. He laughed and then she laughed and she didn't know why.

"Do you"—she couldn't believe she was about to say this to a model-gorgeous upperclassman from California— "want to sit down?"

"Yeah," he said instantly, then glanced up at the window where the lights were on and the party was happening. "You wouldn't happen to know about a soccer party going on somewhere in there?"

Luce pointed, slightly crestfallen. "I was just there. It's right up the stairs."

"No fun?"

"It was fun," she said. "I just—"

"Thought you'd catch your breath?"

She nodded.

"I was supposed to meet a friend." Daniel shrugged, looking up at the window, where Nora was flirting with someone they couldn't see. "But maybe I already have."

He squinted at her and she wondered, horrified, if she'd been talking to him with flower pollen dusting her nose. Wouldn't be the first time.

"Are you taking cell biology this semester?" he asked.

"No way. I barely got out of there alive in high school." She looked at him, at his eyes, which were most definitely a shade of violet. They glowed when she said, "Why do you ask?"

Daniel shook his head, as if he'd been thinking something that he didn't want to say aloud. "You just—you look so familiar. I could have sworn we've met somewhere before."

EPILOGUE

THE STARS IN THEIR EYES

"I love this part!" Arriane squealed.

Three angels and two Nephilim were sitting on the forward edge of a low gray cloud above a U-shaped dormitory in central Connecticut.

Roland grinned at her. "Don't tell me you've seen this one before?"

His marbled gold wings were extended and folded flat like a picnic blanket at a drive-through in the sky, so that Miles and Shelby could sit on them and stay aloft.

The Nephilim had not seen the angels in more than a dozen years. Though Roland, Arriane, and Annabelle bore no physical signs of this passage of time, the Nephilim had aged. They wore matching wedding bands, and the sides of their eyes were creased with the laugh lines made by years of happy marriage. Under his very faded blue baseball cap, Miles's hair was slightly gray around the temples. His hand rested on Shelby's belly, which protruded with a baby due the following month. She rubbed her head like she'd narrowly escaped a concussion. "But Luce doesn't eat pepperoni. She's a vegetarian!"

"That's what you took away from this scene?" Annabelle rolled her eyes. "Luce is different now. She's the same girl with different details. She doesn't see Announcers, and she hasn't been to every shrink on the Eastern Seaboard. She's much more 'normal,' which bores her to tears, but"—Annabelle grinned—"I think, in the long run, she's going to be really happy."

"Does this popcorn taste burnt to you?" Miles asked, chewing loudly.

"Don't eat that," Roland said, plucking the popcorn from Miles's palm. "Arriane got it out of the trash after Luce set the dorm room kitchen on fire."

Miles began spitting frantically, leaning over the edge of Roland's wings.

"It was my way of connecting with Luce." Arriane shrugged. "But here, if you must, have some Milk Duds."

"Is it weird that we're watching the two of them like a movie?" Shelby asked. "We should imagine them like a novel, or a poem, or a song. Sometimes I feel oppressed by how reductive the filmic medium is."

"Hey. Roland didn't *have* to fly you out here, Nephilim. So don't act smart, just watch. Look." Arriane clapped. "He's totally staring at her hair. I bet he goes home and sketches it tonight. How cuuute!"

"Arriane, you got way too good at being a teenager," Roland said. "How long are we going to watch for? I mean, don't you think they've earned a little privacy?"

"He's right," Arriane said. "We have other things on our celestial plates. Like . . ." Her smirk faded when she couldn't seem to think of anything.

"So do you guys see each other anymore?" Miles asked Arriane, Annabelle, and Roland. "Since Roland's, you know . . ."

"Of course we see him." Annabelle smiled at Roland. "Because we're still working on him. Even after all these years. The Throne invented forgiveness, you know."

Roland shook his head. "I don't think Heavenly redemption is in the cards for me anytime soon. Everything's so *white* up there."

"You never know," Arriane chimed in. "We get to being mighty open-minded sometimes. Swing by and say hello. Remember: It's because of the Throne that Daniel and Luce are getting together right now."

Roland grew serious, looking past the scene below,

into the dark and distant clouds. "The balance between Heaven and Hell was perfect last time I checked. You don't need me tipping the scales."

"There's always at least the hope of us all coming together once again," Annabelle said. "Luce and Daniel are an example of that—no punishment is eternal. Maybe not even Lucifer's."

"Anyone heard from Cam?" Shelby asked. For a few moments, the clouds were quiet. Then Shelby cleared her throat and turned to Miles. "Well, speaking of things that aren't eternal—our babysitter's shift is almost up. She charged us overtime last week, when the Dodgers game went into extra innings."

"Do you want a heads-up when Luce and Daniel have their first date?" Annabelle asked.

Miles pointed down to Earth. "Aren't we supposed to leave them alone?"

"We'll be there," Shelby said. "Don't listen to him." To Miles, she said, "Don't talk."

Roland wrapped the Nephilim under each arm and prepared to take flight.

Then the angels, the demon, and the Nephilim flew off to distant corners of the sky, leaving a moment's brilliant flash of light behind them, as below, Luce and Daniel fell in love for the first—and the last—time.

TURN THE PAGE FOR A SNEAK PEEK
AT *UNFORGIVEN*, THE NEW BOOK IN THE
BESTSELLING FALLEN SERIES

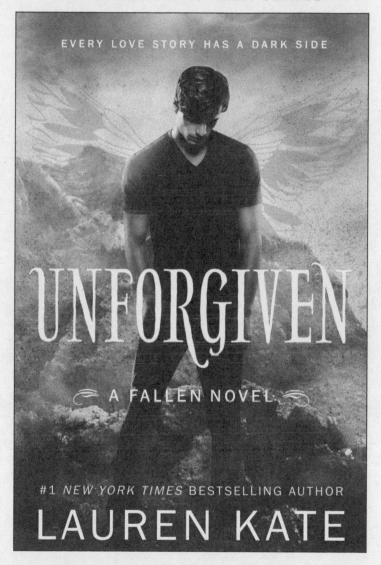

EVERY LOVE STORY HAS A DARK SIDE

UNFORGIVEN

A FALLEN NOVEL

#1 *NEW YORK TIMES* BESTSELLING AUTHOR
LAUREN KATE

ONE

WASTELAND

LILITH

Lilith woke up coughing.

It was wildfire season—it was always wildfire season—and her lungs were thick with smoke and ash from the red blaze in the hills.

Her bedside clock flashed midnight, but her thin white curtains glowed gray with dawn. The power must be out again. She thought of the biology test awaiting her in fourth period, followed immediately by the sucky fact that last night she'd brought home her American history book by mistake. Whose idea of a cruel joke was it to assign her two textbooks with precisely the same color spine? She was going to have to wing the test and pray for a C.

She slid out of bed and stepped in something warm and soft. She drew her foot up, and the smell assaulted her.

"Alastor!"

The little blond mutt trotted into her bedroom, thinking Lilith wanted to play. Her mom called the dog a genius because of the tricks Lilith's brother, Bruce, had taught him, but Alastor was four years old and refused to learn the only trick that mattered: being housebroken.

"This is seriously uncivilized," she scolded the dog, and hopped on one foot into the bathroom. She turned on the shower.

Nothing.

Water off till 3 p.m. her mom's note proclaimed on a sheet of loose-leaf taped to the bathroom mirror. The tree roots outside were curling through their pipes, and her mom was supposed to have money to pay the plumber this afternoon, after she got a paycheck from one of her many part-time jobs.

Lilith groped for toilet paper, hoping at least to wipe her foot clean. She found only a brown cardboard tube. Just another Tuesday. The details varied, but every day of Lilith's life was more or less the same degree of awful.

She tore her mom's note from the mirror and used it to wipe her foot, then dressed in black jeans and a thin black T-shirt, not looking at her reflection. She tried to remember a single shred of what her biology teacher had said might be on the test.

By the time she got downstairs, Bruce was tilting the remains of the cereal box into his mouth. Lilith knew those stale flakes were the last morsels of food in the house.

"We're out of milk," Bruce said.

"And cereal?" Lilith said.

"And cereal. And everything." Bruce was eleven and nearly as tall as Lilith, but much slighter. He was sick. He had always been sick. He was born too soon, with a heart that couldn't keep up with his soul, Lilith's mother liked to say. Bruce's eyes were sunken and his skin had a bluish tint because his lungs could never get enough air. When the hills were on fire, like they were every day, he wheezed at the smallest exertion. He stayed home in bed more often than he went to school.

Lilith knew Bruce needed breakfast more than she did, but her stomach still growled in protest. Food, water, basic hygiene products—everything was scarce in the dilapidated dump they called home.

She glanced through the grimy kitchen window and saw her bus pulling away from the stop. She groaned, grabbing her guitar case and her backpack, making sure her black journal was inside.

"Later, Bruce," she called, and took off.

Horns blared and tires squealed as Lilith sprinted across the street without looking, like she always told Bruce not to do. Despite her terrible luck, she never worried about dying. Death would mean freedom from the panicked hamster wheel of her life, and Lilith knew she wasn't that lucky. The universe or God or *something* wanted to keep her miserable.

She watched the bus rumble off, and then started walking the three miles to school with her guitar case bouncing against her back. She hurried across her street, past the strip mall with the dollar store and the drive-through Chinese place that was always going in and out of business. Once she got a few blocks beyond her own gritty neighborhood, known around town as the Slump, the sidewalks smoothed out and the roads had fewer potholes. The people who stepped outside to get their papers were wearing business suits, not the ratty bathrobes Lilith's neighbors often wore. A well-coiffed woman walking her Great Dane waved good morning, but Lilith didn't have time for pleasantries. She ducked through the concrete pedestrian tunnel that ran beneath the highway.

Trumbull Preparatory School sat at the corner of High Meadow Road and Highway 2—which Lilith mostly associated with stressful trips to the emergency room when Bruce got really sick. Speeding down the pavement in her mother's purple minivan, her brother wheezing faintly against her shoulder, Lilith always gazed out the window at the green signs on the side of the highway, marking the miles to other cities. Even though she hadn't seen much—anything—outside of Crossroads, Lilith liked to imagine the great, wide world beyond it. She liked to think that someday, if she ever graduated, she'd escape to a better place.

The late bell was ringing when she emerged from the tunnel near the edge of campus. She was coughing, her eyes burning. The smoldering wildfires in the hills that encircled her town wreathed the school in smoke. The brown stucco building was ugly, and made even uglier by its papering of student-made banners. One advertised tomorrow's basketball game, another spelled out the details for the after-school science fair meeting, but most of them featured blown-up yearbook photos of some jock named Dean who was trying to win votes for prom king.

At Trumbull's main entrance stood Principal Tarkenton. He was barely over five feet tall and wore a burgundy polyester suit.

"Late again, Ms. Foscor," he said, studying her with distaste. "Didn't I see your name on yesterday's detention list for tardiness?"

"Funny thing about detention," Lilith said. "I seem to learn more there staring at the wall than I ever have in class."

"Get to first period," Tarkenton said, taking a step

toward Lilith, "and if you give your mother one second of trouble in class today—"

Lilith swallowed. "My mom's here?"

Her mom substituted a few days a month at Trumbull, earning a tuition waiver that was the only reason she could afford to send Lilith to the school. Lilith never knew when she might find her mom waiting ahead of her in the cafeteria line or blotting her lipstick in the ladies' room. She never told Lilith when she would be gracing Trumbull's campus, and she never offered her daughter a ride to school.

It was always a horrible surprise, but at least Lilith had never walked in on her mother substituting in one of her own classes.

Until today, it seemed. She groaned and headed inside, wondering which of her classes her mom would turn up in.

She was spared in homeroom, where Mrs. Richards had already finished the roll and was furiously writing on the board about ways students could help with her hopeless campaign to bring recycling to campus. When Lilith walked in, the teacher shook her head wordlessly, as if she were simply bored by Lilith's habitual lateness.

She slid into her seat, dropped her guitar case at her feet, and took out the biology book she'd just grabbed from her locker. There were ten precious minutes left in homeroom, and Lilith needed them all to cram for her test.

"Mrs. Richards," the girl next to Lilith said, glaring in her direction. "Something suddenly smells awful in here."

Lilith rolled her eyes. She and Chloe King had been enemies since day one of elementary school, though she couldn't remember why. It wasn't like Lilith was any kind of threat to the rich, gorgeous senior. Chloe modeled for Crossroads Apparel and was the lead singer of a pop band called the Perceived Slights, not to mention the president of at least half of Trumbull's extracurricular clubs.

After more than a decade of Chloe's nastiness, Lilith was used to the constant rain of attacks. On a good day, she ignored them. Today she focused on the genomes and phonemes in her bio book and tried to tune Chloe out.

But now the other kids around Lilith were pinching their noses. The kid in front of her mimed a retching motion.

Chloe swiveled in her seat. "Is that your cheap idea of perfume, Lilith, or did you just crap your pants?"

Lilith remembered the mess Alastor had left by her bedside and the shower she hadn't been able to take, and felt her cheeks burn. She grabbed her things and bolted from the classroom, ignoring Mrs. Richards's ravings about a hall pass, and ducked into the closest bathroom.

Inside, alone, she leaned against the red door and closed her eyes. She wished she could hide in here all day, but she knew once the bell rang, this place would be flooded with students. She forced herself to the sink. She turned on the hot water, kicked off her shoe, raised her offending foot into the basin, and pumped the cheap pink soap dispenser. She glanced up, expecting to see her sad reflection, and instead she found a glittery poster taped over the mirror. *Vote King for Queen,* it read below a professional head shot of a beaming Chloe King.

Prom was later this month, and the anticipation seemed to consume every other kid at school. Lilith had seen a hundred of these kinds of posters in the halls. She'd walked behind girls showing each other pictures of their dream corsages on their phones on their way to class. She'd heard the boys joke about what happened after prom. All of it made Lilith gag. Even if she had money for a dress, and even if there were a guy she actually wanted to go with, there was no way she would ever set foot in her high school when she wasn't legally required to be there.

She tore Chloe's poster from the mirror and used it to clean the inside of her shoe, then tossed it into the sink, letting the water run over it until Chloe's face was nothing but wet pulp.

❄ ❅

In Poetry, Mr. Davidson was so excited about the faux café he was setting up for the open mic later that week that he didn't even notice Lilith come in late.

She sat down cautiously, watching the other kids, waiting for someone to hold their nose or gag, but luckily they only seemed to notice Lilith as a means for passing notes. Paige, the sporty blond girl to Lilith's left, would nudge her, then slide a folded note onto her desk. It wasn't labeled, but Lilith knew, of course, that it wasn't meant for her. It was for Kimi Grace, the cool half Korean, half Mexican girl sitting to her right. Lilith had passed enough notes between these two to glimpse snatches of their plans for prom—the epic after-party and the sick stretch limo they were pooling their allowances to rent. Lilith had never been given an allowance. If her mom had any cash to spare, it went straight to Bruce's medical care.

"Right, Lilith?" Mr. Davidson asked, making Lilith flinch. She shoved the note under her desk so she wouldn't get caught.

"Could you say that again?" Lilith asked. She really did not want to piss off Mr. Davidson. Poetry was the only class she liked, mostly because she wasn't failing it, and Mr. Davidson was the only teacher she'd ever met who seemed to enjoy his job. He'd even liked some of the song lyrics Lilith had turned in as poetry assignments. She still had the loose-leaf paper on which Mr. Davidson had written simply *Wow!* beneath the lyrics for a song she called "Exile."

"I said you've signed up for the open mic, I hope?" Davidson asked.

"Yeah, sure," she mumbled, but she hadn't and hoped not to. She didn't even know when it was.

Davidson smiled, pleased and surprised. He turned to the rest of the class. "Then we all have something to look forward to!"

As soon as Davidson turned back to his board, Kimi Grace nudged Lilith. When Lilith met Kimi's dark, pretty eyes, she wondered for a moment if Kimi wanted to talk about the open mic, if the idea of reading in front of an audience made her nervous, too. But all Kimi wanted from Lilith was the folded note in her hand.

Lilith sighed and passed it to her.

She tried to skip gym to study for her bio test, but of course she got caught and ended up having to do laps in her gym uniform and her combat boots. The school didn't issue tennis shoes, and her mom never had the cash to get her any, so the sound of her feet, running circles around the other kids who were playing volleyball in the gym, was deafening.

Everyone was looking at her. No one had to say the word *freak* out loud. She knew they were thinking it.

By the time Lilith made it to biology, she was beat down and worn out. And that was where she found her mom, wearing a lime-green skirt, her hair in a tight bun, handing out the tests.

"Just perfect," Lilith said with a groan.

"Shhhhhh!" a dozen students replied.

Her mom was tall and dark, with an angular beauty. Lilith was fair, her hair as red as the fire in the hills. Her nose was shorter than her mother's, her eyes and mouth less fine. Their cheekbones sat at different angles.

Her mom smiled. "Won't you please take a seat?"

As if she didn't even know her daughter's name.

But her daughter knew hers. "Sure thing, Janet," Lilith said, dropping into an empty desk in the row nearest the door.

Her mom's angry gaze flicked to Lilith's face; then she smiled and looked away.

Kill them with kindness was one of her mom's favorite sayings, at least in public. At home, she wore a harsher manner. All that her mom loathed about her life she blamed on Lilith, because Lilith had been born when her mom was nineteen and beautiful, on her way to a remarkable future. By the time Bruce came along, her mom had recovered enough from the trauma of Lilith to become an actual mother. The fact that their dad was out of the picture—no one knew where he was—gave her mother all the more reason to live for her son.

The first page of the biology test was a grid in which they were expected to map dominant and recessive genes. The girl to her left was rapidly filling in boxes. Suddenly Lilith could not remember a single thing she had learned all year. Her throat itched, and she could feel the back of her neck begin to sweat.

The door to the hallway was open. It had to be cooler out there. Almost before she knew what she was doing, Lilith was standing in the doorway, her backpack in one hand, her guitar case in the other. *Another class bites the dust.*

"Leaving class without a hall pass is an automatic detention!" Janet called. "Lilith, put down that guitar and come back here!"

Lilith's experience with authority had taught her to listen carefully to what she was told—and then do the opposite.

She bumped down the hall and hit the door running.

About the Author

LAUREN KATE is the internationally bestselling author of the TEARDROP and FALLEN series. Her books have been translated into more than thirty languages. She lives in Los Angeles. Visit her online at laurenkatebooks.net.

Follow Lauren Kate on

LOVE NEVER DIES

FALLEN

A FALLEN NOVEL

#1 *NEW YORK TIMES* BESTSELLING AUTHOR

LAUREN KATE

Some angels are destined to fall . . .

A LOVE TO DIE FOR

TORMENT

A FALLEN NOVEL

#1 *NEW YORK TIMES* BESTSELLING AUTHOR

LAUREN KATE

Love never dies . . .

ALSO BY LAUREN KATE

"Every single lifetime, I'll choose you.
Just as you have always chosen me. Forever."

THEIR HEARTS WON'T BE BROKEN

FALLEN
in
LOVE

A FALLEN NOVEL IN STORIES

#1 *NEW YORK TIMES* BESTSELLING AUTHOR

LAUREN KATE

New tales from the FALLEN *world*